ALSO BY STELLA RIMINGTON

FICTION
Illegal Action
Secret Asset
At Risk

NONFICTION
Open Secret

DEAD LINE

DEAD LINE

STELLA RIMINGTON

Alfred A. Knopf   New York   2010

THIS IS A BORZOI BOOK
PUBLISHED BY ALFRED A. KNOPF

Published in the United States by Alfred A. Knopf,
a division of Random House, Inc., New York.

www.aaknopf.com

Originally published in Great Britain by Quercus, London, in 2008.
Published by arrangement with Quercus Publishing PLC (U.K.).

Library of Congress Cataloging-in-Publication Data
Rimington, Stella.
Dead line / by Stella Rimington. —1st U.S. ed.
p. cm.
ISBN 978-0-307-27254-6 (alk. paper)
1. Great Britain. MI5—Fiction.   2. Women intelligence officers—Great Britain—Fiction.
3. Arab-Israeli conflict—Fiction.   4. Peace—Congresses—Fiction.   I. Title.
PR6118.I44D43 2010
832'.92—dc22
2010006977

Manufactured in the United States of America
First United States Edition

For my grandson Felix

DEAD LINE

1

In his flat near the British embassy in Nicosia, Peter Templeton woke early. For a few minutes he lay staring at the ladder pattern on the wall of his bedroom made by the sun shining through the venetian blinds. Then, with an anticipatory jolt, he remembered the message he'd received yesterday: the code word from Jaghir that called him to an urgent meeting. Templeton was MI6's head of station in Cyprus, and Jaghir was one of his most important agents.

There was little traffic in Nicosia this early, so when Templeton's black saloon pulled out of the car park beneath his block of flats it had the street to itself. But within thirty seconds a small, battered hatchback swung round a corner and began to follow closely behind the saloon.

The two cars went south through the old walled city, a cautious convoy, avoiding the UN Green Line and the Turkish sector in the north. They took the narrow side streets, past old stone houses with ornate balconies, their tall wooden shutters still firmly closed, and shops that were not yet open for business. Driving through an opening in the old Venetian wall, former boundary of a once much smaller city, they crossed the Pedieos River. The two cars proceeded carefully, their drivers alert and tense; another vehicle could have followed their labyrinthine progress, but not without being detected.

As they emerged from the outskirts of the city, a hinterland of white concrete apartment blocks, the cars accelerated and drove on towards the Troodos mountains. Slowly the road began to climb, and at the base of the range it split, its main artery moving north around the mountain, a smaller track heading in a tortuous zigzag up the mountain itself. In the crook of the junction sat a small café, just half a dozen tables in a dusty courtyard under an overhanging *tourathes* rigged to block the sun.

Templeton lifted his hand briefly from the wheel in a quick salute to his colleague, and drove on up the track. The hatchback pulled into the café's small parking lot and the driver got out to sit at a table, ordering a coffee when the proprietor emerged blinking in the bright light. But the driver's eyes watched the road he'd come along. It was barely seven o'clock and cooler here than in Nicosia, but already the temperature was nearly 90 degrees.

As Templeton made his way up the treacherous track that cut through the large stands of umbrella pines lining the mountainside, he kept an eye on his rear-view mirror, but all he could see was the cloud of dust his car was stirring up. It was just three miles to his destination, yet he knew it would take at least another fifteen minutes. He manoeuvred carefully up the incline with its seemingly infinite twists and curves, catching glimpses through the trees of an ancient monastery ahead of him, nestled neatly into a wide ledge halfway up the mountain. Its walls of white ashlar blocks seemed to grow out of the mountain, enfolding a group of buildings, their tiled roofs aged over the years to a dark mocha brown.

After a final twist of the road, he reached the walls and, driving through an arch, he left his car parked at the base of a short, steep flight of steps. He climbed them slowly, allowing his eyes to adjust to the shade after the blinding sunlight of the hillside. At the top, on a long terrace tiled in white stone, he stopped and gazed down at the road he had come along. Beside him a roofed portico stretched to a large squat chapel with a cloister on one side, from which came the sound of the monks going to prayer. That would keep them occupied for the half hour Templeton required for his meeting.

He sat down on the ledge that overlooked the mountainside and the valley below, picking a shady corner where the terrace joined the portico. The air was scented by the dry, dropped needles of the pines and by the thyme growing in cracks in the walls. Perched here, he could see the café, not much bigger than a speck. As he waited, the mobile phone in his jacket pocket vibrated.

"Yes," he said quietly. He could hear the whirr of cicadas on the hillside below.

"On his way. Alone so far."

"Okay. Keep me posted."

He watched patiently, until far below him he saw dust kicking up in small clouds from the track, then a moving dot that gradually turned into a car, a Mercedes, grey with dust. The noise of its tyres grew louder as it came quickly up the track, and braked with a small squeal next to Templeton's car.

A moment later, an Arab in a smart light-grey suit appeared at the top of the stairs. He was in his forties, trim and thin, his hair short but expensively cut, and even in the heat his shirt was crisply pressed, the collar uncreased. Seeing Templeton, he came over to the corner, his eyes alert.

"Salam aleikum, Abboud," said Templeton as he stood up to shake hands. He spoke classical Arabic, learned in six months' intensive tuition at the language school in the hills outside Beirut, then honed to fluency by twenty years of postings in the Middle East.

"Aleikum-as-salam," the man named Abboud replied, then switched to English. "We are alone, I take it."

"Entirely," said Templeton. He gave a small smile and nodded at the chapel. "The brothers are all at prayer."

They sat on the ledge, Abboud peering warily down the mountainside. Templeton said, "You must have something important to tell me." Their next meeting had not been due for a month, but the message from Abboud—Jaghir—had been unambiguously urgent.

"I do," said Abboud. He took a cigarette case from his pocket, waving it towards Templeton, who shook his head. Lighting a Dunhill with a gold lighter, Abboud inhaled deeply, then blew smoke in a long snow-coloured stream over the ledge. A hundred yards out a hunting kestrel hovered high over the mountainside, its wings fluttering slightly to steady itself against the movement of the thermals. "I was in Damascus last week. Tibshirani called me back."

Templeton nodded. Tibshirani was the deputy director of Idarat al-Mukhabarat, one of Syria's dreaded secret services, and Abboud's direct superior. He was a man who mixed intellectual sophistication (he had been a postgraduate student at Berkeley in California) and peasant brutality.

"What did he want?"

"We are having some problems with the Turks. They arrested one of our agents last month in Ankara. It could have consequences— especially here in Cyprus." He took another drag on his cigarette. "But that is not why I wanted to see you. I had dinner with Tibshirani on my second night. In the old quarter. No wives, though there was some other female entertainment." He gave the briefest flicker of a smile. "Afterwards Tibshirani started talking about another operation. I thought he was just drunk and being indiscreet—he's known me since I joined the service—but then the next morning in his office he briefed me formally about it."

He paused for a moment, looking down the mountain, then stood up to gain a better view. Satisfied that nothing was coming up the track, he sat down again on the ledge, throwing down his cigarette and grinding it out with the heel of his tasselled loafer.

He said, "You've heard about these talks between my country and the Americans."

"Yes," replied Templeton. It was a sore point in Whitehall, since the British had been excluded from the discussions.

"It's commonly thought they are going nowhere—without Israeli involvement, it's said, the Americans cannot agree to anything. If they do, the Jewish lobby will just block it in Congress. That's what the media says, at any rate."

This was true. The original enthusiasm that the two hostile governments were actually talking to each other had gradually given way to a widespread cynicism that nothing of consequence would emerge from the "secret" meetings the whole world now knew about.

Abboud tugged at one of his cuffs and stared out at the arid valley towards Nicosia. The kestrel was lower in the sky now, moving patiently above the slope, like a gundog working a field. He said, "I tell you, my friend, this time the *on dit* is wrong. For once talks may lead to something—the administration in Washington seems determined to break the impasse in the Middle East at last, even if it means standing up to Israel. They want a legacy and they have chosen this to create it."

Was this why Abboud had called an urgent meeting? wondered

Templeton. It was all interesting stuff, but hardly worth the risk each man had taken coming here.

Sensing Templeton's impatience, Abboud held out a reassuring hand. "Do not worry—I am coming to the point. I don't want to stay here any longer than I have to." He looked at his watch, a sliver of gold that glinted in the harsh, still-rising sun. "In two months' time there is going to be an international conference in Scotland. You may know about it. It has not attracted much interest so far because only the moderates have agreed to attend. But my government wants progress. We need a settlement for the stability of our country. So we have decided to attend. I am to be part of our delegation, which is why Tibshirani told me the story." He raised his eyes to the sky.

"What story?"

"We have information that certain parties are working to disrupt the process. We know of two individuals acting to prevent any peaceful solution to the current stalemate. They intend to blacken the good name of Syria and thus to destroy all trust at the conference."

"How will they do that?"

"I don't know. But I can tell you, my friend, that if they succeed there will be a bloodbath in the region."

"Do you know who they are, who is directing them?"

"I know they have connections to your country, and I know their names. But Tibshirani does not know who is controlling them. He does not think it is the British." He smiled, a gleam of white teeth in the sunlight. Then he gave Templeton two names, reciting each one twice, quite slowly, to make sure there was no misunderstanding. Nothing was committed to paper by either man.

"Okay," said Templeton, having memorised the two names. "Where does this information come from?"

"That I cannot tell you." Abboud laughed as he saw the irritation spreading across Templeton's face. "But only because I do not know myself. Believe me, it's not worth my trying to find out; I already know more than I should. I believe it to be true, and so does Tibshirani. But listen to me; here is the most important thing. These people, these two parties who are working against us—my colleagues are going to move against them before they can do harm."

"Move?"

Abboud merely nodded. They both knew full well what this meant.

"When will they 'move'?"

"Soon, very soon. They will do it in the United Kingdom. Secretly. So it will not be known who has acted. My side does not want anything to disrupt this conference. We see much for Syria to gain—we hope to get back our country from the Israeli invaders. So my superiors consider that action against these people is worth the risk if it keeps the conference alive. Personally, I fear that if they make a mistake it may have the opposite effect, which is why I am telling you. But now I must go," said Abboud, standing up.

Templeton stood up too, looking down the mountainside. The kestrel was no longer circling; it must have found its prey.

2

iz Carlyle was not in the best of humours as her taxi came to a grinding halt in a traffic jam in Trafalgar Square. She had spent the morning at the Old Bailey giving evidence in the trial of Neil Armitage, a scientist who had been arrested in Café Rouge in St. John's Wood, in the act of handing over a briefcase of top-secret documents to a Russian intelligence officer.

It was her first time as a witness in court, an experience that once had rarely come the way of MI5 officers, though now with frequent arrests of terrorists, it was more common. Liz had not enjoyed it. She was at her happiest when she was using her analytical and intuitive skills to make sense of complicated intelligence—working to put the case together that led to arrests. Court no. 1 at the Old Bailey was not her natural environment, and she had found it surprisingly stressful.

Knowing that her identity and appearance would be protected, she had expected to sit behind some sort of screen. Instead, the court had been cleared of the press and the public and she'd emerged from a rear door straight into the witness box, where she stood directly facing the defendant in the dock. Although he didn't know her name, he knew he was there largely because of her work. She felt like an actress entering from the wings onto a stage, without a script, exposed and not in control. For one used to working in the shadows, it had been an unnerving experience.

So she was not best pleased when, just as she was recovering with a strong coffee and the *Guardian* crossword puzzle, her boss, Charles Wetherby, had rung to ask her to go and represent the service at a meeting in Whitehall.

"It's about that Middle East peace conference in Scotland," he had said.

"But, Charles," she had protested, "I hardly know anything about it. Aren't the protective security lot dealing with that?"

"Of course. They've been working on it for months and they're completely on top of it. But they've got no one available to send this afternoon. Don't worry. There's nothing to be decided at this meeting. The Home Office have called it at the last minute just so they can demonstrate they're in charge, before the Home Secretary goes to Cabinet tomorrow. I knew you'd have finished in court and you were close by, so I volunteered you."

Thanks very much, Liz had thought ruefully, for dumping this on me after the morning I've had. But though she was irritated, she couldn't feel cross with Charles for long. She'd worked with him for a good part of her ten years in MI5, and he was everything she admired— calm, considered, professional and without vanity. He made people feel part of a committed team, working with him as much as for him. It was more than admiration, she had to admit to herself. She was strongly attracted to him and she knew he cared about her too. But it was an unspoken affection, an invisible thread that neither acknowledged. Charles was an honourable man—one reason why she admired him—and he was married to Joanne. And Joanne was very ill, terminally ill perhaps. Charles, she knew, would never contemplate leaving her, and Liz couldn't have respected him if he had.

Meanwhile, Liz, at thirty-five, was not getting younger and a series of unsatisfactory relationships was not what she wanted. Why had she allowed herself to fall for someone so unavailable?

So here she was, stuck in a cab, likely to be late for a meeting about something she wasn't briefed on and probably about to get soaked into the bargain, she reflected, as the lowering clouds began to deposit their first drops of rain on the taxi's windscreen. Typical, she thought; the summer had so far been unusually dry and she had not brought an umbrella.

But Liz was not one to be gloomy for long. There was too much in her job that she found genuinely fascinating. And when, as was the way with London traffic, the jam suddenly cleared and the cab moved on, her mood lightened; by the time she was dropped halfway down Whitehall, outside the door of the Cabinet Office, in good time for the meeting after all, she felt positively cheerful.

A vast square table dominated the first-floor meeting room, which would have had a fine view over the gardens of Downing Street had the windows not been obscured by yellowing net blast curtains. Good thing, thought Liz, remembering the mortar shell that had landed on the back lawn, fired in the 1980s by the IRA through the roof of a van parked less than a quarter of a mile away.

"I suggest we begin now," said the senior civil servant from the Home Office in a dry voice that made it clear he had chaired countless meetings like this before. Liz had missed his name when he introduced himself and now, gazing at his bland, unremarkable features, she mentally named him "Mr. Faceless."

"As you all know, the Gleneagles conference will take place in two months' time. We have recently learned that, contrary to previous expectations, all the main players are likely to attend, which of course greatly raises the level of the security issues. I believe all the departments and agencies represented here are already in close touch with each other and with the allies." And here Mr. Faceless nodded towards two men, obviously Americans, sitting together on the opposite side of the table from Liz.

"The purpose of this meeting is to emphasise the importance the Home Secretary and the Prime Minister attach to the success of this conference. It is vital that nothing should occur to disrupt it. Ministers feel, and I believe their colleagues in Washington feel the same, that this conference, given the wide attendance, represents the first real possibility of a fundamental breakthrough in the region."

As Mr. Faceless continued his remarks Liz discreetly scanned the table. He had not troubled to begin with the normal chairman's courtesy of going round the table for everyone to introduce themselves, so she amused herself by working out who everyone was. A deputy commissioner from the Metropolitan Police—she'd seen his photo in the newspapers though she'd never met him—was sitting next to a man she guessed was also a policeman, probably a Scot. Then there were the two Americans. They must be from the CIA London station; they didn't look like FBI and anyway she knew most of the FBI characters at the embassy. One of them wore horn-rimmed glasses, a khaki summer suit and a striped tie that shouted Ivy League. The other, older than his colleague, was a heavyset, balding man, who seized on the opportunity of a pause in the chairman's remarks to say, "I'm Andy Bokus, head of station at Grosvenor." CIA, as she had suspected. He spoke in a flat, uninflected voice. Like a Midwestern car dealer in a film, thought Liz. "And this is my colleague, Miles Brookhaven. To date we have received no specific negative information relative to the conference."

Liz suppressed a groan. What was it with so many Americans? Met informally, they could be the friendliest, least pretentious people in the world, but put them on a stage and they turned into automatons.

Bokus went on. "Liaisons with the Federal Bureau of Investigation are ongoing. So far, also negative. A representative of that agency will attend any future meeting." He paused. "The Secret Service may also attend."

"Really?" asked a tall, sandy-haired man, leaning back languidly in his chair. *Oh God!* It was Bruno Mackay, an MI6 officer Liz had run up against before. She hadn't seen him for several years but he hadn't changed at all in that time. Still the deep tan, the sculpted nose and mouth, the beautifully cut suit that spoke of Savile Row. Mackay was clever, smooth, charming and infuriating in equal measure—and also, in Liz's experience, deeply untrustworthy. Now he caught her looking at him, and he stared back into her eyes with cold, professional detachment, until suddenly he gave an unmistakable wink, and his face broke into a wide grin.

Ignoring him, Liz turned her attention back towards the rest of the table, and realised that Mackay's intervention seemed to have flustered Bokus, who was now silent and frowning at the chairman. Clearing his throat, Mr. Faceless remarked in hushed tones, "Although it is not widely known, even among departments and agencies—and I would ask you all to protect this information for the present—there is a strong possibility that the President will attend the conference."

Well, perhaps there is a chance of a breakthrough after all, thought Liz. The President certainly wouldn't be attending if this was going to be just another pointless summit. As if to confirm that this was something different, the door to the room opened and a man came in, walking briskly towards the chairman's seat.

He looked familiar to Liz, and she was at a loss for a moment until realising why. It was Sir Nicholas Pomfret. She had never seen him in the flesh, but recognised him from his many appearances on television and in the press. A saturnine figure, bald and dark-skinned, with coal-coloured eyebrows, a hawk nose and sharp, intelligent eyes, he was a near legendary political Mr. Fixit. But he also had a solid core of government experience; for many years he'd been a civil servant at the Home Office, before becoming senior political adviser to the prime minister before last.

He'd left government for a while, becoming first CEO then chairman of a leading investment bank. Then, after the election of the new Prime Minister, he'd returned to number 10 Downing Street. The PM had sent him on several overseas missions as his personal ambassador—soothing ruffled Saudi feathers when an arms deal was threatened by a hostile U.K. press, helping various British firms with difficulties doing business in Hong Kong under mainland Chinese control.

Most recently, he had been named as the new security major-domo, reporting directly to the PM. His appointment had caused muttering when announced, since he was a political veteran rather than a security professional. But long tenure in the Home Office meant he knew the ins and outs of both the police and the intelligence services and his status as the PM's personal advisor meant that he had influence with foreign heads of government, so he was now generally accepted as a good thing among that most closed of worlds, the security community.

His presence at this meeting suggested an urgency. Liz found herself sitting slightly more upright as, after a nod to the chairman, Sir Nicholas began to speak.

"Sorry to miss some of your proceedings, but I've just come from the Prime Minister. One of the things we've been talking about is this conference, and I wanted to say a few words to you before you go."

He paused dramatically, knowing he now had everyone's attention. "A month ago one might have been forgiven for thinking the prospect of another conference on the Middle East distinctly ... unpromising. With only the usual participants lined up, it was hard to see how any progress could be made.

"Today, however, I'm very pleased to say that things have changed. It now seems increasingly likely, thanks to prolonged and intensive lobbying by Her Majesty's Government, lobbying in which I was privileged to play a part, that *all* the relevant parties to the conflict in the Middle East are likely to be at Gleneagles. Israel, Jordan, Syria, Lebanon and even Iran have indicated their intention to participate."

He's revelling in this, thought Liz, though there wasn't any doubting the importance of what he was saying. "Gleneagles could be the breakthrough that's so desperately needed. It's a great opportunity, but if it fails, there won't be another peace initiative any time soon. I'm sure the seriousness of what I'm saying is apparent to us all.

"That's why I'm here. I must tell you in the utmost confidence that we have very recently received intelligence—highly classified intelligence—that an attempt will be made to abort the conference, possibly before it even begins. I can't be more precise than that for the moment—the intelligence is vague, but highly reliable. Those agencies who have a need to know will be briefed in greater detail by our colleagues in MI6. I can assure you that the threat is real. *Nothing* must be allowed to derail the talks. Thank you for your time." He stood up. "Now I have to get back next door."

Later, when the meeting broke up, Liz looked out of the corner of her eye at Bruno, who was lounging back in his chair, looking immensely self-satisfied. It wasn't hard to guess why. How typical, she thought, feeding intelligence in at the top for maximum dramatic impact, rather than briefing colleagues in the normal way.

Making her way downstairs, through the familiar glass security doors and out into Whitehall, Liz found herself in the company of the younger of the two CIA men, the Ivy Leaguer with the horn-rimmed glasses and the striped tie. It had been raining and there were puddles on the ground. He was wearing a Burberry raincoat that looked absurdly new.

Smiling, he held his hand out. "Miles Brookhaven," he said in a soft voice, his accent mid-Atlantic. The afternoon traffic was light and they had the wide pavement to themselves. "Going this way?" he said, indicating the gates of the Horse Guards building, twenty yards up Whitehall.

She hadn't intended to, but found herself reflecting that she could just as well get back to Thames House by walking across Horse Guards Parade as by going down Whitehall and getting involved with the complicated crossings around Parliament. They turned into the gates together, passed the sentries in their boxes and emerged through the dark archway into the sunshine reflected off the red gravel of the parade ground.

"Your Sir Nicholas," Brookhaven said appreciatively. "Is that what they mean by a mandarin?"

Liz laughed. "Strictly speaking, a mandarin is a civil servant. He was a mandarin once, but now he's got himself a profile—these days he's a politico."

Brookhaven was walking quickly. A shade under six feet, he was lean and athletic-looking. He seemed to glide effortlessly over the pavement and though Liz was hardly a dawdler, she found it hard to keep up. As they crossed the gravel she saw Bruno Mackay climbing into the driving seat of a flashy-looking car. How on earth had he got one of the special passes that entitled him to park there? In fact, how had he got out there so quickly?

"What do you make of what he said?"

"Sir Nicholas?" Liz shrugged. "Oh, I think we have to take him at his word, for the time being anyway. No doubt Six will pass on the intelligence when it's been assessed. There's nothing we or anyone can do until we know more."

She changed the subject. "How long have you been stationed here?"

"Just two months," he said, before adding quickly, "but I know England well. My school had an exchange programme with a school here. I had a lovely time and I've often been back."

Lovely—not usually a favourite word of the American male. Brookhaven was an Anglophile, thought Liz, and keen to show it. They were always quick to tell you that they knew the place.

"Which school?" she asked.

They had reached the corner of Birdcage Walk and Parliament Square. Brookhaven pointed almost directly ahead of them.

"Right here. Westminster," he said. They stopped. "I'm off that way," he added, gesturing up Birdcage Walk.

"Right. I'll see more of you, no doubt."

"I hope so." He smiled quickly and walked off.

Liz had intended to skirt Queen Elizabeth Hall and then set off diagonally towards the far corner of the square, but on an impulse she continued straight ahead, passed the front of Westminster Abbey and walked through the arch into the great courtyard of Westminster School. On the green in front of her a group of uniformed fifteen-year-olds was casually throwing a ball around. To her mind there was something maddeningly upper-class about the scene, something that she knew she could never quite understand or like.

Feeling somehow out of place, out of time, she crossed the court, out through the tiny gate at the far end and into the sunlit maze of eighteenth-century houses that led her out opposite the House of Lords and the long, tapering wedge of a little park, convenient for peers of the realm and members of parliament to take the air. She remembered the fateful afternoon when she'd sat on one of its benches with Charles Wetherby, and tried calmly to relate to him her discovery that the thing he had feared most—a traitor working in their midst— was true. He'd taken the news with an outward show of calm, but she'd known how shaken he must have been.

She was thinking of that now when a car pulled up abruptly on the street right next to her. It was the Mercedes 450 cabriolet—a low-slung sports model, silver with an amazingly loud ketchup-coloured top—that she'd seen Bruno Mackay getting into on Horse Guards Parade.

Her heart sank as she watched the front passenger window slide down. The driver leaned over.

"Want a lift?" he shouted out.

"No thanks," she said, as cheerily as she could. The only way to deal with the man, she had learned before, was to make it clear that nothing he said mattered at all.

"Come on, Liz, lighten up. I'm going right by your building."

"I'm going to walk, Bruno," she said firmly, as a van started to hoot its horn in protest at the hold-up. "You go on. If you stay there much longer you'll get arrested."

He shrugged. "Suit yourself. But don't think I didn't see you back there consorting with the enemy." He said this with the mock-reproof of a headmaster.

"Nonsense," said Liz, tempted to use a stronger word. "Miles Brookhaven isn't the enemy. He and I have a 'special relationship.'" And she walked on, certain that for once she had left Bruno at a loss for words.

3

That morning the Reverend Thomas Willoughby hoped for rain. Earlier in the year, during the flooding in May, he had wanted never to see rain again. But now in late summer the grass had curled and died, yellowed from the heat and drought, and the gnarled old apple tree in the front of the churchyard looked pained, its carpet of wizened windfall fruit picked at by hovering wasps.

When he had first moved from his Norfolk village parish to St. Barnabas, on the edge of the City of London, Willoughby had feared the worst—endless traffic and noise, vagrants, a secular culture that would have no time for his religion. Yet St. Barnabas had been a surprise. It had turned out to be a refuge from the fast-paced urban world. Built by an anonymous student of Hawksmoor, the church had the baroque grace of the master, and a characteristic towering spire. It was just a stone's throw from the bustle of the old Smithfield meat market and the thrusting steel and glass of the world's greatest financial marketplace.

But the church figured on no tourist map and was visited only by the occasional aficionados, working their way through a weighty architectural guidebook. It was almost wilfully obscure, tucked away at the end of a small side street of eighteenth-century terraced houses, not yet gentrified. "Bit of a backwater, really," the previous incumbent had said on Willoughby's first visit, then pointed at the small graveyard in one corner of the churchyard. "It's been full up since Victorian times. That's one service you won't have to conduct."

Like any city church, St. Barnabas was locked overnight. Approaching the vestry door, the Reverend Willoughby was just reaching for his keys when he noticed that the door was already open. Not again, he thought, his heart sinking. The church had been burgled the autumn before—the collection box stolen, along with a silver jug that had been left in the vestry. Worse, though, had been the vandalism: two brass rubbings that hung on the chancel wall had been hurled to the floor, their frames smashed to smithereens; one of the ornate family memorial plaques had been badly chipped by a hammer blow; and—he shuddered at the indignity of it—human excrement deposited on a pew.

He entered the vestry apprehensively, confident the intruders would be long gone but worried about the destruction they might have left behind. So he was surprised to find the room untouched—the collection box (kept empty now) in its proper place, the cassocks hanging on their hooks; even the Communion articles sat on the dresser apparently unmolested.

Still anxious, he went cautiously through into the choir, dreading what he might find. But no, the altar stood unharmed, its white marble shining in a shaft of sunlight, and the delicately carved wooden pulpit seemed undamaged. He looked up and saw to his relief that the stained-glass window in the chancel still had all its panes. Willoughby looked around, mystified, searching for signs of an intruder. There were none.

Yet there was a smell in the air, faint at first, then stronger as he moved down the centre aisle to the front of the church. Something pungent. Fish? No, more like meat. But Smithfield's days as a meat market were over. It was being converted into smart apartments. And this was meat gone off. Ugh. The odour intensified as he examined the pews on either side of the aisle, all pristine, the kneelers neatly hanging on the backs of the wooden benches, hymnals in the low racks on every row.

Puzzled, he walked down to the front door of the church. Lifting the heavy iron bar that secured the massive oak door from inside, he swung it open, letting light flood into the nave. It was as he turned away, blinking from the sudden harsh sunlight, that he saw something odd. It was next to the large wooden box (a vestment chest originally, he'd always supposed) in which the extra hymn books were stored. Two or three times a year—at Christmas, or for the memorial service of a local dignitary—the church was filled to capacity, and then these spare books were pressed into service. But now they lay in a higgledy-piggledy heap on the ash-coloured paving stones.

He walked cautiously over to the pile, wrinkling his nose at the smell, which was almost overpowering now. In front of the box he hesitated; for the first time cold fingers of fear touched his spine. *Trust in the Lord,* he told himself, as with both hands he slowly lifted the heavy oak lid.

He found himself looking at a young man's face—a white face, an English face perhaps, in its twenties, with thinnish blond hair combed straight back. It would have been a conventional, perfectly usual sort of face, except that the eyes bulged like a gruesome parrot's, and the mouth was set in a rictus of agony, lips stretched wide and tight over the teeth. The tendons of the throat strained against the skin of the neck like tautened cords. There was no question: he was dead.

As Willoughby stepped back, horrified and frightened, he saw that the man's legs had been bent at the knee, presumably to cram him into the chest. The knees were pressed together, drawn up almost to the chin, held by a cat's cradle of rope that encircled his throat, then passed down his back and around his legs again. The man had been trussed like a chicken, though since both his hands were gripping one end of the rope, it looked as if he had trussed himself. If that were so, who had put him in the box?

4

n her fourth-floor office at Thames House, in the counter espionage branch, Liz was telling Peggy Kinsolving about yesterday's experiences at the Old Bailey.

"Gosh, thank goodness it was you, not me," said Peggy, shuddering. Peggy had also played a key role in the investigation that had brought Neil Armitage into court.

It had been over a year since the young desk officer had transferred from MI6 to MI5. After leaving Oxford with a good 2:1 in English and vague scholarly ambitions, Peggy had taken a job in a private library in Manchester. There, with few visitors using the library, she had been free to pursue her own researches, which was what she had thought she wanted to do. But the solitary days and evenings soon began to pall and when, quite by chance, she had learned of a job as a researcher in a specialised government department in London, she had applied. At the age of twenty-four, still with the round spectacles and freckles that had made her family call her Bobbity Bookworm, Peggy had found herself working for MI6.

Peggy was a girl who thought for herself. She had seen enough of life to take no one at face value. But for Liz she felt something like . . . she had to admit it to herself—something like hero worship. Or was it heroine worship? No, that didn't sound quite right. Liz was something Peggy would have liked to be. Whatever happened, she always seemed to know what to do. Liz didn't have to keep pushing her spectacles back up her nose whenever she got excited; she didn't wear spectacles. Liz was cool. But Peggy knew that Liz needed her, relied on her—and that was enough.

Peggy had applied to transfer to MI5 after working with Liz on a particularly sensitive case—a mole in the intelligence services—and though MI6 were not best pleased, MI5 had welcomed her with open arms. Studying her junior's eager face, Liz realised that Peggy now felt completely at ease in Thames House. She's one of us, she thought.

"When will we hear the verdict?" asked Peggy.

Liz looked at her watch. "Any moment now, I should think."

As if on cue, Charles Wetherby poked his head through the open door. Smiling at Peggy, he said to Liz, "Armitage has got twelve years."

"Quite right, too," said Peggy with conviction.

"I suppose he'll serve about half, won't he?" asked Liz.

"Yes. He'll be retirement age by the time he gets out. How did it go in the Cabinet Office yesterday?"

"I was just writing it up. We had a guest appearance by Sir Nicholas Pomfret. Apparently there's something hot off the press from Six."

Wetherby nodded. "So I gather. I've just had a call from Geoffrey Fane. He's coming across in half an hour. I'd like you there."

Liz raised an eyebrow. Fane was one of Wetherby's counterparts at MI6, a complicated, intelligent and tricky man, primarily a Middle East specialist, but with a wide-ranging brief covering MI6's operations in the U.K. She'd worked with him before and had come to realise that it was safest either not to sup with Geoffrey Fane at all or to do so with a long spoon.

Now Liz said, "Why's he talking to us about this? Shouldn't it go to protective security?"

"Let's wait and see what he has to say," said Wetherby calmly. "You know the PM's pinning a lot on this conference. God knows what happens if it fails. I think the Middle East is in what the Americans call the Last Chance Saloon."

"There were two men from Grosvenor at the meeting."

"Was Andy Bokus one of them?"

"That's right."

"Head of station. They call him Bokus the Bruiser," said Wetherby with a smile.

"He had a sidekick with him, a guy called Brookhaven. He seemed rather nice."

"Don't know him. See you shortly."

"I'll be there," said Liz. She paused a beat before asking, "Is Fane coming on his own?"

"Yes. Why do you ask?"

She shrugged. "He sent Bruno Mackay to the Cabinet Office meeting."

Wetherby grimaced, then gave a wry smile. "No, it's just Fane, thank God. He's hard enough to pin down without Mackay muddying the waters. See you in a bit, then."

He went off down the corridor and Peggy left to return to her desk in the open-plan office.

What a relief to have Charles back in charge, Liz thought. Charles Wetherby, formerly director of counter terrorism, had spent several months earlier in the year on compassionate leave, looking after his two boys when his wife was thought to be dying from an incurable blood disease. At the same time, Liz had been transferred to the counter espionage branch, working for the dreadful Brian Ackers, a long-time Cold War warrior who couldn't get it into his head that the relationship with Russia had changed. Liz had had to manage Brian Ackers and Geoffrey Fane as well. That Irish business! She still shuddered at the thought. If Charles hadn't come back at the last minute it could have been the end of her. It was bad enough as it was. Anyway, Charles had taken Ackers's place, since his wife seemed to have turned another corner. It wasn't clear how ill she was—Charles never spoke about it.

Liz looked again at the summary report she had started to prepare the day before for her weekly meeting with Charles. A lot was going on: yet another pass had been made by a Russian intelligence officer, this time to a low-level clerk in the Foreign Office who had reported the contact straightaway; an Iranian posing as a Saudi was suspected of trying to buy anti-tank weapons from a U.K. manufacturer; the numbers in the Chinese embassy continued to grow suspiciously. She'd finish it tomorrow, she thought, as Charles phoned to tell her Fane had arrived.

She stood up and locked the file in her cupboard, running a quick hand through her hair, pulling down her jacket.

5

Many years of working with Geoffrey Fane of MI6 had taught Wetherby self-control. He knew that however annoying Fane might be, with his lean, elegant figure, his well-cut suits, his languid air and above all his habit of dumping embarrassing situations on Charles at a late stage, the worst thing to do was to show irritation. Managing Geoffrey Fane was a fine art and Charles rather prided himself that he was as good at it as anyone.

That said, however, he had hoped that his move to counter espionage would mean seeing less of Fane, most of whose time was spent on Middle East issues, particularly terrorism. But now, after only a few weeks back at work, he found himself again gazing across his desk at Fane, who was reclining comfortably in one of the two padded chairs in Charles's office as they waited for Liz Carlyle.

Avoiding his visitor's eye, Charles looked over Fane's shoulder, through his office window at the wide view of the Thames at low tide with a bright sun scattering diamond sparkles across the small, receding waves. At least he had one thing to thank Brian Ackers for. Traditionally the director of counter espionage had one of the best offices in Thames House.

Ackers, in his curious, obsessive way, had turned his desk so that his back was to the view, and one of Charles's first changes had been to turn it round. After that, he had removed Ackers's lifelong collection of Sovietology from the bookshelves and replaced it with his own eclectic library, assembled over his years in the service. The one extravagance he still allowed himself was buying books and he had long since filled up all the space in the house near Richmond, which now had to accommodate the assorted possessions of his teenage sons as well as his and Joanne's.

The door of his office opened and Liz Carlyle came in, bringing, for Charles at least, a breath of fresh air and a noticeable lightening of the spirit. Charles had by now admitted to himself that an important part of the pleasure he got from his work came from the proximity of Liz. He found her deeply attractive—not just her appearance, her level gaze, her slim figure and her smooth, brown hair, but her straightforward, down to earth personality, her honesty and her quick intuition.

He thought she felt for him too, but she gave little away. He knew that she expected nothing of him and, while Joanne was alive, he could not expect anything from her. But that did not prevent the tinge of jealousy he always felt when he saw another man's attraction to her.

The two men stood up. "Elizabeth," said Fane warmly, shaking her hand. "You're looking well."

Charles was aware that Liz hated to be called Elizabeth and he suspected that Fane knew it too. He waited to see how she would react. Fane, with his sophistication and his style, was an attractive man; he was also divorced. But Charles knew he was ruthless in pursuit of operational success and probably in his pursuit of women too. Liz and Fane had worked closely together in his absence on a case without a happy outcome for either. Charles, coming in at the end, had seen how it had shattered the confidence of both of them and in doing so had drawn them together. He hoped that Liz would be careful. Fane was not the man for her.

"Thank you, Geoffrey," Liz said frostily as Charles waved her to the second chair in front of his desk.

"Liz, I thought you should hear what Geoffrey's just been telling me. It strikes me as rather important."

Liz looked levelly at Fane, her eyes narrowing slightly with concentration.

Fane said, "We've had an intriguing report from Cyprus. Our head of station there is Peter Templeton—he's been in the Middle East for years, so I don't think you'll have met him." She shook her head. "He's been running a very sensitively placed source for some time. It's someone who's given us excellent intelligence in the past."

Fane paused again, hesitant, and Charles could see that not all of his old arrogance had returned; once, he would have known exactly what he would or wouldn't say.

Settling himself in his chair, Fane went on. "This source has high-level access. The day before yesterday he called an urgent meeting with Templeton. What he had to say was rather concerning."

And Fane related in economical fashion what Templeton had learned from his source—that two people in the United Kingdom were working to blacken the name of Syria and so to destroy trust and wreck the peace conference. And that Syrian intelligence was going to move against them.

"And that," said Fane, ending his account with a dramatic flourish of one cuffed wrist, "is the reason I came to see you."

No one spoke for a moment. Then Liz asked, "Is this the threat Sir Nicholas Pomfret was talking about at the Cabinet Office?"

Fane nodded. "Yes. Bruno told me Pomfret had addressed you all." He smiled knowingly.

Charles was tapping his pencil on his notepad. He looked thoughtfully at Liz, who said, "If it's a matter of protecting two people, that sounds like a job for the police, not us."

"This is delicate source material, Elizabeth. It can't possibly be handed to the police," replied Fane. "Anyway, I'm not sure whom we should be protecting."

"You said these two lives are at risk," she responded.

He ignored the implication. "This is about the future of the Middle East. If there is some sort of plot to disrupt the conference, and the Syrians snuff it out, who are we to complain?"

Typical of Fane, thought Charles, and seeing Liz's hackles rising he spoke quickly to pre-empt her response.

"Did this source have any sense of what these two are planning to do? Are they working together? Who is controlling them? And above all, how did the Syrians find out about this plot?"

"I've told you everything we know, Charles, and I've given you the names." Charles pushed a paper across his desk to Liz, while Fane leaned back in his chair. Fane said, "It's over to you now." And as if the ensuing silence confirmed that the ball had been placed in MI5's court, a smile bordering on the smug settled on Fane's lips.

Charles ignored him and started tapping his pencil again, his eyes drifting over to the window and its view of the Thames. "It could just be an old-fashioned set-up. God knows, we've seen them before, especially from the Middle East."

Liz spoke up. "But what would the point be, Charles? I mean, other than sending us on a wild-goose chase, why would anyone want to plant disinformation of this sort?" Unusually, Charles noted, she was arguing on Fane's side.

Fane snapped, "They wouldn't."

"Possibly," Charles said. "But whoever told them may have had their own motives—or some reason we can't imagine at present."

"In my experience, Charles, fathoming motives in the Middle East is the equivalent of building sandcastles." Fane was emphatic. "You can erect the most impressive structure, and then one big wave can wash it all away."

Charles suppressed a sharp reply and Liz broke in. "These two names," she said, looking at the paper, "do we know anything about them?"

"Not a lot," said Fane.

"Sami Veshara—well, I think we can say he's not Anglo-Saxon."

"Lebanese perhaps," said Charles. He added drily, "Curiouser and curiouser."

Fane shrugged again. He's being purposely irritating, thought Charles.

Liz went on, "And Chris Marcham. That has a familiar ring to it—or is it just because it sounds English?"

Suddenly Fane looked slightly flustered. "Actually, that's a name we do know something about. He's a journalist, specialises in the Middle East. Freelance now; used to be on the staff of *The Sunday Times*. We have talked to him in the past. Not often. Bit of an odd fish, frankly."

"Why's that?" asked Liz.

"He made his name reporting first-hand on the Falangist massacres in the South Lebanese refugee camps. For a moment, the world was his oyster. He's extraordinarily knowledgeable about the Palestinians, and one of the few Western journalists all their factions seem to trust. He could have become another Robert Fisk, but something seemed to hold him back. He doesn't write that much nowadays."

"Personal issues?"

"I don't know," said Fane. "He's a loner—no wife that we know of. He travels a lot—must be out there at least half the year."

"We should be able to find him easily enough."

"Yes, I'd suggest you start with him."

"Start?"

Charles caught Liz's outraged gaze. But he had already made up his mind. "Geoffrey and I have agreed this story needs looking into, if only to establish there's nothing to it. I want you to do the looking." He shrugged and knew that when she calmed down Liz would realise that he had no choice. To be told that people, operating in the United Kingdom to disrupt a peace conference, were also targets for assassination required some response—even if, as he suspected, it all proved to be absolute balls.

Fane's smug expression made it obvious that whether he was passing along a ticking bomb or a damp squib, he was in the clear now.

"When do you want me to begin on this?" asked Liz, knowing the answer.

"Right away," Charles told her and added what he hoped would be a consolation. "Have Peggy Kinsolving help you."

Liz suppressed a laugh. She knew Fane had been irked when Peggy had switched allegiances from MI6 to Thames House.

But Fane seemed unfazed. "Good idea," he declared. "She's a clever girl." He stood up. "In the meantime, I'll ask Templeton to try and get more out of this source of ours." He grinned at Liz. "It will be good to work with you again, Elizabeth."

"It's Liz," she said curtly.

"Of course it is." Fane was still smiling. "How could I forget?"

Honours even, I think, said Charles to himself as Fane left the room.

6

This is really good!" Peggy exclaimed, and Liz had to suppress a smile. Only Peggy could be delighted by a cheese sandwich bought from a deli on Horseferry Road.

They were lunching at Peggy's desk in the open-plan office, surrounded by reference books and working papers. Liz glanced with distaste at her own lunch, a grim salad of lettuce, cherry tomatoes and a piece of rubber passing as a hard-boiled egg.

"All right," she said to Peggy. "Let's start with the Syrians. What do we know about their people here?"

"Not much," replied Peggy, riffling through her papers. "I spoke to Dave Armstrong in counter terrorism, but he says the Syrians aren't one of their priority targets, so they haven't done any close work on them recently. And we haven't had a counter-espionage case involving them for many years. All we know is what's on their visa applications. I've checked the names with European liaison and the Americans and got three possible intelligence traces."

"We'd better get A4 to take a look at them and get some better photographs, so we can begin to build up an idea of who we've got here."

Peggy nodded and made a note.

"Now," went on Liz, "what about these two names? How have you got on with Sami Veshara?"

"I've found out quite a bit about him. He's a Lebanese Christian who's lived in London for about twenty years. He's a prominent member of the Lebanese community here, and runs a very successful business importing foodstuffs from the Middle East: olives and pistachios from Lebanon, wine from the Bekaa Valley—all sorts of items, not just from Lebanon. He seems to supply virtually every Middle Eastern restaurant in London; speciality shops take his stuff, and even Waitrose carry his olives. He has a wife and five children, and he travels a lot—Lebanon, of course, but also Syria and Jordan."

"Politics?"

"He doesn't seem to have any, though he gave a lot of money to the Labour Party, and supposedly he was in line for some kind of gong until the Honours scandal erupted."

"Any trouble with the law?"

"No, but he's sailed pretty close to the wind. I talked to the Revenue, and they said they'd audited him four times in the last six years, which is pretty unusual. They wouldn't say much, but I had the feeling they didn't think Veshara was completely straight. His is the kind of business where cash changes hands and transactions aren't always recorded."

"Anything else?"

"Yes. Customs and Excise have been keeping an eye on him—apparently some of his shipments come in by boat."

"Something wrong with that?"

"No. But these aren't large containers. Some of these boats are no bigger than a fishing trawler, and they're sailing from Belgium and Holland, then offloading in East Anglia—Harwich mainly. It seems an odd way to bring in olives."

"What did they think he was bringing in?"

"They wouldn't speculate. But drugs is the obvious possibility."

"If they think that, they'll be checking him out themselves. Better watch out for crossed wires. But we do need to know more."

Peggy nodded. "How about you? Have you managed to locate Marcham?"

"No. I gather he's been away on some sort of assignment for the *Sunday Times Magazine*. He's just interviewed the President of Syria, and he's supposed to deliver the piece next week. That may explain why he's not answering his phone. He lives in Hampstead, so I thought I might try to root him out there."

"Maybe he drinks."

"What makes you say that?" asked Liz, slightly surprised.

"I don't know. Don't all journalists drink too much?"

Liz laughed, as the phone on Peggy's desk rang. Peggy picked it up and listened for a minute.

"Where are you?" she said. "Waitrose would have been much better."

Waitrose? What was this about? thought Liz, amused. Peggy was listening intently, then suddenly erupted. "No, *not* broccoli. *Green beans.*"

And then it dawned—Peggy had a boyfriend. Well, blow me down, thought Liz. It had barely occurred to her that Peggy had any personal life at all; she seemed so utterly caught up in her work. Good for her.

Suddenly remembering Liz's presence, Peggy blushed deeply, her face the colour of beetroot. "I have to go," she said tersely and put the phone down.

Liz grinned. She couldn't resist teasing her. "He's not good on vegetables, then?"

Peggy shook her head. "Hopeless."

"Still, I'm impressed if you've got him doing the shopping. Can he cook?"

Peggy sighed. "He can't make an omelette without using every bowl and frying pan in the kitchen. Deep down he thinks he's Gordon Ramsay. Are all men like that?"

"By and large," said Liz. "What does he do when he's not destroying your kitchen?"

"He's a lecturer in English at King's. He's only just started."

"That's nice. How did you meet?"

"At a talk he gave at the Royal Society of Literature. It was on John Donne—that's Tim's speciality. Oxford University Press are going to publish his book," she added proudly. "I asked a question, and he came up to me afterwards. He said he didn't feel he'd answered it properly."

I bet, thought Liz. She could imagine it: earnest but pretty Peggy, with her freckles and glasses; the worthy Tim, impressed by her clever question, but also attracted in a strictly unintellectual way. The time-honoured way of all flesh, thought Liz.

7

Wally Woods knew this depressing block of 1930s flats just off the North Circular Road. Years ago when he was a young A4 surveillance officer, starting his career, he'd often sat outside it. In those days, at the height of the Cold War, the block had been home to a group of East German intelligence officers and their families. When the wall had come down in 1989 they had melted away like snow.

Wally and A4 had moved on to other targets. New, younger surveillance officers had been recruited and now he was a team leader. Apart from his partner, Maureen Hayes, he was the only one of the team who actually remembered the Cold War. Halton Heights had moved on too, though it still looked just as down at heel. Now it was home to some Syrian diplomats and their families.

It was a quiet day for A4. For once they had no big operation on, and Wally and his team had been briefed to observe the comings and goings at Halton Heights. The briefing officer, Liz Carlyle of the counter-espionage branch, had told them that this was part of establishing background information on a new target. The job was to photograph anyone going out or coming in. But if any one of three men suspected to be intelligence officers appeared—and she had handed out rather poor-quality photographs which looked as if they had come from passports or visa applications—they were to follow him and report on his movements, as well as photograph whoever he met. It was the sort of job A4 hated—vague and promising little action.

By ten a.m. on this hot, sultry morning, nothing at all had happened. Wally was happy with his position, parked in a lay-by outside a line of small shops at the side of the flats. He had a good view of the ends of the semi-circular drive that led to the front door. Maureen was in the launderette, one of the shops in the row, putting some old clothes from the A4 store through a wash. If the call came to move, she'd just abandon them.

From where he sat, Wally could see Dennis Rudge apparently dozing on a bench just opposite the flats, with a full view of the front door, while a few yards behind him, in a little park, the youngster of the team, Norbert Bollum—they called him Bollocks—sat on another bench reading a paper. Other members of the team were parked up in nearby streets or driving slowly around in the vicinity.

Wally yawned and looked at his watch. Another four hours before the shift ended. Then his eye caught a movement—Dennis Rudge, whose head had been sunk on his chest, had suddenly looked up.

Wally's radio crackled. "There's action at the front door. One male. I think it's Target Alpha."

The door of the launderette swung open. Maureen came out and got into the car beside Wally. Several streets away a car did a three-point turn and two others that had been parked started their engines.

"He's standing at the door. Looks as though he's waiting for someone," came through from Dennis on the radio. As he spoke a black people carrier with smoked windows turned into the semi-circular drive.

"There's two, no, three men getting out," reported Dennis a few minutes later. "Leather jackets, short hair. They look military. They're unloading big holdalls. I think they're going to go inside."

"Get pictures—including the luggage," ordered Wally. Clutching her handbag, Maureen got out of the car, walked briskly across the road and past the flats. The camera concealed in her handbag would supplement the pictures Dennis got from his bench.

After everything was unloaded and all the men had gone inside, the people carrier drove away. Following his brief, Wally let it go, and kept his team at Halton Heights in case anyone left the flats. But by two o'clock, when their shift ended, no one had emerged, and Wally withdrew his people. Control at Thames House would make a preliminary report of their findings; Wally and his team would be debriefed in detail the following day.

8

Sami Veshara sipped his demitasse of Lebanese coffee and gave a small appreciative belch. The lunch celebrating his friend Ben Aziz's forty-fifth birthday was almost over, and it had been a feast worthy of the name.

Not surprising, thought Sami, since most of the ingredients had been supplied to this London restaurant by his own company, and he had made sure nothing but the best was used for this meal. The *mezze* had been first-rate, especially the *babaganoush* and the *fatayer*, pastries stuffed with minced duck and spinach. Then the main course, lamb *shawarma*, had been mouth-wateringly tender after its two-day bath in a spicy marinade. Dessert eventually followed: muscat ice cream and a sesame tart with berry-rose mousse. All of it washed down with mineral water and vintage Château Musar from the hillside vineyards above the Bekaa Valley, north of Beirut.

Beirut—you would not have had a better meal even there, he thought with some satisfaction. He looked idly at the plate of Turkish delight on the table, and decided he should show some self-discipline. So he took only one.

He sat back and lit a small cheroot, chatting from time to time with the dozen or so other friends of Ben Aziz gathered here. They were all fellow Lebanese, and often congregated for lunch in this small restaurant on a side street off the Edgware Road, just a few streets up from Marble Arch. Once the neighbourhood had been full of Yanks, Little America they'd called it. But those days were long gone, thought Sami with satisfaction, and now Arabs outnumbered the Westerners.

He contemplated the afternoon ahead of him. Business had been very good during the last twelve months, both the food-importing side of things that he was known for, and other activities he preferred not to be publicly associated with. He had been to the Bayswater offices of his import company that morning for a meeting with the accountants, and had been pleased by their low estimates of the year's tax liability. A lot of thought had gone into that. He felt an afternoon off was well deserved.

Outside, his chauffeur waited in the Mercedes saloon. Sami's wife and children were in Beirut for a pre-Ramadan visit to family and friends, staying in the large villa he had built off the Corniche when the troubles had subsided in the 1990s.

Normally, Sami would have found distraction in the arms of his mistress, an Italian beauty whose modelling career he was happy to subsidise. But she was on a shoot in Paris for two days, so he would have to find some other way to pass the afternoon. He thought fleetingly of other possible distractions, but he remembered there was a phone call due about a shipment coming in. And later a private meeting, where he would need to have his wits about him. Better to go home, snooze a bit and read *Al Nabad* until then.

Gradually the lunch party dispersed. Sami went outside and stretched his arms, his eyes blinking in the bright sun. His driver jumped out of the car and ran around to hold the door open. Malouf was Egyptian, an obsequious man, eternally grateful to his benefactor. He was almost seventy years old and he had a heart condition. Sami's wife, Raya, wanted her husband to get a younger driver, but Malouf had been with him for twenty-five years, and Sami valued his loyalty. He also knew that at least half of the salary he paid the man was sent back to relatives in the slums of Giza, not far from the pyramids. They would suffer if he let Malouf go.

Now Malouf asked, "Where to, Mr. Veshara?"

"Just home. Then you can have the rest of the day off." He would drive himself to his early evening meeting, since he trusted no one, not even Malouf, to accompany him there.

The call came on his mobile as Malouf turned the car around and headed north, towards the Vesharas' twenty-room mansion on Bishops Avenue in the Highgate hinterland.

"Yes," he said into the mobile.

"The shipment arrives tonight." The voice was low and respectful.

"How many?"

"Five."

"That's one short."

"I know. There was an accident."

"Accident? Where?"

"In Brussels."

Not on his watch then. Sami was relieved: the last thing he wanted was Interpol sniffing around. He asked, "Is the ground transportation all arranged?"

"It is. And we have a house in Birmingham."

"Let me know when the packages arrive there."

"Yes." And the line went dead.

Malouf was watching in the mirror. "Forgive me, sir, but there is a large car behind us, a limousine. It's staying very close. Could it be one of your friends from lunch?"

Sami looked back over his shoulder. Sure enough, there was a black limo almost on their bumper, and as they went under the flyover and through the green light it momentarily flashed its lights. Who could it be? Not one of his lunch companions, he was sure of that. They were businessmen, but none of them could run to a stretch limousine. Yet he was not alarmed; London was full of idiots in cars. This wasn't Baghdad, after all.

"Relax, Malouf. It's just some fool showing off."

Suddenly a Range Rover pulled out sharply from the right, and cut in ahead of them on Edgware Road, forcing Malouf to brake. After its initial burst of speed, the Range Rover slowed, forcing them to cut their own speed even further.

"I don't like this, Mr. Veshara."

Neither did Sami. For the first time he sensed a threat; they were being boxed in. "Take the next right turn. But do not indicate." That should shake them off.

Malouf nodded. He angled slightly to make the turn but suddenly a large 4 × 4 appeared on their right side, drawing up alongside. When Malouf slowed, so did the 4 × 4. It hogged the middle of the road, and cars coming the other way were forced to move over, one blinking its lights furiously and its driver giving a vigorous two-finger salute.

Sami wondered who could be in these cars surrounding him. Had they mistaken him for someone else?

"Turn left," he ordered. His throat felt dry, constricted.

But on that side, too, another car suddenly appeared, almost close enough to clip the Mercedes' wing mirror. It was a white van, like the kind the police used to shuttle prisoners around, with smoked windows that screened its occupants from view.

The Mercedes was now effectively surrounded and Sami no longer had any doubt they were working together. Who were these people? The Russian mob had been making noises lately about his little sideline, the one that needed small boats running across the North Sea to the dock he'd rented near Harwich. Who else could it be? For a brief moment, he wondered if his deeper, darker secret might have been discovered. No, it was impossible. He had always been exceedingly careful. So maybe it was the Russians, after all. But what did they want? And for Allah's sake, what did they intend to do? They couldn't be trying to murder him in broad daylight, and a kidnapping seemed equally preposterous. They're just trying to scare me, he thought, and if that was their aim they were doing a good job.

"Hold on, sir," Malouf said, and gripped the wheel tightly with both hands. On their left ahead, a man in a green shirt was getting out of a parked car. He seemed oblivious to the tense convoy approaching them and, though the white van honked its horn furiously in warning, made no effort to get out of the way.

The white van was forced to slow down, and it was then Malouf made his move, swinging the wheel sharply and steering the car fast into a side street, its wheels screeching like a B-movie car chase. Narrowly missing a trio of mothers crossing the road, buggies pushed before them, Malouf accelerated and sped on. When Sami looked back, only the white van was following, now a hundred yards behind.

When they reached the junction with a large avenue, the light was green, but inexplicably Malouf slowed down. "Go, go," shouted Sami. He noticed the older man was sweating.

But Malouf knew what he was doing. The van was closing behind them, and Sami was about to shout again, when Malouf floored the accelerator and joined the main road just as the light turned amber. The flow of traffic on the larger road meant there was no way the van could run the red light. It gave them at least a minute head start.

Sami leaned forward and spoke urgently. "Malouf, do not drive to the house. There may be others waiting for us there. Find a hiding place, but quickly." He noticed the Egyptian was now sweating even more profusely.

They drove through a bewildering maze of side streets. God knows where they were. Sami kept looking back, but they had lost the van. At last Malouf pulled into a small mews, and turned the car around so they could exit rapidly. He left the engine running while Sami thought what to do next.

He didn't want to call the police. What could he tell them? "Officer, four cars surrounded me, and I am sure they wanted to . . ." what? Kidnap him? Murder him? The police would think him paranoid—he could give them no evidence of what had happened. Besides, it was important to keep his profile as low as possible with the law enforcement authorities.

No, he needed security of a private sort, which wouldn't ask for evidence, and wouldn't pose difficult questions. Mahfuz came into his mind, a cousin who ran several nightclubs in the northern suburbs of London. He employed all sorts of "muscle" to sort out trouble in his clubs. Once he had shown Sami a handgun he carried when he had large amounts of cash to transport.

"I need to make a call, Malouf. Then I'll tell you where to go next."

There was no reply from the driver. Sami dialled Mahfuz's home, but got his wife. He was doing an inventory at one of the clubs, in Finchley, she said. He thanked her and was about to ring there when he noticed that Malouf was still sitting upright in his driver's seat.

Sami said sharply, "Malouf." The man didn't move. Sami leaned forward and touched the old retainer gently on the shoulder, but there was no response. He could have been a statue.

"Oh no," said Sami. The old man's heart had given out. The excitement had killed him.

9

Geoffrey Fane disliked visiting the American embassy in Grosvenor Square. The litter of concrete blocks and ill-shaped flower tubs spread all over the road and round the gardens offended his aesthetic sense. What a mess we've made of London in the name of "the war on terror," he reflected.

His taxi dropped him on the opposite side of the square from the embassy. "Can't get any nearer, Guv," the driver told him, echoing his thoughts. "New barriers up since last month. If the Yanks didn't go round the world interfering where they're not wanted, we could have our streets back. No one wants to live round here now, you know. Used to get top whack for these properties, now they can't give 'em away."

Well, not quite, thought Fane, as he walked towards the police post in front of the weighty, white building that filled one side of the square. The huge gold eagle on the top shone in the late summer sunshine, loudly announcing the presence of Britain's dominant ally.

Today, Fane had a lunch engagement at the nearby Connaught Hotel, so instead of summoning Andy Bokus, the CIA station head, to his office in Vauxhall Cross, he had decided to call on him. By the time he had emerged through the slow, deliberate security measures at the door, he was regretting his decision. The breezy cheerfulness of the long-legged, squeaky clean American girl who collected him on the other side, with her wide grin of perfect, white teeth and her *Good morning, sir,* did not improve his humour. Utterly sexless, he thought to himself.

It was five years now since Fane's marriage had broken up and Adele had gone off to live in Paris with her rich French banker. In some ways it had been a relief. Quite frankly, he could now admit to himself, she had been a drag on his career. She had never taken to being an MI6 wife. She had had no sympathy for his work or any wish to understand it and was merely irritated by the frequent postings abroad and her husband's mysterious and unpredictable absences.

All the same, now she was gone he was lonely. He hated the vulnerability and he disguised it. His thoughts often turned to the MI5 woman, Liz Carlyle. She would be an attractive companion. She understood him, he knew—perhaps too well. She appreciated how important his work was. For a time last year he thought they were growing closer, but now that Charles Wetherby was back, it was damned obvious that he was the one she was keen on. What a waste, thought Fane. A dry old stick, Charles, and too cautious by half. Well not old perhaps, he thought ruefully, since Charles was a good five years younger than Fane.

Down in the depths of the building, in the CIA station, Andy Bokus was waiting for him in his office with Miles Brookhaven, a young CIA officer whom Fane had met only once, a couple of months ago, when Brookhaven had paid his courtesy calls on arrival in the country. Fane, standing taller than either of them, his heron-like figure clad elegantly in a dark grey suit, his tie sporting the discreet stripes by which Englishmen communicate with each other, surveyed them with his sharp blue eyes.

He had heard about Brookhaven from Bruno Mackay, who'd met him at the Downing Street meeting about the Gleneagles conference. Fane could take in the man at once: a classic East Coast WASP, Anglophile, another Yank keen to show he was at home in Britain—doubtless, like others Fane had known, Brookhaven would soon be pressing him to sign the book on his behalf at the Travellers Club.

Bokus he found infinitely more interesting, and harder to read. When it came to Americans he preferred someone who was not trying to be a European, someone like Bokus, who had amused Fane when they had had lunch at the Travellers by asking for a Budweiser. From the framed team photographs lining the office wall, he saw that Bokus had played American football (unsurprising given his bulk and obvious strength) at some university Fane had never heard of, somewhere in the Midwestern sticks. Perhaps that was the origin of his remarkable accent. He didn't speak English as Fane recognised it, but rather as Fane imagined a stevedore on the Great Lakes might speak. It was an act—wasn't it? Behind the beefy, balding exterior of the man, Fane suspected—though he couldn't be sure; he had dealt with some dozy CIA officers—there lay a first-rate intelligence, one with enough confidence not to need to show itself, except when absolutely necessary. It would be very easy to underestimate Mr. Andy Bokus, Fane concluded. He might be as stupid as he looked, but there would be no harm in assuming the opposite.

"Gentlemen," Fane said now with a practised smile, deciding that if Bokus could act like a professional football player, he would adopt his most patrician manner, "it's most awfully good of you to see me. I don't want to take up too much of your valuable time, but I thought you'd want to know a little more about what was behind Sir Nicholas's intervention at the Cabinet Office meeting the day before yesterday. Perhaps we might withdraw and I will expand a little."

This was the signal for the three of them to move into the safe room, that insulated bubble that intelligence stations in embassies keep, where they can speak without fear of eavesdropping. It always slightly amused Geoffrey Fane to think that the normal function of a safe room in an embassy was to prevent eavesdropping by the intelligence services of the host nation. Whenever he penetrated the Grosvenor Square bubble, Fane, from the heart of British intelligence, felt like the cat invited into the goldfish bowl.

Fane took his time telling his story of Jaghir's revelation of the threat to the Gleneagles conference, drawing it out to disguise how much he was leaving out. When he had finished neither Bokus nor Brookhaven would have known from which country, much less which source, the information came.

Bokus scratched his forehead, as if he still had the hair that had once grown there. "What are these two individuals meant to be planning to do to screw up the conference?" he asked.

Fane shrugged. "It's not clear. We're pushing our source to try to find out."

"I mean, is it supposed to be a bomb?" demanded Bokus. "Or a bullet? Or maybe an embarrassment? One of your newspapers catching a president or a prime minister in bed with an eight-year-old girl."

Fane laughed politely, noticing that Brookhaven could only manage a wan smile. There was nothing very subtle about Andy Bokus. Fane said, "If the *News of the World* was the extent of the problem, I wouldn't be troubling you with this. No, we can only assume that it's something dramatic—and lethal." He sat back against the taut padding of the couch, adding almost casually, "I was hoping you might know something about these two people."

Brookhaven looked surprised, but Bokus responded stolidly. "What are their names again?" he asked nonchalantly.

"Veshara and Marcham."

"Sounds like a vaudeville act," Bokus said, and this time Brookhaven made a better show of laughing.

"I'm afraid these two have rather limited comic potential," Fane said, letting his tone slowly frost. "Veshara is Lebanese; lives here in London. That's all we know so far. Marcham's a journalist." He looked at his watch. "We'll find out more about them in due course, but I thought you might save us some time." There was nothing casual about his tone now. "Can you?"

Bokus looked questioningly at Brookhaven. The younger man shook his head at once. "Neither rings any sort of bell. I'll check the files, of course."

"Of course," said Fane and looked again at Bokus.

Bokus stared at him blankly, but then his mouth opened, as if it were not being controlled by his brain. "We'll check it out with HQ in Langley if there's nothing here, but maybe . . ."

"Right," said Fane, accepting defeat. But he wasn't through yet. "I'd like to stay in touch with this. Our protective security people are already liaising, but this is highly sensitive intelligence and I want to keep it like that for the time being."

Brookhaven interjected hesitantly. "I'm talking to MI5 about the conference. Are you suggesting something else?"

Fane lifted his palms about an inch and a half from his knees to indicate reassurance. "No, no," he said, "Charles Wetherby is completely au fait. I told him I was coming to see you. He's got one of his best people on this already—I'm sure he'd want you to deal with her."

"Liz Carlyle?"

Was there a hint of eagerness in Brookhaven's voice? Fane hoped not. "That's the one," he declared.

"Okay, okay," said Bokus. "Miles here will intermediate with Carlyle." His voice took on a peremptory tone. "Anything else?"

"No," said Fane, as they left the bubble and returned to Bokus's office, "though if we could have a quick word à deux, I'd be grateful." He smiled at Brookhaven to show it was nothing personal. Turning slightly red-faced, the younger man made his excuses and left.

Fane remained standing as Bokus went back to sit behind his desk. "As I hope I've made clear, strictly speaking this is a matter between you and Thames House."

"Strictly speaking, yes," said Bokus, giving nothing away.

"Well, what I'd like to suggest—that is, if we can speak off the record?"

"Off the record?" Bokus seemed amused for the first time. "You sound like a reporter from one of those . . . what do you call them, red tops?"

Fane inclined his head slightly. "Well, perhaps. But between us, I think you and I should have a sort of *informal* channel of communication. Just to keep in touch—about this matter, of course, and anything else that might crop up. It seems important, given the possible urgency."

"Sounds okay to me," said Bokus without enthusiasm.

10

When Fane had left, Andy Bokus picked up the phone and dialled an extension. "Miles, could you come back for a minute?" he said, though it wasn't really a question.

There was something puppy-like about Brookhaven that annoyed Bokus almost as much as his East Coast manners, his English-style clothes (elbow patches for Christ's sake) and his open admiration for all things English.

What kind of a name was Miles Brookhaven anyway? His people were probably landing in Massachusetts while Bokus's forebears were shovelling shit in the Ukraine. "Miles" for godsake—anybody with a first name like that had ivy twined round his head.

Bokus hadn't been poor, but unlike most of his Agency colleagues he had come from America's small-town heartland, where "sophisti-cated" was not a word used admiringly. But he had always believed in himself, and in the American promise that anyone in that country could, if they worked hard and put their mind to it (and, he admitted to himself, enjoyed a fair share of luck), do anything. When a football injury in his second year at college had put paid to his hopes for a pro-fessional career, Bokus had for the first time in his life paid attention to his studies. A political science major, he had known he wanted to see a bigger world than rural Ohio had to offer, so when one of his profes-sors had suggested he take the Agency's exams, he had seized the chance.

And by now, he'd seen a fair amount of it. His most recent posting before London was Madrid. He spoke Spanish fluently and he had liked the Spanish people—the men were dignified but straightforward, the women often beautiful and full of grace. He'd been there at an interesting time, too—the Madrid train bombings had been a real wake-up call in that country and had put the Agency's Madrid station into the front line at Langley. He'd done well in Madrid, which was why he'd got this plum job of London.

But he wasn't as happy here. The English struck Bokus as a sour bunch; snooty, devious when it suited them, willing to rely on Ameri-can firepower while making it clear they had the superior intellects. Like Fane, who couldn't ever disguise his obvious conviction that Bokus was an idiot.

Yet it wasn't Fane's patronising manner that was worrying him now; it was what Fane had said. You didn't have to like the Brits—which God knows Bokus didn't—to respect them. Once they got their teeth into something they shed all their "jolly good this" and "jolly good that" and acted like old-fashioned bloodhounds. They didn't give up.

Bokus could not be seen to refuse to help the Brits with this high-alert threat to the Gleneagles conference, but he was going to have to walk a tightrope. There would be no doubt at Langley that "Tiger," the source Bokus had spent the last eighteen months running in London under the nose of MI5, was too valuable to jeopardise. If the Brits even got a sniff of him, the shit would hit the fan with a massive splat. Tiger was a source so sensitive that no one else in the CIA's London station was aware of it. Tiger's reports went directly to a small group in Langley, who controlled the case. This was topflight "need to know" and only a handful of people were indoctrinated. If the Brits learned about Tiger, then Langley would, to use an English expression that Bokus actually liked, have his guts for garters.

There was a tap on the open door and he turned and motioned Brookhaven to come in. Brookhaven stood in front of the desk as Bokus, standing behind it, shuffled papers while he thought. "Listen," he said at last, "I want you to do something."

"What's that, Andy?"

"I want you to get close to this MI5 woman, Carlyle. Okay?"

"Sure," Brookhaven said dutifully. "I met her at the Cabinet Office meeting. She seemed perfectly competent, nice actually."

Where did he learn to talk like that? At prep school? "Yeah, well, competent's just dandy, but make sure you get close to her, and not the other way around. These people act like they're your best friends. They aren't, right?"

"Okay," said Brookhaven, but Bokus was warming to his theme. "Sure, this Carlyle lady will be 'perfectly charming.' She'll coo and chat and give you tea." He looked sharply at Brookhaven. "She may even act like she'll give you more than that. But if you close your eyes for the first kiss, when you open them you'll find she's swiped your shoes. You got me?"

"I got you, Andy."

You better, thought Bokus, but only grunted in reply.

11

Ben Ahmad left the Syrian embassy in Belgravia a little before three o'clock, telling his secretary he would not be back until the morning. She was used to his sudden departures and had learned not to ask questions. On his way out, he was glad to see the ambassador was not in. Ahmad reported to him in his capacity as a trade attaché; they both knew his real reporting line ran back to Syria, to the headquarters of the Mukhabarat, the Syrian secret service. The ambassador did not disguise his unhappiness with this arrangement.

Outside, Ahmad glanced at his watch, a handsome Cartier given to him by his wife, who was in Damascus looking after their three small children. His meeting was not until four-thirty, but it would take him at least an hour to get there, since there would be several diversions en route.

He was dressed neatly in a dark suit, and carried a raincoat over one arm. With a trim haircut and neat moustache, he was indistinguishable from the thousands of other Middle Eastern men going about their business in London that afternoon. He had worked hard to cultivate this anonymous air.

Walking up to Hyde Park Corner he went down into one of its labyrinthine underground tunnels, and emerged several minutes later on the far side of Park Lane, where he walked to the Hilton. There he joined a bunch of high-spirited American tourists waiting in a small queue for taxis in front of the hotel, giving the doorman a pound coin when it was his turn to enter a cab. Out of earshot of anyone but the driver, he gave his destination as Piccadilly Circus.

There, he got out, and stood for a minute against a disused doorway at the bottom of Shaftesbury Avenue, watching for other taxis that might have followed him. It was difficult in so much traffic to be sure he was not under surveillance; equally, in the hurly-burly of the streets here, following him without being noticed would be a difficult task.

He saw nothing untoward, and walked quickly to the Underground entrance. He disliked the area, which he thought epitomised the baffling English love of sleaze. He was faithful to his wife, teetotal, and he simply couldn't understand a culture that gave such value to infidelity and alcohol.

He had hoped to be back in Syria by now, for his posting had originally been intended to last only six months. Tibshirani had promised him that; otherwise Ahmad would never have left his family behind. But then "Aleppo"—code name for a source that had appeared out of the blue—had arrived, full of information so extraordinary that Ahmad had distrusted it at first and relayed only bits and pieces, while he tried to confirm its authenticity.

Yet even these titbits had caused consternation in Damascus, enough that Tibshirani had tried to insist on flying to London to manage Aleppo personally. But Aleppo had refused to meet anyone but Ahmad, stressing that if the Syrians tried to push him, he would break off all contact. Tibshirani didn't dare risk that, especially once the authenticity and value of Aleppo's information had become indisputable.

Aleppo had forecast the assassination of a senior Lebanese politician, information which subsequently proved of intense interest to that part of the Syrian secret services that was widely (and erroneously) thought to have been responsible for the murder. He had exposed a fundamentalist cell of Saudi extremists in Germany who were plotting to kill Bashar-al-Assad, Syria's young President, during a forthcoming trip to Paris; the result was the discovery of four men shot dead in a Hamburg flat, killings put down by the German police to internal Wahhabi feuding. And Aleppo had revealed the facility location of Iran's research into limited plutonium-based explosions, information Syria kept carefully in reserve.

So when Aleppo had revealed that two agents were actively working against Syrian interests in the United Kingdom with the intention of blackening Syria's name before the Gleneagles peace conference, Ahmad had ignored the vagueness of the information and promptly passed it back to Tibshirani. He had long ago learned that when an agent had a perfect record, there was no point in trying to pick and choose; he would leave that to his superiors at home, while he got on with trying to control this gold mine on his own.

In the Underground, Ahmad bought a ticket from the manned booth rather than a machine, then stopped to buy a copy of the *Evening Standard* before descending on an escalator into the cavernous depths of the Piccadilly Line.

He stood on the platform, almost empty at this time of day. He did not board the first train that came in, but took the next one, and stood up in the compartment, holding his paper in front of his face, until he got off at Acton Town. Here he went upstairs and through the ticket machines, then made a show of looking at his watch, before going back into the station. He caught a train heading north and after a single stop got off at Ealing Common. There he remained on the platform until the others who disembarked—there were only three of them—had taken the lift and gone. Then he caught the next train.

At Park Royal, he got off again, but this time he left the station. He took the pedestrian subway to the south side of the roundabout for the North Circular, and walked along Hangar Lane until he suddenly turned around and reversed his steps, stopping just short of the subway and going down a dingy side street of small shops.

Near the end of the line of shops was a small premises, with a hanging sign outside reading G. M. OLIKARA. On the front pane of the shop were dozens of manufacturer's stickers for every conceivable make of vacuum cleaner, and the window was packed with old and new models. On the glass window in the door, next to the small sign that said OPEN, was another sign, hand-lettered and stuck on with sticky tape. It read *We Fix Hoovers!*

Inside an assistant was demonstrating a Dyson machine to a customer, deliberately tipping the contents of an ashtray onto the thinning carpet of the shop before sucking up the mess into the vacuum's transparent tank with a single pass of the machine.

Ben Ahmad ignored both men and walked straight through the shop to the rear, through a bead curtain, past the stockroom and the single, squalid lavatory and out into the yard at the back. Here, in contrast to the shabbiness of the shop, a new Portakabin had been installed, freshly painted, its door unlocked. Ahmad found it prepared for his visit; a full kettle sat waiting to be boiled, and in the miniature fridge in one corner was a fresh carton of milk.

He switched the kettle on and sat down, suddenly tired by the tension of his trek. He knew he had to take every possible precaution. British surveillance was legendary, a daunting mix of the latest technology and intelligent legwork—and agents of Mossad were also all over London. But he was confident he had not been followed to the shop, which was rented in the name of the Syrian Christian who managed the business, but paid for in full by the Syrian Arab Republic.

He did not have long to wait. Before the kettle came to the boil, there was a sharp rap on the door. "Enter," commanded Ben Ahmad, and he was joined by the man he knew as Aleppo. Aleppo was wearing a black leather jacket, his face was flushed and he was breathing heavily. Without removing his jacket or so much as glancing at his host, he sat down hard in one of the two director's chairs on either side of the cabin's small desk. He was clearly on edge: "It's not convenient for me, meeting here," he complained angrily.

Ben Ahmad shrugged. They had had this conversation before. "It's safer out here. You know that. I have to insist on it."

Aleppo frowned and shook his head in disgust but did not argue further. His mind and his eyes seemed elsewhere, and he suddenly switched to the classical Arabic spoken from Morocco to the Gulf. He spoke it beautifully, while Ahmad, who had grown up in a poverty-stricken village on the Hawran Plateau, could never entirely shed all traces of the demotic from his speech. Aleppo said tersely, "There's been a leak from your people."

"A leak?" Ben Ahmad was shocked; this was the last thing he had expected. "What d'you mean?"

"Someone's been talking. To the West—the British, most likely. They know the two names I gave you and they know they intend to derail the conference in Scotland."

"How did you learn this?" asked Ben Ahmad. He was beginning to tremble, as the awful implication of what was being said hit him.

"It's my business to know." Then, sarcastically, "It's not as if I can expect your people to protect me."

"How do you know the leak comes from Syria?"

Suddenly, Aleppo's eyes turned hot and angry, fixed thunder on the man across the table. His voice was biting. "Where else could it come from? Unless your Damascus masters are in the habit of sharing secrets with their enemies."

Ben Ahmad was trying to think, though panic was slowing his brain. He must reassure and pacify Aleppo. "I will report this at once," he declared. "I give you my word, we will root out the traitor."

Aleppo was unappeased. "You'd better, or this is the last you'll see of me. And why has no action been taken against these two people yet? I took great risks to get that information. I assumed you would see its importance. But the two are still operating. Against you, I need hardly say."

"I appreciate that. But my superiors are cautious."

"Why? Do they doubt my information?"

He said this challengingly, and Ahmad's palms sweated as he felt the situation running out of his control. It was a cardinal rule for an agent runner to stay in charge, to make it clear that he, not the agent, was running the show. But with this man, Ahmad found it impossible. He was not just prickly and quick to take offence, but there was something dangerously unpredictable about him, an air of menace that Ahmad feared. Had his superiors not valued Aleppo so much, Ahmad would have been happy to break the contact. But he knew that if he lost Aleppo, his career would be finished.

"Not at all," he said reassuringly. "No one doubts the truth of what you say. But it has been hard for us to know what these people could do that would damage our interests in any substantial way." And, he decided not to add, that would justify the risks of moving against them on foreign territory.

"So they'd rather take their chances, your masters? Fools."

"I didn't say that. In fact, you can expect action to be taken soon." Ahmad thought this was likely, though in truth he didn't know what would happen or when, and he daren't give a hostage to fortune by promising the man a timescale. *Soon* would have to do for now.

Aleppo was clearly unimpressed. "Make sure it does." He got up from his chair, moving towards the door. "Now this has been leaked to the West, I am in danger. I have little confidence that you can plug this leak, which makes it all the more urgent that these people are dealt with right away. Otherwise, you may find it is too late. Tell your superiors that, from me." And he went out, banging the door so hard that the flimsy walls of the Portakabin shook.

Was that a threat? Ahmad wondered. Not quite, he decided, and he wouldn't pass it on to his superiors in Damascus—they might try to insist again on meeting the source, even try and take him over, and then Ahmad would return home without any of the credit he knew he had earned. But he would have to tell them about the leak.

After waiting ten minutes to make sure he would not trip over Aleppo on his way home, Ahmad left the Portakabin and walked through the shop, along the dingy side street and back towards Park Royal station.

He was alarmed by what Aleppo had said. It was desperately worrying if his own service had been penetrated by the West—worrying but not inconceivable. The British were good and Mossad also had infiltrated all its enemies at one time or another. At the station, he bought another copy of the *Standard,* his attention caught by a late, lurid headline. As he waited for the next train, he read the story, half-fascinated, half-repelled by its details. Auto-asphyxiation—why would anyone want to play at that? And in a church, no less. These English, he thought as he saw the amber beam of the approaching train fill the distant tunnel, they were beyond bizarre.

12

At least she knew where she was, not that it helped. Seventy feet below ground, thirty seconds out of Chalk Farm station, stuck in a tunnel with no sense they would be moving any time soon.

Across from her a morose-looking woman in a brown cardigan stared at the floor apathetically, while next to her a builder in dust-covered boots noisily turned the pages of the *Sun.* The headline read MAN IN BOX MYSTERY. How ghoulish, thought Liz, then she remembered how an ex-boyfriend, a journalist at the *Guardian,* had claimed that such headlines were reassuring. "If I land at Heathrow and the headline on the *Evening Standard* reads NURSE FOUND STRANGLED, then I know all's right with the world. No terrorist bomb has gone off, no threat of impending nuclear war. Just a humdrum sex murder to titillate commuters."

Looking at her watch, Liz saw they had been motionless for more than ten minutes. Thank God she wasn't claustrophobic; Peggy would be climbing the walls by now. Thinking of Peggy, she pondered the girl's mix of shyness and delight as she'd described Tim. Liz could imagine their first dates, all in suitably intellectual places (the National Gallery, the Soane Museum). They'd have chatted earnestly over flapjacks and mugs of tea, discussing the comparative merits of the Metaphysical Poets, or the late Beethoven string quartets.

It was easy to be patronising, but Liz had to admire Peggy's initiative—going to talks, meeting new people. Meeting men. There was no point in being stuffy about it, thought Liz, not if it worked for Peggy. And it had. And look at her own mother. Sixty-plus, a widow with a lovely house, an interesting job—even she had found company.

For years after her father had died Liz had felt responsible for her mother. Not enough for her to agree to give up what her mother regarded as her "dangerous" job to go back home to Wiltshire to share the running of the garden centre her mother managed. But enough for her to make the tedious journey every month and keep in touch regularly by phone. Then earlier this year, out of the blue, her mother had acquired a boyfriend, Edward, and now she seemed contented and less dependent on her daughter.

Liz knew she should be pleased for her mother, but when she thought of all those weekends she had forced herself to drive down to Wiltshire when she would much rather have stayed in London, the anxiety when her mother had had a cancer scare just as Liz was in the middle of a complex and worrying case, she felt a flash of resentment. It was irrational, she knew it was, but she felt it just the same.

Liz tried to picture this new boyfriend of her mother's, whom she'd never met but knew she would not like. He'd wear tweeds and be ex-army, a major perhaps, or even a colonel. He'd go on and on about the Aden campaign or wherever. God, how boring, thought Liz, and possibly venal—she was sure part of her mother's appeal to Edward must be the creature comforts she could provide for him in her cosy house in Bowerbridge. Still, she thought grudgingly, her mother seemed to be enjoying this late romance of hers.

Whereas I'm just stuck in a rut, Liz brooded, watching as the woman in the cardigan yawned and closed her eyes. The only men she met were at work, and yet at work she found her emotions already engaged. By Charles, a man she saw only in the office and who was unavailable anyway.

It suddenly seemed ridiculous. I can't go on this way, thought Liz, surprised at how obvious this realisation was. She couldn't blame any-one but herself—it wasn't as if Charles had ever encouraged her, or asked her to wait for him. She supposed he'd made his feelings clear, in his discreet and dignified way, but equally, he'd never pretended he could do anything about them.

All right then, thought Liz, cut your losses and move on. Time's a-flying, however young I feel. There must be men I can meet. The image of Geoffrey Fane flitted briefly through her head. There was something undeniably attractive about him—he was good-looking in an arrogant way, clever, quick-witted, amusing when he wanted to be. And best of all, Fane was no longer married.

But it wasn't for nothing he was known in MI5 as the Prince of Darkness, and she knew she could never altogether trust him. No, like Peggy, she needed to meet someone outside the service, and she cheered up briefly at the prospect. There was just the small matter of how to meet this new someone.

A hissing noise of escaping air came from the tunnel, and the train slid forward as if on ice. The builder looked up from his sports page and briefly met Liz's eyes. Across the carriage the older woman was sound asleep, her hands clasped in her lap.

13

It was nearly seven in the evening when Hannah Gold got off the Underground at Bond Street station and started to walk slowly towards Piccadilly. She could have changed lines and got a lot nearer to her destination, but she loved walking in London on these late summer evenings. The weather had been a surprise—she had come to England armed with sweaters and a raincoat and umbrella, but so far she had needed none of them. She might still have been in Tel Aviv, to judge by the climate.

Now, as she walked down Bond Street, she stopped from time to time to admire the clothes and shoes in the smart shops and, as she got nearer to Piccadilly, the watches and jewellery and the paintings in the windows of the galleries. She still found it hard to get used to the idea that she had enough money of her own now to buy practically anything she liked, and the independence to spend it as she pleased.

She hadn't seen Saul for more than a year—not since she'd sold their home in Beverly Hills, banked her final settlement from the divorce and upped sticks and left for her new life in Israel. Looking back on it all, she could see that she'd been in a state of shocked anger when she left America for good. Thirty-three years of marriage had been suddenly ended by one late-night conversation with her husband. She couldn't believe her ears. It was no surprise that he was having an affair—he'd had affairs before, often—but this time he wanted a divorce. All those shared years, the experiences, the help she'd given him as he built up his business . . . all gone in the forty-five seconds it had taken him to deliver his prepared speech. It was over, he'd said, and that was final.

After the first shock came the anger and it was anger that had fuelled her through the drawn-out wrangling of the divorce proceedings. She had finally been awarded her twenty million dollars, enough for a complete change of life. She could have gone to live anywhere. She could have come to London, where her son, David, lived with his wife and small children. But she'd finally chosen Israel, though it was not the obvious choice. She was proud to be Jewish, but she was increasingly upset by the way Israel behaved. The situation in that part of the world seemed to be worsening every year, and she simply couldn't believe that none of it was Israel's fault. The settlements seemed to her to be madness and the unwillingness of many Israelis to concede that the Palestinians had a grievance, more madness still.

If she was honest, she'd really chosen to live there because she thought it might give her the chance to do something in her own right. She wasn't naïve enough to think she could change the world single-handedly, and she knew she would come across people who disagreed strongly with her. But she hoped that she could have some influence by working for moderation and compromise and listening to the other side's point of view.

And so far she was convinced she was doing some good in her new homeland. She had joined a peace movement and was taking an active part in organising meetings and debates and helping to write the literature they put out. She had even practically forgotten about Saul—that is, until Mr. Teitelbaum had come her way.

It had all started at a drinks party in Tel Aviv given by one of her new friends, another American woman called Sara. Hannah had met a man there, Sidney something, who at first had asked her the usual polite questions about how she found life in Israel, but as they'd talked he had seemed much more interested to hear about her former husband's doings—particularly about the satellite communications company that Saul had founded and still ran.

After the party, Sara had told her that Sidney was a Mossad officer, and when he'd subsequently rung and asked Hannah to meet him for what he called "a chat," she'd known his interest wasn't social and had politely but firmly declined.

But then news had come of Saul's remarriage, and Hannah had learned in a phone call from one of her less tactful Californian friends that the new Mrs. Gold was a tall, twenty-three-year-old blonde with a golden tan. For Hannah, who was short and dark and didn't like the sun, that was the last straw. Twenty minutes later she had rung Sidney and agreed to meet him, though when she'd turned up at the outdoor café he'd named, she'd found another man waiting for her.

His name was Mr. Teitelbaum—she knew only his surname, and since she was Mrs. Gold to them, she reciprocated with a "mister," which gave an old-fashioned flavour to their meetings. Teitelbaum was short and squat and reminded Hannah of a toad. His bald head, which gleamed in the sunshine, sat like a bowling ball on massive shoulders, and his hands were rough as a peasant's. From the open neck of his shirt, hair sprouted like dark, curly weeds. He said very little, but he listened hard, apparently mentally recording everything Hannah had to say, for he took no notes. There had been a lot for him to remember.

Her ex-husband's company sold satellite systems all over the world—Saul had never been choosy about his customers. Many of them were in the Middle East and some were the enemies of Israel. It was these customers Mr. Teitelbaum had wanted to hear about, and since Hannah had been the one person to whom Saul had confided all his business secrets, she'd had a lot to tell; she'd seen Mr. Teitelbaum once a week for almost three months.

Now as she reached Piccadilly and walked east towards Haymarket and the theatre, she felt she deserved a treat. It was lovely to be here in London. After all the experiences of her first year in Israel she'd badly needed a rest, and after only a week she felt her energy was coming back.

The Stoppard play was tremendous fun—fast-paced, witty and verbally ingenious. All that was missing was someone to share it with; looking around the audience, Hannah felt surrounded by couples.

At the interval she worked her way through the scrum at the bar to buy a glass of wine, which she carried carefully to the safety of a corner. She was just about to take a sip when her arm was knocked sharply and her glass went flying, landing with a small pirouette on the carpet.

"I am *so* sorry."

Hannah turned to find a man behind her looking upset. He was fortyish, tall, with floppy black hair, dressed in a black suit and a charcoal turtleneck. Reaching down, he picked up her glass, which was miraculously unbroken. "I am so sorry," he said again.

"Don't worry about it," said Hannah. "It doesn't matter."

"But of course it does," the man insisted. "I'll get you another."

"Oh please don't—" Hannah started to protest, but he was already halfway to the bar.

Despite the crush he was back in a minute, bearing a new glass. This one had bubbles. "I hope you like champagne," he said, handing the glass to Hannah with a small bow.

She felt embarrassed. "It's very good of you," she said, taking a sip.

"The least I could do."

Hannah was slightly discomfited to find that he didn't move away but stayed standing beside her. She said, "You've been very kind. But please don't let me keep you from your friends."

He smiled. "I'm here on my own." He spoke fluent English, but with a very slight accent that she couldn't place.

"So am I," said Hannah.

"Where do you live?"

"Tel Aviv."

"No," he said with disbelief. "You are Israeli? So am I."

"Well, I'm American actually. But I moved to Israel last year."

"How interesting," he said. "You have reversed the trend. Half of my generation seems to be immigrating to the States."

They continued talking, rapidly discovering several mutual acquaintances in the small world of Israeli society. Hannah was quite disappointed when the bell rang for the start of the second act.

"Oh dear," he said. "What a pity. I should introduce myself. My name is Danny Kollek. I work at our embassy here in London."

"Hannah Gold." They shook hands.

"I wonder," said Kollek hesitantly.

"Yes?" said Hannah, noticing the bar was almost empty now.

"Would you like to have supper with me after the play?"

Hannah had been thinking of taking a taxi back to David's house and having an early night. But she liked this man, and was flattered to be the object of attention for a change. Why not take advantage of it?

"I'd like that very much," she said at last.

Again there was the smile—even more than his good looks it was this that made the man appealing. "I'll meet you in front then," he said, as the last bell rang before the second act.

When the play ended, Hannah half-expected to find that Danny had disappeared; why would someone his age want to take a woman half as old again out for dinner? So she was pleasantly surprised to find him standing on the edge of the pavement, looking out for her.

They went to a restaurant in St. James's—a large, modern place with a high ceiling, bright pastel columns and mirrors on the walls. Danny proved an easy conversationalist: amusing, entertaining, yet willing to talk about serious things. And to listen—he seemed to take a real interest in what Hannah had to say, which after thirty years of Saul was a refreshing change. Their conversation ranged widely: the theatre, music and the strange ways of the English. When he asked for her impressions of London—he said he had been there two years himself—she said, hoping it didn't sound too banal, "It feels very different here. It's almost as if something's absent."

He looked at her as their starters arrived. "You know what's missing, don't you?"

"Halva?" she asked playfully.

Danny laughed out loud and Hannah noticed how white his teeth were, in contrast to the walnut colouring of his skin. He was probably Sabra, a native-born Israeli. Who knew where his parents had come from? It could have been almost anywhere.

Suddenly Danny's face sobered and his expression grew serious. "What's missing here is *fear*. Oh I know they had IRA bombs for years, and after the July bombings you could see the apprehension on the Underground, the mistrust in everyone's eyes. But it didn't last, because the status quo here is peace. When people leave home in the morning here, they expect to return home safe and sound in the evening."

"Spoken like a true Israeli," she said. It was true; life in Tel Aviv was constantly tense. It was the one thing she didn't like about living there. Danny nodded and she went on. "Unfortunately, I don't see the situation in Israel changing any time soon."

"Not while the two sides are at such loggerheads," he said, and she was gratified that at least he understood that there were two sides to the issues. Mr. Teitelbaum would never countenance that; he was a hawk through and through.

She said tentatively, wondering if he would disapprove, "I've joined the peace movement." But far from disapproving, it turned out that he knew some of the people involved well and was sympathetic to their ideas. He even allowed that yes, he was related to Teddy Kollek, the late mayor of Jerusalem and a famous dove, though he stressed that he was a distant relation.

"Did you ever meet him?"

"Yes," he said, looking down modestly. "But only once or twice. He was very kind, but I was just a boy then."

Dinner seemed to pass in minutes and when Danny called for the bill, he raised his wineglass and proposed a toast. "To the genius of Mr. Stoppard, and to my elbow."

"Your elbow?"

"Yes, for inadvertently spilling your glass of wine."

She laughed and he added, "And thus for providing me with your company this evening."

As she smiled at him he asked, "I wonder if by any chance you would be free two evenings from now. I am sure you are very busy with your family, but a colleague at work has given me two tickets to a chamber concert at St. John's church in Smith Square. I am told the acoustics are marvellous."

"I'd like that very much," she said, this time without hesitation.

Outside Danny hailed a taxi, and Hannah gave the driver the address in Highgate. Danny said good night and shook her hand formally. As the taxi drove off, Hannah found herself thinking what a nice man he seemed, and how pleasant dinner had been.

But she was not naïve—not after thirty years of life with Saul—and inevitably part of her wondered what Danny Kollek was after.

Her body? she wondered, then suppressed a giggle at the thought. It seemed most unlikely; Hannah was flattered by the attentions of this good-looking young man, but she had too little vanity to think he was really interested in her sexually. Could it be her money, then? She thought not. She wasn't dressed expensively this evening, or wearing any jewellery, and nothing she'd said would have indicated personal wealth. And Danny had picked up the cheque for dinner at once, refusing her offer to share.

No, it couldn't be money attracting him—a conclusion confirmed beyond doubt when the taxi arrived at her son's house. As Hannah got out her purse to pay the driver he shook his head. "It's all been taken care of, luv," he said, waving some notes that Danny Kollek had given him as he said goodbye to her.

So neither gigolo nor gold-digger, thought Hannah contentedly as she entered the Highgate house. Just a companion—and a very amusing one at that. Best of all, he hadn't asked her one blessed thing about Saul.

14

It was a very small house for Hampstead, a cottage really, single-storey with one Gothic gable. Nineteenth century, perhaps even older, and Liz wondered if the roof had once been thatched. The cottage sat behind a tall, shaggy yew hedge. The wooden entrance gate moved slightly in the breeze, its hinges squeaking mournfully; when she gave a push, it swung wide open.

Liz took two tentative steps and found herself in a small front garden hidden from the street by the hedge. A path of old paving stones led to the front door of the cottage, which seemed to be badly in need of repair: several roof tiles were slipping, and the windowsills on either side of the front door looked rotten.

She rang the bell and heard it echoing loudly. No sound of

movement inside. She peered through the letter box but couldn't see any post lying uncollected on the mat inside. She waited a little while, then rang again. Still no response.

It was while she was wondering what to do next that some second sense made her turn round and see the man standing in a corner of the garden, next to a small circular rose bed. He was over average height and wore a baseball cap, tilted down, making it hard to see his face or tell his age—anywhere from thirty to fifty, Liz decided. Around his waist a gardener's apron was wrapped, and in his right hand he held a pair of secateurs. He waved them casually at Liz, before turning to prune one of the tall roses.

"Excuse me." Liz raised her voice as she crossed the lawn.

He turned around very slowly, but didn't look her in the eye. "Yes?"

"I'm looking for Mr. Marcham. Is he in?" She wondered if this could be Marcham himself, tending his garden, but no—Marcham's photographs had shown an angular English face. This man looked slightly foreign; dark-skinned, Mediterranean.

The man shook his head, turning away from her. "I haven't seen him today. Did you ring the bell?"

"Yes, but no one answered. You don't happen to know where I might find him?"

The man now had his back to her. "Sorry. He's not often here when I am."

"Right," said Liz, wondering if she should leave Marcham a note. "Thanks very much," she said, and the man merely nodded, continuing with his pruning. I hope you're a better gardener than communicator, she thought as she left.

She walked out and looked both ways along the street, as if willing Chris Marcham to appear. Where could he be? The source at *The Sunday Times* had said there was no wife or children, no family that he'd ever heard about. "A bit of a loner," he'd added for good measure. Liz cursed Marcham—if he was so bloody unsociable, then why couldn't he stay at home?

But he couldn't be doing too badly, she concluded as she started the long walk back to the Underground. His house was small and pretty run down, but it was in Hampstead, and right on the edge of the Heath. It should provide a handsome pension in his old age. And he could afford a gardener, though from the look of the ragged flower beds this one didn't seem to be up to snuff. A funny bloke, thought Liz, suddenly realizing the man hadn't even been wearing proper shoes for the job—they were slip-ons, shiny-looking ones, more at home in a wine bar than a flower bed. What had he been doing anyway? Pruning the roses, that was it.

Liz stopped suddenly and stood still. Her mother ran a nursery garden, but you didn't need her knowledge to see what was wrong. No one prunes roses in August—not bush roses, that was for sure. The man had been a fake. Whatever he was, he wasn't a gardener.

She wondered what to do. Looking back, she saw that she was barely a hundred yards from the house. Ought she to ring the police? She paused. Better to go back herself, right now, before he'd sloped off, and see what he was really up to.

She hesitated, since if he wasn't a gardener, then he couldn't be up to anything good. But she made up her mind to ignore her apprehension, and started half-running towards the little house. When she got to the gate she saw the front door was wide open. She slowed only momentarily, then walked quickly inside, calling out "hello" loudly as she entered.

Silence. She stood in the small hallway next to a living room remarkable for its lived-in drabness. Through the door she could see a television perched on an MDF cabinet in one corner, covered by a thick layer of dust. Along the far wall sat a shabby, stained sofa badly in need of reupholstering. The low coffee table in front of it was covered with newspapers and magazines. Never mind the gardener, thought Liz, Marcham should get himself a cleaner.

Directly ahead of her the short hall led to a closed door. She walked up to it, quietly turned the knob and pushed it open. She was looking into a small, square kitchen. Dirty dishes sat in the sink; an open box of cereal stood on the pine table in the middle of the room. Beyond were two more doors, one also closed, the other open and leading to a bedroom. She walked across the kitchen and, peering in, saw a brass bed, neatly made. On the bedside table there was a dog-eared copy of *England's 1000 Best Churches,* and on the wall a framed picture of Jesus on the cross.

Then she heard the noise. Something being moved, or pushed, the sound of wood sliding, coming from the room next door. Retreating to the kitchen, she looked around for something to defend herself with. Not a knife, she thought; facing a stronger man, she might find a knife turned against her. But there was a heavy frying pan on the stove. Grabbing its handle, she moved to the closed door and opened it cautiously. She was just in time to see a man drop from the back window.

"Stop!" she shouted, knowing he wouldn't, and by the time she got to the window, the man was scaling the low wall that separated the rear garden from Hampstead Heath. All she got was a glimpse of his shoes. Slip-ons, still shiny.

Her pulse racing, she put the frying pan down and looked around the room, which was a small study. In contrast to the squalid sitting room, the study was tidy and well organised. Books lined two of the walls, neatly arranged, and a small antique bureau sat next to the window, its lid down to double as a writing surface. On it sat a closed laptop computer, a digital tape recorder the size of a cigarette lighter, an A4-sized notebook and three HB pencils, sharpened and aligned in a row. The arsenal of a professional writer.

She examined the tape recorder, but it was empty. Noticing a pile of file folders on the bookcase, she extracted the top one, which lay askew across the neat stack. She read its label with sudden interest. *Al-Assad Interview, Notes and Final Copy.* The article on Syria's President that *The Sunday Times* was waiting for so eagerly. Yet when Liz opened the file it was empty. Was that what the "gardener" was after?

"What the hell do you think you're doing?"

Liz jumped at the sudden noise behind her. She turned and found a middle-aged man in jeans and a white shirt standing in the doorway. He was tall and he was very angry—an accomplice of the burglar she'd just surprised? Liz looked quickly around, but the frying pan was out of reach.

It seemed best to take the initiative; maybe she could catch him off-guard long enough to get past him. "Who are you?" she demanded.

"My name's Marcham. Now perhaps you'll tell me just what the hell you're doing in my house?"

1 5

Sophie Margolis sat in the kitchen of her large Highgate house, thinking of her mother-in-law. For once, Sophie had time on her hands, a cup of coffee in front of her and Hannah for the moment out of the way—the attentive granny, walking little Zack on the Heath.

Sophie had always liked Hannah, but she reflected how little she really knew about her. For one thing Saul had always got in the way—Hannah's former husband, a bullying missile of a man who mistook pugnacity for energy, monopolised attention and had done his best to undermine everyone around him. Not least David, his son, Sophie's husband, whose gentleness had so attracted her, and still did. In the end Hannah had called "time" on Saul. It had been a contested divorce, a fiery business, full of animosity. Had it wounded Hannah? Not to all appearances, thought Sophie. She was full of enthusiasm about her new life in Israel; acting in fact as though she was only just beginning to live life to the full.

A pair of blue tits was picking greenflies off the roses. Sophie got off her stool to watch them and to cast an eye at the pram containing her latest offspring.

There was something, though, about Hannah—something not so much worrying as puzzling. When she'd first arrived in London it had been hard to get her out of the house on her own. She'd gone with Sophie and David to the theatre, to dinner with a few friends, that was all. But now there seemed to be a man in the picture. Where had he come from? Sophie had first spotted the two together when she had been pushing the buggy down Highgate High Street and to her great surprise her mother-in-law had emerged from a coffee shop in the company of a male at least twenty years her junior—attractive, too. There had been no attempt at concealment. Hannah came straight up and introduced her companion—Danny Kollek from the Israeli embassy. And from there it had taken off. It soon transpired that Hannah was seeing a lot of Mr. Kollek. They went to concerts, to restaurants, sometimes for walks and once, amazingly, to the zoo.

Well, thought Sophie, resuming her stool and running her eye over the *Times 2* crossword puzzle, was it really so surprising? At least Mr. Kollek was as unlike Saul as it was possible to be. He seemed intelligent and cultured and he was, frankly, handsome. Surely he couldn't be after sex with Hannah, could he? She hadn't spent a night away from the house. Money? Well, Hannah had fought Saul tooth and nail for a good settlement. She was worth the best part of twenty million dollars, Sophie knew for a fact. So Kollek could be after her money, but he seemed to be going an odd way about it. Hannah had told her that he always insisted on paying for their entertainment. Still, twenty million dollars justified a careful, tactical courtship. It was with this in mind that Sophie decided that she'd better do something.

They were on the Heath by the dog pond, taking turns pushing the baby in the buggy, when she broached the subject. The sun had moved from behind the clouds, warming the air, and Sophie took off her pullover, feeling frumpy in an old T-shirt and jeans. Hannah was dressed casually too, but smartly—in linen trousers and a silk shirt.

Sophie remarked, as if by the way, "What exactly does your friend Danny do at the Israeli embassy?"

Hannah gave a small smile. "He's a trade attaché. Not very senior, but he's still quite young."

"So he's just a friend?"

"Yes. What else would he be? I have my vanity, my dear, but it doesn't extend to boy toys. I'm sure he's not interested in me in that way. And if you're thinking it's my money he's after, you can relax. He seems perfectly well-off, and besides, he doesn't know I have money of my own. No, I think it's just that he's lonely over here; English people aren't always that welcoming, present company excepted. And Israelis aren't very popular anywhere these days. He and I just get on well— we both love music, for one thing."

Sophie knew she should have been relieved by this, but in fact it only made her more suspicious. It simply didn't make sense to her that Kollek would want to spend so much time with a woman twenty years older, especially if he had none of a gigolo's objectives in mind. Yet how could she put this to Hannah, without causing offence? It would be too insulting to insist that he must be pursuing a hidden agenda, rather than mere friendship.

It niggled at her for several days, until now, staring idly out as the blue tits were joined by a couple of blackbirds, she felt she had to act. In the old days, when she was still working, she would have been able to do some digging herself, but as a Highgate housewife, she felt powerless. Hang on, she thought, there must be somebody from the past who could give me some advice. Even if it was just to tell me to mind my own business and stop worrying. And she realised that of course there was someone, a sort-of friend, whom she hadn't seen for a while but knew well enough to ring up out of the blue. Someone whose judgement she respected, too, which was more important now than simple moral support. She got up and went to the wall phone by the kitchen door.

"Liz Carlyle," Liz said mechanically, for she had been immersed in an agent runner's report when her phone rang.

"Liz, it's Sophie Margolis."

"Hi there," said Liz, surprised. It had been a couple of years since she'd seen Sophie, and probably six or seven since Sophie had left the service. They'd kept in touch, at least at first, meeting for the occasional lunch. When the baby had been born, Liz had sent a present. What was his name? Zack, that was it. Hadn't there been another one since? Liz felt a pang of guilt, since she hadn't sent a present the second time round.

They exchanged pleasantries for a few minutes. Sophie told Liz about her children, and how David was doing in the City (very well, apparently), and about a recent holiday in Umbria. Liz did her best to sound cheery about her own single existence, and realised she had yet to plan a holiday for herself.

Then Sophie said, "Listen, it would be wonderful to see you. David and I were hoping to get you over for supper. Any chance?"

"Of course. I'd love to."

"David's mother is visiting from Israel. She's American but moved to Tel Aviv when she got divorced last year."

"Oh, I'm sorry."

"Don't be. He was the monster from hell. Even David would admit that, and he's his son. Listen, I know it's not much notice, but could you come this Saturday?"

"Oh, Sophie, I'm sorry but I'm going down to my mother's this weekend." Yes, thought Liz, to meet this Edward man at last. She wasn't going to miss that.

"What a pity. How about next week some time? Say Wednesday?"

Liz looked at her diary. It was accusingly empty. "That would be fine."

"Great. You know where we are. Shall we say eight o'clock?"

"Fine."

But Sophie wasn't ready to ring off. "Liz, we do want to see you, but I'd better confess—I have a slight ulterior motive."

"What's that?" Maybe Sophie was going to set her up with some City friend of her husband. Liz stifled a yawn. She could arrange her own romantic life, thank you very much.

"Well, it's about David's mother. You see, she's been going around with a man from the Israeli embassy. A much younger man. And apparently . . ."

Two minutes later Liz had a pencil and was writing carefully. "K-o-l-l-e-k. Got it. Let me look into it, and I'll let you know on Wednesday."

Sophie was just putting the phone down when Hannah came in, holding Zack's hand.

"Hi, Hannah," she said cheerfully. "I was just talking to an old friend I haven't seen in ages. I've asked her to dinner next week; I think you'll like her. Her name's Liz Carlyle."

"That's nice," said Hannah, steering Zack to a chair by the table, while Sophie went to start on his supper. "How do you know her?"

"We used to work together. In Personnel." She switched the kettle on. Hannah seemed to like the English habit of a cuppa in the late afternoon.

Hannah nodded. "Oh yes. That job you used to do."

She said this with such irony that Sophie turned and stared at her.

"Sophie, I've always had a pretty good idea of what you did for a living. The idea that you were in Personnel is just absurd." She held a hand up. "And no, David didn't tell me anything."

"Oh," said Sophie, since it was all she could think of to say. She was annoyed her ruse had been found out. The sooner Liz checked out Danny Kollek the better.

1 6

So much for leaving early, thought Liz, as the roadworks signs appeared and the traffic began to slow. She had left her desk in Thames House at four, collected her dark blue Audi Quattro from the underground car park and headed off, hoping to reach her mother's house in Wiltshire in time for a walk before supper.

It was a beautiful late summer afternoon, the sky an unbroken blue, but the Audi, which she had bought secondhand several years ago with some money her father had left her, had no air-conditioning. To take her mind off the traffic fumes sucked in through the open window, she tried to imagine the smell of the countryside around Bowerbridge and of her mother's house, filled as it always was with flowers.

But something was spoiling the picture. It was the thought of this man Edward. What would she find when she got there?

The invitation had arrived the week before. *Susan & Edward— Drinks*, handwritten on an *At Home* card. A joint invitation, she had noticed with dismay—had this man Edward actually moved into Bowerbridge? Would everything there be different?

It was easier to think about work, and as she sat waiting for the car in front to move, her mind drifted back to the previous day's troubling conversation with Chris Marcham, after he'd surprised her in his Hampstead house. Marcham had turned out to be a man in his fifties, she reckoned, tall with longish hair, casually, almost raffishly dressed—a yellow jumper with a hole in one elbow, cracked brogues and trousers that could do with a wash.

After the first shock and the discovery that Liz wasn't actually a burglar, Marcham had relaxed a bit. She had introduced herself as Jane Falconer, her standard cover, but rather than claiming to be from the Home Office, as she would normally have done, she'd said right away that she was from the Security Service. After all, she knew this man to be a casual source of MI6.

"Do you work for Geoffrey Fane?" he'd asked suspiciously.

"No, I'm with the other service."

"Ah, MI5."

"Do you have a gardener?" Liz had begun.

"No," Marcham had replied, looking mystified. "Why do you ask?"

Liz explained how she'd disturbed a man apparently working in the garden. She'd noted with interest that Marcham had shown no sign of wanting to report the intruder to the police.

As the traffic freed itself and she swung the Audi into the fast lane, Liz recalled the conversation that had followed. She'd decided beforehand that there was no point in alarming him about a threat she couldn't be sure was real, so she'd explained instead that she'd come to see him about the forthcoming peace conference at Gleneagles. Intelligence sources, she'd said, without being specific, had picked up a higher level than usual of "chatter," much of it relating to Syria, and there was concern that there might be an attempt to derail the conference. Since he was an expert on the country, she'd remarked flatteringly, and had just come back from interviewing President Assad, she wondered if he could help.

It turned out he knew already from sources in Damascus that Syria planned to attend the conference, but he claimed no insight into who might try to keep that from happening. The country certainly had plenty of enemies, he conceded, but since all of them seemed to have decided that it was to their advantage to attend the conference, none seemed likely to want to sabotage it.

Marcham had been impressed by President Assad, who'd seemed to him far savvier than his detractors allowed, not at all the puppet of his late father's henchmen, much more his own man. It didn't sound to Liz as if the journalist was writing anything about Bashar Al-Assad that would prove particularly provocative, either to the Syrians or their enemies.

Yet there had been one odd exchange which, as the Audi picked up speed, Liz was puzzling over. Marcham had said at one point, "You might want to talk with your counterparts in Tel Aviv. Though doubtless you already have."

"Doubtless," she had replied drily. "Have you?"

He wasn't expecting the question, for he had suddenly seemed unnerved, stammering hesitantly, before finally saying, "I talk to lots of people."

Including Mossad, Liz concluded, making a mental note of this. If he was talking to Mossad as well as MI6, God knows who else he knew in the intelligence world. Including the Syrians, perhaps.

There'd been something else strange too. They'd been sitting at the kitchen table and suddenly without warning or explanation, Marcham had got up and firmly shut the door to his bedroom. He hadn't wanted her to see inside, not realising of course that she already had. What was he trying to hide from her? There was nothing remarkable in there that she could remember, except perhaps the crucifix on the wall. But what was wrong with that?

There was something not quite right about the man. She felt it instinctively. Something he wasn't saying. Something worth exploring further. I'll think about it after the weekend, she thought. First I need to concentrate on Mother and this Edward character.

As she came in through the back door of Bowerbridge she was met with a strong smell of cooking. Curry, with a spicy tang that made her hungry. What was her mother up to? She was a competent cook, but old-fashioned and very English. Stews, soups, shepherd's pie, home-made fishcakes, a Sunday roast—these were her standard dishes. Now, on the stove, a large casserole was bubbling, the source of the delicious smell. Rice sat in a measuring cup, waiting for a saucepan to boil. On the table there was a half-drunk glass of white wine, and a copy of the *Spectator*.

"You must be Liz," said a voice, and she looked up as a man entered from the direction of the drawing room. He was tall and slim, with tidy greying hair and thin-framed glasses. He had a long, sun-burned face with high cheekbones and friendly eyes, and was wearing a beige jumper and dark corduroy trousers.

"I'm Edward," he said, extending a hand. "I'm afraid your mother's been delayed at the nursery."

"Nice to meet you," said Liz, thinking he didn't look at all how she had expected. No tweeds, no pipe, no bufferish moustache.

"I hope you like curry." He sniffed the air. "A bit overpowering, I'm afraid." He grinned disarmingly, and Liz found herself grinning back.

"I'll just take my bag upstairs," she said.

Up in her room, Liz put her bag down and looked out the window at the tulip tree, its flowers over now at this late stage of the summer; the tree itself was almost the height of the house. They had grown up together, she thought. Her father had planted the tree when her mother had been pregnant with Liz.

She looked around at her bedroom, unchanged since she was a little girl. There was a watercolour on the wall of the Nadder River, painted by her father, a keen naturalist who had fished the river every summer. Liz would often accompany him, and he'd taught her how to manage a rod and the names of flowers and trees and birds. He'd have been sad that she had ended up living in London.

Next to the painting was a framed photograph of Liz, aged nine, sitting on Ziggy, her pony, wearing a black velvet riding hat and smiling toothily for the camera. Liz laughed at the sight of her younger version's pigtails, and remembered how bad-tempered Ziggy had been. Once he'd even bitten the riding instructor.

She unpacked quickly and changed out of her office clothes into jeans and a T-shirt. Before she went down, she took a quick peek in her mother's room. She was expecting the worst: Edward's brushes on the dressing table, a trouser press in one corner. But it looked unchanged. And across the landing in the spare room, she saw a suitcase next to the bed. Edward's, still unpacked. He must have just arrived today, she realised, remembering he lived in London. Perhaps he hadn't moved in after all.

She went downstairs, noticing on her way through the living room a framed photograph on one of the side tables. It showed a posed group of Ghurkhas, wearing dress uniform and sitting in three neat rows, their bayoneted rifles held upright. Two English officers were at the end of the front row, presumably their commanding officers. One looked like a younger version of Edward.

"There's an open bottle of Sancerre in the fridge," Edward declared when she joined him in the kitchen. She poured herself a glass and sat down at the table, while he bustled about the stove.

"You've had some sun, I see," Liz ventured, feeling pasty and pale by comparison.

"Comes with the job."

"Are you still in the army?" asked Liz with surprise.

"No, no. They packed me off in '99. I work for a charity now; we help the blind in developing countries. At least we try to help them—you wouldn't think politics could get in the way of something so straightforward, but it does. I travel a fair amount because of it—India, Africa once in a while. Funny how people think if you've got a tan you must have been lolling about in a deckchair in the Bahamas. Sadly not."

"I saw the photo in the next room."

"Ah," he said, looking slightly embarrassed. "I brought it down to show your mother. She insisted on seeing a picture of me in uniform."

"Were you with the Gurkhas for long?"

"Thirty years," he said, with a touch of pride. "Very fine soldiers," he added quietly.

"You must have got around a bit," said Liz, sipping her wine, which was deliciously dry and cold. Here we go, thought Liz: tales of Aden and derring-do. She wished her mother would hurry up.

"A bit," he said. "The Falklands, the first Gulf War, six months in Kosovo I'd sooner forget."

But that was all he said. Liz gratefully noted how adroitly he changed the subject, asking her where she lived in London. Within minutes Liz found to her surprise that she was telling him all about her flat in Kentish Town, when she'd bought it, how she'd done it up, what she still had to do to it. He was a sympathetic listener, interjecting only occasionally, though at one point he made Liz laugh out loud with an account of living in a leaky tent while on manoeuvres in a Belize rainforest.

The ice was broken, and though Liz sternly reminded herself to reserve judgement, they continued to talk about all sorts of things, including music, and she saw Edward's face light up as he described a Barenboim concert he'd been to recently at the Barbican. They were talking about acoustics, of all things, when Susan Carlyle came through the back door, a bunch of freshly cut flowers in her arms and a look of relief on her face to find the two of them chatting.

They had supper in the kitchen, then sat together in the sitting room, reading and listening to Mozart. By ten, Liz found herself stifling a yawn. "I'm for bed," she declared. "Is there much to do tomorrow to get ready for the party?"

Susan shook her head. "All in hand, dear. Thanks to Edward."

Upstairs Liz fell quickly into a light sleep, then woke up as her mother and Edward came up the stairs. Doors closed, another opened; Liz gave up trying to decipher what was going on, and this time fell soundly asleep.

In the morning she drove into Stockbridge, having established that there really wasn't anything she could do to help. When she came back her mother was at the nursery, but Edward was busy—the wine had arrived, and he'd put a clean tablecloth on the dining-room table, vacuumed the sitting room and dusted. My God, thought Liz, instead of the Colonel Blimp she'd been expecting, Edward was turning out to be a New Man.

The party was a success, full of long-standing friends of her mother's, most of whom seemed to know Edward already. There had been a few new faces, and even someone Liz's age—Simon Lawrence, who owned an organic farm nearby. They'd been at school together, but Liz hadn't seen him in almost twenty years. He'd grown immensely tall, but still had the apple-cheeked fresh face she remembered.

"Hello, Liz," he'd said shyly. "Do you remember me?"

"How could I forget you, Simon?" she declared with a laugh. "You pushed me into Skinner's pond the summer I turned fourteen."

They'd chatted for half an hour, and when he'd left Simon asked for her number in London. "I try and avoid the place as a rule," he confessed cheerfully, "but it would be lovely to see you again."

On Sunday, for once Liz slept very late, and realised work had been taking a physical toll. When she came down to the kitchen Edward was just starting to fix lunch, and declined all offers of help, giving her a welcome cup of coffee and a hot croissant instead. He explained Susan had popped over to the nursery garden for a minute; Sunday was its busiest day.

Liz sat and read papers, noticing a column about the Gleneagles peace conference. BREAKTHROUGH OR BREAKDOWN? was the headline, and Liz thought again how fragile were the prospects of peace and how important it was for the conference to be a success.

After lunch she and her mother walked up the hill at one end of the Bowerbridge estate. Edward stayed behind; he seemed to sense that Liz wanted some time alone with her mother.

At the top, they paused to look down at the Nadder Valley stretching below them. The long, dry summer meant the trees were turning early, and the oaks down in the valley were already a palette of orange and gold.

"I'm so glad you could come down," her mother said. "Edward's been wanting to meet you."

"Likewise," said Liz. She could not resist adding, "He seems quite perfect."

"*Perfect?*" Her mother looked at Liz sharply. "He's not perfect. Far from it." She paused, as if considering his faults. "He's sometimes very vague—you know what men are like." She paused. "And sometimes he gets awfully sad."

"Sad? What about?"

"I imagine it's his wife. She was killed, you see, just after he retired. In a car accident in Germany."

"Oh, I am sorry," said Liz, regretting her slight sarcasm. "It must have been awful."

"I'm sure it was, but he doesn't talk about it. In the same way, I don't talk to him about your father. There doesn't seem much point. We enjoy each other's company, and that's what seems important now."

"Of course. I didn't mean to sound unkind. He seems very nice. I do mean that."

"I'm glad," Susan said simply.

"And, Mother, one other thing." Liz hesitated for a moment, feeling slightly embarrassed. "I don't want you to feel that Edward has to be exiled to the spare room when I'm around."

Her mother gave a small smile. "Thank you. I told him it was perfectly ridiculous, but he insisted. He said it was your house, too, and that he didn't want you to think he was invading."

"That's very tactful of him," said Liz with surprise, though she was becoming increasingly aware that there was rather more to Edward Treglown than she had supposed.

"He *is* very tactful. That's one of the things I particularly like about him."

"He said he does some work for a charity."

"He *runs* the charity. I didn't discover that until I'd known him for months. He's very modest; you'd never know he won the DSO."

Her obvious pride in her new beau started to nettle Liz, but she stopped herself. Why shouldn't Susan be proud of him? It wasn't as if Edward were the boastful type—far from it. And he obviously made her mother happy. That was the important thing.

And when she left for London, Liz found herself saying to Edward not only that she had enjoyed meeting him, but that she looked forward to seeing him again soon.

"Perhaps you and Mother could come for supper sometime," she said, thinking of all the clearing up she'd have to do in her flat if they were to visit.

"You let us take you out first," he said gently. "From what I gather you work awfully hard. The last thing you need to worry about is entertaining. I'll let your mother make a date."

She drove back to London in a more cheerful mood than she'd been in driving down. Edward had turned out to be rather a good thing, actually, and her mother seemed happier and surer of herself than she'd been in ages. It was funny to think that she didn't have to worry so much about Susan now, not with Edward in loyal attendance. Funny, but why wasn't it more of a relief? In a flash of self-knowledge that made her shift uneasily in the driving seat, Liz admitted that now she would have no excuse not to sort out her own personal life. She'd already resolved that it was time to move on from her fruitless hankering after Charles Wetherby, but could she do it? And move on where, she asked herself, move on to whom? She wondered if Simon Lawrence would actually use the phone number she'd given him. She wasn't going to worry about it, but it would be nice if he did.

She opened her front door to the usual muddle of last week's newspapers and letters spread all over the table and the faint air of dusty unlovedness that the flat always had after she'd been away for a weekend. The light on the answer machine was blinking.

"Hi, Liz," the voice said. It was American but polished, and sounded slightly familiar. "It's Miles here, Miles Brookhaven. It's Sunday morning, and you must be away for the weekend. I was wondering if you'd like to get together for lunch sometime this week. Give me a call at the embassy if you get a chance. Hope to hear from you."

Liz stood by the machine, quite taken aback. How did he get my number? she thought. Was this work-related? The call had been oddly ambiguous. No, she decided, he wouldn't have called her at home if this was just professional, much less rung on a Sunday, not unless it was something extremely urgent. She suddenly remembered that she'd given him her home number after it had been decided that he would be her contact on the Syrian case, and immediately, in a quick change of mood, she began to feel flattered, rather than suspicious.

17

hacun à son goût," said Constable Debby Morgan. DI Cullen scowled at her, wondering whether to admit he hadn't a clue what that meant. She liked using foreign phrases, but then she had a degree, like so many of today's recruits, and he supposed they couldn't help showing off a bit.

Not that he really minded with young Morgan, for he had a soft spot for her. He got a bit of stick from some of his colleagues on the subject, and it was true that Debby Morgan was an attractive girl, with big blue eyes, cute features and an athletic figure. But DI Cullen had been married twenty years and had three daughters of his own, one almost as old as Debby. He was fond of his junior colleague, but in a completely avuncular way.

Now he said, "Goo is the word for this one." He pointed to the open file on his desk, with the photos of the corpse that had been found in a box in one of the City's churches. "This bloke met a sticky end all right."

"Weird to think he did it to himself."

"I've seen weirder." Which was true—he'd worked vice for six months once in Soho, and had never got over what some people were up to. He looked at young Morgan, thinking she had a lot to learn about life. "So what are you thinking?"

She shrugged. "The obvious, I guess. Who put him in the box?"

DI Cullen nodded. "There's that, of course, but does anything else strike you?" She looked blank, so he supplied the answer. "Someone else put him in the box, but the death was self-inflicted. So why didn't this other person help the victim? The pathologist said death wasn't instantaneous at all—the poor bugger took several minutes to go. Where was our Good Samaritan then?"

"Maybe they didn't know the victim," she offered hopefully.

"If you found a dead stranger in a church, what would you do? Call the police? Run for help? Try the kiss of life? Or would you cram him in a box and walk away?"

"I see what you mean."

There was a knock and the door to Cullen's office opened a foot. A young sergeant stuck his head in.

"Excuse me, guv, but I thought you'd want to know." The sergeant looked at Constable Morgan with frank admiration.

"What is it?" demanded Cullen shortly.

"We had an anonymous call giving a name for the man in the box."

"And?"

The sergeant looked at his pad. "Alexander Ledingham."

"Who is?"

The sergeant shrugged and looked at Cullen helplessly, as if to say "beats me." "Lives in Clerkenwell, according to the caller."

"What else?"

"That's it. They hung up."

"Write down everything you can remember about the caller," said Cullen, standing up abruptly, and the young sergeant nodded and withdrew. Cullen looked out the window, where the sky was turning a threatening shade of grey. "Grab your coat," he said to Morgan. "It looks like rain."

They ended up going to Clerkenwell twice, the second time with a search warrant and a locksmith. The previous afternoon, with the help of the local police station, they had located the residence of one A. Ledingham, in a brick warehouse that had been converted into new flats. No one answered the buzzer, which made sense if Ledingham was indeed the man in the box. Two neighbours said they hadn't seen him for a couple of days. He was a new tenant, who kept himself to himself. Neither recalled ever seeing any visitors to Ledingham's flat.

This time DI Cullen and Constable Morgan went straight to the flat on the third floor. They waited impatiently while the locksmith went to work; five minutes later the flat's front door sprang wide open.

A powerful odour greeted them as they stepped into the small hall. "Phew," said Debby Morgan, holding her nose and stepping into the blue haze that filled the flat. Straight ahead of them was a large, wooden-floored open area that seemed to be dining room and sitting room combined. It was sparsely furnished, a sofa and two wooden armchairs at one end, a cheap-looking dining table and four chairs at the other. On the walls, just visible through the haze, were framed posters, bright Op Art geometric constructions.

DI Cullen screwed up his eyes and stepped forward into the small kitchen, which seemed to be the source of the smell. He saw with alarm that the electric cooker was on, and opening the oven door he was greeted by a cloud of black smoke. Once he'd stopped coughing he looked again. There seemed to be something in a roasting tin.

"Let me," said Debby, turning off the cooker at the wall. Holding her handkerchief in front of her face and grabbing a pair of oven gloves, she reached carefully into the oven and pulled out the tin, which contained the remains of some unidentifiable roast, now shrunken to a smouldering black heap. She dumped the entire pan without ceremony into the sink and turned on the cold tap. A loud hissing noise resulted and clouds of steam rose up and gradually began to disperse as Cullen switched on an extractor fan.

"What do you think that tells us?" asked Cullen.

"That he's not much of a cook?"

DI Cullen shook his head. "It means he was planning on coming back here. Whatever he was getting up to wasn't meant to take very long."

"This is one of those ovens with a time delay," said Morgan, who was examining the controls. "So he could have set it to come on at a certain time."

"Whatever. He was expecting to come home and eat it." He was looking round. A bookcase on one wall held a row of paperback novels, and several larger books on computer graphics. That must be his work, thought Cullen, and he noticed a laptop open on a small desk in one corner.

"Let's look in the bedroom," he said, pointing to a door in the corner of the room. "We can do a detailed search here later."

He opened the door gingerly, and the cautious look on his face turned to astonishment as he peered in.

"What on earth?" exclaimed Constable Morgan as she came in behind him.

The room was dominated by an enormous bed, neatly made, with brass posts at its feet and a canopy supported by intricately carved wooden posts above the head. Dangling from one of the brass uprights was a pair of silver handcuffs.

DI Cullen said, "He must have been a right weirdo."

"But a religious weirdo," Debby said, pointing to the wall facing the bed, where a painted triptych of wooden panels hung. Christ was on the cross, depicted in gory detail; blood dripped from his side and crucified hands and feet. The panels were cracked and faded—antique, thought DI Cullen; he'd seen things like it in a church in Italy, where his wife had insisted on going one summer, overruling his preference for Marbella.

That wasn't the only strange thing: on the other walls were dozens of architectural drawings, held up by masking tape. They were all of churches, many of them detailed floor plans, heavily annotated in black ink in a small, precise hand, notes mostly, but also a series of lines that converged near the altar, marked by arrows and large Xs.

If the bed hadn't been there, you would think this was the office of an ecclesiastical architect. But there was nothing sacred about the overall effect—sinister, rather.

Shaken, DI Cullen opened a cupboard door in the corner of the room, half-expecting to find a skeleton hanging from a rail. He was relieved to discover only clothes, neatly folded on shelves, with a few jackets and shirts on hangers.

Constable Morgan had put on a pair of latex gloves and was searching through the drawers of a pine dresser. She turned with a triumphant look on her face, holding up a little black book. "Don't tell me," said Cullen, "you've found a guide to black magic rituals."

"Not so exotic. I think it's his diary." She flipped through the pages, then suddenly stopped, holding it out for Cullen to see.

Each page covered one week and Morgan had stopped at the current week. There were only two entries. Sunday said *1 p.m., Marc.* Which sounded like a lunch date. But Tuesday made Cullen's eyes open wide. *St. B. 8 p.m.*

"What was the name of the church where they found this bloke?"

"St. Barnabas."

He pointed at the diary with an angry finger. "There it is." Morgan continued going through the diary. There was no other mention of "St. B." But on several pages she found initials that could be churches—"St. M," "St. A" and "Ch Ch" appeared.

Cullen gave an appreciative whistle.

"What are you thinking?" asked Constable Morgan anxiously.

He looked into her big blue eyes and smiled. "You've done well, Debs. Drop that in an evidence bag and let's take a look at Mr. Ledingham's computer to try and find out where he worked. Maybe someone there can explain all this . . ." He raised a baffled hand to take in the room.

1 8

Liz had dressed up for her lunch with Miles Brookhaven. She was wearing the flared silk skirt and the strappy sandals that she'd bought for her mother's party. She'd been determined to put Edward in his place with her sophisticated elegance. But as it turned out, that wasn't necessary. Now she was giving the clothes an airing for a different reason.

But looking at the CLOSED sign on the front door of Ma Folie, a bistro on the South Bank, she wondered if they'd be wasted again. What had happened to American know-how and where was Miles Brookhaven? When he'd rung to arrange lunch, he'd said he'd booked the restaurant. "You'll love the place. The food's so good you could be in France." You certainly could, thought Liz now, since like many of its French counterparts, Ma Folie turned out to be closed for the entire month of August.

She was wondering what to do next when she heard footsteps hurrying along the pavement, and saw Miles approaching.

"There you are!" he cried, with such a friendly smile that Liz couldn't be annoyed. He cut an eye-catching figure in a light grey summer suit with a bright blue shirt and yellow polka-dot tie. Gesturing towards the bistro, "I take it you've seen the bad news," he said. "But never mind: I've got an alternative I think you might enjoy. I hope you have a head for heights."

Twenty minutes later Liz was a third of the way up the London Eye, sipping a glass of fizz. Miles had booked a private "pod" with a champagne lunch.

The ascent of their capsule was so gradual that they didn't seem to be moving at all, though Liz noticed that the top of Big Ben, which a few minutes before had been at eye level, was now below them. It was a perfect day for the Eye, sunny and clear, and all that was preventing Liz enjoying herself was the thought of how much this must have cost. Had Miles paid for it himself or was this on the expenses of the CIA station in Grosvenor Square? She suspected the latter and if she was right, why was she worthy of such extravagant cultivation? What were they hoping to get out of her?

"I have a small confession to make," she said, as Miles offered her a plate of smoked salmon sandwiches.

"What's that?"

"I've never been on the Eye before."

He laughed. "Most New Yorkers have never been up the Statue of Liberty. Now have some lunch."

She sat down on the banquette next to him. "Is that where you're from—New York?"

"Nothing so flash. I am a native of Hartford, Connecticut." He paused, then added with a smile, "The insurance capital of America. As interesting as it sounds."

"How long have you been with the Agency?"

"Five years. I joined two years after 9/11. I graduated from Yale and was doing an MA in international relations at Georgetown. Being virtually next door, it's a natural recruiting stop for Langley. Plus, I speak Arabic . . . I'm sure that's why the Agency was interested in me in the first place."

"It's quite unusual for an American to know Arabic, isn't it? No offence."

"None taken. You're quite right—when I joined you could count the number of Arabic speakers in the CIA on the fingers of one hand. Seven years on, you now need *two* hands to count them."

"How did you get interested in it?"

"My father was an insurance broker; he specialised in oil tankers. One summer he took all of us with him on one of the super tankers. We went all around the Gulf, then through the Suez Canal. I just fell in love with the region, and the language." He gave a shy grin.

"Is this your first posting abroad?"

"I was in Syria for three years. In Damascus." He looked out the pod's window dreamily. "It's the most beautiful country, Liz. Much maligned by my countrymen."

Even sitting down, Liz could see the distant suburbs to the north and south come into view. From the Eye, the city was curiously flattened, stretching out like a pancake in every direction.

She said, "London must seem very humdrum. A different world altogether."

"Not really. Sometimes it seems half the Middle East has moved here." Miles stood up and pointed west towards the horizon. They were at the apex of the Eye's trajectory and seemed dizzyingly high. "What is that? It looks like a castle."

Liz said drily, "Well done. It's Windsor Castle."

"Of course it is." He laughed. "And down there are two other fortresses." He pointed down at the long block of Thames House on the north bank, its copper roof shining gold in the sun, and a little further along, on the South Bank, the trendy green and white lines of MI6's post-modernist towers.

After a pause he said, "Andy Bokus, my head of station—you saw him at the meeting the other day—Andy says the French have complained for years that even though London is a hub of Middle East terrorist activity, you guys have been far too slow to get onto it. He says he thinks they're right."

"Do you agree with him?" asked Liz. She'd heard that view too often to react.

"No. I don't. I think you do a good job between you. It must be a nightmare trying to keep track of all the foreigners you have here, each with a different agenda. And it's your side that has come up with this threat to the peace conference. I suppose that came from a source here?" With his back to her, Miles looked out through the window of the capsule.

Liz said nothing. If Geoffrey Fane hadn't told the Americans where the information came from, she certainly wasn't going to. She was surprised at Miles's crude approach. They must think I was born yesterday, she thought. Maybe this style of intelligence gathering worked well in Damascus—lush up your potential source and then pop the question—but he'll have to get a lot more subtle if he's going to be successful here. She wondered with a smile whether Andy Bokus would refuse to pay the bill for lunch if Miles came back empty-handed.

The silence dragged on. Liz had done enough interviews to know about silences—this was one she was not going to break. Eventually Miles said, "I guess we just have to watch for anything unusual that crops up. I know, for instance, that there's at least one senior intelligence officer Damascus has sent over here recently."

"Who's that?"

"He's called Ben Ahmad. He was a senior counter-espionage officer in Syria. His presence here doesn't make much sense to me."

But it did to Liz. Brookhaven didn't know that the threat to the conference came from anti-Syrian forces—according to the MI6 source in Cyprus. For that reason, a counter-espionage specialist was precisely what Damascus would be sending. Backed up by the muscle Wally Woods and his team had seen arriving at Halton Heights.

They were slowly descending now, the buildings below seeming to grow larger as they grew closer. Miles was tidying up the lunch things while Liz thought about what he'd said. Yes, Ben Ahmad would be worth having a look at, she decided, making a mental note.

When they left the Eye the river was full of boats, taking advantage of the fine weather. "Back to the farm?" he asked, and she smiled at the Americanism, then nodded.

"Me too. I'll walk with you."

They went along the South Bank, with its view of Parliament across the river. Miles said, "We haven't talked about you at all. When did you join your service?"

As they walked, she gave him her own potted history—how she'd answered an advert initially, then found herself progressing through interviews until suddenly she had been offered a job. She'd had no specialist expertise, and would never have predicted during her university years that MI5 was where she would end up.

"You must be doing very well there."

She shrugged. She liked Miles, in spite of his rather crude intelligence-gathering technique, but she didn't need his flattery. She knew she was good at her work: she had strong analytic skills, worked well in the field (especially when interviewing people) and could get along with almost everyone—except, she thought, people like Bruno Mackay, but she hadn't met many of those. Any pride she took was always tempered by the realisation that her work was never done, and that the successful resolution of one case just meant the introduction of a new challenge. But that was what made it all so interesting.

They'd reached Lambeth Bridge, and Liz stopped. "I'd better cross here," she said. "Thank you for lunch."

"A little unorthodox."

"It was fun," she said simply.

"How about dinner sometime?" Miles seemed slightly nervous.

"I'd like that."

As she crossed Lambeth Bridge, watching two barges adroitly miss each other just upstream, she wondered about Miles. Asking her to dinner seemed unequivocal enough, but was it all part of a CIA attempt to cultivate her? If it was, it didn't matter. She felt quite confident that she could see Miles coming, well, miles off. She had a date, she thought, the first in some time. Nice, but she wasn't going to get very excited. More interesting, for now at least, was this news of a Syrian counter-intelligence officer in London.

1 9

Lucky Sophie, thought Liz, taking in the oak cupboards, the granite tops and the slate floor. The kitchen of the large Edwardian villa seemed enormous and bright, as the sun, low in the sky now, glanced between two tall trees at the bottom of the garden. It was a far cry from Liz's Kentish Town basement.

She was sipping a glass of wine while Sophie moved back and forth between the stove and a large chopping block—she'd always liked to cook, Liz remembered. An elegant woman came in through the French windows from the garden, holding the hand of a small pyjama-clad boy. Dressed casually in well-cut trousers and a cashmere cardigan, she was still handsome in her mid-sixties. Liz liked her at once. Watching her sitting in the kitchen with her grandson on her knee, she admired how the older woman seemed to manage to be an attentive and devoted grandmother while simultaneously conducting an adult conversation. While Sophie put the little boy to bed, Liz and Hannah sat on the terrace and talked about Israel, which to Liz's surprise, Hannah seemed to regard with very mixed feelings. Now Liz took another pistachio from the bowl between them and said, "Sophie tells me you've made a friend here, from the Israeli embassy."

"Yes. Danny Kollek. Have you met him?"

"No. I don't think I have," said Liz. "Where did you meet him?"

"Quite by chance, really. We got talking in the interval of a play at the Haymarket theatre. He's very nice. Much nicer than any of the officials I've met in Tel Aviv, that's for sure."

"Do you know a lot of them, back in Israel?"

"Well, not really. Most of those I know are Mossad. They came to talk to me about my husband, Saul—ex-husband I should say—almost as soon as I arrived in Tel Aviv. I expect Sophie told you. Sophie thinks Danny may be Mossad too," added Hannah disarmingly.

"Did he tell you he was?"

"No, and I don't believe it. He's far too nice and we met quite by chance."

Liz said nothing but she was thinking, I bet that was no chance meeting. She'd checked before she came out and Kollek was at the embassy all right, and he wasn't on the list Mossad provided of their London-based officers. But what Hannah had described was a classic intelligence officer's pickup. He's probably been asked to keep a discreet eye on her while she's in London, she thought.

Hannah went on, "I've told Mossad I don't want to talk to them anymore." She lowered her voice. Why? thought Liz. There was no one to overhear.

"Saul and I split up, you know. He did business throughout the Middle East, probably still does; computer systems. I couldn't help them much because I didn't understand the detail, but they told me that though the systems were innocent enough by themselves, they were capable of helping a country develop sophisticated counter-radar weapons."

"Did he deal with the enemies of Israel?"

Hannah shrugged and, looking at Sophie, who was now back in the kitchen and seemed preoccupied with her daube, she said, "Saul wasn't very choosy about his customers. He was only interested in making money."

Liz nodded sympathetically. "Is that what Danny Kollek talks to you about?"

Hannah gave a sudden laugh. "Goodness, no. Danny's only interested in music. Even more than in me," she added loudly enough for Sophie to hear. "Seriously, he's just a friend. We have lunch, we go to a concert—there's nothing professional about it at all. If anything, he's sympathetic to the movement."

"The movement?"

"The peace movement. I got involved almost as soon as I arrived in Israel. Everyone seems to think Israel is full of right-wing hawks, determined to keep the occupied territories. But it's not that way at all. There's plenty of dissent there. In fact, I'd say most intelligent Israelis are adamantly opposed to government policy. I don't know anyone who doesn't think a negotiated settlement is the only way forward. The Likud people are just nuts."

"And your friend Danny thinks that way, too."

"Absolutely. But of course his hands are tied. That's one of the drawbacks, he says, of being at the embassy. He's not allowed to have an opinion, really. But I can tell he's on our side."

"I see," said Liz as politely as she could, reluctant to say that this didn't seem a very professional way for a diplomat to behave. Could this apparently switched-on woman be so easily taken for a ride?

At this interesting point in the conversation Sophie intervened. "Here we go," she called from the kitchen, putting a large cast-iron casserole on the table. "All I can say, Hannah, is thank heavens you're not kosher. I had to brown the beef in bacon fat."

Thinking afterwards about her conversation with Hannah Gold on Sophie's terrace, Liz concluded that Sophie had been perfectly right about Danny Kollek. To the professional eye, too many things didn't fit, quite apart from the implausibility of the whole relationship. Charles Wetherby agreed. "He must be Mossad," he said. "But you say he's not on the list—he's undeclared to us?"

"Well, it's not the first time the Israelis haven't played by the rules. Presumably his head office have asked him to keep an eye on Mrs. Gold while she's here. But there's not enough there so far for us to complain."

Charles looked at her. "What's the matter? What are you thinking? Is this important?"

"I'm just worried about this peace conference. There's too much noise around it. Too many odd leads that don't seem to take us anywhere. I don't know what it is, but I'm going to keep in touch with Sophie Margolis."

"Yes," said Charles, turning back to the papers on his desk. "Do. And keep me informed."

2 0

Dear Peggy, thought Liz, as the younger woman entered her office clutching a thick stack of notes. She *has* been busy. Liz motioned her to take a seat.

"All well with you?" she asked.

"Yes, thanks."

"Tim still cooking up a storm?"

Peggy turned a light shade of pink, then sighed. "We're onto Jamie Oliver now."

Liz laughed, then turned to business. "So what have you got?"

"I've been looking some more into Sami Veshara, our Lebanese food importer. He leads quite a life. There's a girlfriend in Paris, so he's made a couple of trips there recently. And he's been to Lebanon three times in the last six months—nothing unusual there. But on the last occasion he flew home via Amsterdam."

"Is that suspicious? Maybe he couldn't get a direct flight."

Peggy shook her head. "I checked that. There were plenty of seats that day. He went to Amsterdam for a reason."

"And what do we think that was?"

"It's more what Customs and Excise think. I told you about these shipments Veshara's been making by boat. The Excise people now think they are a cover for something else. Some other boats that don't come into Harwich; Harrison, the officer I spoke to, has been investigating them and he thinks they drop anchor in a deserted spot further down the coast, then offload the cargo there."

"What does he think they're offloading?"

"He doesn't know for sure, but Amsterdam suggests the obvious. Harrison's planning to intercept one of them next time they sail. They've been coming out of Ostend, and he's liaising with the port authorities there."

"Any idea when the next one's going to be?"

"Yes, as a matter of fact." Peggy consulted a printed e-mail she had on her lap. "Tomorrow night, they think."

Liz thought for a moment. It might prove a wild-goose chase, but right now it was the only solid lead they had.

Liz was beginning to feel sick. It was high tide in the little cove, ten miles south of Harwich on the Essex coast, and though the curving bend of this stretch of shoreline made for a natural harbour, it was still fully exposed to the North Sea. It wasn't rough but the slow swells lifting and lowering *The Clacton*, the little Customs cutter, seemed to have a worse effect on her stomach even than the violence of a storm.

"Should be any minute now," said Harrison to Liz, who was the only other person on deck, besides the helmsman. Harrison's team of half a dozen were below, drinking tea, immune to seasickness. The helmsman stiffened, though he kept the boat idling gently in the curve of the little bay, under the shadow of the cliff face that loomed directly above them. A crescent moon darted in and out of the patchy clouds that spread across the sky like fat puffballs.

Liz had driven up in the afternoon to Harwich, where she'd met Harrison and been introduced to his men. She had been kitted out with a yellow uniform parka, which was warm and cosy—and about three sizes too big. The odd look had come her way during Harrison's briefing, but no one had asked her why she was there; perhaps they'd been told beforehand not to ask questions, or maybe they were used to unexplained visitors. Harrison himself was a model of discretion, making polite small talk over sandwiches, then excusing himself to get ready. Liz killed the wait before they embarked by reading dog-eared copies of *Hello* and the *Sun*, which were lying around in the canteen.

The helmsman spoke. "There's a boat over there, sir," he said, pointing out towards the North Sea. "Coming this way."

Liz looked seaward and saw a tiny light, like an illuminated pin bobbing against the horizon. The pin grew larger, and Harrison took two steps and banged loudly on the hatch door. A minute later it opened, and the six Customs men came up the stairs quickly. Liz noticed that two of them were armed with Heckler & Koch MP5 carbines.

Looking through binoculars, Harrison spoke to the sailor at the helm. "Time to move. But take it easy at first."

The pin light was now well into the cove and Liz could make out the shape of a small trawler. Almost a quarter of a mile from shore it stopped and sat motionless in the water.

Harrison tapped Liz on the shoulder and handed his binoculars to her. "Have a look."

She peered through the infra-red glasses, and could see the trawler clearly in an eerie greyish light. It was a fishing boat, with a flat-backed stern and a hoist to haul its nets up. The bow was snub-nosed, and she could read its name on the side—*The Dido*. The entire vessel couldn't have been more than forty feet long. There was no sign of anyone on board, though the wheelhouse was sheltered, so whoever was steering was hidden from view.

She handed the glasses back to Harrison. "She's sitting pretty low in the water, isn't she?"

He nodded. "Whatever she's carrying must be heavy. Or else there's just a lot of it." He turned to the helmsman. "Okay, let's move in."

The Clacton surged forward, and Liz felt the sting of salt spray and cold wind against her cheek. Her nausea had turned into a familiar rush of excitement. About one hundred yards short of *The Dido*, *The Clacton* slowed, and at a command from Harrison, a pair of spotlights positioned on her bow suddenly pierced the darkness, throwing out penetrating streams of light, illuminating the trawler against the background of night like a film set.

Harrison was ready in the bow with the loud hailer. He had just shouted, "This is her Majesty's Customs and Excise," when the engine of the trawler erupted and the boat suddenly turned sharply and headed at speed toward the open sea.

"Go!" ordered Harrison, and *The Clacton* accelerated in pursuit. Liz clung to a brass rail as the boat surged forward. But they didn't seem to be gaining on the trawler, and she feared they would lose her once they were out in open water. Then ahead of them, heading in an intercepting line, appeared another boat.

"Who is that?"

"One of ours," Harrison reassured her. He gave a short laugh. "It always helps to have some backup when the buggers cut and run."

As the other Customs boat drew near, the trawler was forced to turn and slow down, allowing *The Clacton* to draw ahead of *The Dido* on its port side. The trawler gave a sudden burst of speed, and for a moment Liz was convinced it would cut through the converging Customs boats and get away. But a rapid sequence of flashes crossed in front of the fleeing boat, and Liz heard the sound of an automatic weapon firing.

"Tracer bullets," explained Harrison. "That should get their attention."

The Dido seemed to hesitate, as if trying to make up her mind, then she slowed almost imperceptibly. As they sailed farther out into the open sea, Liz realised that *The Clacton* and the other Customs boat were forming a V, which held the trawler trapped between its arms. The two then began to turn almost imperceptibly to port, perfectly in synch, keeping the trawler nestled between them, until Liz saw that they were heading back into the quieter water of the cove.

"Keep alert," Harrison called out to the men on the bow. "They may try it again."

Now down to idling speed, *The Dido* was covered by searchlights from both Customs boats. There was still no sign of anyone on deck. Harrison stepped to the outside rail. Lifting his hailer he called to the trawler.

"We are armed, and will board you by force if you don't come out. You have thirty seconds to show yourselves."

This is like a Western, thought Liz, as they waited tensely. After about fifteen seconds, a man emerged from the wheelhouse; he was followed almost immediately by another man. They both wore black sou'westers, with knee-high gumboots.

"Stay where you are," Harrison commanded. "We're coming aboard."

In a moment *The Clacton* drew alongside. The two armed Customs men stood with their rifles pointed at *The Dido,* and a third man moved forward, holding a rope in his hand. Carefully judging the gap, he suddenly jumped and landed on the deck of the trawler, then moved to the bow, out of the line of any possible fire. Pulling hard, he brought *The Clacton* towards him until it bumped the trawler gently. In the stern another officer jumped onto *The Dido* and between them they brought *The Clacton* parallel.

Harrison turned to Liz. "You're welcome to come aboard, but please stay behind me. You never know what they may have waiting below."

Following Harrison, Liz jumped from the gunwale and landed lightly on *The Dido*'s deck. The other Customs boat had drawn up on the far side, and soon there were a dozen officers on board, though Liz noticed that an armed man remained on each Customs boat, covering them. Three of the Customs men on board were also carrying weapons—Glock 9mm pistols.

The two men who stood in the glare of the spotlights were Middle Eastern in appearance. The older one was heavyset with a thick stub of moustache. He looked to be in charge.

"Do you speak English?" Harrison asked him.

He shrugged, feigning incomprehension. When Harrison turned to his companion, he received the same response.

There was a broad hatch on deck that clearly led below, though it was bolted shut. Harrison pointed. "What's down there?" he demanded.

The moustached man spoke for the first time. "Is nothing below."

"Nothing?"

"Nothing. I swear."

"You are the only two on board?"

The man nodded.

"We'll see about that," said Harrison. He gestured at the hatch. "Open it."

They waited tensely while the younger man moved grudgingly across to the hatch. If there is someone below who's armed, this guy will get the first bullet, thought Liz. The man reached down and slowly pulled back the hatch bolt, then lifted open the square hinged top, letting it fall with a loud bang on the deck. He stood back, and looked away toward the sea, with a resigned expression on his face.

Suddenly up the ladder a figure emerged—a head first, wrapped in a plain brown scarf, then a cloth coat. A woman, Liz realised, as the figure climbed the last rung and stepped out on the boat's planks. She looked absolutely terrified.

Another figure appeared, also female, and then another and another . . . There were seven in all, all blinking in the bright search-lights, some shaking with fear or cold, though the sight of Liz seemed to calm them.

All of them were young. Liz was certain they were not from the Middle East—though they were dark, they had high cheekbones that were more European than Arab. Romanian, Liz guessed. Maybe Albanian.

Harrison said to them, "Who are you and why are you on this boat?"

Silence. Then a plump younger girl with dyed blond hair stepped forward. "I speak English," she said. She pointed to the other women. "They don't."

"What are you doing on this boat?"

"We come for work," she declared.

"What kind of work?"

"Modelling," she said seriously, and Liz winced. Is that what she really thought? Had a woman like this really believed the lies told her back in her village—the vision of a glamorous life in the West, high wages and innocent work?

Liz thought of what had been lying in store for this "cargo"—the journey to some strange English city in an overcrowded van, the squalor of their new accommodation, the coercive threats, the "initiating" rapes, until they were sufficiently degraded to be put to work in the sex industry. What industry? thought Liz angrily. This was white slavery.

21

They reached Harwich at three a.m. Gradually the spirits of the female "cargo" had lifted, and there was even a small cheer when *The Clacton* tied fast in the harbour. The two Middle Eastern men looked a lot less happy. They'd been searched for weapons on board, and once inside the terminal Harrison had them searched again.

Both were carrying British passports, with addresses in London suburbs—Walthamstow and Pinner. The men's names were Chaloub and Hanoush, which sounded Lebanese to Liz—Veshara's men.

Not that they were talking: Chaloub, the more senior man, was an old pro, and asked at once to see a lawyer. When he turned and spoke tersely in Arabic to Hanoush, Liz sensed it was to tell the younger man to keep his mouth shut.

Liz saw no point in hanging around; she'd hear from Harrison in due course what he'd managed to get out of the two—not very much, from the looks of it. But there was plenty to charge them with, and the link to Veshara was indisputable; his company was the registered owner of *The Dido*. What Liz couldn't see was any connection to Syrian intelligence, or to the Gleneagles conference, which was now just six weeks away.

Though it was now the middle of the night, she decided to drive straight back to London; three hours' sleep in a Travelodge wasn't going to do her much good. The A12 was virtually empty, and even the M25 proved comparatively painless, so Liz made good time: the sun was just tipping over the horizon as she reached the outskirts of London. This early, the city looked deserted, like the landscape of a post-apocalypse film.

She drove across north London through Dalston and Holloway towards her flat in Kentish Town, passing a solitary milk float wobbling along Fortess Road. As she turned into her own street, she saw a minicab waiting outside one of the houses. An early-morning start for some young City type, she thought, off for a meeting in Zurich or Rome.

Inside her flat, Liz put the kettle on and ran a bath. Though her bed called seductively, she rejected the idea of a nap; it would just leave her groggy for the rest of the day. Better to soldier on and collapse early in the evening.

An hour later, she slammed her front door, climbed the basement steps and turned towards the Underground station. The neighbourhood was slowly waking up, and she was surprised to see the minicab still waiting farther down the street. Her neighbour must have overslept.

There was some traffic now on Kentish Town Road, though not many people on the pavements—it was another week or so before the school term began, and most people still seemed to be away on holiday. Even at work, people were thin on the ground at the moment, though Peggy wasn't going off until the autumn, doubtless on some cultural jaunt with her new friend Tim.

Charles was still at work, even though his boys must be on holiday. Joanne's condition meant they didn't go away on family holidays these days. Liz would see him later this morning, to tell him about the previous night's escapade off the Essex coast. Sami Veshara must be wondering where his "cargo" had got to, and Liz imagined that Harrison was looking forward to interviewing and then arresting the Lebanese businessman about the covert side of his business. She intended to suggest to Charles that she should see Veshara as well, and try within the rules to leverage the charges he was certain to face, against cooperation with the service.

She stopped at a newsagents' to buy the *Guardian* and exchange her daily hello with the cheerful Pakistani owner. She was about three hundred yards from the Underground station now, thinking of how best to squeeze Veshara, when she looked up and saw a woman standing still on the pavement not more than ten feet away. She was looking at Liz with an expression of absolute horror.

Then Liz realised the woman wasn't looking *at* her, but *behind* her. Instinctively she turned around, just in time to see a car, off the road and on the pavement, coming rapidly straight at her.

She leaped desperately to get out of the way, but too late. The car hit Liz side-on, sweeping her legs from under her and catapulting her onto its bonnet, where she bounced like a floppy doll, hitting her head with a sharp crack against the windscreen. She felt a horrible pain in her temple and in her hips, then realised she was rolling off the car. She flailed her arms, but there was nothing on the bonnet to grab onto. As she fell to the pavement her one thought was that the car hitting her had been the minicab. And then she didn't think at all.

22

Charles Wetherby looked up with a frown. He was in the middle of a phone call to the deputy head of GCHQ and there was his secretary, normally the most discreet of women, standing in the doorway waving her hands. Her face was a map of anxiety.

"Hold on a moment, please," he said into the phone, and cupped his hand over the receiver. "What's the matter? I'm busy at the moment."

"There's a policeman on the line. He's at the Whittington hospital. Liz Carlyle's been brought in. She's been hit by a car."

"My God. Is she okay? Is she badly hurt?"

"I don't know. He won't say."

"Put him on," Charles said, rapidly cutting off his other call. "This is Charles Wetherby. Who am I speaking to?"

"It's Sergeant Chiswick, sir, Special Branch. We had a call from Camden District about a woman named Carlyle who was brought into A and E. She was carrying Home Office ID, but they didn't get very far when they rang there. So we were brought in."

"Is she alive?"

"Yes, though it was a close-run thing—if the ambulance had been ten minutes slower she wouldn't have made it. She's in surgery now, and the doctors seem to think she'll pull through."

"Can you tell me what happened?"

"She was hit by a car in Kentish Town. Near the Underground." He paused briefly. "The car hit her on the pavement, sir. A witness said it looked as if the vehicle left the street deliberately."

"Did the driver stop?"

"No. We haven't got much of a description, I'm afraid. It was a man—and that's about it. The closest witness is a woman and she's still in shock. But one thing she did say is that the car was a minicab. It had the sticker on the back window."

Charles thought quickly. "Now listen carefully, Sergeant Chiswick. When Miss Carlyle comes out of surgery, I want her put in a single room and kept under police guard—armed guard. There may have been an attempt on her life; I don't want another. If you have any questions, or if there is any problem, ring me back straightaway. Is that understood?"

Once he put the phone down, Charles sat for a moment, tapping a pencil on his desktop, collecting his thoughts. He called his secretary in and asked her to find Peggy Kinsolving, get DG on the line, extract the contact details for Liz's mother from her file (though he'd wait to ring her until after Liz was out of the operating room) and get the head of media relations to come and see him right away. The presence of Special Branch at the Whittington and now an armed guard on Liz's room might well draw a reporter, tipped off by a member of staff, and he wanted that possibility closed down straightaway.

There was one other call he needed to make. He got through right away.

"Fane," said the voice, in that slow drawl Charles always found annoying.

"Geoffrey, it's Charles Wetherby. Liz Carlyle's been hit by a car."

"No! Is she all right?"

At least his concern sounds genuine, thought Charles, though the last thing he was interested in right now was sharing his worry about Liz with Geoffrey Fane. "The thing is, Geoffrey, the police say this may not have been an accident. It looks as though a car tried to run her down."

"Are they sure?"

"Well, they've got a witness and the car didn't stop."

"But who would do this?"

"That's why I'm calling." Charles's voice was cool now. "Is there anything you haven't told us? When you briefed us on your source, you didn't give the slightest indication that one of my officers could be in danger."

"Steady on, Charles. There wasn't any reason to think so. As far as I can see, there still isn't. It may not have anything to do with that."

"Nonsense." Charles was emphatic. He could picture Fane in his office, high as an eyrie in the central block of MI6, reclining in the padded leather chair he favoured. The image infuriated him. "She's got nothing else on that could pose this kind of a threat."

"I know you're upset—"

"Upset? There's a very real possibility she may be injured for life.

We certainly knew nothing of any danger. You were obliged to let us know if there was even a possibility of this."

"I know my obligations," Fane protested.

"If you've held anything back, I want to know what it is. Is that clear? Otherwise, I'll consider you to have placed one of my officers in danger quite unnecessarily."

They both knew how serious a charge that would be. Charles was about to say something further, then thought better of it. He knew he'd got his point across.

Charles sensed Fane was trying to stay composed. "I certainly hear you, Charles," he said carefully. "I'll be in touch."

2 3

Fane put down the phone. He was more badly shaken than he would have expected. Liz Carlyle had somehow got under his skin. This accident, attack, whatever it was, affected him badly. He knew as well as Charles that it almost certainly came from her investigations, ones that he had set in train. He didn't blame himself for that—if he hadn't passed on the information from Cyprus, he wouldn't have been doing his job.

But it gnawed at him nonetheless. Cross as Charles had been, he'd refrained from saying what they both knew to be true: this wasn't the first time an MI5 officer had been put in danger in a case where Fane was involved. As they both knew to their cost, the previous time it had proved fatal, arguably because Fane had not been entirely forthcoming.

There must have been a leak somewhere, one that had almost resulted in Liz being killed. Where could it have been? he thought. Not within Vauxhall Cross, he was confident of that. He doubted there were more than four people in his building who knew Liz was working on the case. And only two, himself and Bruno Mackay, knew any detail of what she was doing.

No, the leak must have come from outside. And there was only one place, other than Thames House, where he'd talked. Grosvenor Square.

He picked up his phone and dialled an internal extension. "Bruno, it's Geoffrey. Got a minute?"

Mackay arrived in short order, spruce in a blazer and club tie. Fane said, "Someone's had a go at Liz Carlyle—ran her down."

For once Bruno Mackay's aplomb deserted him. He looked horrified.

"I know, I know," said Fane, "it's perfectly awful. She's hurt, but it looks as if she'll recover. The thing is, she's been working on this Syrian business, and I think somewhere, somehow, somebody's talked. Nothing else explains it. I'm wondering if it could be Grosvenor Square. Maybe just loose talk, possibly something more sinister. Either way, we need to plug that leak and do it quickly. I want you to take a closer look at young Mr. Brookhaven—check him out very thoroughly. His last posting was Damascus, and he may have more contacts than we realise. If you need more resources let me know. But keep it strictly to yourself at present. All right?"

"Don't worry," said Bruno, his composure restored. "I'll get onto it now." Fane knew he didn't think much of the Americans. "Let me know how Liz gets on. I'd like to take her some grapes." He grinned.

As Mackay got up to go, Fane said, "Be discreet, Bruno. I don't want Bokus in here like some mad bull."

24

Sami Veshara was frightened. Not for his safety—since the attempted hijacking of his car, he'd surrounded himself with bodyguards—but for his liberty. He had an appointment that morning at Paddington Green police station, and he was pretty sure he knew what it was about.

When Chaloub hadn't rung at midnight as scheduled, Sami hadn't been particularly perturbed: sometimes the trip from Holland took longer than expected; once Hanoush had got the tides wrong and the trawler had been forced to wait four hours before disembarking its passengers.

But when Sami had still not heard from them by breakfast, he knew something was up. He began to make inquiries, and by supper-time he'd learned that Chaloub and Hanoush were both in custody. The "cargo," too, had been impounded, and he'd had an angry call from the owner of a Manchester massage parlour demanding to know where his new employees were.

It had still been a shock to be asked to come in for "a chat" the following morning. Why Paddington Green? Wasn't that where terrorists were questioned? A big solid block of a place under the flyover of the A40 as it tipped down to Marylebone Road—Sami passed it every day on his way home—which seemed to feature on the television each time the Prevention of Terrorism Act was pressed into service.

He left home in plenty of time, wearing one of his smartest Milan suits and a Hermès tie. One could not be intimidated, he decided. He was driven by his new chauffeur, Pashwar, the son of an Afghan refugee who owed him a favour. Behind them another car followed closely, a Mercedes sedan with two of his cousin Mahfuz's heavies. They were probably armed, but Sami made it a point not to know.

As he got out of the car at the police station, he scanned the pavement nervously, before realising that this was probably the one place in London where he was unlikely to be attacked. Above him, cars thundered along Westway.

Inside, he gave his name to the receptionist, and immediately a uniformed policewoman led him down two flights of stairs, along a corridor bleakly lit by overhead bulbs, to a small, windowless room containing a table, two chairs and nothing else. She closed the door behind her as she left.

Claustrophobic at the best of times, Sami had a moment of panic, wondering if he would ever breathe fresh air and see grass again. This modern-day dungeon seemed designed to play on his fears. Pull yourself together, he told himself sternly; this is England, not Saudi Arabia. I can always ask to see my lawyer.

He waited twenty minutes, sitting on one of the hard chairs, growing more anxious every minute. The door opened and a man came in. Middle-aged, conservative suit, his face business-like but not unfriendly. He was carrying a folder. Sami relaxed just a touch.

"Mr. Veshara, my name is Walshaw. Thank you for coming in." The man sat down on the other side of the table and looked at Sami, his eyes fixed and expressionless. Sami shifted uncomfortably. Perhaps he was not so friendly after all.

"I am happy to help in any way I can," said Sami. He tried to make a joke—"You know, to assist the police in your inquiries."

The man gave a fleeting smile but said, "I'm not a policeman, Mr. Veshara. They'll be along in a little while to speak to you. I think you may know what it's about."

"No," Sami said theatrically, turning both hands, palms up, in a gesture of innocence. "I have no idea."

"I see," said Walshaw. He fixed Sami with a stare of such intensity that the Lebanese felt unnerved. The man's eyes seemed to look right through him like an X-ray.

Then Walshaw shrugged. "It's up to you, of course. From what I understand, the police think you have a good deal to answer for. *The Dido* has been seized, in case you didn't know. There were seven women on board, entering the country illegally."

He opened the file in front of him and looked briefly at the top page. "They were heading for Manchester, I understand, though the work they would have found there might not have been what they were expecting." He gave a wry smile. "I understand several people are in custody. The crew of *The Dido* and a man in Manchester. Who knows what they will say?"

Sami's heart began to beat faster and he could feel perspiration on his palms. He rubbed them on his immaculate trousers. Walshaw looked at him, this time thoughtfully. Suddenly, putting both his hands together, he leaned across the table, speaking softly but directly. "We haven't got much time, Mr. Veshara, so let me come to the point. In a few minutes you are going to be interviewed, and very probably charged. Like it or not, we take a dim view in this country of the kind of trade you're involved in. Frankly, I'm not sure they'd think much of it in your country either. You need to make a decision."

Sami gulped. The situation was running out of his control. Who was this man and what did he want? "What sort of decision?"

"You can take your chances with the British justice system, or you can talk with me. I'm not in a position to offer you anything, but I am not . . . without influence. If you help me, it will be taken into account and it could prove useful to you."

There was something lulling about this voice. Sami felt as if he were trapped in a pressure cooker and had suddenly been shown the safety valve, but without knowing how to turn it on. What did this man want?

"What would my talk with you consist of?"

Walshaw took his time replying, picking up a pencil and tapping it lightly on the table. At last he said, "We already knew a bit about your business interests, and after the seizure of *The Dido* we know a lot more. But that's not what interests me." He added lightly, "Neither does your personal life, for that matter.

"What does matter to me is where you've travelled in the Middle East in the last few years. What you've seen there, and who you have been talking to about it. In Lebanon, of course. But in other countries as well. In fact, why don't we start with Syria?"

Sami stared at this man Walshaw, whose eyes were unyielding now. It was tempting to start talking straightaway, to calm his nerves, but if he told this man everything, the next time he set foot in the Middle East his life wouldn't be worth a Lebanese piastre. He hesitated.

Walshaw said, "If we're going to be able to help you, Mr. Veshara, then you need to start talking. Otherwise, I'll tell the inspector that you're ready for him."

It would be a great gamble. He would effectively be putting his life in this Englishman's hands. But if he didn't, he knew he faced arrest, trial, a prison sentence. Prison. The prospect was too ghastly to bear. He could live with the disgrace; he knew his wife would stand by him; conceivably his businesses might even survive his absence. What he couldn't contemplate was the physical fact of incarceration. It was his worst nightmare.

He exhaled noisily, then sat back in his chair. "I hope you are not in a hurry, Mr. Walshaw. It is a long story I have to tell."

As Charles Wetherby listened, making the occasional note, Sami Veshara told him how, five years or so ago, two Israelis had come to his office in London. They had threatened that if he didn't help them, they would report his people-trafficking business to the British authorities. It was at a time when he was cultivating some government ministers through a charity he had founded, and he was hoping to be recommended for a peerage.

The men were from Mossad. They knew about his regular visits to Lebanon and his contacts there. They knew he travelled around the country buying figs and other produce. They wanted him to go to Lebanon whenever they asked him to, to travel to the south and, using some equipment they would give him, to send signals which they told him would help them locate the positions of Hezbollah rocket launchers.

He had done what they wanted. He had not seen them again in London, but had met them in Tel Aviv from time to time. He described two men, one built like a squashed bowling ball, the other lean.

But to Charles's enquiries about his contacts with Syrians, Sami gave a flat denial. He had no contact with Syrian intelligence people or with government officials and had to the best of his knowledge never met any. He had no particular hostility or friendship towards them, he said, and Charles could not shake his story.

2 5

Remarkable," the consultant had said. "You are very lucky, Miss Carlyle. You're making a truly remarkable recovery."

Liz wished she felt quite so remarkable now, as she sat drowsily in a deck chair in her mother's garden at Bowerbridge on her fourth day out of hospital. She had wanted to go back to her flat, but Susan Carlyle wouldn't hear of it. What Liz didn't know was that Charles Wetherby had met Edward in London. The two men had liked each other immediately and Charles had been frank with Edward about his concern that Liz might still be at risk from whoever had attacked her. Edward had undertaken to keep a very close eye out for anything unusual around Bowerbridge and to contact Charles immediately if he had any anxieties. Now Susan sat knitting on a garden bench, watching Liz carefully, like a mother hen.

It was September now and the apples were swelling on the trees at the bottom of the lawn. The huge white flowers of a hydrangea paniculata were attracting heavy, slow-moving bees and the musky scent of an old-fashioned climbing rose was wafting down from a wall. Liz had been in the Whittington two weeks, though the first few days were not even a memory. Amazingly, she had not broken a single bone in her "accident"—but she hadn't escaped unscathed. Far from it: she'd had severe internal bleeding and, most ominously, a ruptured spleen. A quick-thinking paramedic had spotted that as she lay half-conscious in the ambulance. On arrival she had been whisked straight into emergency surgery. The consultant told her later that another ten minutes and she would not have made it.

So I shouldn't complain, thought Liz, though even walking from the house to the garden still tired her. She'd realised for the first time that just because she was out of hospital, it didn't mean she was well again.

In the first few days, between the lingering effects of the anaesthetic and the codeine-based painkillers, Liz had been entirely out of it. She'd sensed her mother's presence, and in the background saw a man she dimly recognised as Edward Treglown. Once she could have sworn Charles had been sitting in the chair at the foot of her bed.

As she'd slowly come to, more visitors had arrived—Peggy Kinsolving, trying to act her usual positive, cheerful self, but more subdued than Liz had ever seen her. Flowers had arrived from Geoffrey Fane and, typically, a bottle of champagne from Bruno Mackay. Miles Brookhaven had sent flowers too, and Peggy said he'd rung twice to ask after Liz.

She had had ample time to think about what had happened to her.

Her mind kept flashing back to the sight of the oncoming car as she'd turned around, but she could remember nothing after that. There was no doubt in her mind that she had been deliberately run down, but no one had come up with any clue as to who had done it, or why.

It would not have been easy to plan. Someone would have had to follow her to find out where she lived. How long had they been watching and waiting? She might easily have stayed that night in Harwich. Or taken her car instead of the Underground to work. Presumably they would have just come back another day. Liz fought back a shudder at the thought they might try again.

She couldn't stop going over it all. It must be someone she'd encountered in the course of work. She reviewed what she'd been doing in the past few months, but nothing pointed to any explanation. Was it some kind of revenge attack? No doubt Neil Armitage, the scientist convicted of passing secrets to the Russians, in whose case she'd given evidence, nursed a massive grudge, but he was safely behind bars and in any case he didn't know who she was.

Which left the Syrian Plot, as she was beginning to think of it, even though it had a dearth of suspects who might want Liz out of the way—only two, in fact: Chris Marcham and Sami Veshara; and possibly the Syrians.

Marcham had certainly been peculiar, and she had sensed there were secrets he didn't want her to know. But not about Syria, which was her only real concern with the man. He seemed so chaotic (she thought of the mess in his house) that for him to engineer a carefully plotted murder seemed wildly improbable. He hadn't got a motive and the means of doing it would be well beyond him.

That wasn't true with Sami Veshara, whose respectable front as a food importer belied his involvement with an especially vicious trade. He'd be no stranger to violence, but unlike Marcham he wouldn't have had the faintest idea Liz was investigating him. If he'd had someone watching out for the trawler, who had somehow witnessed its capture, and even spotted Liz, would Sami's reaction really be to order a hit on her? Not within a few hours. It didn't make sense. Especially since the minicab was already sitting on her street in Kentish Town when she got back from Essex.

What about the Syrians? How could they possibly know who she was, and even if they did, why attack her?

Lying in hospital during her second week there, Liz had kept mulling all this over, without coming to any satisfactory conclusion. When Charles came to see her in the second week, as she was just starting to feel human again, she'd tried raising it with him. But he had proved frustratingly elusive. "Let's talk about that when you're better," he'd said, over Liz's protests that there was nothing wrong with her brain. Even Peggy couldn't be drawn, and she'd avoided any serious talk about what was going on at Thames House in Liz's absence.

She heard the front doorbell and her mother sprang up, returning a moment later with Edward, who was carrying two bags of groceries. "I've brought you the papers." He waved copies of the *Guardian* and the *Daily Mail*.

"Let me help you put things away," said Liz, standing up a little unsteadily.

"You sit still," her mother commanded. "I'll get you a nice cup of tea."

"Don't be ridiculous. I'm perfectly all right," Liz snapped, knowing she wasn't, but annoyed that people kept mollycoddling her. It was becoming intolerable.

"That's a very good sign," Edward interjected, coming out of the kitchen. "A cranky patient is usually a recovering patient."

For a moment Liz felt furious—who was he to intervene? But there was such a twinkle in Edward's eye that she couldn't stay cross, and she found herself laughing, for the first time since the accident.

"That's better still," said Edward, and this time all three of them laughed. "Leave it to me," he said to Susan, and while he busied himself in the kitchen Liz looked at the newspapers.

Edward emerged holding a tray, with two mugs and a tumbler. "Susan," he said, handing her one of the mugs.

He handed the tumbler to Liz. "Very medicinal," he said. "Your mother says you prefer vodka, but I hope a hot toddy will do."

She took a careful sip. Just what she needed.

"Anything in the papers?" Edward enquired, sitting down on the sofa next to Liz.

"Just the usual. I see the Man in the Box has been identified."

"Who's that?" asked Susan.

Liz laughed. "Someone they found dead in a church, Mother. In a box, as I say." She glanced at the paper, interested that the police had finally decided to release the victim's name. "He's called Ledingham. I don't suppose you knew him," she said with a smile.

Her mother smiled back. "I'm sure I didn't."

Liz looked at Edward, but he wasn't smiling. "Did you say Ledingham? Is it by any chance *Alexander* Ledingham?"

Liz was slightly nonplussed. She looked at the article again. "That's right."

"Could I?" asked Edward, and reached out for the paper. He read the article quickly, then gave a small sigh.

Liz said, "I'm awfully sorry for joking. Did you know him?"

Edward shook his head. "I met a man with that name several times." He reached for his drink and took a sip. "Oddly enough, it was in Kosovo. One of my duties was to liaise with the Serbian Orthodox in the area. They'd had an awfully rough time—the Albanian Muslims had burnt down many of the churches, and the clergy had really got it in the neck. Mind you, it was all dwarfed by Serbian atrocities, but it was unpleasant nonetheless.

"One day I was told a journalist wanted to see me about it. His name was Marcham and he was out there for a newspaper." Liz tried not to react, and kept her eyes fixed on Edward. He went on, "I met him, and he seemed an intelligent chap, a bit eccentric perhaps—he seemed more interested in what had happened to the churches than to any people.

"After that, I seemed to run into Marcham all the time. It was a bit like when you're reading a book that mentions something obscure, like fishing in Iceland, and after that 'fishing in Iceland' seems to crop up in everything you read.

"Marcham often had a much younger chap with him—a sort of sidekick, if you will. At one point, Marcham introduced me. He said, 'This is Alex Ledingham,' and I remember wondering if the fellow was his partner."

"You mean journalist partner?"

Edward shook his head with a smile. "No. We weren't *that* narrow-minded in the army, Liz. I mean partner as in lover."

"And was he?"

"Who knows? It's quite likely, because he wasn't a journalist and it was a jolly dangerous time to be out there without any reason. What I most remember is that Ledingham shared Marcham's interest in churches. He said he was making a survey of the Serbian Orthodox churches—which ones had been destroyed, which had been damaged."

"Wasn't that a bit risky? You'd have to admire him, though."

Edward took a swallow of tea and Susan said, "You're rather keen on churches yourself, Edward."

He acknowledged this with a nod. "That's true. Though I'm not a fanatic and I certainly wouldn't take the risks Ledingham took to visit them. With him it seemed much more than an intellectual interest."

"Perhaps he was very pious," suggested Liz.

"It seemed more like fervour than piety, if you ask me. It's not as if he were Serbian Orthodox—he made a point of telling me he was Anglican. Yet I saw him once after he'd visited a church in Musutiste, and he seemed incredibly excited. Almost possessed. There was something almost . . ."

"Sexual?"

He nodded with a smile. "Yes. Now that you say that, it did seem sexual."

"Did you ever see him again after Kosovo?"

"No. And for that matter, I never saw Marcham again, either."

"They both sound perfectly creepy to me," said Susan Carlyle. She got up, holding her empty mug. "I'm just going to make some supper."

But Liz's mind was somewhere else.

She rang Peggy Kinsolving early the next morning, and told her what she'd learned about the connection between Ledingham and Chris Marcham.

"What a coincidence," said Peggy.

"I know. Let's go with it, shall we? I want you to get onto the Met. Speak with the officers investigating Ledingham's death, and tell them about Marcham's relationship with him."

"I'll do it right away. They'll want to speak to Marcham, won't they? Shouldn't I go along, too?"

"No. *I'm* going to go. I've already met Marcham; I want to see what he has to say."

"But Liz, you can't—"

"Yes I can, and that's final." Then, softening, Liz added, "Let me know when they want to see him."

And as she rang off, Liz felt a small surge of adrenaline. Thank God, she thought, exhilarated. I can always convalesce later.

26

Whatever its ups and downs—and recently there had been plenty of downs—Geoffrey Fane made it a rule not to let his personal life intrude into his professional affairs. But this morning he was finding it difficult.

A letter had come from Adele, his ex-wife, now living in Paris. It had opened cordially enough, but on the second page she had dropped the bombshell:

> *I have been thinking about the farm in Dorset. Frankly, it's becoming more and more apparent that Philippe and I are unlikely to go there very often in future, if at all. We've been looking for our own place in Brittany and in the*

*circumstances it doesn't make much sense for me to retain
my interest in the farm. Before doing anything, I would of
course want to offer you the chance to acquire it—at a fair
market price of course!*

The farm had been in Fane's family for generations. Since the war, the actual farming of its six hundred acres had been leased out to a neighbour, but the house—a large stone building at one end of a valley five miles from the market town of Blandford—had been used by generations of Fanes at Christmas and Easter, almost every half-term, and throughout the summer months.

Not for much longer, thought Fane, since he couldn't see any way he could afford to buy Adele out. If there had been one consolation in the financial disaster of his divorce, it had been Adele's willingness not to force the place's sale. But now that's just what she was doing.

He didn't understand why it bothered him so much. He hardly ever went there anymore, and the prospect of retiring there in a decade's time or so had always been more imagined than likely. His son, Michael, loved the place when he was young—even spoke touchingly, if unrealistically, as a teenager about trying to make a go of farming it. But that wouldn't happen now, and with the news that Adele no longer had any interest, Fane had no one to share it with.

Perhaps that was the problem. If he'd built another life, even had another family, then he might have felt some urgency about protecting his legacy. Instead he just felt a depressing lassitude. He was engaged with his work again, felt his old confidence had largely returned. But outside it there was a void that work didn't fill.

Who could fill it?

There was no shortage of candidates: he'd tried some of them. Adele had half a dozen friends in London whose marriages had also split up. But none of them appealed to Fane; they were too like Adele, interested mainly in clothes, restaurants, the latest holiday in Verbier or Provence. He knew too that his appeal to them was based entirely on his supposed status and (he had to laugh, thinking of what the divorce had cost him) the money they thought he had.

No, he knew now that he wanted a companion he could talk to, one with a head on her shoulders, one he could share his work with—something he'd never been able to do with Adele, who'd resented the constant moves round the world, the secrecy and above all the fact that as an MI6 officer he was most unlikely to become an ambassador, so she could never be "Her Excellency." All those problems disappeared if one's partner had the same kind of job. But he was too senior now, too experienced, to find solace in some junior denizen of Vauxhall Cross, and the eligible women nearer his own rank and age were either thin on the ground or, inevitable in MI6, stationed abroad.

There had been one possibility. Liz Carlyle had always struck him as refreshingly intelligent, forthright, very much her own woman. And very attractive. Best of all, she worked across the river, so there would be none of the competition and the incestuous gossip that characterised romantic relationships between colleagues.

But it had all gone wrong somehow. Well, not "somehow"; rather, in the specific debacle of Fane's own involvement in what he thought of as the Oligarch Operation. He knew some of it was his fault. But no one could have foreseen the disastrous consequences, and surely no one could have thought Fane indifferent to them. Yet a coolness had resulted between him and Liz, just when he had thought they were growing close. And now she was in hospital, and Charles Wetherby was blaming him.

His secretary came in. "This has just come from Bruno," she said, and handed him a sheet of paper.

Fane found Bruno Mackay just as irritating as most people did. But no one doubted that, given a task, Bruno was utterly reliable. He was going off on two weeks' leave, but had promised to come back first to Fane with whatever he'd unearthed about Miles Brookhaven, and here it was.

Bruno had begun with Washington, talking both to MI6 there and then to friendly American sources they'd put his way. It seemed that Brookhaven was well thought of in the CIA, and had risen rapidly at Langley. Intelligent, personable—and he spoke Arabic, which made him a rarity.

It was Brookhaven's Syrian posting that interested Fane most, and he read on carefully. In Damascus Brookhaven had stood out both for speaking the local language and for his eagerness to learn all about Syrian life and culture. With few colleagues to share his enthusiasm, he had made friends instead among the larger community of diplomats, international businessmen and intelligence officers. Among the latter, one in particular became a close friend—Edmund Whitehouse, the head of MI6's Syria station.

Whitehouse had been a mine of information for Bruno. He was an old Middle East hand; he'd worked in Jordan, Israel and Saudi Arabia before running the station in Damascus. Whitehouse had been happy to take Brookhaven under his wing; after all, a friendly source in the CIA station was always useful. Brookhaven struck him as enthusiastic but, as an intelligence officer, naïve. He'd been surprised by how little supervision Brookhaven seemed to get from his own head of station.

But Whitehouse had been positively dumbstruck when Brookhaven had met him for a drink one evening in the bar of the Champ Palace Hotel, and told him he'd received an approach from a man in the heart of Syria's labyrinthine intelligence network. There had been nothing boastful in the American's account, for he soon made it clear that this potential agent did not want to work for the Americans—he wanted to be put in touch with the British, which was why Brookhaven was telling Whitehouse about him. Whitehouse could not help but look with new respect at the young American he'd thought so naïve; his protégé now turned patron.

For that's what it had been—a gift, handed over to the Brits, with the understanding that the donor, the CIA, would also be the recipient of whatever secrets this new source turned over to the British. And MI6 had lived up to its end of the bargain, for the most part. Reading the report, Fane thought about the pains he had taken to disguise from Andy Bokus and Brookhaven the source of his information about the threat to the conference—or was it a threat to Syria? He'd been hiding a source from the very man who'd given it to them in the first place.

When he had finished reading, Fane stood up and walked to the window. On the Thames a barge chugged upstream at low tide, and a covey of gulls hovered hopefully around its stern. A group of young schoolchildren, marshalled by three teachers, was crossing north on Vauxhall Bridge, probably heading for the Tate. Fane watched them, but his thoughts were elsewhere.

He went to his desk and picked up the phone, confident he was delivering useful news. He got through right away. "Charles, it's Geoffrey Fane. We've done some checking into the background of our American colleagues in Grosvenor Square. The younger one in particular. I think you might find it makes interesting reading."

2 7

It had been raining continuously since four. Now it was evening, and Ben Ahmad left the Park Royal Underground with his raincoat soaked. The front had come in from Ireland, a day earlier than forecast. He supposed it was difficult predicting weather on an island, but he missed the certainty of the forecasts in Syria, where there were no surprises and it stayed dry for months on end.

The vacuum cleaner shop was just closing when he arrived, and he exchanged the briefest of nods with Olikara, the "owner." In the backyard he hurried to the Portakabin, and was surprised to find when he put his keys in that the metal door was already unlocked. When he opened it, to his astonishment Aleppo was sitting behind the desk.

"How did you get in?" he started to demand.

Aleppo dismissed the question with a curt nod of his head. "Sit down," he said sharply. His black leather jacket and charcoal high-necked pullover made him look especially sinister in the fading light.

Ahmad found himself with no option but to take the seat in front of the desk. He was alarmed. The control of the meeting had already slipped from him and Aleppo's steely gaze unnerved him.

"I want you to listen very carefully." Aleppo put his hands on the desktop and leaned forward threateningly. His voice was icy. "I have at great personal risk supplied your government with crucial information. I did this on the clear understanding that they would act upon it—otherwise I would be a fool to have taken such risks. I am not a fool."

Ahmad fought to keep his mind clear. He'd been right to be frightened of this man. There was something so ruthless about him that it seemed pathological. He said earnestly, "No one has suggested you're anything of the sort. But these things take time. I have explained that to you before."

Aleppo chopped the air abruptly with his hand, as if mincing the argument. "Time is the one thing neither of us has."

What was the urgency? wondered Ahmad. Was something going to happen soon that he didn't know about? Before he had summoned up the nerve to ask, his thoughts were cut short by Aleppo. "I do not want lies, I do not want waffle. I want action. Do you understand?"

Ahmad took a deep breath. He had never found himself so dominated by an agent before. "Yes," he said reluctantly.

But Aleppo was dissatisfied; that was clear from the impatient way he shook his head. "Let me tell you something. The last man who told me yes while meaning no was South African. They found his torso washed up on a beach near Cape Town. They never found the legs."

"I give you my word. Something is going to happen this very week."

When Aleppo stood up suddenly, Ahmad felt uncomfortable. Would Olikara hear him if he shouted out? No, the shop was closed and he would have gone home by now. He glanced out of the dusty window of the Portakabin and saw that it was dark outside. No one would still be at work in this squalid little precinct of shops.

Aleppo stepped forward and Ahmad tensed, waiting for the assault. But the agent laughed harshly. "Don't be so frightened," he ordered. "Not yet, that is." And he walked straight out of the Portakabin door, leaving it swinging and squeaking gently on its hinges as the Syrian sat still, trying to regain his composure. Aleppo might be a valuable source, but Ahmad was now convinced he was also crazy.

He sat there for several minutes until his breathing returned to normal. The odd thing was, he thought as he left the Portakabin, locking the door carefully behind him, he had been telling Aleppo the truth. Something *was* going to happen that week. Only it wasn't going to happen in England.

28

Peter Templeton was hot, even sitting in the shade of the portico in the corner of the monastery's long terrace. He could hear cicadas on the slope beneath him, but the heat must be too much for the kestrels, for the sky was empty of life. As Templeton peered down the valley the air shimmered slightly, oscillating jelly-like in the unremitting glare of the high noon sun.

He had come, as always, in convoy with his colleague. The other car sat two miles below at the café, waiting for Jaghir to drive past. Just outside Nicosia a large Peugeot saloon had joined them, making Templeton nervous. He had been relieved when it had finally turned off, and sped south towards the coast.

His mobile vibrated. "Yes," he said, keeping his voice down, though he had the terrace to himself—the monks were all at prayer.

"A couple of miles away. I can see the dust. I'd say five minutes to here; twenty to you."

"Okay. Keep an eye out for any other cars," he added, thinking again of the Peugeot.

Templeton waited tensely, resisting the temptation to look at his watch. He had called this meeting, prompted by Vauxhall Cross's agitated requests for confirmation of Jaghir's original story and, if possible, more detailed information. Against Templeton's better judgement, Jaghir had insisted on meeting him here at the monastery again. Vauxhall Cross had been so adamant that he talk with Jaghir right away that he hadn't protested.

Something stirred in the far corner of the terrace, and Templeton turned quickly, alert. A lizard hopped once, then twice into the shadows cast by the rough stone wall. Then Templeton's phone vibrated.

"Yes."

"He's just passed."

"Anything else around?"

There was a pause. "Negative."

Soon Templeton saw the first dust cloud stirring from the track at the base of the hill. He peered across the valley and could just make out a dark saloon edging its way carefully up the slope. Gradually the image magnified as the car approached, taking the sinuous bends carefully, since the track was narrow and perched on a knife-edge high above the valley. On the few short straight stretches the car accelerated briefly, and now Templeton could see the solitary figure at the wheel. Jaghir.

The car disappeared momentarily where the track cut into the hillside, then reappeared in the last big bend before the final precipitous climb to the top. Templeton could hear the tyres gripping on the sandy surface, the rough throttle of the engine as the automatic transmission slipped in and out of gear. Then a flat thud, like a hand giving a short sharp slap against a rubber mat.

Suddenly Templeton saw the car veer like a child's toy out of control. It headed at a sharp angle for the edge of the track, then the tyres' seemed to catch themselves and the car moved away from the edge. Like a slow-motion film replay, the car now slewed across the thin wedge of track in widening swerves.

Templeton held his breath as he watched Jaghir desperately trying to regain control. But the Syrian must have swung the wheel too sharply—the car now careered towards the edge. A front tyre left the track and hung briefly in mid-air, then the back tyre joined it.

For a moment the car teetered perilously, tilted at an angle, as if in suspended animation. Then the entire vehicle tipped sideways and fell through the air, descending for almost a hundred feet until it just caught the protruding edge of a large boulder sticking out of the hillside. This flipped the saloon 180 degrees and it landed on its side on the sharp downward slope, gaining momentum, crashing through the brush, with a noise like dry cereal crushed by a spoon. The car rolled over and over until it came to the bottom of the valley, where it flipped over with a final movement onto its roof, and stayed completely still.

Whoomph! The shockwave of its crash landing rose up the valley, filling the hot moist air with a blanket of sound. Staring down, Templeton saw flames begin to creep from the bottom of the wrecked saloon, licking the side windows, then reaching the tyres that sat like circles of dark chocolate on top of the upended car. The fire spread over the exposed chassis, and Templeton, watching horrified from the terrace above, waited for the petrol tank to catch fire.

It did, in a series of muffled explosions. Now the entire vehicle was ablaze, and Templeton realised that while it was improbable that

Jaghir had survived the descent, it was inconceivable he could survive the fire.

Templeton's phone vibrated and an agitated voice said, "I see smoke."

"I bet you can. The target went off the track."

"Did he get out?"

"No."

"Is there anything I should do?"

Soon someone would spot the blaze—if not below in the valley, then here at the monastery when the monks came out of prayers. Fires were no joke in this tinderbox of arid scrub—people would watch to make sure the fire didn't spread; someone would go down to investigate and then the police would be called. There was time, but not much.

"Leave at once. And go back a different way. Meet me back at the office."

"You okay?"

"Yeah. Just go." And he switched off his phone.

Templeton left the terrace immediately and got into his car. He was shaking as he drove as quickly as he dared down the track, stopping when he came to the bend where Jaghir's saloon had left the road. He left the engine of his own car running while he got out and looked quickly at the tyre marks that ran through the dust until they stopped, on the edge of the cliff. Templeton peered down, stunned by how steep the fall had been. He could see the massive, obtruding boulder that the car had hit on its way down, leaving a smear of dark paint on the rock. His eyes followed the vertical trail as the saloon had somersaulted, crushing the scrub in its way, until it came to a halt on the bottom where it blazed now, like a final punctuation mark.

Templeton turned and quickly walked along the track, following the twists and turns of the tyre marks until he came to their first erratic move. What had gone wrong? A blowout? Possibly, though at such relatively low speed it should have been possible to control the saloon until it had stopped safely on the narrow road.

He looked carefully around the track to see what might have caused the accident. A nail, broken glass, something sharp; perhaps, he thought, even a small remote-controlled explosion. He found nothing.

He had better get going. He jogged back up the fifty yards of track, climbed into his own car, then drove down towards the junction, anxious to get away before a patrol car arrived and trapped him on the one-lane track.

Five minutes later, he was far enough away to think about what had happened. Could it have been a simple puncture after all? Realistically he had to admit that the odds of a blowout at low speed on the way to a covert meeting, resulting in Jaghir's death, were minimal. Far more likely that Jaghir's work for a foreign agency had been discovered and his Syrian masters had extracted the penalty. But he'd found no evidence to support that theory, either. It was only as he saw the residential apartment blocks of Nicosia appear on the horizon that he remembered something else—the dull crack he'd heard just before the ill-fated saloon first veered. His hands shook. If Jaghir had indeed been killed, how had he been detected?

29

Charles Wetherby was sitting in his armchair by the window of his office reading the draft JIC papers for the next day's meeting, when his secretary tapped on the door and put a tentative head in. "It's Geoffrey Fane on the line."

Wetherby was a patient man, but even he had his limits. What did Fane want now? Yesterday he'd revealed that the two "names" and their threat to the Gleneagles conference had come from some highly placed Syrian source whom the Americans had actually *donated* to Fane's people. And who had done the donating? Miles Brookhaven for pity's sake, seemingly a bit of private enterprise. And what were these two names up to? Just about everything except threatening the conference, so far as MI5 had been able to find out. But Fane had calmly come over and asked him to protect them. From what, exactly? To judge by the attack on Liz, it was MI5 who needed the protection. Just who was deceiving whom? And why in the name of hell and damnation had Fane not found out sooner about Brookhaven's links to Syria—if that's what he had—while that young man was enjoying a ringside seat on all the security arrangements for Gleneagles? He'd asked Fane that and got no plausible response. But at least Fane had volunteered to talk to Andy Bokus about it. That might be a tricky conversation. How did you tactfully tell someone like Bokus that his man might be working for the opposition? Well that was Fane's problem, thank God. And now what did the man want?

He walked over to his desk and picked up the telephone warily. "Hello, Geoffrey," he said.

"Charles, I'm afraid there's been a further development. Not a good one, either. Our Syrian source has been killed in the Troodos mountains in Cyprus. He was on his way to a meeting with Peter Templeton, head of our Cyprus station, who was running him."

"Was he assassinated?"

"It's starting to look like it. He drove off a narrow track that leads to the monastery where Templeton was waiting to meet him. The car was completely smashed up, and then there was a fire. Naturally Peter didn't wait around to investigate, but he's been talking to his sources in the Cypriot police. Apparently, the rear tyres in Jaghir's car were both shot out—there must have been a sniper somewhere on the hillside."

"What have the Syrians said?"

"That's the interesting thing. They cooperated only minimally with the police. Didn't seem to want to go into it much."

"Perhaps they were hoping to hide the fact that he was an intelligence officer."

"Perhaps. But in Syria they've hushed it up as well. I think they must have killed him."

"Which means we have another leak somewhere," said Wetherby bitterly.

"Possibly," said Fane. "Or it could be the same one."

3 0

Liz knew she'd made a mistake. She'd insisted that she felt perfectly well enough to do the interview with Marcham, though everyone—Charles, Peggy, her mother and even Edward, though he'd admitted it wasn't his business—had disagreed.

Now, sitting in the taxi on her way to Hampstead, she knew they'd been right. She felt weak and shaky, her head hurt if she moved it too quickly and the yellowing bruise down one side of her face still attracted looks, if not comments. Why had she been so obstinate? Charles could have done the interview, or even Peggy in a pinch. But they wouldn't have done it as well, she'd told herself, though now she wasn't so sure. She couldn't stand feeling that she was on the sidelines. Was it a fear of not being needed? She shook her head painfully to get rid of her thoughts. This wasn't the time to psychoanalyse herself; she needed to focus on Marcham.

He had cleaned up his house. It now looked bohemian rather than tatty—no overflowing ashtrays, the books and magazines once strewn on the coffee table were stacked neatly and the filthy carpet looked professionally cleaned. Marcham had made an effort, or paid someone to make it for him. Liz wondered if the clean-up had extended to his bedroom, remembering the religious relics and icons in there when she'd looked in on her last visit. But now the door was firmly closed.

She sat uncomfortably on the lumpy sofa while Marcham flitted back and forth between the sitting room and the kitchen, making himself the cup of coffee she had declined. He seemed nervous. He'd tidied himself up, too, she noticed, observing the blazer with shirt only slightly frayed, flannel trousers and brown brogues. He looked almost respectable.

At last Marcham sat down in an old patched armchair. Sipping from his mug carefully, he winced, then, smiling ingratiatingly at Liz, he sat back and said, "So how can I help you now, Miss Falconer?"

"I'd like to talk to you about Syria," said Liz. Marcham's eyes flickered and she felt sure that whatever he'd been expecting, it wasn't this. "You've been there often, I understand, and I know you've just come back. What I wanted to ask you is whether on any of your visits there you've been contacted by the intelligence services."

He paused. "No. Not as far as I know. I interviewed the President recently for an article I'm writing and I had to go through various official hoops, but as far as I know none of them were the intelligence services."

"Did you meet any hostility there? Did anyone make any threats or ask you to do anything for them?"

"No. I can't remember anything like that," Marcham replied. His voice, which had been deep and rather hoarse, rose an octave. "Why are you asking me these questions?"

Liz ignored him. "Have you ever been approached by any intelligence services on your visits to the Middle East?"

"Miss Falconer," he said, putting down his mug and rubbing the palms of his hands together, "in my job you're always being approached by spooks of all sorts. I've learned to see them coming and I don't get involved. It's more than my professional reputation is worth."

"I know you've spoken to MI6 in the past," said Liz, in case any unnecessary loyalty was holding him back.

"Yes I have. But I've never done more than talk in general and I've never done anything for them."

"Any others you've just spoken to without doing anything?"

"No," he replied and leaping to his feet he said, "I'd like another cup of coffee."

There's something here, thought Liz while he was in the kitchen. I'm sure there is. Her head was beginning to ache and she didn't feel up to a long interrogation, so she decided to exert a bit of pressure. While he was in the kitchen she leaned forward and put a photograph on the coffee table in front of Marcham's chair.

When he came back he picked it up. "It's Alex," he declared. "I read about his death in the papers. What's he got to do with you?"

"You knew Mr. Ledingham, then?"

Marcham nodded. "Of course. For a while I knew him fairly well." He added regretfully, "Lately, we hadn't been in touch while I'd been travelling."

"Could you tell me how you came to know him?"

"I'd be happy to," he said, looking unfazed. But Liz sensed he was acting—a good performance so far, she thought, but a performance all the same.

"Alex was very interested in churches. So am I. Not perhaps to the same degree—he was something of a fanatic." There was a patronising, distancing effect to this. "We met at a Hawksmoor Society meeting. Alex was very active in the society, particularly in its efforts to raise money for renovating the Hawksmoor churches in London. To some purists, of course, renovation is a dirty word, but not to Alex. Or me for that matter. And for a time I was rather involved as well." He gave a slow smile, as if confessing a juvenile aberration he had outgrown.

Liz was getting impatient. This wasn't leading anywhere. So she said, "You were in Kosovo, weren't you?"

Marcham looked startled. "Yes, I was. Why?"

She ignored the question. "You were there as a reporter, as I understand. For *The Observer,* and the *Los Angeles Times.*"

Marcham seemed less complacent now, but was struggling not to show it. He said archly, "You've been doing some research, Miss Falconer."

You can thank Peggy Kinsolving for that, thought Liz. She continued, "You were in Kosovo on assignment, but could you tell me why Alexander Ledingham was also there?"

Silence hung in the room like a weight. For a moment, Marcham stared at Liz, and she could sense his antipathy. He said slowly, "A pity you can't ask him that question."

"Yes, but that's why I'm asking you."

Marcham sipped his coffee mechanically. He said, keeping his face burrowed in his mug, "Alex was very het up about the Serbian churches that were being destroyed. People forget that the violence cut both ways—and Alex was keen to do what he could to preserve the Orthodox places of worship."

"Even if it meant putting himself in danger? Lots of people are appalled by war without wanting to see it for themselves."

"Alex wasn't one to be put off by danger. He'd knocked around a bit. He was gentle, sure, but he didn't scare easily."

Liz said pointedly, "Did your being there have anything to do with it? My understanding is that you two went around together in Kosovo."

"I wouldn't put it quite like that."

"Oh, really? I gather you were virtually inseparable."

"For a time we were very close." He added, unnecessarily, "I'm not married, you know."

He gave her a knowing look. She didn't care if Marcham had been intimate in that way with Ledingham; she wanted to know if he'd been there when he'd died.

"So he was there as your . . . companion?"

Marcham didn't look at her, and Liz felt he was milking the drama for all it was worth. He clearly thought a confession that he and Ledingham had been lovers would seem shameful enough to persuade her that this was the secret he was hiding.

"I understand. But I doubt other journalists brought their partners."

Marcham thought about this. Then he said, "He was desperate to come. He was obsessed with the churches. He had all these *theories.* He started by thinking there was a code in Hawksmoor's churches— then it became a code in almost every baroque church of the time. I tried to tell him it was nonsense. Alex started to like to have . . ." He paused.

"Sex?" asked Liz, determined to get on with this.

"How delicate of you, Miss Falconer," said Marcham with a flash of his former insouciance. "But yes, for lack of a better word. Sex."

"But that night in St. Barnabas, the, um, sexual part of things seemed to have been solitary."

"I know," said Marcham. "That was because of me." He looked

stonily at his hands in regret. "That sort of thing wasn't my scene. He said I should take a walk and come back when he'd . . . finished." He shivered in distaste.

"And when you came back from this walk, what did you find?"

"He was dead. He'd misjudged, apparently . . . only I wasn't there to save him."

As he said this, he broke down. Between sobs he managed to say, "If only I'd stayed, it never would have happened."

"I'm sure no one could blame you," said Liz, "but why did you put him in the box?"

Marcham looked up, red-eyed. "What else could I do?" he asked plaintively.

At last, thought Liz and she said, "Mr. Marcham, you realise that concealing a death is a very serious offence. I shall have to report what you've said to my police colleagues. But I would just like to go back to my earlier question. Are you sure that on your various travels you have never undertaken any covert task for an intelligence service or anyone who might have been acting on their behalf? I am in a position to help you in various ways," she added unspecifically, "if you have anything to tell me."

But by now Marcham was sobbing uncontrollably and he just shook his head.

Liz had had enough. The interview hadn't gone the way she'd planned and she hadn't learned anything to move her inquiries on. The police would have to deal with Marcham now.

31

Wally Woods looked more bleary-eyed than usual that Friday afternoon when he came into Liz's office. She still had faint traces of bruising round her eyes, but Wally looked a lot worse. "I can't blame work," he declared, in response to her question whether he was all right. "Our dog's just had a litter and she's not a very good mother. I was up half the night feeding the puppies. Makes a change from watching some hairy-faced youths in a terrace in Battersea."

Liz laughed. She liked Wally: he was an old hand, who'd survived all the changes of targets and technology without fuss or resistance. *They also serve who stand and wait* seemed to be his motto, and Liz respected both his competence and his interest in maintaining it.

"So what's up?" she said.

Wally waved a manila envelope. "I wanted to show you some photographs we took yesterday. We've been following this chap Kollek from the Israeli embassy, as you know. Nothing unusual at first—he seems to have lunch twice a week with that woman you told us about, but everything was above board. Then three days ago it changed."

"How was that?"

"I wish I could tell you," said Wally wistfully. "We lost him." He shook his head in frustration.

Liz could sympathise. Following a target who was determined to lose you was never an easy job.

"Do you think he knew he was being followed?"

Wally shook his head. "I think he was just being very, very careful. In the end, we couldn't stay with him or we'd have been spotted. I knew you didn't want that."

"No, you're right," said Liz, a little discouraged. Kollek must be Mossad—why would a trade attaché carry out sophisticated counter surveillance? She wondered who he could have been meeting.

"Cheer up, Liz. That's not the end of the story." His voice was brighter now, and Liz looked at him hopefully. He said, "Yesterday we followed him as he left the embassy mid-morning. He took us as far as the Oval cricket ground, but that's where we lost him—when he went inside. Don't know if you like cricket, Liz, but the One Day Internationals are on, so the place was packed.

"By this time I and the other backup cars had got there as well. It took us two hours of searching row by row, but we found him," Wally said proudly. "Sitting in the corner stand with a drink in his hand, and a programme, acting like he'd grown up watching cricket. Which seems a bit unlikely for an Israeli.

"Nothing happened for an hour or so, but then another guy came and squeezed in right next to Kollek. Dressed up—more Lord's than the Oval."

"Oh no," said Liz, her heart sinking. Israeli penetration of foreign intelligence services was legendary. "You'd better show me the pictures then," she said, though she already had an image in mind.

Wally passed over the envelope he had been holding, and said, "I don't know who it is, but I reckon he's American."

The first picture had been taken from below. Kollek was caught prominently, holding a large plastic cup—gingerly, it had to be said, like someone trying to fit in. She looked at the men on either side of him: on Kollek's left sat an Asian man in a yellow windcheater; he was staring intently at the play, seemingly oblivious to his neighbour. Kollek was turned towards the man on his right, his head tilted down as if he were listening carefully.

"It's the tie," she said numbly.

Wally looked at her curiously.

"Look at the stripes," she said, pointing to Kollek's other neighbour. "They go the opposite way from ours. That's how you can tell he's a Yank."

"I'm afraid he left at lunchtime, Liz. He tends to work at home on Friday afternoons these days." The tone of Wetherby's secretary made it clear they both knew the reason for this—Joanne.

"Right. I'll ring him there."

"Do you want the number?"

"That's all right—I've got it. Thanks." Liz thought for a moment. She was loath to interrupt Charles at home, but felt he needed to know at once.

"Charles," she said when he answered, "it's Liz. I am sorry to ring you at home, but something's come up."

She listened for a moment. "The morning's fine—that's no problem. Of course I can. No, I think I'll drive down." She paused, then wrote down the directions he gave her. "Got it," she said as he finished. "Ten-thirty will be fine. See you then."

She hung up, relieved he'd understood the urgency at once. It was unfortunate to disturb his weekend, but there it was—and it wasn't as if she'd had anything planned herself. It would be odd seeing Charles at home. More to the point, she wondered what Joanne would be like. Well, she thought, at last I'm going to find out.

32

There was little traffic this early on Saturday morning, which made it a rare pleasure to meander south in the Audi through the centre of London. Shops were just opening, and along Bayswater Road artists were hanging their pictures from the iron railings of Hyde Park ready for the weekly art sale. Liz drove south through Earls Court and over to the Hammersmith roundabout, then crossed the river at Chiswick with her window down, though a cloudless night meant a chill hung in the air.

Within a quarter of an hour she entered the leafy, affluent belt of the Surrey suburbs. The houses grew larger, as did their gardens, separated from each other by the occasional woodland or pony paddock.

It always amazed her how many pockets of green had been preserved within twenty miles of Westminster.

At Twickenham she crossed the river again; the Thames was snake-like in this stretch. As she got farther on, traffic started to build up in the high streets and on the outskirts of towns, as cars headed for the shopping centres, or "retail parks" as they described themselves on the signposts.

After Shepperton she looked at Charles's instructions and took a small road, then a smaller lane; she could sense the river was not far off. Taking a final left onto a track that ended in a cul-de-sac, she parked, and looked across a large lawn to a mid-sized Arts and Crafts house, with high wooden gables. A small sign on the front gate said MILL RUN.

She walked along a path of paving stones with rose beds on either side, and up some steps to the front door. Ringing the bell, she waited until eventually she heard light steps approach in the hall. Then the door opened.

A woman stood in the doorway, wearing a simple blue cotton dress with an unbuttoned cardigan. She was thin—too thin; this must be Joanne. She had a handsome, gentle face, and her hair, chestnut turning grey, was tied back in a ponytail. Her eyes were a rich, deep blue and set wide apart, which made her look vulnerable.

"Hello, I'm Liz Carlyle. Here to see Charles."

The woman smiled. "I'm Joanne," she said, extending her hand. "Do come in. I've just put the kettle on."

Liz followed her down a hall that stretched past a large oak staircase. The house seemed lived in, and comfortable.

In the kitchen a tabby cat lay asleep in a basket next to an enormous, ancient-looking Aga. There was a refectory table in the middle of the room, half-covered by sections of newspaper and a jar of marmalade. It was quiet, peaceful and sunny.

"What a pretty cat," said Liz, wondering where Charles was.

"That's Hector, though he's too old for the wars now. Coffee or tea?"

"Coffee please," said Liz, and sat down at the table while Joanne filled two big blue-and-white-striped mugs.

"Charles had to go out," she explained, as she joined Liz at the table. "We've had a minor family emergency." She smiled to make it clear nothing dire had happened. "One of my sons broke his foot playing cricket. He's decided to come home for the weekend so we can suffer with him." She gave a small laugh. "Normally he'd walk here from the station, but his foot's in a cast, so Charles went to fetch him. They'll be back soon."

Liz looked around the cosy room. It had old wooden cupboards, copper pots hanging from hooks along one wall and a vast corkboard covered with notes and phone numbers and a crayon drawing of a horse.

"It's very nice to meet you at last," said Joanne. "I've heard a lot about you." She gazed penetratingly at Liz, but her voice seemed friendly.

"Likewise, and I've seen your picture. Charles has one on his desk."

"Really?" She seemed pleased. "I wonder which it is."

"You're by a river, with a straw hat on. The boys are on either side of you, and each one's holding an oar."

"Oh, I know that one. We bought them a little rowing boat once they knew how to swim. For a couple of summers they seemed to live on the water."

"I imagine the boys must have loved growing up here."

She nodded. "Sam—that's the one Charles is picking up—says he wants to live here when we're gone. He's the one who takes after Charles. He's a worrier, though he doesn't like to show it. Just like Charles."

"I must say he hides it very well." This was true; even in tense situations, Charles was a model of calm.

"Does he?" Joanne's face brightened. "I wouldn't know. I do know that he enjoys working with you."

Liz didn't know how to respond. "We were in different departments until recently."

"Yes, and he's delighted to have you back again."

It was said so frankly that Liz struggled not to blush.

Joanne went on, "It's funny, sometimes I think life would be a lot easier if we moved into town—it's quite a long commute for Charles. And as you probably know, I haven't been very well the last few years. But Charles won't hear of it. He says if he didn't have the garden to come home to he'd go mad."

She paused, and looked wistfully at the mug she held in her hands. "I know between his job and looking after me it must be an immense strain. I worry about him—and about how much he worries about me." She paused, then laughed and looked at Liz. "Have you ever been married?"

Liz shook her head, and felt suddenly awkward.

"Well, I recommend it."

They sat silently for a moment, then Joanne cocked an ear. "They're back," she said. A moment later Charles came into the kitchen followed by a gangly boy who must have been sixteen or so. He wore a school uniform of blazer and grey trousers, but his right foot was encased in a plaster cast. The boy had inherited his mother's large blue eyes, but otherwise took after Charles.

"Hello, Liz," said Charles. "This is Sam."

She got up and shook hands with the boy. Joanne said, "Why don't you go into the garden, darling? Take your coffee with you, Liz. I'm so glad we had time for a chat."

Outside the brisk air of the morning was turning mild, and

Charles took off his coat and left it on a bench by the kitchen door. A wide herbaceous border ran down one side of the garden and a small ring of tall roses stood in the centre of the lawn.

"How beautiful," she said.

"I'm not sure I'd go that far," said Charles mildly. "But I'm glad you like it. We do have some help," he admitted.

"I should think so," said Liz, thinking her mother would appreciate this garden. She stood still and listened. "What's that noise?"

He stopped too, and listened. "Just a boat. The river's on the other side of the garden. We don't quite make it to the water, I'm afraid. There's a public footpath over there. Still, it means we have access."

He led her to a stone bench under a towering tree and they sat down. "So," he said, putting an ankle across his knee. "What's the problem?"

"We've had this Israeli, Kollek, under surveillance, as you know. Nothing untoward has come up, though on a couple of occasions he has gone to great lengths to lose A4. Wally said it was clear he knew what he was doing. I'm certain now he's Mossad."

Charles's jaw set in anger. "We'll have to make a protest about this."

"I'm afraid that's not all. Two days ago Wally and his team followed him to the Oval."

Charles smiled. "New Zealand. We slaughtered them." Across the garden, a blackbird was singing, somewhere in the upper branches of a hornbeam tree.

Liz handed him the manila envelope she had brought with her from London. Charles took his time, looking at the stills. Then he put them down on the bench between them. "I take it you know who that is?"

"He was at the Gleneagles meeting in Downing Street."

"So you said." Charles leaned back and breathed out noisily. Hector the cat had appeared, and was moving slowly towards the horn-beam, where the blackbird continued to trill. "This opens up such a can of worms."

"I can see that," said Liz.

"We've been looking at Brookhaven while you were away. Our assumption was there'd been a leak about the Syrian threat—we couldn't see any other reason for someone to try and run you down. Brookhaven looked up to his neck in potential conflicts: Arabic speaker, time in Syria, and one of only two at the Grosvenor station who knew about the threat." He shook his head wearily. "It just goes to show you mustn't jump to conclusions."

Liz looked thoughtful.

"Is there something else?" asked Charles.

"The Syrians are supposed to be at the heart of all this but I'm beginning to think that it's actually the Israelis. There's what Sami Veshara told you and now we see an undeclared Mossad officer meeting a CIA officer." The thought that the problem might include the Americans lay unspoken between them.

Charles said nothing. Hector had arrived at the base of the tree, and was looking up. The blackbird was a good thirty feet above his head, and the cat seemed to recognise the futility of his hunt, for he lumbered off towards the ring of roses. Charles laughed. "Look at him. He's too old to catch anything, but still likes to pretend he can."

He turned towards Liz, serious again. "The first thing I'd better do is ring DG—this is too important to wait. I think it's fairly safe to predict he'll want me to talk to Langley. It will have to be in person, given the circumstances."

He pointed at the photograph, and Liz looked at it once again. It showed Kollek with his head down in the stands at the Oval, listening to his neighbour. When Wally Woods had first shown her the photo, she knew she had seen the neighbour's face before, but for a moment hadn't been able to place it. Then she had remembered, and an image had entered her head—of a middle-aged man, balding, and heavyset, leaning across a conference table in Downing Street and announcing in the nasal tones of America's Midwest, "To date we have received no specific negative information relative to the conference."

Liz turned now to Charles. "You'll have to go to Washington?" she asked, suddenly mindful of Joanne. It didn't seem a good time for her to be alone.

"I don't see I have much choice." He gave her a wry smile. "I can't really talk to the CIA's head of station here about whether he's working for Israel."

Charles got up from the bench. "Why don't I show you the river? Then we can go inside. Joanne wants you to stay for lunch."

33

Wetherby had decided to keep his visit to Washington very low-key so, unusually, no one met him at the airport. After the usual lengthy wait, Immigration accepted him for who he said he was: Edward Albright, a London businessman in town for a couple of meetings, staying just the one night.

He'd picked a hotel in Virginia, on the airport side of the city, not far from Langley, where he was due first thing in the morning. With any luck he'd catch the early evening flight back to London the following day.

His hotel, one of a vast American chain, was comfortable, clean and entirely soulless. He phoned home and spoke to Joanne who, five hours later, was getting ready for bed. Then he ate an early dinner in the hotel restaurant—an overcooked steak and a glass of California cabernet. Back in his room, he lay down for a while on one of his room's two large double beds and clicked idly through what seemed to be several thousand television channels.

He thought with amusement how he could have squeezed the entire Wetherby family into this ample room. When the boys were small, they'd often stayed in more cramped quarters on their trekking holidays in Europe. They'd made walkers of the boys early on, and he remembered fondly how the then-healthy Joanne had put them all to shame when it came to stamina in the Tuscan hills or Pyrenees, where they'd go for two weeks in August. Now, he thought sadly, she ran out of puff after twenty minutes in their garden.

In the morning he made the short drive to Langley, stopped at the security sentry post, then parked his hired car where he was directed near the headquarters building. The CIA's director of counter intelligence was Tyrus Oakes, a long-time Agency veteran, lacking any public profile but famous within the halls of Langley. He had many quirks, most notably a habit of taking voluminous notes throughout even the most pedestrian meeting, all collected on the yellow legal pads that American attorneys in pre-computer days had used to compose their briefs.

Physically, too, he was unusual—a small, slight man with a razor-edged nose and big ears that protruded from each side of his head like satellite dishes. To his friends, mainly fellow senior officers, he was known as Ty; to those who knew him only by repute, he was The Bird.

Wetherby had come to realise over the years that the different reactions he sometimes received from Oakes had nothing to do with Wetherby's position as an intelligence officer of a foreign country, but only with the extent to which he shared Oakes's views about the matter under discussion. This gave Wetherby slight forebodings about his forthcoming conversation, since he couldn't believe Oakes was going to be very happy with what he had to say.

"Charles, it's real good to see you." Oakes came out from behind the desk.

"And you, Ty."

"Take a seat," said Oakes, pointing to a chair in front of his desk, while he retreated behind it. He said, "This must be kind of important for you to fly over."

"It is. I think we may have a serious problem."

Wetherby outlined the sequence of events as succinctly as he could. As he spoke, Oakes rapidly discarded his yellow pad, fishing out of his pocket a small spiral-bound notebook, in which he wrote quickly in tiny writing, lifting his head occasionally to look at Wetherby.

At least he's not moved to a laptop, thought Wetherby, as he continued his account of Fane's relayed message from Jaghir, that two rogue elements were acting against Syrian interests in London, and were threatening to sabotage the impending peace conference.

Oakes's eyes widened at this, then widened further still when Wetherby recounted the attempt to run down one of his female officers with a car. He stopped writing momentarily, then resumed, head down, scribbling furiously, though when Wetherby explained that Jaghir had been killed the week before in Cyprus, Oakes stopped writing altogether. This time he even put his pen down.

Wetherby said, "Here's where the difficulty starts. All this information about a threat was held very tightly. In MI5, fewer than half a dozen officers were indoctrinated and Geoffrey Fane has said that in his service it was strictly 'need to know.' But the attack on my officer, and now the murder of Jaghir, makes it look as if there's been a leak. The only others told were two of your officers in Grosvenor Square."

Oakes looked up again, but didn't speak.

"I'm not suggesting anything. Just stating facts. And I'm sure you'll understand that we had to look into this. After all, one of my officers was almost killed."

Oakes nodded. Wetherby continued: "Fane talked with two of your officers there. Andy Bokus and Miles Brookhaven."

"I know them," said Oakes noncommittally.

"We've had dealings with both of them, of course, on many things, and Brookhaven has been liaising with one of my officers on this business." He added flatly, "The same officer, in fact, who was almost killed."

Oakes frowned, but remained silent. Wetherby went on, "We noted, too, that Brookhaven had recently come from Syria. A coincidence we felt compelled to pursue."

"So you put him under surveillance," said Oakes bluntly. It was not a question.

"I'm sure you would have done the same. We get particularly concerned if people are undeclared. For example, somebody we've been watching recently is a man named Kollek. He's an attaché at the Israeli embassy, and is supposed to be a trade officer. But we're confident he's actually with Mossad."

Oakes looked puzzled. "I don't follow you, Charles. What has this got to do with Miles Brookhaven?"

"Nothing whatsoever, and that's not why I'm here. Last Thursday one of our teams followed Kollek to a cricket match in south London. Funny place for an Israeli to go, we thought. But he wasn't there for relaxation." An envelope materialised in Wetherby's hand and he handed it across the desk. "Have a look, if you don't mind, Ty."

And he watched as Oakes extracted the photographs and looked at each in turn. You had to hand it to him, thought Wetherby, Oakes made a good show of looking unperturbed. But when he put the photographs down Wetherby noticed Oakes's right hand was tensed into a fist.

Oakes said, too casually to convince, "There could be a perfectly innocent explanation for this." He stared directly at Wetherby, but his eyes were curiously unfocused.

"Of course there could. It's just that in that case, we would like to know what it is."

Oakes pursed his thin lips, then put a hand to his forehead, the first indication of the tension Wetherby knew he must be feeling. Oakes said quietly, "I've known Andy Bokus a long time." He sighed, as if he knew this was irrelevant. "I don't know what to say, Charles. Except that these"—and he pointed at the photographs—"are as much a surprise to me as they must be to you."

They sat in silence for a long time. At last Oakes said, "I haven't got an answer for you. And I'm not going to have one today—or even tomorrow. But I will have by the end of the week. Will that do?"

"Of course." Charles rose to his feet. "I'll head back to London. It goes without saying you should deal only with me on this."

"Understood," said Oakes, and Wetherby sensed that as soon as he'd left the man would spring into action.

3 4

The director's office was on the top floor of the Old Headquarters Building, with a clear view of the Potomac and its tree-lined banks. Tyrus Oakes waited impatiently in a leather chair in the anteroom, ignoring the magazines neatly displayed in a fan on the credenza in front of him.

"Come in," said a man's voice from the doorway, and Oakes stood up and followed the slightly stooping white-haired man into a large corner room, which had a view on two sides. They walked to the far end, where the director pointed to the chair on the near side of his large, antique rolltop desk. Oakes sat down reluctantly, since the director, a towering figure, stayed standing, moving to the window, his hands clasped behind his back.

"Thanks for seeing me on such short notice, General," Oakes said.

The director nodded, but his gaze remained locked on the grass plaza below. It was as if he smelled trouble brewing, and wanted to take his time before following the scent.

General Gerry Harding was a West Point graduate who had risen to be one of the Joint Chiefs of Staff, having served with distinction at the tail end of the Vietnam War and been a senior commander in the first Iraq War. Showing an aptitude for Washington infighting, he had then served administrations of different political stripes, first as number two to the UN ambassador, now as director of the CIA.

His appointment had been a sudden, unplanned affair, since the President's first choice—an obvious political appointment, a man with neither military nor intelligence experience—had fallen at the first hurdle of Senate approval. Harding had sailed through, since his war record had made him an all-American hero, and the only partisan ideology he had ever evinced was ruthlessness.

Now he turned around and eased his long frame into his high-backed leather chair. He pushed it back easily from the desk, then stretched his legs out in front of him.

"What's on your mind, Ty?" he asked, with an edge that poked out through the folksy veneer.

"I've had a visit from our British friends. Their director of counter espionage—Charles Wetherby. He's an old hand, and a good one. They think there's a leak of information about the threat to the Gleneagles conference. You'll have seen the report on that, General. One of their officers working on the lead has been attacked. It seems they've been following a Mossad agent operating in London." He said significantly, "Danny Kollek."

"Kollek?" Harding's equanimity was fast receding. "How the hell did they get onto him?"

"I don't know. He didn't say. Kollek's undeclared, which has the

Brits' dander up. They don't trust the Israelis. And unfortunately, their surveillance found Kollek meeting with one of our own."

"Andy Bokus runs him, doesn't he? You mean they saw them together?"

"That's what makes it so difficult. The photographs the Brits took show Kollek meeting Andy. It was hard for me to explain that away to Wetherby. I didn't know what to tell him."

Harding thought hard for a moment. "How about the truth?"

"I can do that. But I figured I needed your approval first."

"You've got it."

Oakes hesitated before saying, "It will involve a fair amount of risk."

"How's that? You don't trust the Brits?"

Oakes shrugged. "It's not that. They're hyper-anxious about this conference. It's top of their priorities. They'd tell the Israelis anything, even that we're running one of their people, if they thought it would help them protect the conference. That could do us a lot of damage. Mossad gives us some very valuable intelligence. They'll close up like clams if they find out we've been running Kollek."

He could see the General calculating this. Harding was relentlessly, clinically logical, something not always true of the directors Oakes had known. Harding said, "What if we throw them a bone?"

"Who, the British?"

"No. Mossad. If there isn't much more we can get out of Kollek, maybe we should just turn him over to his own service. We can say he approached us, and we turned him down. That might earn us some brownie points in Tel Aviv."

Oakes was appalled. He struggled to hide his outrage at the suggestion they throw an agent to the wolves. The logistics of what Harding was proposing were impossible—Mossad would see through the subterfuge at once—but that was not what bothered Oakes the most.

He prided himself on his realism, but he also held firm to certain principles. Foremost among them was a loyalty to his agents, especially penetration agents, who risked their lives to help.

He knew any argument with Harding would all too easily be lost. So he said slowly, "Not sure that would work, General. And anyway, I don't think we've got the best out of Kollek yet. It would be a pity to let him go prematurely." He thought ruefully of what "let him go" would mean for the Israeli, once put under Mossad's notorious methods of questioning.

Harding seemed to think about this, then glanced at his diary, open on the desktop before him. He looked intently at his watch, and Oakes realised his time was up.

"Okay, Ty, let's keep him in place then. You can come clean with the Brits, but make it clear we expect them to keep it to themselves. If they tell the Israelis, then we might as well have got some credit by telling them ourselves."

35

Aleppo had told no one where he was going. He would be coming here again in three weeks' time, but that would be official and with colleagues. Now he needed to see the lay of the land for himself. He had his own agenda.

He caught the train at King's Cross, and promptly fell asleep for three hours. He was tired. Although his meetings rarely lasted long, the tension and the painstaking counter surveillance before and after each rendezvous exhausted him.

He woke up in Northumberland, or so the old man across the aisle was telling his wife, and he looked out the window as the countryside grew hilly, wilder, starker. He didn't understand the British: if he'd been in charge, he would have placed the bulk of the population up here, rather than in the tame, cramped environs of the Home Counties.

The border came and went unnoticed and it was only as he heard the train guard announce Edinburgh that he knew he was in Scotland. As the train left the city behind, Aleppo, knowing he was nearly at his destination, watched intently, noting with surprise the rolling land-scape, soft and agricultural. He had expected crags and mountains; they formed his image of Scotland.

But when he left the train at a small station farther north, an hour later, he could see the Cairngorms in the distance. There were no taxis in this remote place, but a minibus waited in the small station yard to pick up Aleppo and the two obviously American couples, laden with luggage and golf clubs, who left the train with him. The driver, a plump man with a uniform cap, was chatty.

"Here for the golf?" he asked amiably, eyeing his passengers in the mirror.

Aleppo didn't feel the need to reply as his fellow passengers were only too willing to talk. They said they were.

"Greens are very quick just now," said the driver.

"I've booked a hack with the riding school," said one of the women.

"We're forecast lovely weather. You'll get great views of the hills out there." They chatted on as they drove towards the setting sun, which was casting the nearby low hills in a rose-coloured light.

Soon, the bus turned in between two low stone walls surmounted with gold letters: GLENEAGLES.

A vast golf course lay to the left of the drive, its clubhouse a hand-some, low building of cream stucco with a grey slate roof. On the other side of the drive, on the wide sweep of lawn beside two lakes, were more golf holes. He seemed to be entering a golf obsessive's paradise.

Dominating the scene was a vast nineteenth-century pile, with a castle tower on its front corner, flying a blue and white flag, waving in the stiff evening breeze. The driver turned at a little roundabout, down a formal drive that ended at the hotel entrance. Across the manicured lawns were long hedgerows of rhododendrons and tall trees.

Aleppo was amazed to hear the sound of bagpipes playing as the minibus drove up to the door; a huge doorman in a kilt and green tweed jacket, who had been standing with the piper at the top of the steps, came down to take the luggage. As he checked in at the reception desk in a wide panelled hall, lit by vast saucer-shaped Art Deco lamps hanging from the ceiling, Aleppo felt as if he had arrived on the set of an American musical.

He had purposely booked one of the best rooms, at the front of the hotel. It was spacious and comfortable, with a view of the golf courses and behind them, only a couple of miles farther on, green hills that rose gradually from the valley.

Aleppo looked over his quarters with care. The bathroom was large and brightly lit, with a white porcelain bath and a steel-framed shower in the corner. Taking his shoes off, he climbed onto the closed seat of the lavatory, then carefully pushed at the square tiles of the ceiling above it. One gave way; moving it aside, he raised both hands and carefully pulled himself up to look into the horizontal ventilation shaft. Inside its long tunnel you could fit a small suitcase; at a pinch, lying flat, a man could fit as well. It would take a professional about twenty seconds to find anyone hiding there, but it was good to know nonetheless.

Climbing down, he stripped and showered, then changed into smart casual clothes—a blazer, cotton trousers, slip-on shoes—and went downstairs in search of food. From the various restaurants he chose the middle-range Italian-style trattoria, where he sat in the middle of the room and ate supper while looking carefully through the brochure he had found in his bedroom.

His waitress was middle-aged, polite and wore a wide wedding ring, but Aleppo paid more attention to a younger girl who was waiting on the tables across the room. She was sandy-haired, big-boned, with an attractive smiling face and a confident air as she moved around the room, chatting with the people at her tables. She had noticed him, too, the only single male in the room, and glanced his way on each occasion she came out from the kitchen carrying plates of food.

When Aleppo had finished his meal, he waited to get up to leave the dining room until she came out of the kitchen. He caught her eye and she looked back at him. Nothing was said but something invisible passed between them. A plucky kind of girl then, even forward, and he made a mental note of her.

In the morning he ate breakfast in the same restaurant, but there was no sign of her. He had a lot of ground to cover and only one day to cover it. He'd expected a grand hotel and a golf course, but Gleneagles was so much more than that. The place was a resort, more on the American model than the usual British version. It was set on hundreds of acres of coniferous woodland, with hotel rooms, chalets, time-shares, private apartments and literally dozens of recreational activities. This was a bigger task than he'd expected.

Finishing his coffee, he walked through the oak-panelled corridors of the hotel's ground floor, past shops that catered without inhibition to an affluent clientele—diamond jewellery, cashmere sweaters, rare and exotic whiskies—emerging at the back of the hotel next to a swimming pool enclosed in glass. Already guests were reclining on wooden poolside chairs as if on a Mediterranean beach, while children splashed and played in the water.

Outside again, Aleppo paused. He knew there were time-share villas, grouped in a village-like settlement across the road, but they could wait until his next visit. As could the equestrian centre farther down the road, of no use to him now. He sensed the answer to his own search lay outdoors, not in, so he set to work exploring the grounds.

It took him till mid-afternoon, walking round all three golf courses, intrigued especially by the biggest, the famous King's Course, which sloped gradually upwards towards the ridge of hills that he had seen from his bedroom. He walked to the farthest edge of the course, as near as he could get to the hills, and there, from a secluded spot under an oak tree by the tenth tee, he peered through a small pair of Leica binoculars he produced from his jacket pocket.

The slopes in the distance were unfarmed and looked untended, though there were a few sheep lower down. The grass was bleached yellow from the summer sun, and the slopes looked bare, but careful examination revealed a few pockets of trees, and the odd dip in the hills' contours. Enough to keep someone out of sight for a while, especially in bad weather—he'd noted the sign warning of the sudden advent of fog and mist.

At lunchtime, he stopped for a sandwich in the clubhouse, looking out again at the hills, gauging whether they'd be considered a possible threat when the multiple security agencies scoured the area in a week's time. They would certainly not be ignored. He looked again at the activities listed in the brochure. There was clay pigeon shooting, croquet, fishing supplied on request, off-road driving, a gundog training school, even a falconry centre.

Aleppo visited them all, in the guise of an interested foreign tourist, but spent the most time at the gundog school and the neighbouring falconry centre. He watched for half an hour as a posse of young black Labradors, agile and keen, practised retrieving. Then he moved off through a line of trees to a two-storey wooden building, with a green metal roof and purple pillars at each end. It looked like an oversized chicken coop, or a prison for dwarves, with small, individual cells with metal bars across their windows. In each cell, a bird of prey sat unwinking on a wooden perch, staring at any observer free to move about in the world.

A small boy and his father came out the front door, followed by an instructor wearing a padded glove on one hand, on which was sitting a hawk. Aleppo watched as they proceeded to a mown circle of grass, where the keeper raised his hand slowly until the bird suddenly took off. It flew round in a big arc and then swooped back down again to snatch at the lure the man held at the end of a long cord, the bait an ounce of raw grouse meat.

He heard the little boy's father ask, "What happens if they don't come back?"

"They're carrying a radio transmitter. It's tiny—just a microchip," the man said, pointing to the hawk now back on his extended hand. "I can hear it through my earpiece. The closer I get to him, the louder the transmitter squawks."

"What's the range of the signal?"

"The manufacturer claims it's twelve miles." He scoffed. "But that's because the manufacturer is in Salt Lake City. In this landscape it's more like twelve hundred yards."

"Do they go that far?"

The instructor shook his head. "Not usually. They *can* go up to thirty miles away, but most of the time we find them in the woods."

Aleppo moved away and strolled, deep in thought, towards the golf courses, coming shortly to the edge of a little lake, no more than a few hundred yards square, which was nestled in a long hollow beside the main drive. A small island in the middle of the lake boasted a solitary cedar tree surrounded by low rushes that went down into the water. On Aleppo's side of the lake was a wooden landing stage with a rowing boat tied to an iron ring. Across the water, on the golf course side, sat a small putting green. This could be useful, he thought, suddenly open to yet more possibilities.

When he returned to the hotel there were three men at the reception desk, wearing suits and ties, white shirts and tasselled loafers. One had an earpiece, and wore a miniature American flag pinned to his lapel. Aleppo stopped at the desk, ostensibly to ask for a newspaper in the morning, but really to confirm his suspicions that these were Secret Service men.

"It's just preliminary," one of them was saying to the manager. "Next week we'll be up to check every room thoroughly. For now, it's just to acquaint ourselves."

He moved away casually and went up to his room, thinking hard. The Secret Service men would be back for their room-to-room inspection of the place; they'd be followed by British police, using state-of-the-art detection equipment and sniffer dogs.

It simply wouldn't be possible to hide anything in the hotel itself. The IRA had done that at the Grand Hotel in Brighton, almost managing to murder Margaret Thatcher and most of her Cabinet. They'd concealed a long-fuse bomb behind the panelling in the bathroom of one of the central tier of rooms. It had been put there so far in advance that it had escaped the sweeps made just days before the Conservative Party Conference had begun. But things had moved on a lot since then in the security world.

So any action would have to take place somewhere else on the grounds. They'd be heavily policed, of course, and a perimeter would be established out on extended boundaries. But with hundreds of acres to police, it might just be possible to think of something that would escape the combined efforts of the U.K. police, foreign security, sniffer dogs and state-of-the-art detection machines. But it wasn't going to be easy and to do that he'd need help—and from someone who knew the place far better than he was ever going to. Someone with access. He'd need a local ally, with local information.

That night he dined again in the Italian trattoria, but this time he asked the maître d' for a table towards the back of its big room, where he knew he would be waited on by the pretty sandy-haired girl.

"Good evening," she said, as she came to take his order.

"Good evening, Jana," he said, reading the name tag on her blouse. She gave a faint smile.

Each time she came to the table, he greeted her approach with an admiring gaze that he was glad to see her reciprocate. At last, as she brought his after-dinner coffee, he said quietly so no one else would hear, "What time do you get off?"

"And why would that be of interest?"

"Oh, I don't know," he said, looking down at his demitasse, "I thought you might let a foreigner buy you a drink. In return for some local knowledge."

"Oh I see, you're looking for a tutor, are you?" She gave a knowing smile, but then just as quickly frowned. "Seriously, though, we're not allowed to fraternise with the residents. It would be more than my job was worth."

"Maybe it wouldn't have to be in public." He opened his hand; in his palm lay his room key, with its number face up—411. "You have a good memory, don't you, Jana?"

She looked a little startled by his boldness. "Well, I don't know about that."

"It's just a drink. I have a rather enormous minibar. Too much for me on my own."

"I thought I'd heard them all," she said with a laugh, then went off to see to another table.

But later, as he sat in his room, reading the local paper, he was unsurprised by the slight tap at the door, and when he opened it, the girl Jana was standing there. She was out of uniform now, wearing jeans and a pink crop top. As she slipped quickly into the room, he closed the door behind her.

"I'm not sure I should be doing this—" she began.

"Shhhh," he said, putting a finger to his lips and leaning over to kiss her waiting lips.

Much later, when it was closer to morning than midnight, but while it was still pitch-dark outside, the door of 411 opened, and Jana came out silently, then walked speedily down the corridor to the back stairs. She felt happy to have conducted her rendezvous unobserved, and a little exhilarated, especially since the man had said he would be back in three weeks' time.

36

Peggy was being so solicitous that Liz found herself growing impatient. "I'm fine," she protested again in the face of her junior colleague's repeated offers of aspirin, ibuprofen, paracetamol. "If you don't leave me alone, I'm going to call the Drug Squad."

Mercifully, Charles Wetherby appeared in the doorway and Peggy went back to her desk.

"Liz, Tyrus Oakes is flying in from Washington. He's due here at ten tomorrow morning, and I'd like you to join the meeting."

"That was quick," she said. Wetherby had been back from Washington only two days.

He nodded. "I think we'll be getting an answer this time, or he wouldn't be taking the trouble to come in person."

. . .

The next morning, when she entered Wetherby's office, she was unsurprised to find a stranger sitting there, but she was utterly astonished to find Andy Bokus with him. What on earth was going on?

Wetherby made the introductions. Tyrus Oakes looked dapper in a grey summer suit. He exuded the old-style charm of a Southern plantation owner—he shook her hand, gave a gallant little bow, then pulled back a chair for her. Wetherby watched the performance with barely suppressed amusement. Bokus, looking hot in a khaki suit, just nodded at Liz. "We've met," he said curtly.

"Good to see you, Charles," Oakes said affably as they all sat down again. "As I promised, I've come with an explanation and to clear up a misunderstanding."

Wetherby's eyebrow lifted, almost imperceptibly. "Thank you," he said mildly. "That's good."

The thoughts flashing through Liz's mind were less charitable. Were they questioning the authenticity of the photographs she saw lying on Wetherby's desk? It was certainly true that thanks to computer technology, pictures could tell all sorts of lies: you could morph images to seat people next to each other when in fact they were on different continents; you could delete whole mountains from landscapes, or remove entire buildings from an urban panorama. But in this case the camera was telling the undeniable truth: Andy Bokus was sitting next to a suspected Mossad officer at the Oval cricket ground.

Or would Oakes try and suggest that Bokus had run into the Mossad man "by accident"?

Oakes said, "What I am about to tell you is of course completely confidential and I hope I can count on its remaining that way."

Wetherby said sharply, "We are looking forward to what you have to say. To put your mind at rest, Liz is here because she is in charge of our investigation of the Israeli trade attaché in the pictures. As I told you in Washington, Ty, we have reason to suspect he is not a trade attaché at all." He pointed to the incriminating photographs on his desk. "That's how these came to be taken. She has also been liaising with your chap Brookhaven about this Syrian business and the Gleneagles conference."

Oakes said, "My concern is not about who knows what here in MI5 or in MI6. It's to do with the Israelis." When Wetherby looked at him questioningly, Oakes explained, "What I'm saying, Charles, is that yes, your people saw Andy meeting with a Mossad officer—Kollek."

Wetherby didn't say anything. Liz noticed Bokus had reddened and was looking uncomfortable, like an oversized schoolboy who'd been caught with his hand in the biscuit tin.

Oakes said, "What the photographs don't show is that he's *our* agent."

Silence fell over the room. Wetherby looked stunned. "You're running a Mossad officer in London?" he asked at last. His surprise was undisguised.

"That's right. And until these came to light"—Oakes pointed to the photographs—"this was a very closely held operation. Only a very few in the Agency knew of it. As you'll well understand, this type of operation is our most sensitive."

"Quite," said Wetherby crisply. "Thank you for being frank with us. I'll need to inform DG of course and Geoffrey Fane, who is aware of the photographs and has I think been frank with you about other things." He glanced momentarily at Bokus, then looked back at Oakes with a steady gaze. "But there's no need for anyone else outside this room to be told. Though there are some things we'd like to know about this agent you're running under our noses," he said with the slightest of smiles.

"Such as?" said Bokus, speaking for the first time.

"Why is Kollek undeclared by the Israelis? There has to be a reason or they'd never do it—Mossad knows what our reaction would be if we discovered they had an undercover officer operating here. What is Kollek doing that's so important for them to take the risk?"

Oakes looked over at Bokus and nodded. The big man was sweating slightly, and he hunched his shoulders and leaned forward as he said, "Kollek's role here is to look after Mossad sources living in the United Kingdom, or passing through. He's their local point of contact."

"How long has he been working for you?" Liz asked.

Bokus shrugged. "Not long. Maybe nine months, a year."

Wetherby was rolling a pencil in his fingers, considering this. "May I ask what his motivation is for working for you?"

"He made the approach." Bokus seemed unabashed. He's regaining his confidence, thought Liz, now that he knows he's in the clear.

"What reason did he give?" asked Wetherby. Liz was glad to see he was taking nothing on faith. He added with a hint of acidity, "Or was it money?"

"Good God no," Oakes interjected, with what Liz felt was contrived horror. "I'm not exactly sure of his motives. Andy?" He turned to his head of station.

Bokus put a large hand under his chin, pensive. "I think he feels things are moving too slowly in the Middle East for there ever to be peace. He sees things getting worse. He thinks it will take America to make his leaders move, and unless we have the full picture that's not going to happen."

Wetherby asked, "And how is he helping to paint this 'full picture'?"

When neither American answered, Wetherby stared down at his pencil dourly. He seemed to be avoiding looking directly at Oakes, as if not to challenge him unnecessarily. But when he spoke his voice was firm: "I said you can count on our discretion, Ty. But in return we need to hear what Kollek is telling you. He's operating in our territory undeclared—both by the Israelis *and* by you—in a clear breach of protocol," he said, raising his eyes now and staring fixedly at Oakes.

Liz understood what Wetherby was getting at: a quid pro quo. They'd say nothing to the Israelis, but in return the Americans would relay the information they got from Kollek.

Bokus hunched down farther in his chair, but Oakes looked entirely unfazed. He might have been at a golf club committee meeting, discussing an application for membership. "Of course," he said rapidly—too rapidly, thought Liz, who knew they would get only selected excerpts of Kollek's information. Still, excerpts were better than nothing.

Oakes turned again to Bokus. "Why don't you start the ball rolling, Andy?"

Bokus reached for his briefcase and brought out a file. He extracted a single page and handed it across the desk to Wetherby. "These are the people he's been running in London."

Wetherby scanned it intently, then handed it across his desk to Liz.

There were six names. Liz had never come across any of them, though two were international businessmen she'd heard of, and a third was a Russian exile who was always in the press. She looked at Wetherby and shrugged.

"Are they known to you?" asked Oakes a little anxiously.

"I'll have to check," she said. "Obviously, I've heard of some of them." She looked at Wetherby, who nodded to confirm this. Then she pointed a finger at the sheet. "Markov owns a football team in the north. His personal life is always in the papers—I'm surprised he has time to talk to Mossad."

Wetherby put his pencil down. "What sort of intelligence are these people providing?"

Bokus didn't answer, letting Oakes reply. "Well, it's early days, Charles. Certainly nothing very dramatic has come down the pike to us yet. Nothing about the United Kingdom or of course we'd have made sure you had it . . . in one way or another." Wetherby inclined his head minutely in acknowledgement. "But we can brief you in more detail if you like." He looked at Bokus. "If Miles is the liaison with Miss Carlyle here, why don't we have him come over and take her through your reports on Kollek?"

Bokus nodded, though Liz could see that he was not at all delighted by the idea of Miles being involved. From the sound of it, there wouldn't be much for Miles to tell her, but Liz's thoughts in any case were focused on something else. It was not the names on the list that had caught her attention, but the names that weren't there. Sami Veshara wasn't there—perhaps not so surprising as he'd told Charles he met the Israelis only in Tel Aviv—but neither was Hannah Gold. What did that mean? Perhaps I was wrong, she thought. Maybe Kollek had no ulterior motive for his careful courting of Sophie Margolis's mother-in-law. Perhaps it was just friendship, as Hannah had said. Even intelligence officers need friends, she told herself. Though from what she knew of Kollek, sentiment played little part in his character.

Liz tuned in to the conversation again to hear Wetherby saying to Ty, "That will be fine."

"How often do you meet Kollek?" she asked Bokus, her mind still on Hannah.

The big American looked annoyed by the question. When Oakes didn't come to his rescue, he replied tersely, "Once a month. Sometimes less often."

A sudden intuition made her follow this up—she could not have said why. "Before your meeting at the Oval, when was the last time you'd seen him?"

Now Bokus's irritation was obvious. He hesitated, then said crossly, "Not since June. He was away for a while."

There was a brief silence, which Wetherby ended. "Anything else we need to discuss, Ty?"

"There is one thing. As Andy can testify, Kollek is kind of a nervous guy, very careful, almost to the point of paranoia. If he had an inkling of this conversation we've been having, then I think he'd stop talking to us right away. Isn't that right, Andy?"

Bokus's big head nodded vigorously. "Tighter than a clam."

"I told you, knowledge of this meeting is going to be very restricted," Wetherby said, adding pointedly: "There's no possibility of a leak from our end."

"Sure. But it would also be helpful if you could call off your surveillance of Kollek. It'd be a disaster if he spotted it, and this guy's a real pro. If he thought he was being watched he'd assume we'd told you about him. And anyway, I can't really see that surveillance would serve any useful purpose now, not when you know we're running him."

Charles digested this for a moment. "All right. I'll put that in hand."

After the Americans had gone, Liz stayed behind. Wetherby stood up and took off his suit jacket, hanging it around the back of his chair. He walked over to the window and looked down at the Thames. "So what do you make of that?" he asked.

"I suppose they felt they had to come clean. Ty Oakes must have seen he had no option—otherwise, we'd think his London head of station was playing away."

"As we did for a moment, yes. Though as you'd expect Ty put as good a face on it as he could. He did his best to make it look as if he was here to cut a deal."

"Even though he wasn't holding any cards to speak of."

"Exactly. I'm told Oakes loves a game of poker." Wetherby gave a brief smile. "You have to admire his brio. Ty's a great survivor."

"I can see why. But I'm not sure Andy Bokus was very happy. He must have felt completely exposed. He won't choose a meeting place as public as the Oval next time."

Wetherby gave a happy laugh. "Probably it was its public nature that appealed to him. Wasn't it Sherlock Holmes who claimed that if you want to hide in a crowded drawing room, you should sit on the sofa in plain view, while the people looking for you are scouring the corners and poking the curtains?"

"That's wonderful advice, until one of them gets tired and sits down on the sofa right next to you."

Wetherby gave an appreciative grin. "Now you know why I can't take detective stories seriously."

"What I don't quite understand is how this connects to the Syrian threat. If at all."

"I think we should assume that Bokus told Kollek more than he should have. Obviously with us, he wanted to act as if he was in complete control, and information was passing strictly one way. But I doubt it, somehow. I got the feeling Bokus is a lot closer to Kollek than he was willing to let on. I'll need to find out exactly what Geoffrey Fane told Bokus about the source of the information about the Syrians. But if Bokus passed any of that on to Kollek, then the leaks might have come from Mossad. Though what would the Israelis gain from tipping off the Syrians?"

"Perhaps there's some factional fight we don't know about. You know, hawks who don't want the peace conference to go ahead."

Wetherby considered this, then shook his head. "I doubt it. Mossad has always stayed well clear of politics. That's one of the reasons they're so good."

Liz said, "Still, there's something not right." Wetherby looked at her, and she shook her head in mild frustration. "I can't say what it is, because I don't know. It's just a feeling I have."

"I've learned to trust those feelings of yours." He walked back to his desk looking contemplative. "I think we'll continue watching Kollek for a little while more."

37

Charles was working at home that day, which gave Joanne the opportunity she needed. It was time they had what she thought of as "the conversation," if only because there wasn't much time left.

She was sitting, as she did on most fine mornings, on the small patio outside the kitchen, facing the garden. She had taken to having coffee here after Charles had left to catch his train. She liked to watch the birds swooping down over the river at the end of the garden, catching insects, and the robin that came to drink and wash in the birdbath on the lawn. Sometimes she'd doze off, and wake chilly, to find that almost the entire morning had gone.

The day was already heating up—the forecast said it would reach the seventies by noon—but she was always cold these days, and wore a thick cardigan over her long-sleeved blouse. She had a pillow wedged against the back of her chair; it lessened the pain, which was constant now in her lower back.

She heard the kitchen door swing open, then bang shut, and a minute later Charles appeared, carrying a tray with a full cafetière and two mugs.

"Well done, darling," she said cheerfully. Charles smiled in ironic acknowledgement that he had never been a dab hand in the kitchen. Though Joanne thought ruefully of how many duties he had taken on in what had formerly been her preserve.

"Here you are," he said, handing her a mug and sitting down with one himself. "Milky and sweet."

"Just like me," she said lightly. An old joke, but one that still made him smile. She added, "I'm certainly not complaining, but I worry about you being at home today. It seems to me you've got a lot on."

"Don't you worry."

"If you flew to Washington on such short notice, and then they flew here, it must be important."

He shrugged tolerantly. She went on, "And for Liz to come all the way out on a weekend . . ."

He nodded. "Yes, it is busy, but I have these annual confidential reports to write and I can do them more easily at home, where I'm not disturbed, than I can in the office." Joanne had once worked in the service. She'd been Charles's secretary. That was how they had first met. But they had long ago established a convention about his work—he sometimes told her what was going on, but she never pressed to learn more. It had always worked well that way; he was never indiscreet, and she never felt entirely excluded.

"I liked Liz, by the way." She looked at her husband steadily. "Very much. I'm glad to have met her." She wanted to be absolutely clear about this; it was one of the things she wanted him to know for later.

He nodded and looked thoughtful. Then he said, "Well, anyway, the Americans have been and gone, thank goodness. I think that problem is sorted out."

They sat in silence for a minute. From the river they could just hear the ducks squabbling. Charles finished his coffee and stared down at his mug. "Do you remember when we bought these?" he asked, holding the mug up in the air. It was bright, with a honey-coloured stripe around the rim, and blue and red mermaids painted along its side.

"How could I forget? It was in San Gimignano, and the boys thought we were mad—they didn't realise eight thousand lira wasn't eight thousand pounds."

"They were so little then," Charles said slightly wistfully. "I was worried how they'd manage a walking holiday, but they surprised me."

"They always do," she said with a mother's transparent pride.

"I was thinking about that holiday the other day, when I was in Washington staying at the hotel—or maybe it was a motel; I'm never precisely sure of the difference. My bedroom was enormous; it could have held the whole family. I kept thinking about that night near Siena, when we thought we'd never find a place to stay."

"Sam was worried we'd have to sleep in a hay loft. And we almost did."

"We found a room in the end," he said.

"Don't remind me." She shuddered at the memory of the four of them squashed into a tiny attic room. It had been at the top of a farmer's "villa" which had seen better days.

"I wonder what that village is like today."

"Teeming with tourists, and half the houses owned by the English."

"Probably," he acknowledged ruefully. "Still, it would be nice to see it again. Maybe in the spring, if you're better, we could think about a few days there. You always loved Italy. I bet the boys would like to come along."

She recognised the eagerness in his voice, a tone he liked to adopt when he thought she most needed cheering up. Usually she went along with the optimistic pretence, his determination that any half-filled glass was actually half full. But she wasn't willing to go along with him today, not when there was no longer any way to deny that the glass was almost empty.

"I don't think so, darling," she said quietly. He looked at her, surprised by the certainty of her tone, and she could see the fear entering his eyes.

"I saw Mr. Nirac yesterday," she said. Her consultant.

"You didn't say you were going," he protested. "I'd have taken you."

"I know," she said. "But I'm perfectly capable of getting there on my own. Especially when you have a lot on at work." She left the real reason unsaid: she had wanted to see the consultant alone so she could hear the truth, unsoftened by Charles's insistent optimism.

"So what did the old quack have to say?"

She reached across the table and put her hand on his. "He said it's not going to be very long now."

"Oh," he said reflexively, and she saw his shoulders slump, and how he wouldn't look her in the eye.

He had been the strong one, keeping her going through all these years of illness, cajoling her, teasing her, making her laugh, always there whenever she'd been tempted to succumb to despair. Now she had to be strong for him.

"I wanted you to know that I know now, too. I wanted to feel neither of us had to pretend. Are you all right?" she asked gently.

He nodded with his eyes down. She could see he was struggling to keep control. At last he raised his head and looked at her. "Is there anything you want? Anything I can get you? Somebody you'd like to see, perhaps. Your sister?"

She chuckled. "Ruth will be around whether I like it or not. But no, what I'd really like most of all is to have you here, and the boys. Just the family." She hesitated. "And if it's possible, I'd like to be here, at home, when . . . it ends. I've seen enough of hospitals to last a lifetime." She smiled at the unintended play on words.

"Of course," he said.

"There's something else. It's to do with . . . after. I want you to promise me that you'll have a life." He looked surprised and seemed about to speak, but she pre-empted him. "I mean it. I want to feel confident that you won't go to ground—I know you, Charles. Given half a chance you'll be working eighteen-hour days and sleeping at your ghastly club. But that's no good. You must promise me you won't do that. The boys need you, for one thing, so you mustn't hide away. This has always been a happy home for them; I don't want that to end simply because I'm no longer here. I want you here for them, Charles, and I don't want you living on your own forever. You're still young, you know."

"Hardly," he said, with a rasp in his throat.

Undeterred, she kept speaking. "I like to think you'll have happy memories of our time together, and of all the fun we've had. But life's here to be lived; if I've learned one thing from all this, it's exactly that. I don't want you living with a ghost, Charles." She leaned over, though it hurt her back so much she had to struggle not to wince. Looking into his eyes, she said, "Promise me that?"

He looked back at her now, sensing she needed him to. She noticed his eyes were moist, and he blinked once, then twice, in an effort to subdue his tears. "It's all right," he whispered at last, "I promise."

She sat back, and shivered slightly. "I'm feeling cold. Do you mind awfully if we go in now?"

3 8

Thank God she'd finally gone. He'd just about managed to keep the woman at bay, but her visit had left him very, very frightened. She had made it clear that she knew something. Had MI5 discovered what he'd managed to keep secret for ten years? But why did she keep asking about Syrian intelligence, or was that just a blind?

Ever since that day in Jerusalem when those two men had come to his hotel room, he'd lived in fear of being found out. It was long before he'd "come out" and admitted he was gay. He was still married then—to Hope, his girlfriend at Cambridge. She'd long gone; he'd been on his own for years. The men had had photographs of him on the bed, with a boy he'd met in a club. He knew now of course that the boy had been working for them and the whole thing was a setup. They were

Israeli intelligence and they'd said if he didn't co-operate they'd publi-cise the photographs and make sure he could never work again in the Middle East. He would have lost his job and his marriage. Now of course that kind of photograph wouldn't matter much, but they had him well on the hook and too much else had happened for him to get off it. At the time, he'd been working in Syria as a correspondent. The Israelis had wanted to know everything, particularly personal infor-mation about high-up Syrian officials—weaknesses, sexual proclivi-ties, all that sort of stuff—no doubt so they could try on them what they'd done to him.

Now MI5 had found out something, but that woman hadn't said what they knew. If she was telling him that the Syrians knew what he'd done, then his life expectancy had diminished dramatically. She'd left him worried sick, but in the dark.

Since she'd left, he'd taken precautions. He'd double-locked the front and back doors, made sure the windows were shut tight and locked. He'd stayed in, hadn't answered the phone, and had kept the curtains drawn. But he couldn't live like this forever and this morning he'd been forced to venture down the hill to Hampstead village. The cupboard was bare, and that was not a metaphor—there wasn't even a packet of dried pasta left.

Not that he'd bought much in the way of groceries, for he had decided he would have to leave his house until the immediate danger had passed. Though how would I know when it was safe to return? he wondered anxiously, as he walked slowly back along the edge of the heath, dotted at this time of the morning with dog walkers and East European nannies pushing babies in buggies.

Where should he go? It would probably be possible to secure another assignment, provided MI5 didn't scupper him. What he needed was something that would take him abroad. *The Sunday Times* people had liked his Assad profile and had suggested further assignments—Merkel in Germany was high on their list. But it would be impossible to keep a low profile working on that, not when he'd need to be in Berlin making appointments to see the Chancellor, interviewing her friends and colleagues, digging into her background in East Germany. Anyone who wanted to find him could do so within days.

But *was* there a threat? The rational, experienced side of Marcham struggled to convince himself there wasn't. After all, he had only just come from Syria, and there'd been no sign anyone knew anything about his covert activities. If they'd known, they could have killed him there. He could have been easily dealt with in Damascus—discovered dead in a hotel room, a fatality declared an accident by a compliant doctor, under orders from the country's authorities.

He thought some more about where he should go, as he walked circuitously back to his house, ensuring that the people behind him on one street were not the same ones he noticed when he turned around casually on the next. There was always Ireland, where young Symonds, a churchgoing friend he'd made through Alex Ledingham ironically enough, had a cottage outside Cork he'd always said Marcham was welcome to use. If he went there for a month, things might calm down. Should he tell anyone where he was going? No, he'd just say he was away. He could always check e-mails at an Internet café in Cork; he couldn't be traced doing that—he hoped.

But there was one person he wasn't going to tell about his departure, and he shuddered at the reaction of the man if he did. He called himself Aleppo, which Marcham knew as one of the most peaceful and beautiful cities in Syria. It seemed such an inept name for the man; there was something ruthlessly clinical about him, an air of controlled menace that didn't seem entirely human.

On his own street he saw no one, but was careful nonetheless as he approached the house, stopping on the paved path once he'd gone through the gate in the hedge, looking and listening for signs that anyone was waiting outside. Nothing.

He carefully unlocked his front door, then with equal care doublelocked the door behind him. He walked straight through to the kitchen and made sure the back door had not been disturbed. He unpacked his two bags of groceries, boiled the kettle and made himself a strong cup of tea, which he took into the sitting room. It was only as he sat down with a sigh that he saw the man in the wing chair by the unused fireplace. It was Aleppo.

"God, you scared me!" he exclaimed, leaping to his feet and spilling his tea on the coffee table.

"You'll recover," the man said. He wore a black leather jacket and a black pullover and black jeans. The effect was European rather than English; he might have been a lecturer at the Sorbonne, though equally, the dark hair and swarthy countenance could be Middle Eastern as easily as French.

"How did you get in?" asked Marcham, his heart beating frantically. He wanted to be angry at the intrusion, but he was too frightened to protest.

"I'm paid to get in," said Aleppo. "Relax. Sit down."

Marcham did as he was told, starting to feel a prisoner in his own house.

"So have you had any other visitors lately?"

Marcham hesitated. He didn't want to say anything about Jane Falconer's visit, but he sensed it would be a great mistake to be caught lying and Aleppo always seemed to know more than he let on. "Actually, I have. A woman came from MI5. She wanted to talk to me about a friend of mine who died."

"Anything else?"

He hesitated for a split second. "Yes," he admitted. "That was the strange thing. She wanted to know if I'd had any contact with Syrian intelligence."

"*Syrian?*" Aleppo looked up sharply. "What did you tell her?"

"Nothing," he said hastily. "Nothing that matters. I told her about the profile I wrote on Assad."

"And did you tell her what else you'd done in Syria?"

They both knew what he meant.

There was a chill in the room now, and Marcham realised his answer was going to be crucial. Crucial to what? He didn't like to think. "Absolutely not," he said forcefully.

Aleppo looked at him thoughtfully. "She didn't want to know anything about your history there?"

"I'm sure she did. But I diverted her. My friend Ledingham died in rather bizarre circumstances. You may have read about it in the paper. They called him 'The Man in the Box.'"

He was glad to see that Aleppo's eyes widened. Marcham continued, "What the papers didn't say is that I was the one who found his body. I put him in the box.

"So, when this woman started pressing me about Syria, I got upset. I think she thought I was breaking down. I told her it was over Ledingham. I said that we'd been close—lovers, in fact. I told her I'd been hiding that. As well as the fact I hid his body."

"She swallowed this?"

"Absolutely. She didn't ask me anything more about Syria." He looked intently at Aleppo. "I give you my word."

To his immense relief, Aleppo nodded. He believes me, thought Marcham, feeling almost grateful. He sensed that if he'd given a different answer, something awful might have happened.

Aleppo said, "This woman's been in the house before. Is there anything she might have seen she shouldn't have?"

"No. There's nothing secret here at all."

Aleppo stood up. "Let's just make sure, shall we? Let's do a quick tour."

"Of course." Marcham led the way down the short hall to the kitchen, feeling calmer now, his worries largely dispelled. He'd told Aleppo the truth, and the truth seemed to have been accepted.

Marcham walked into the bedroom and switched the central light on. Aleppo paused in the doorway, surveying the room. Then he pointed past Marcham, to the small painting of Jesus on the cross that hung on the far wall. "I like that. Where did you find it?" he asked, with a voice full of curiosity.

"Funnily enough, I found it in Damascus," Marcham began, moving closer to the painting. "There's an interesting story associated with the shop where I first saw it," he added, preparing to tell Aleppo the tale—it should amuse even this dour, dark man. As he started on his story, he didn't notice Aleppo quietly close the bedroom door.

39

The call came just as Liz arrived in her office. She was juggling a mug of coffee with the same hand that held a newspaper; her other gripped her handbag and she had her office pass in her mouth. She managed to pick up the phone on the fourth ring.

"Ms. Carlyle? It's DI Cullen. It's about Christopher Marcham, that friend of Alexander Ledingham, the man who was found in St. Barnabas."

"St. Barnabas? Oh, the Man in the Box," she said instinctively. Then she tensed a little: something must have happened if Cullen was calling her.

"I've got some bad news. Christopher Marcham's been found dead."

What? She was shocked by his simple declaration. It hadn't been forty-eight hours since she'd seen the man. "Where was this?"

"In his house in Hampstead."

"How did he die? Was it a heart attack?"

"No, no," said Cullen, hastening to put her right. "That's the peculiar thing. He asphyxiated himself. Just like Ledingham did. Looks like he was involved in auto-eroticism too. He was tied up to the bed posts, and, um, he didn't have any clothes on." The policeman coughed to cover his embarrassment. Liz sensed that DI Cullen thought dimly of such practices. She asked, "Are you sure it was an accident? It seems quite a coincidence."

"Well, I don't think he was trying to kill himself, if that's what you mean. There're a lot of simpler ways to do that. But it's not that unusual for people who go in for that sort of thing to get it wrong. It's a dodgy business."

"I didn't mean that," said Liz, forcing herself to restrain her impatience. "I meant, are you sure that no one else was involved?"

"As sure as we can be at present, though the scene of crime boys will be going in later this morning. They'll find anything there is to find. But there were no signs of forced entry; the house was all locked up when the cleaner arrived—she's the one who found him."

"I saw him the day before yesterday, as we agreed. He was perfectly okay when I left."

Cullen coughed again. "Yes, I'll need to take a statement. You may have been the last to see him alive. But we should be able to keep it quiet if it's as open and shut as I think it is."

"When was he discovered?"

She heard him turning the pages in his notebook. "About four p.m. yesterday. We haven't got the pathologist's report yet, but the attending physician said he'd probably been dead less than twenty-four hours. It's a good thing it was the day the cleaner came, or he might have been lying there quite a while. Apparently she's new. Gave her quite a shock. She's wondering what she's got herself into."

When Cullen had rung off, Liz sat at her desk, wondering why Chris Marcham was dead. *Another* freak accident? She didn't believe it for a minute. The coincidence was too great and he'd told her he didn't go in for the same practices as Ledingham.

Trust your bones. That's what her father had always said about intuition. And Liz felt in her bones that this was no accident. She couldn't prove it, she knew that, but that just meant that Marcham's killer was not only ruthless, he was also clever. Which made him even more dangerous.

Perhaps it was her fault. She shouldn't have insisted on doing that interview. She wasn't thinking clearly. She'd been too oblique. She should have warned him instead of just asking him vaguely about Syria. Well, there was no point in worrying about that now. The only thing worth thinking about was whether his death had any connection with the Syrian plot. After all, that had been what initially stirred her interest in the man. If this was all part of it, what was going to happen next?

She remembered her first visit to the small Hampstead house, and an image came to her, of that mysterious gardener. Tall, lean, dark, with those giveaway shoes—slip-ons, last seen disappearing over the back wall of Marcham's garden.

There was something troubling about the picture, almost a form of déjà vu—a sixth sense linking it to some other image stored in her head. She sat thinking fruitlessly, trying to place the face in another context. Had she seen him somewhere else? Could it have been in Essex, where she'd gone in pursuit of Sami Veshara's illicit business? Or even Bowerbridge, when she'd first tentatively emerged from her sickbed, visiting the nearby village shops with her mother?

No, she couldn't place it. And then suddenly she understood why.

She hadn't seen the man in another place; she'd seen him in a *photograph*. And the photograph was sitting in an envelope in the cupboard in the corner of her office. She twirled the combination lock to open the cupboard and took out the envelope, tipping the prints onto her desk impatiently.

There he was, sitting next to Andy Bokus, high in the stands of the Oval. Suddenly two different worlds collided, and the name Danny Kollek, which had come to represent Mossad for her, joined the image of the sinister man snooping around Marcham's house.

So Kollek had known Marcham. Why? Had he been running him for Mossad? There seemed no other conceivable explanation. In which case, why wasn't Marcham's name on the list Bokus had supplied, of all the agents run by Kollek here in London? And what about Hannah?

There were too many questions she couldn't answer. But what bothered her most was that she didn't think the Americans—Andy Bokus or Miles Brookhaven—could answer them either. She was sure Bokus hadn't been holding out on MI5; he simply didn't know. He thought he was running Danny Kollek, but it was starting to look the other way round.

40

A nd that's the lot." Miles Brookhaven threw the file down onto Liz's desk, and sighed wearily.

She was tired too. They'd spent all morning reviewing the reports of what Danny Kollek had passed on to Andy Bokus, and the experience had been unedifying. It was very low-grade stuff; little more than gossip. Even Markov, the Russian-Jewish oligarch now based in Lancashire near his newly acquired football team, had nothing to say about his fellow émigrés that MI5 didn't know already.

"Are you thinking what I'm thinking?" said Miles knowingly.

"Probably." Liz pointed to the files. "There's not a lot there."

"Actually, I was thinking how hungry I am." He laughed, adding, "How about you?"

"Yes, I could use some lunch. There's a good sandwich shop round the corner. We could sit on a bench and watch the river go by."

"Aren't we near the Tate Gallery?"

"It's just down the road. Why?" She'd noticed how Miles always seemed to be ready with irrelevant questions and tangential remarks.

"I haven't been there in a long time. Couldn't we get a sandwich there?"

Twenty minutes later, Liz and Miles were staring at a large oil by Francis Bacon, of a grotesque satyr-like male figure whose face was set in a rictus of agony.

"I don't know about Bacon," said Miles at last. "I know he's very gifted and so on, and his pictures go for millions. But I can't help wondering what he's done that Hieronymus Bosch didn't do centuries before."

Downstairs they gave the formal restaurant a miss and bought sandwiches from the café, finding a place to perch on the line of stools against the corridor wall.

Liz, casually dressed in a skirt and blouse, was amused by Miles's smart blazer and cream linen trousers. Did his taste for formal clothes hark back to his time at Westminster school? All he needs is a boater, she thought, and he'd fit in well at Henley regatta.

"Not long now till the conference," said Miles as he cast a cautious eye at his smoked salmon sandwich.

"Two weeks."

"I'm not going to be here for it, I'm afraid."

"Really?" she asked, startled.

"I'll be in the Middle East. It's part of my job to stay up to date with things, and follow up any business I've come across here in London. I'll be in Damascus. Anything I can do for you there?"

"I'd be interested in what you could find out about Marcham's time there."

"Oh," he said, "I meant anything *personal*. Damask silk from the Old City, say."

Liz gave an inward sigh. She liked Miles, but having tried to hustle information out of her on the Eye, was he now going to make romantic overtures? It was flattering, and she was not averse to his interest in her, but she wished he'd picked a better time.

"Besides, I could use a break from Andy Bokus." He grimaced.

Liz looked at him, and he returned her gaze. "That bad?" she said lightly, intrigued but not wanting to press. Miles had never struck her as the complaining type.

He shrugged, then folded his paper napkin and put it on his plate. "One of the myths about America is that it's a classless society. Bokus carries a hell of a chip on those big shoulders of his."

"Really? What's he chippy about?" She wasn't going to pretend to understand the social intricacies of American society.

"Half the time it seems to be me. It's not that I'm grand. I don't mean that. It's more to do with education. Bokus likes to call me Ivy."

Ivy? thought Liz. She was surprised. Miles had none of the macho swagger of his boss, but there wasn't anything effeminate about him. Had she missed a trick?

She must have looked puzzled because Miles explained. "As in Ivy League. He likes to think I must be some rarefied snob because I went to Yale—he went to a state university."

"Isn't that all a bit passé?"

"Of course it is. Though I suppose Bokus can remember the days when half the staff went to Yale. A bit like your services and Oxbridge, I suppose."

"It changed here a long time ago," said Liz. And a good thing too, she thought to herself.

"And Andy's feeling especially touchy ever since Tyrus Oakes briefed me about Kollek."

"He must be rather embarrassed that we caught him out. Though it was pure chance we were watching Kollek that day."

"You can say that again. Andy got caught with his pants down all right." Miles took a careful sip of his coffee, looking thoughtful. "The thing is, I've never understood what this threat to the conference is supposed to be about. These two men, Veshara and Marcham, don't strike me as the types to do anything significant. A businessman and a journalist."

"Though both had connections with Mossad." Liz had briefed Miles already about Veshara's admission that he had reported rocket positions to the Israelis. Now she explained Marcham's links to Kollek—how she had only belatedly realised the Israeli in the surveillance photograph was the same man she'd seen scaling Marcham's garden wall.

"Okay, so they both gathered information for the Israelis," said Miles when she'd finished. "But I can't picture either of them actually taking any action. And their Mossad links don't explain why they'd be working to disrupt the peace conference. They wouldn't be doing that on Israel's behalf, surely. There's no reason to think the Israelis want to disrupt the thing. Why should they? They're part of it."

"Search me. I don't see it, either," Liz admitted.

"You know, when we were told about this threat we didn't have any idea where this information was coming from. Fane wouldn't tell us," he complained. "Is he always that buttoned up?"

"Pretty much," said Liz. "*Need to know,* is written on his heart."

Bookhaven sighed. "That causes problems, believe me."

You can say that again, thought Liz, keenly aware of the drawbacks to Fane's perpetual secretiveness. Something Brookhaven had just said was niggling her, but she wasn't sure what it was. So she filed this part of the conversation away in the back of her mind, promising herself to come back to it when she was alone.

"What do you know about Kollek?" said Liz casually. She didn't want to sound too interested in the man, or give any indication that he was still being watched by A4.

"Not much. And there isn't a snowball's chance in hell of my ever meeting him."

"Bokus wants him to himself?"

"Yes, though in fairness, that's really because of Kollek—the secrecy has been at his insistence as much as ours. Not that I can blame him. I wouldn't want to be in his shoes if Mossad ever found out he was talking to us."

"I wonder about his motivation," said Liz, remembering what Bokus had said in their meeting with Oakes and Wetherby—that Kollek felt only America could make peace in the Middle East, and therefore needed to know what Israel was thinking. But it was hard to see how Kollek was doing that in practice. The dribs and drabs of intelligence she had spent the morning reviewing with Miles wouldn't be of significant help to any country trying to find a solution to the Middle East crisis.

Miles seemed to read her thoughts, for he said, "Maybe he's just got an inflated sense of his own importance. God knows, nothing you or I read justifies all this hush-hush business. He could be just another egomaniac; there're enough of them in this business."

He looked at his watch. "I'd better be going." They put their trays back and left the Tate by its side entrance.

"How long will you be away?" asked Liz as they reached the corner with the Embankment.

"Ten days or so. But I'm not going until next week."

She nodded. "It might be a good idea to touch base before you go."

"Maybe you'd like to have dinner one night?" he asked.

Miles looked slightly awkward, more like a teenager than a rising star of the CIA. There was something boyish about him, thought Liz.

It was attractive in some ways, enormously preferable to the man-of-the-world cockiness of Bruno Mackay. Yet once again Miles was mixing business and pleasure in a way Liz found discomfiting. She wished he wouldn't.

So she said, "I'm a bit tied up until after the conference." Miles could not contain a look of disappointment, so she added more brightly, "Let's meet up when you're back from Damascus. Give me a ring at home."

Liz turned and walked along the river towards Thames House, thinking about their conversation. It was the business side of it that held her attention. The Mossad involvement in all this continued to puzzle her: again and again that connection came back to one person, Danny Kollek.

She wondered how to find out more about him. I'll put Peggy Kinsolving onto it, she thought—she'll rootle out whatever there is to find. And I should check again with Sophie Margolis, and see if Hannah's been in touch with Kollek recently.

All that seemed clear enough, but something was still bothering her. Then she stopped dead on the pavement. Of course, she saw what it was.

The attack on Liz, and the murder of Fane's Syrian source in Cyprus, must mean that someone had leaked the fact that the British knew of the threat to the conference. Who knew about the threat? Only a few people in MI5 and MI6 and Miles and Bokus. At first she had thought that they were prime suspects—particularly Bokus, once A4 had photographed him meeting Kollek.

And even when Tyrus Oakes had admitted that Bokus was running Kollek, rather than, as they had first suspected, the other way round, Charles had continued to suspect that the CIA man might have unintentionally revealed more than he should have done to Danny Kollek.

But there was a problem with this scenario, Liz suddenly realised. Even if Bokus *had* talked too freely, that couldn't explain the Syrians' discovery of a double agent in their midst. Geoffrey Fane had disguised the source of the original information—from everybody. And as Miles had just said, neither he nor Bokus had had any idea where the intelligence came from. It could have been any one of a number of countries or—Liz thought of Hamas and Hezbollah—political organisations. If Bokus had told Kollek about the threat to the peace conference, then even if Mossad had wanted to leak it back to its originating source, they wouldn't have known who to leak it to. They couldn't have spilt the beans when they didn't even know whose beans they would be spilling.

So how on earth had the Syrians learned about the double agent in Cyprus?

She saw Thames House ahead of her, its stone pale in the midday sun. The questions of this case were starting to seem maddeningly circular; Liz had a sense that ultimately there would be something simple—a person, she was sure of that—linking them all together. Yet each time she peered into the mystery she saw only a hall of mirrors, reflecting something so far unrecognisable.

41

Dougal had been warned by the hotel manager that Israelis could be rude. But the three he was showing around Gleneagles that morning were perfectly polite—if uncommunicative. They spoke to each other in Hebrew, and to Dougal barely at all.

The three Israelis were not staying in the hotel; they had taken one of the Glenmor time-share houses, where their country's delegation would also be staying during the peace conference. Normally the manager himself would have been escorting them, but he had even bigger fish to fry: the Secret Service had arrived the night before, and were already combing the hotel, where the American President would be staying.

The time-shares were pleasant, high-gabled houses, laid out in a meandering line around a pond and little stream just across a road behind the hotel grounds. When Dougal had collected the three visitors first thing that morning, they had no complaints about the accommodation.

The woman in this trio, Naomi, was about forty, a little haggard-looking, and perpetually talking on her mobile phone. She seemed to be consulting her superiors in London or Tel Aviv about every detail, from the way each room should be arranged to the food and kitchen utensils required to make two dozen kosher breakfasts. The younger of the two men, Oskar, seemed to be her assistant; he deferred to Naomi in any discussion, and agreed with everything she said.

It was the other man whom Dougal found unsettling. He kept himself aloof, and spoke to Dougal only when he had a question. He didn't say much to Naomi or Oskar either, and Dougal had the distinct impression that the other two were a little nervous of the man. They called him Danny.

During the morning they focused on finalising domestic arrangements, inspecting each of the houses assigned to the Israeli delegation, the catering arrangements for those who might want to cook for themselves, and a tour of the hotel—Dougal showing them the restaurants, the pool and the small arcade of shops.

Dougal left them to themselves as they lunched, claiming he had to check in with the office—it wasn't true, but he needed a break, especially from the dark-haired Danny, whose blank eyes Dougal found unnerving.

When they reconvened after lunch, on the gravel drive by the hotel entrance, Dougal sensed that something had been decided. Naomi was no longer on the phone, and she hung back as Danny stepped forward.

The Israeli said, "On the evening before the conference begins, we are planning to give a dinner for one of the delegations. We think the golf club restaurant would make a nice venue."

Dougal nodded. "That can be arranged. The view of the hills is grand. Would you be wanting to go down there now and look at it?"

"Later," said Danny, a little curtly. Dougal wondered if he'd been in the military, but then, hadn't all Israelis? "We also want to provide some entertainment for our guests. Something local to this region that they might enjoy."

"Would you like live music?" He could rustle up some pipers in kilts to give an "authentic" Scottish flavour to the entertainment.

But Danny shook his head. "No, no music. We'd like something *before* the dinner. Something outside."

"Outside? The weather can be up and down, you know, especially now it's autumn." And chilly, thought Dougal.

"We'll take the chance. Let's go to the falconry centre," Danny said. The preoccupied man of the morning had given way to the leader, somebody who knew what he wanted. It was clear now that Danny was in charge of this curious trio.

"They say all Arabs like birds of prey," Naomi said.

"Is it Arabs you'll be entertaining?" asked Dougal as they stood waiting for Danny to finish his conversation with the head of the falconry centre. They had been there for over an hour; Dougal had had to struggle to look interested as Danny asked the falconry man another of his countless questions. How much did the birds weigh? Did their transmitter bother them? Would they mind being handled by strangers? This assuming the guests of the Israelis would want to have a go themselves.

"Actually, I'm not supposed to say," said Naomi, looking guiltily towards Danny, who fortunately was listening intently to the falcon man. But Dougal noted that she had already nodded.

At last Danny was finished. He spoke sharply to Naomi and Oskar in Hebrew. Turning to Dougal, he said, "Now we need to look at the golf club restaurant. But on the way, let's stop at the gundog school."

Danny strode confidently towards the school, and Dougal followed with Naomi and Oskar. He was beginning to feel like a spare part. *You'd think he knew this place better than I do,* thought Dougal crossly.

They stood outside a large fenced compound as a dozen black Labradors, cooped up inside the fence, jumped around friskily. The handler, a smiling woman with a mop of blond curly hair, came out to meet them. Danny took her to one side, talking earnestly to her, and Dougal could hear only snatches of their conversation. *A retrieval display . . . duck decoys . . . no problem.*

Gradually it dawned on Dougal that the Israeli wanted the dogs to be part of the entertainment he was planning for the evening before the conference began. He was surprised. In his experience, Arabs didn't like dogs, regarding them as barely a step up from vermin.

The handler led one of the Labradors out of the pen on a lead, and walked to the kennel building, where she left the dog tied to a post and went inside, emerging a minute later carrying a couple of decoys and a large rag. Behind her another dog followed obediently, without a lead. It was bigger than the Labradors, and short-haired, with a rich chocolate coat and a white-and-brown-speckled face.

"This is Kreuzer," the handler said, walking towards the edge of the adjacent lawn, a wide grassy square of several acres, dotted by the small greens and sand bunkers of the pitch and putt golf course. "He's a German pointer. Give him one smell of something and he'll find it half a mile away."

She stopped and called the pointer to her. Kreuzer came up and sat obediently, his keen face looking up awaiting his orders. The handler took the rag she held in one hand and passed it once, then twice, in front of Kreuzer's nose. She stood back, then handed the rag to Oskar,

Naomi's sidekick. "If you go across the field I'll distract the dog." She pointed towards the distant trees across the expanse of lawn. "Hide it wherever you like."

As Oskar set out, she turned around and faced the kennel building in the opposite direction. Kreuzer obediently did the same. Danny stood beside her and they talked for a minute, while Dougal wondered what was going on. He looked across to the trees and saw Oskar go round a clump of rhododendrons then emerge again, no longer holding the rag.

The handler turned around as Oskar rejoined them. "Now watch this," she said, and gave a sharp high whistle. At once the German pointer began moving agitatedly in circles, its nose held high in the air as it sniffed carefully. Suddenly it turned and raced at high speed across the grass, heading straight for the shrubs where Oskar had been. The dog charged right into the middle of the dark foliage and was lost from sight; when it came out seconds later, it had the rag in its mouth.

"Bravo!" shouted Naomi, as the dog trotted back with its find.

The handler nodded with satisfaction. "Good enough?" she asked Danny, who was watching the dog intently.

"Let's try the decoys," Danny said, pointing with one arm in the direction of the small lake near the entrance drive.

"Okay," said the handler. "I'll just get the Labrador." As she walked off, Danny looked at Dougal. "There is no need for you to stay with us," he declared.

"Oh," said Dougal, taken aback. "I'll be getting back then. You know how to find me if you need me."

Danny started towards the lake before he could even shake his hand. Graceless kind of bloke, thought Dougal, as he walked back to the hotel and his office. I don't mind if I never see him again.

. . .

But he did, that very evening, as Dougal drove home to the small grace and favour cottage he lived in on a neighbouring estate. He had just left the hotel grounds and was passing the equestrian centre when he saw the Israeli, under the cover of some trees. He was talking urgently to a girl—a pretty girl with strawberry blond hair who was certainly not haggard-looking Naomi from the delegation. There was something about the look on the Israeli's face that made it obvious he knew this girl; he wasn't just casually saying hello. As he drove past, Dougal saw the girl's face in his headlights, only fleetingly, but enough to recognise her at once—it was one of the waitresses in the hotel's Italian restaurant. A foreign girl, very attractive. Janice? Something like that. Danny, you sly bastard, thought Dougal, not without a note of envy.

42

She had been a forward kind of girl ever since she was small. Her father had died when she was four, and after that it had been her mother and little Jana all on their own. Her mother had told her you get nowhere by being shy, and from an early age she had been comfortable with adults—especially men, for it was men she mainly met. She'd started helping in the Moravian tavern where her mother worked almost as soon as she could read; taking her cue from her mother, she would talk easily with the customers, tease them when they wanted to be teased, play coquette when they wanted her to be a Shirley Temple. She'd even imitate the saucy way her mother spoke to Karl, the tavern owner, though it wasn't until she was nearly twelve that she realised her mother's duties included more than being a barmaid.

Moravia and her home town seemed a million miles away now. Her mother had been bitter when she'd told her that she was off to work in the West. "You can take the girl out of Ostrava," she'd warned, "but never Ostrava out of the girl. You will be back."

Fat chance, thought Jana now, comparing the opulent surroundings of Gleneagles with her all-too-vivid memories of the smoke-filled, sour, beer-soaked confines of the tavern that had been home. She worked hard in the restaurant here, but no harder than she had at home, and the pay was a fortune by Moravian standards; she'd even sent some money to her mother. She was fed well, and she got every seventh day off. Other waitresses complained about the quarters in the staff hostel behind the hotel, but to Jana they seemed positively luxurious.

True, the social life was a bit limited: the pubs in nearby Auchterarder were not exactly lively or even particularly friendly, especially when the locals heard her foreign accent. The other staff at the hotel were perfectly nice, but she didn't have much in common with the girls, many of them Poles, and the boys were too young for her taste.

Not that she was looking for a serious romance. "You think you will find a knight in shining armour to sweep you away?" her mother had demanded. "You think that's what happens to waitresses and chambermaids?"

Of course she didn't think that, though funnily enough the knight had appeared. He hadn't exactly said he was going to sweep her away—but Sammy was a good lover, and he had said they'd see each other again.

And sure enough, he had texted her that he was coming back. But she was still surprised when she glimpsed him walking across the lawn towards the tennis courts that afternoon. She'd been tempted to call out to him, but didn't when she saw that he was with some others—including young Dougal, who had tried to chat her up that night at the staff's darts evening. He was sweet and not bad looking, but much too young for her.

There was a woman with Sammy, but she felt no need to be jealous. She was a real old frump.

Jana kept her mobile phone on while she served lunch and at three, while she was still clearing up after the late customers, there had been a text message: *6 p.m. by the equestrian centre. S.*

There was no sign of him on the road outside the equestrian centre and she waited impatiently. Then from a clump of dark fir trees at one side of the building came a low whistle. She moved cautiously towards the trees until she could make out a lean figure standing underneath a branch. Her heart lifted as she realised it was Sammy.

"What are you doing in there?"

"Shhhhh," he replied, stepping out from underneath the trees. He merged into the background in his black jeans and a grey turtleneck, but she could see his face clearly. Once again she thought how handsome he was.

"What's the matter? Are you embarrassed to be seen with me?" she demanded huffily.

"Of course not," he said. "But we need to be careful, for your sake as well as mine. I'm here on business this time, with colleagues, and if they saw me with you it would be a bit hard to explain. They're very strict about this sort of thing. I could be suspended, or even worse."

"Oh," she said, now sharing his concern.

A car accelerated on the road behind her and Sammy started, moving quickly back into the shelter of the trees. She followed more slowly and the car's headlights just touched her as it passed. They stood under the bough of a tall spruce. She felt like a teenager on a furtive rendezvous. There was something thrilling about the whole encounter.

"I didn't know you were coming," she said a little petulantly.

"I didn't know myself, honestly. I only arrived last night. Anyway I'm here now," he added firmly.

"How long are you staying?"

"Only until tomorrow, I'm afraid."

"Well, at least that gives us tonight."

"Don't you have to work?"

"You're in luck. I've got the night off." She had managed at the last minute to switch nights off with Sonja, one of the Polish girls. "What's your room number this time?" she asked, smiling up at him.

But he was shaking his head. "I'm not in the hotel. I'm sorry, but I'm in a Glenmor house with my colleagues. I can't try and smuggle you in there; we'd get caught."

"Oh," she said, unable to disguise her annoyance. Why had he bothered to contact her then? "But you'll be back for this conference, won't you? Don't tell me you'll be staying with these people then."

"I won't be staying at all. Officially I'm not going to be at the conference," he said flatly, then looking at her his tone softened. "But don't worry—I'll be nearby. Only no one's to know that I'm around. It's strictly hush-hush. Do you understand?" There was a hard edge to his voice which scared Jana a little, and she nodded right away.

"Good. Now listen to me," he said, putting an arm around her shoulders. She tried to snuggle up against his chest, but he held her away. She could feel the strength of his arms, and wished they could be somewhere more private. "There's something I want you to do for me during the conference. Two things actually—things I can't do myself, because I won't be here. Will you do them for me?"

She looked up at him and said, "That depends."

"Depends on what?" There was that hint of coldness in his voice again.

She detached herself from his arm, then took him by the hand. "It depends on how nice you are to me now." And she pulled him in the direction of the woods behind them.

"What are you doing?"

"You know. Come on," she said, "the pine needles back there are very soft."

It was dark when she walked back to the hotel, brushing off the pine needles from the back of her skirt. She laughed inwardly at the ridiculousness of it all; she could have been a schoolgirl again, meeting Franz, the lawyer's son, by the river near the tavern. But she couldn't help herself; she had never been able to.

Besides, the man was *so* attractive, far too much so for her to miss the opportunity. He could be a little cold, Jana decided, almost steely, but then, that was part of his attraction.

She thought of what he had asked her to do. It certainly seemed odd, but she reassured herself that it couldn't be anything wrong, or else he wouldn't be coming back after all these international bigwigs had been and gone. She was a bit frightened, but she hadn't wanted to admit that. She'd have to find someone else to do the other thing—how could she be five miles away at the same time she was waiting on tables at dinner? But she knew that her friend Mateo, one of the busboys, would do it for her. He was Spanish and he had an enormous family. What had he said? Twelve brothers and sisters. Five hundred pounds wasn't to be sneezed at and all he had to do for it was walk up some hills.

43

You've been shopping," said Liz, as Peggy Kinsolving walked into her office in a new trouser suit with a short jacket that showed off her figure.

Peggy blushed. "Do you like it?" she asked.

Liz nodded. "It suits you," she said, thinking that things must be going well with Tim. Peggy didn't usually bother much about clothes; but now, thought Liz, with a tinge of jealousy, she had someone to appreciate them.

They discussed what they'd come to call the Syrian Plot, Liz voicing her frustration at the lack of obvious leads. "Now that Bokus and Brookhaven are in the clear, the only element that keeps recurring is

Mossad—or Kollek, actually. I think we need to home in on him. Why don't you do some digging?"

"Can I talk with people in Israel?"

"I'd rather you didn't for now."

"That won't help," said Peggy.

Liz understood the complaint, but shook her head. "If we tell Mossad we're interested in Kollek they'll want to know exactly why, and we've promised the Americans to be discreet."

"What about other sources there? You know, his school and university."

"Sorry, no. It's such a small country they'd soon find out we'd been asking. We can't take the risk. I'm afraid you'll have to stick to his time in the United Kingdom. Start with his visa application."

"Anything in particular I'm looking for?"

"See if you can find out where else he's been posted. Check with the friendlies and see if they know him. Show them his photograph— he might have been using other names. Talk to the FBI. They might have something on him that they haven't shared with the CIA. But for heaven's sake don't blow Bokus's little secret."

"It sounds a bit of a long shot."

Liz knew Peggy wasn't being negative, just realistic. "You never know," she said encouragingly. "Something may turn up and it's all we've got to go on for now."

After Peggy had left, Liz rang Sophie Margolis's home number. Her friend picked up on the second ring.

"Hi, Sophie, it's Liz. How are things?"

She listened patiently while Sophie told her the latest about her two children (school phobia and teething were the current concerns) and about David's recent promotion.

"And how about Hannah?" Liz asked at last.

"She's fine. The peace conference has got her very excited."

"I'll bet," said Liz. "Has she seen anything of our friend Kollek lately?"

"Funny you should ask. She hadn't mentioned him for a while, but they're having lunch just now, while we speak."

"Really?" Liz thought quickly. "I'd like to talk to her about him if I could. He's proving a bit of a puzzle—though please don't say so to Hannah. Is there any chance I could drop in for a bit? Maybe this evening if that's not too short notice."

"Of course. Come after work. You can share our chicken stir fry, if that's an inducement. And don't worry, I won't say anything except that you're dropping in."

One more call to make. She looked through her phone book and found Edward Treglown's work number. She slightly dreaded phoning, since they'd fixed the date almost two weeks before. The switchboard put her through to a secretary, who was frosty when Liz asked for Edward—"Will he know what it's about?" had to be Liz's least favourite telephone response.

But Edward came on straightaway, sounding cheerful. "Hello, Liz. Your mother and I are both looking forward to this evening."

"Oh, Edward," she said with undisguised regret, "that's exactly why I'm ringing. I can't make it. Something's come up at work, and I have to see someone."

The pause was almost imperceptible, and she thanked him mentally for the way he reacted. "Doesn't matter. We'll find another time. But listen, help me with something. If you can't come, I'd like to do something special for your mother. She'll be so disappointed not to see you. Have you any ideas?"

She had a sudden inspiration. "Why don't you take her up in the Eye? There's a special deal where they give you champagne."

"That sounds like the voice of experience," he said with a chuckle. "Splendid idea. Just sorry you can't join us. Ring soon and we'll make another plan."

Hannah seemed excited, drinking white wine and munching prawn crackers she took in handfuls from a large bowl on the kitchen table. Sophie had disappeared momentarily to put little Zack to bed—the baby was already asleep.

"I was just telling Sophie before you came that I've had the most wonderful news. I've been asked to go to the peace conference, as part of the peace delegation." Her eyes lit up.

"That's great. I didn't know there was to be a peace delegation. So you're going to Gleneagles?"

Hannah nodded. "I've even got a place to stay. Some B and B in Auchterarder." She laughed. "Did I pronounce it right?"

"I think so," said Liz, with a smile. "To the Scots I'm as foreign as you."

"Obviously, from the Israeli government point of view it's all just a PR exercise. They've invited a small group of Jewish peace activists to meet the Israeli delegation before the main conference starts. But if they think we're just going to act like yes-men they've got another think coming." She added defiantly, "We'll make our views known, don't you worry. They have no more right to act as if they represent Israel than we do."

"Who invited you?"

"The embassy," she said proudly. "They knew I was here and put my name on the list." Then she looked embarrassed. "I think Danny had something to do with it. He denied it, but he knew how much I'd like to go."

She seemed so enthusiastic that Liz waited a moment before asking, "Did Danny say if he'd be going to the conference, too?"

"Yes. I mean no, he won't be. It's a shame in some ways, though I think it would have been difficult for him—you know, having to act as a member of the official delegation, while your heart was really with the peace movement people."

Liz tried to look sympathetic, but inwardly she was puzzled. Why wasn't Kollek going? "Did he say why he won't be there?"

"He's going to be in Israel. There's some trade conference he has to attend. That's his specialty after all."

"Of course." She added, trying to make it sound like an afterthought, "Is there anything he asked you to do at the conference?"

Hannah shook her head. "Not really. He said we'd talk on the phone—I know he wants to know how we get on up there."

"So you're going to ring him from Gleneagles?" asked Liz, trying to keep the tension out of her voice. If Hannah had Danny's mobile number, they should be able to trace its location—and his.

"No," said Hannah. "He said he's going to ring me. He didn't say when, I'm afraid," she added, sensing that Liz wanted to know. She smiled wanly.

Damn, thought Liz. Kollek could be anywhere, and she had no way to find him. But if he wasn't going to Gleneagles, then just what was he up to? Sophie had come into the kitchen now, and though she was busy by the stove, starting the stir fry, Liz could see she was listening closely.

Hannah suddenly sighed, sounding exasperated. "Honestly, you two keep acting like Danny's got terrible designs on me. First you think he's a gigolo, Sophie; now you both act like he's some kind of spy."

Liz ignored this, and asked, "Has Danny already left for Israel?"

Hannah looked over at Sophie, who kept her back turned to

them both. "Not yet. In fact, I'm seeing him the day after tomorrow. We're going to a lunchtime concert in St. John's church in Smith Square."

"That should be good," said Liz, making a note to talk to A4 first thing in the morning.

4 4

Two days later at half past two in the afternoon, Liz was in the A4 control room in Thames House, sitting on the old leather sofa that was kept especially for case officers who wanted to hear how their operations were going. This was the domain of Reggie Purves, the A4 controller, and the rules were set by him. Case officers were allowed in, provided they kept quiet. If Reggie needed their contribution, he'd ask for it. That Liz was there at all was a sign of how concerned she had become about Kollek. She would normally have left a surveillance operation to the experts and waited until afterwards for the debrief.

Denis Rudge's team had picked up Kollek as he came out of the lunchtime concert at St. John's Smith Square and were behind him as he walked with Hannah towards the Houses of Parliament. Liz listened to the exchanges between the team and the control room as Hannah and Kollek reached Westminster Underground station, where they bought tickets from the machine and went down the escalator, with A4 in pursuit.

Five minutes later a report came in from the liaison officer on the surface that both had got out at Embankment station and changed onto the Northern Line. Another ten minutes of waiting, then a further transmission passed on the information that at Leicester Square Kollek had got off and changed onto the Piccadilly Line, heading west towards Heathrow. Hannah had stayed on the Northern Line and, as briefed, the teams had let her go, and were concentrating on Kollek. Wally Woods and his team were on the train with him. Backup teams in cars were already well on the way to Heathrow, ready to meet him if he got off there and follow him if he went into the terminals.

In answer to Liz's enquiry, the information came back that Kollek was not carrying a bag of any sort.

Liz knew it was a waste of time for her to sit in the operations room all afternoon, just waiting to see what happened. There was nothing she could do there, so she dragged herself away and went back to her office, having extracted a promise from Reggie Purves that he would ring her immediately if anything significant happened.

She had just sat down at her desk when Charles stuck his head round the door. "I'm really worried about Kollek," she said as soon as she saw him. "Peggy's getting nowhere fast. She's drawn a complete blank with the FBI and she's still waiting to hear from the Europeans. I've told her she can't make enquiries in Israel.

"Now A4 have got Kollek on the Underground, apparently going to Heathrow. Do you think he's leaving the country? He's told Hannah he's not going to the conference but he seems to have set it up for her to go with some sort of a peace delegation. What on earth do you think's going on, Charles? The conference is next week and I've got a really bad feeling about it."

"I've no more idea than you what's going on," he replied. "But I don't like the look of it either and I'm thinking it's time we talked to the Israelis."

"But, Charles. You can't. We promised Ty Oakes that we wouldn't."

"Well, we'll just have to persuade him to change his mind."

She looked at him in surprise and for the first time she noticed how grey and drawn he looked. "Charles," she said, "are you okay? You look really tired."

"Not really," he said, sitting down heavily in her visitor's chair. "There's something I wanted to tell you. That's what I came in for." He paused and looked away from her. "It's Joanne. She's dying. The consultant has said it won't be very long now."

"Oh, Charles. I'm so sorry," said Liz. She was mortified. She'd been so focused on her own problems that she hadn't even noticed how upset he was. "How long?" she asked tentatively, not really wanting to hear the answer.

"I don't know. It's a matter of weeks, I think. No more. It could be days. She's very weak now. Spends most of the time in bed."

Liz reached across and touched his arm. "Oh, Charles," she said again. "How dreadful for you. Is there anything I can do to help?" Knowing that there wasn't.

He shook his head, looked down and his eyes filled with tears. After a few seconds he seemed to shake himself and he looked up, blinking the tears away. "So I'm going to be at home now until the end. She needs me there and so do the boys. I'm really sorry to be leaving you in the lurch."

"I can manage," she said, though something like panic gripped her stomach as she realised what a weight of responsibility had now fallen on her.

"Tyrus Oakes is back in town. You need to go and see him and persuade him that the time has come to talk to Mossad. I've spoken to Geoffrey Fane and I've asked him to go with you. Don't take this the wrong way, but I think there's a better chance of persuading him if Geoffrey's there too. You've met Oakes and I'm sure you know what I mean."

She grimaced but she knew he was right. Oakes with all his Southern charm was a steely customer and he'd think he could run rings round someone who was much younger and a woman. She could probably get her own way in the end, she reckoned, but it would just be much quicker and simpler if Geoffrey Fane was there to lean on him.

"Good luck," Charles said. "I've every confidence in you. I'll be on the end of the telephone any time you want to ring me and DG has said to keep him closely in touch with what's going on. He'll make sure you get whatever support you need. I know you and Geoffrey Fane don't have the easiest relationship—I don't always see eye to eye with him either, as you know—but he is a real professional and he has a high regard for you, so consult him too. I'm sure you can rely on him to help in a crisis."

Liz nodded, thinking that was the first time Charles had ever actually said anything about his opinion of Geoffrey Fane.

"Well, I'd better be going now," he said, getting up. Liz stood up, too, and they faced each other awkwardly for a second or two, then he reached out and took her hand. "You know, I'm really glad you met Joanne, Liz. She liked you so much."

"I'm glad, too," she said, looking up at him. He turned and left the room.

When he'd gone, she sat down again at her desk, put her head on her arms and cried.

. . .

It wasn't until she was back at home in Kentish Town and considering what to eat for supper that Reggie Purves rang. Kollek had got off the Underground at Heathrow. He'd gone to the El Al desk in Terminal One. He must have had a ticket or shown some kind of pass because he was let through airside. By the time A4 had got hold of Special Branch at the terminal to get them through airside, too, he was nowhere to be seen. They'd searched all the shops and the restaurants and the open lounges. Wally's partner Maureen Hayes and a Special Branch officer had been into the El Al lounge, too, but there was no sign of him there either and no one admitted to having seen him. No El Al flight for Israel had departed yet, so he'd either left the airport or gone on some other flight.

"We'll wait until the El Al flight leaves. Boarding's at 21:05 and we can see if he turns up at the gate. But then either we'll have to withdraw or I'll need to allocate some fresh teams. That might be a problem as we've got a lot on for counter terrorism tonight."

"Thanks," said Liz. "Watch till boarding's complete and if he doesn't turn up withdraw and we'll just have to assume we've lost him."

"Okay," replied Reggie.

Liz put the phone down and poured herself a glass of wine. She knew with a sinking feeling that Kollek had slipped through their fingers. He wasn't going to turn up for that flight and now they had no idea where he was or what he was doing.

At 9:30 the phone rang. She was right. Kollek had not boarded. Damn.

45

Andy Bokus was fed up. The last thing he wanted was another visitation from the Brits, and if Ty Oakes hadn't been in town and looking over his shoulder he would have fobbed them off. Hadn't they already had their pound of Bokus flesh?

He felt he'd been made to look stupid. He kicked himself for being picked up by the MI5 surveillance of Danny Kollek. But he'd had no reason to think they'd be watching the Israeli. Kollek was undeclared, after all, and his operations were discreet enough not to have attracted MI5's attention. Or at least, that's what he'd told Bokus.

Now Bokus had to wonder. He kept asking himself what had put MI5 on to Kollek in the first place. Maybe he could learn that today; there had to be something useful he could get out of this meeting.

He looked without appetite at the slab of Danish pastry on his plate, and took a careless slug from his coffee, cursing as he burned his tongue. He was sitting in the embassy restaurant, practically deserted at mid-morning. He'd been in his office before eight, but he'd been too agitated to eat breakfast.

He wondered what the Brits had made of the material Kollek had supplied. Not much, he guessed. It was low-grade stuff. He knew that, but that wasn't the point. You had to take a long-term view, and by that standard Kollek was potentially one of the most important agents the CIA had ever had. The idea of jeopardising all this because the Brits were panicked about a peace conference that no one thought for a minute was going to get anywhere was ridiculous.

At least Miles Brookhaven was away, so he didn't have to put up with meeting the Brits with that preppy jerk in tow. He remembered how self-satisfied the Ivy Leaguer had looked when Ty Oakes had briefed him about the Kollek debacle. Concerned and superior at the same time. Bokus had never been a fan of Miles Brookhaven, but now he actively disliked him. He had managed to get rid of him temporarily by accelerating the junior officer's annual trip to Syria. Bokus had claimed it might be useful, given the imminent peace conference, though that was just an excuse to get him out of his hair.

Now Fane and that Carlyle woman had asked for this meeting and he was worried in case they'd found out something else to his discredit. His reputation at Langley was high, ever since the Madrid bombings, when he'd done so well. He wasn't used to being caught out embarrassingly by his host country.

He felt on edge as he looked at his watch—the Brits were due any minute. Fane he could just about stomach: all that British upper-class stuff grated on him and he was pretty sure Fane considered himself both his intellectual and social superior. It was irritating, too, when Fane played the gifted amateur, whose work in intelligence was just one of many hobbies, like fly fishing or collecting rare books. But beneath that smooth, cynical façade, Bokus knew Fane was a pro—which meant he was a guy you could do business with.

That woman Carlyle, on the other hand, was harder to read. She had none of Fane's snootiness or affectation, and on the surface she seemed much more straightforward and direct. Yet it was hard to know what was going on with her—what she was really thinking. And there was something relentless too, a sort of tenacity that Bokus found uncomfortable, particularly when he was its target. She needed watching, as he'd told Miles Brookhaven.

Oh hell, give me a break, thought Bokus, sighing wearily, as he stood up to go to the meeting. If he had taken just a bit more care, as he would have done anywhere else, the Brits would never have found out about him and Kollek. Hopefully, they were coming today to talk about Gleneagles, not yet again about that bloody Israeli.

As a teenager, Liz had been told by her grandmother to beware of the kind of boy who "wasn't safe in taxis." Geoffrey Fane would once perfectly have fitted the mould. But this morning, as she saw him sitting gloomy and slightly hunched in the corner of the black cab that picked her up outside Thames House, he looked far too depressed to be much of a threat. He barely replied when Liz raised the subject of their forthcoming meeting in Grosvenor Square, grunting his assent when she outlined the approach she wanted to take.

As they moved up the Mall past Buckingham Palace, he gave a loud sigh. "Pity Miles Brookhaven won't be there. I gather he's abroad."

"Yes. He's in Syria."

"Such a clever, handsome youth, isn't he?" said Fane caustically. When Liz did not respond he looked dismally out the window.

Twenty minutes later, as their meeting began, Liz was relieved to see that Fane had emerged from his sulk. That was the redeeming feature of the man: you could grow infuriated by his overdone secrecy, his manipulative ways, his arrogance, but there was never any doubting his professional commitment. Or his competence.

She had explained Charles Wetherby's absence to the two Americans, promised to pass on their messages of sympathy and endured the chitchat about the persisting warm weather, as they proceeded to the safe room. Inside, the air-conditioning, humming loudly, had turned the insulated bubble into an icebox.

Fane kicked off, crossing a leg languidly and saying, "Sorry to trouble you, gentlemen, but we thought a quick meeting before the Gleneagles conference began might be useful." He added pointedly, "Especially since I gather Miles Brookhaven is in the Middle East."

Bokus replied, "Sure. I sent him off to see if there was anything useful to be picked up out there."

"Well, it's more what's going on here that's concerning us at present," said Fane mildly. "Elizabeth?"

Liz leaned forward, concerned to make her points unambiguously. "We've grown very concerned about Danny Kollek. Yes, we appreciate the sensitivity of this, but the fact is that the two people we were told were working against the Syrians were actually working *for Mossad*. And I happen to know that one of them, Christopher Marsham, was in contact with Kollek because I saw Kollek myself outside Marsham's house." She looked at Bokus. "I briefed Miles fully on this."

Bokus gave a weary shrug of his shoulders. "Yeah, I know. But it didn't mean much to me. I never had much faith in the idea that the two guys were working against the Syrians. It looked like a classic piece of disinformation to me."

"Perhaps," Liz conceded. "But whose disinformation? The list you gave us of Kollek's contacts in the United Kingdom didn't include Marcham. And earlier, when Geoffrey told you the two names we'd received, you said you hadn't heard of either of them."

"I hadn't," said Bokus aggressively. "Otherwise, I would have said so when Geoffrey came and told us they were the targets. That's why I'm sure Kollek didn't have anything to do with them, or he would have listed them as contacts he was running."

No one spoke. Liz saw Tyrus Oakes shift his gaze downwards to study his tie—another reversed stripes item. Bokus looked around him with a mystified expression. "What's the matter?" he demanded.

Liz glanced at Fane, wondering if she should say what they were all thinking. Tyrus Oakes's continued inspection of his tie spoke volumes.

At last Fane said coolly, "Maybe Kollek didn't want you to know."

Liz thought for a moment Bokus would explode. His cheeks turned puce and he began to shake his head. "No way," he said emphatically. "Kollek was straight; he wouldn't have dared hold back on me. There was too much at stake for him. If his colleagues in Mossad even got a whiff that he was talking to us, his career wouldn't have been worth five cents. He'd have gone to prison—think of what happened to Vanunu."

The scientist who, having spilled the beans to a British newspaper about Israel's nuclear capability, was lured to Italy in a classic "honey trap," then kidnapped Eichmann-like and brought back to Israel, where he was tried and sentenced, and then spent eighteen years in solitary confinement.

"Listen," Bokus added rudely, pointing an accusatory finger at Liz, "I've run more assets than you've had breakfasts. I know when an asset's holding back, and this guy wasn't."

"Where is he now then?" asked Liz.

"He said he was going to Israel. That must be where he is now. I know he wasn't going to be in the country during the peace conference. If that's what you're driving at."

Liz spoke with deliberate softness. "It seems to me Kollek hasn't always told you the truth about his whereabouts."

"What's that supposed to mean?" Bokus shot back.

"When we met in Thames House, you told me Kollek was away, and had been for a couple of weeks. But he wasn't—he has been cultivating a woman named Hannah Gold here in London. Kollek chatted her up at the theatre on a day you said he was in Israel."

"For Christ's sakes," Bokus exclaimed, exasperated. "I'm not his goddamned nanny. I don't keep daily tabs on him."

"We need to know where he is now." Liz felt if she weren't careful her own irritation would match his. That would be a mistake. So she said as calmly as she could, "Since you can't tell us, I think we only have one option."

"What's that?"

"We need to speak to Mossad."

"No!" Bokus shouted.

She turned to Oakes. "We promised not to go down this route, but I can't see any other choice. That's why we're here. We believe Kollek may present an imminent danger of some kind. I don't know exactly what yet."

Fane intervened now. He said placatingly, "Obviously, Ty, if we're wrong about this, then we'll apologise. But I'm afraid I support Elizabeth here on this. We have to be sure."

"But I *am* sure," Bokus said, in a half-howl.

Liz ignored him and spoke directly to Oakes. It was hard to read what he was thinking. "From our point of view, two people who were supposed to be a threat to Syria and the peace conference had been working for Mossad, and one at least had been run by Kollek. I'm sure that's true—I saw Kollek myself at Marcham's house. And now Marcham's dead in suspicious circumstances. We don't know what any of that means, but we can't afford to ignore it. And given that the conference is now so close, the whole thing has become desperately urgent."

Bokus was looking at Oakes for support, but to Liz's relief Oakes nodded, to show he accepted the argument. Bokus grew more agitated. "Ty, we can't have this. You want the British to tell Mossad we were running one of their officers? Think of the damage that will do. Kollek *is* ours. I'm sure of it."

"Steady on," said Fane equably. He was looking only at Oakes now. Liz realised Bokus had been relegated to observer status; Oakes was going to be the arbiter.

Fane continued, "That's the bad news. But we'd be very happy for you to make the approach to the Israelis. Mossad are much more likely to level with you chaps than with us. And in that way, you can control how much Mossad learns about your dealings with Kollek. All we're looking for is assurance that Mossad has Kollek under control, that they know where he is, and that they can vouch to us that he's in no position to do any damage to Gleneagles."

Bokus was looking intently at Tyrus Oakes. But Oakes wasn't looking at him; he was looking straight back at Fane.

"Okay, Geoffrey. I can see you're right."

Bokus shook his head in disgust.

Liz said, "Miles Brookhaven is in Damascus already, and he knows as much as the rest of us about the situation. Could he do it?"

"Absolutely not," said Bokus, looking despairingly at Oakes.

But there was no help coming from that quarter. "That makes sense," Oakes said. He looked at Bokus, and this time there was a hint of anger in his eyes. "Who else am I going to send, Andy? I can't very well send you to talk with the boys in Tel Aviv, now can I? Not when you're still insisting that Kollek's one of the good guys."

46

Time was running out. There were only five days left before the conference began, and Liz was getting nowhere in finding Kollek.

Then, just as she'd collected her afternoon mug of tea, onto her desk came Miles's report from Tel Aviv, marked URGENT. Twenty minutes later she was still reading, while her tea sat untouched.

At Teitelbaum's suggestion, they had met, not at the Mossad offices, but in a café on the edge of a small plaza in Tel Aviv.

Its equivalent in Damascus, thought Miles, who had only arrived the night before from Syria, would have been a dark hovel, cramped, filthy, foetid—and full of charm. This café was clean and neat, with metal tables and aluminium chairs, and utterly impersonal.

He'd had drinks the night before with Edmund Whitehouse, the MI6 station head in Damascus, and helped by his description, Miles spotted the Israeli at once. Teitelbaum was sitting at an outside table, under the edge of the café's awning, half in and half out of the sun. He wore a short-sleeved khaki shirt, open at the throat—the informal uniform of Israelis from generals to businessmen—and he was smoking a small brown cheroot and talking into a mobile phone. Looking at Teitelbaum, sitting there with his powerful forearms propped on the table, his bald head gleaming in the bright morning sun, Miles thought he was the spitting image of Nikita Khrushchev.

Teitelbaum put his phone in his pocket and stood up as Miles approached the table. They shook hands and Miles felt the man's hand squeeze his with momentary force, then just as quickly relax. See, the gesture seemed to say, I could crush you if I wanted to.

Miles ordered an espresso from the waiter, then said, "Thank you for seeing me."

Teitelbaum waved a dismissive hand. Then he asked, "You have flown from Washington?"

"No. I've come from Damascus." He wasn't going to lie; the old fox knew perfectly well where he'd come from.

Teitelbaum nodded. "Ah, our neighbours." He held up one arm, and Miles could see a long sliver of pink scar tissue, running in a faint crescent beneath the dark curly hair of his forearm. "I have always wanted to see the country that gave this to me. My relic of the Six-Day War." He looked without emotion at Miles. "Now tell me how I can help you and Mr. Tyrus Oakes."

Across the square a man came out of the doorway of a jeweller's shop. He was opening up, and bent down to unlock the steel cage-like grille that protected his window display. Miles took a deep breath and said, "Almost two months ago we received news of a potential threat to the peace conference that starts next week in Scotland. We were told that two individuals in the United Kingdom were working to undermine the Syrians' participation in the conference."

Miles couldn't tell how much of this was news to Teitelbaum, but at least he was listening carefully. Miles went on, "One of these men is a Lebanese businessman based in London. The other was a British journalist, often in the Middle East."

"You say he *was* a journalist?"

"That's right. He's dead. Apparently an accident, though some doubts have been expressed."

Teitelbaum pursed his lips. "What were these men supposed to be doing to damage Syria and affect the conference?"

"It's not clear, and we may never know. The Lebanese man is in custody now—he's facing charges over his business dealings, nothing to do with this. But it's convenient from our point of view that he's being held."

"Yes," said Teitelbaum, nodding slowly like a Buddha. "I can see that. And the other fellow is even more out of the way."

Here comes the hard bit, thought Miles, and waited as the waiter delivered his small espresso.

Miles sipped his coffee—it was bitter and scalding hot. He put two sugar cubes in and stirred the cup while he gathered his thoughts. He could see the jeweller across the way struggling unavailingly with the lock of his grille, then give a gesture of exasperation and go inside his shop.

"In looking into these two men, it was discovered that both of them claimed to be working for your service and one had ties with a member of your embassy in London."

"Oh," said Teitelbaum, as though there was nothing unusual about it. "Who was that?"

"His name is Daniel Kollek."

He watched Teitelbaum's face for a reaction. There wasn't one, which Miles took to be a reaction in itself. Teitelbaum said slowly, "I think I may have heard the name. But then, it's a famous name in this country—you remember the Mayor of Jerusalem."

"Kollek is attached to the trade delegation, apparently."

"Really?" said Teitelbaum with such a show of surprise that Miles was tempted to ask if he'd been to drama school. "But what would a trade officer have to do with such men? A Lebanese businessman and a journalist."

He's going to make me work for it, thought Miles. Every step of the way. "I thought maybe you could tell me."

"Me?" Now the surprise was even more dramatic. "I'm just an intelligence officer six weeks short of retirement, ready to crawl off to my place in a kibbutz. What would I know about this?"

Miles ignored this: Edmund Whitehouse had told him that Teitelbaum had been proclaiming his imminent retirement for the last ten years. Across the plaza the jeweller had reappeared with another man, and the two of them set to work on the recalcitrant grille.

Teitelbaum said sharply, "Tell me, who discovered this supposed set of connections? You or the British?"

"We've been working together on this," Miles said stolidly. What did the Brits like to say? *Keep a straight bat.* Well I'm trying, thought Miles, sensing Teitelbaum would otherwise do his best to drive a wedge between the United States and the United Kingdom, and through Miles's argument.

"Ari Block has not mentioned this at all," said Teitelbaum. Block was the Mossad station head in London, as Miles well knew.

"We haven't spoken to Ari Block."

"I'm surprised. It seems to me that if MI5 imagined that there was an undeclared Mossad officer working in London they would raise the matter with Mr. Block right away. Yet instead you're here, on a confidential mission arranged by Tyrus Oakes himself."

"Yes, but I'm representing the British as well. I'm here with their blessing."

"Ah," Teitelbaum said with a child-like appreciation that did not conceal his scorn, "what an *embarras de richesses* Mr. Brookhaven—to have Langley's authority and a British blessing." He closed his eyes, as if transported by the sheer bliss of the scenario. When he opened them, he gave Miles a sceptical look. "I would not dream of doubting you, Mr. Brookhaven, but I have to say I find your account of this . . . puzzling. And I don't see why it should involve my organisation."

"Oh, that's simple enough: we don't believe for a moment that Kollek is just a trade officer. And we're certain he was running Marcham." When Teitelbaum started to interrupt, Miles overrode him.

"But that's not all, Mr. Teitelbaum. In the course of this investigation, someone tried to kill an MI5 case officer who was directing the British side of things. They came very close to succeeding, too."

"That could have been the Syrians," protested Teitelbaum, though he looked taken aback by this news. "They've never been known for their restraint."

Miles was having none of it. Shaking his head sharply, he said, "Not in this instance. There was a Syrian presence we were worried about—trained heavies. But they've left the United Kingdom now and were closely followed while they were there. No, the attempt to murder the case officer had all the hallmarks of an individual effort."

"And you're accusing Kollek?" Teitelbaum demanded stiffly.

"I'm not accusing anyone. But we are concerned. And if Kollek is one of yours, which we believe to be the case, then we wanted you to know about our worries."

"In the hope that I can somehow provide you with reassurance?" There was a challenge in his voice.

"Yes," said Miles. There was no point denying it.

Teitelbaum was silent for almost a minute. He stretched the fingers on one hand, looking at his nails. Then he said at last, "Let us play hypotheticals for a moment, Mr. Brookhaven. Let us suppose, for example, that there is something in this idea of yours that Danny Kollek is not simply a trade officer. But that doesn't explain your concern, now does it? Both of these men you mention have had Middle Eastern ties—it might well be they knew things that would interest someone like Kollek, assuming as I say for the sake of argument, that he had auxiliary interests to his normal embassy duties. And there's certainly no reason to think he would have anything to gain by trying to kill an MI5 officer; the idea is insane. So just what is it you want to know about Mr. Kollek?"

Miles thought for a moment; he was determined not to be put off by this cunning bruiser. He said carefully, "The bizarre thing about this case is that we don't know whether the person behind it is working to hurt the Syrians, or to hurt other countries, or both. We're sure the person isn't Syrian himself, but whatever is motivating him has something to do with the place. So what I'd like to know about Kollek is if he has any kind of connection with Syria. I know it's a long shot, but there it is."

Silence hung between them, and for a moment Miles was convinced Teitelbaum was not going to answer his question. Miles saw the men across the plaza were still struggling to open the grille. There was something almost farcical about their continuing efforts.

Teitelbaum seemed to make up his mind. He looked at Miles with dispassionate eyes, and said simply, "Let me tell you a story."

47

Liz read on, completely absorbed by Miles's laconic prose. She was there herself, sitting in that Tel Aviv café, listening to Teitelbaum's hoarse voice telling his simple but haunting tale.

Danny Kollek's grandfather Isaac had been a Syrian Jew. A merchant, who traded in rugs and spice, and almost anything that kept his small shop in the ancient city of Aleppo afloat. He stayed in Syria after the War, and survived the murderous riots against Jews in that city in 1947, when synagogues had been burned down and shops, including Isaac's, destroyed.

Life had eventually returned to a semblance of normality. Never prosperous, Isaac nonetheless made a living, and was able to support his wife and sole child, a son named Benjamin.

But after Suez the climate suddenly changed again. Isaac found himself the object of an unofficial boycott by local residents, both Muslim and Christian, and the object of harassment by the government itself. Becoming increasingly anxious and fearing the worst, he sent his wife and boy to Israel, where they settled in Haifa and waited for Isaac to join them. He stayed behind to try and sell his business, and also, as Teitelbaum now acknowledged, "to help us."

After six months, just three weeks before he planned to join his family in Israel, Kollek was arrested. Tried on treason charges, he was found guilty, and six days later he was hanged in a public square in front of a silent crowd of Aleppo residents.

After this, his son, Benjamin, Danny Kollek's father, grew up in Israel, and became a successful retailer of electronic goods in Haifa. Teitelbaum had met him once, not long after young Danny—fresh from university, having served his mandatory years in the army—had been recruited into Mossad. In such a small society, the nature of Danny's job was hardly secret; certainly Danny's father knew—he told Teitelbaum it was the proudest day of his life when Danny joined Mossad. Because his son would be defending the imperilled state, home of the Jews? Not at all, replied Benjamin. Because his son would now be in a position to avenge his grandfather's death.

When Teitelbaum had finished, Miles sat for a moment in silence. Then he said quietly, "I wish we'd known about this sooner."

He said this more in sorrow than in anger, but Teitelbaum's eyes flared. "I wish you'd told us some things as well. I think you've known far more about Danny Kollek than you're letting on."

"What makes you say that?" asked Miles, sensing they were heading into dangerous territory. The one thing Tyrus Oakes's cable had stressed was that he must avoid explicitly admitting that Kollek had been run by Andy Bokus.

"Chance? Coincidence? I don't believe in them. Maybe it is a drawback of belonging to our mutual profession. But that's how I am." He was looking at Miles with hostile eyes. "So the idea that you and British intelligence have homed in on Danny Kollek through observation of two men said to be a danger to Syria, strikes me, frankly, as utterly preposterous."

Miles held his breath, not daring to speak. Teitelbaum gave him a small, sardonic smile, which added to Miles's tension. Then the Israeli said, "I think you know exactly what I'm talking about, Mr. Brookhaven. And if you don't, then I think you'll find your head of station, Mr. Bokus, can illuminate you."

You knew about Kollek, thought Miles, and a fresh wave of agitation swept across him. He had been struggling to keep secret something Teitelbaum had known about for a lot longer than Miles.

Teitelbaum gave a short squawking laugh, but it was without malice. "You look like a rabbit caught in a tractor's headlights. But cheer up, Mr. Brookhaven; I am not feeling so clever myself."

"Why is that?" Miles said hopefully.

"Because if Mr. Andy Bokus feels he's been taken for a ride, I have to admit I feel precisely the same way. He thought he was running Danny Kollek; I thought Danny Kollek was running him."

"*What?*" Miles was astonished. So Mossad *had* thought that Bokus was playing away—Danny Kollek had told them so. Jesus, this was becoming a nightmare, with individuals and entire agencies played masterfully by one twisted puppeteer. It was hard to believe.

Looking equally perturbed himself, Teitelbaum gazed into his empty cup, as if hoping to find something there to soothe his troubles. Sitting back, he clasped his hands and set them on his ample stomach. He said ruefully, "But I see now that I have been as big a fool as—if I may say so—your own head of London station."

"Why?"

Teitelbaum sighed rabbinically. Miles had the sudden sense that this man had seen more aspects of the human comedy than he ever would. The Israeli said, "Partly because of the things you have told me. But for the clincher, as I think you Americans like to say, you'd have to ask Danny Kollek."

"Happily," said Miles eagerly. "Can we call him in?"

"That won't be possible."

Miles's spirits sank. Had he misgauged the conversation? He had been starting to think Teitelbaum was on his side. Then he noticed the expression on the older man's face: he seemed to be enjoying some secret.

Teitelbaum said, "I am not being difficult, Mr. Brookhaven. You're more than welcome to talk to Kollek—if you can find him. We certainly can't."

"What do you mean?"

"Simply that Danny Kollek has disappeared." He stared at Miles, all amusement gone. "It looks as if we have a rogue agent." Just then there was a large bang across the plaza, and looking up Miles saw the jeweller looking triumphant, swinging the unlocked grille against the wall.

As Liz, in her office in London, finished reading Miles's report, she saw how they had all been fooled. Duped by false attachments, phoney allegiances, clever manipulation of national and Agency rivalries. All carried out and encouraged by one man. Who said the Age of the Individual was over? She reached for her mug of tea. It was stone-cold.

48

The Israeli embassy was a white stucco mansion at the High Street Kensington end of Kensington Palace Gardens, barely a stone's throw from the Underground. It took Liz fifteen minutes to get inside. She was asked for identification twice, was hand-searched and scanned, passed through a metal detector arch, had her handbag examined inside and out and only after all that was she allowed into a waiting room.

When she finally reached a room containing Ari Block, Mossad station head in London, it was both a surprise and a relief to find that he was a gentle-looking little man, with a soft voice and mournful eyes.

They sat down on opposite sides of a small, square table. Liz was under no illusion that this was his office. It was clearly a meeting room set aside for visitors who did not qualify to be allowed into the Mossad station proper. Ari Block was not a man to indulge in social chitchat. His voice had a sibilant, almost whispering quality as he said, "My colleagues in Tel Aviv have been in touch, so I know why you're here." A pained look came over his gentle face. "Unfortunately," he said, "I don't know where Danny Kollek is."

"Well, that means that no one does," said Liz. "But we do need to find him, for everyone's sake. I'm sure you will have heard from Israel that we have good reason to suspect that he may be planning some disruption of the Gleneagles conference. We don't know what, but at the worst it could be something very nasty indeed."

Ari Block nodded and said, "I have been instructed to be very frank with you, Miss Carlyle, but I have to tell you that I do not know Kollek well. He is nominally on my staff and he communicates with me when he sees fit, which I have to tell you is not very often. But unusually, his reporting line is directly back to Tel Aviv. It is not an arrangement I like or approve of. And from what I understand, it appears to have turned out to be disastrous."

"That arrangement enabled him to play his cards very close to his chest?"

"Yes. Though he gets on well enough with the other members of my team, he does not share information with them and he is not close to anyone. He can be very charming—when he wants to—but there is also something reserved about the man. A sort of coldness, even. To be perfectly honest with you, though I do not like having a member of my team who does not report to me, in one way it is a relief that I don't have responsibility for him."

Liz said, "What we're particularly concerned about is the peace conference next week. Does he have any involvement with the arrangements for your delegation?"

Block looked at her and his face flushed with anxiety. "Involvement? He most certainly does. On behalf of the embassy, he is in charge of all the planning for our delegation and its programme."

Liz found her jaw tensing involuntarily. "Has he been up to Gleneagles, then?"

"Yes. Last week."

"Did he go alone?"

"No. One of the embassy staff and one of my staff went with him. Wait a minute," Block said, "and I'll try and get hold of them." He picked up a phone on the table and spoke urgently in Hebrew.

While they waited, Liz took the opportunity to ask more about Kollek. "Does he socialise with any other members of the station or the embassy?"

"Not as far as I know."

"Where does he live?"

"In East Dulwich." Block had already sent two men to search his flat, but they had found nothing incriminating, and no sign of Kollek.

There was a knock on the door. A woman came in, big-boned, medium height, a little older than Liz, with a tired, haggard face. She looked nervous as she introduced herself as Naomi Goldstein. Without any explanation, Ari Block told her that they wanted to hear about her visit to Gleneagles. She looked puzzled, but asked no questions and started on a detailed minute-by-minute account of the two days she had spent there.

They'd had a lot to do, with all the domestic arrangements to confirm, everything from beds to bathrooms. They'd also had to tour the resort so they could brief the delegation on the leisure facilities for their spare time. If they had any, said Ari Block, pointing out that if the conference went well, everyone would be very busy indeed.

"And then, of course," Naomi said, almost as an afterthought, "there was the dinner to plan."

"What dinner is that?" asked Liz.

"Oh," said Naomi, as if she had spoken out of turn. She looked at Ari Block.

"It's all right, Naomi. We're working with Miss Carlyle," he said gently. He turned to Liz. "We've decided to host a dinner for the Syrian delegation the night before the conference begins. I am going myself. We're keeping it very quiet, so the press won't make an issue of it. The thinking is, if you've broken bread with someone, it makes it hard to go on wanting to break their bones." He added, "Doubtless that's why Judas left before supper."

Liz smiled. "Did the three of you stay together all the time you were at Gleneagles?" she asked Naomi.

Naomi thought for a moment. "Not the whole time," she said finally. "Danny went off on his own to do things a couple of times."

"Do you know what things?"

"No. And I didn't think it was my business to ask. Once he said he was going for a walk. The other time he just wasn't there." She was thinking hard and Liz waited. Suddenly Naomi raised a hand, as if to ward off anything that might upset her train of thought. "There was something odd about the second time. It was before we had dinner—we ate in the hotel on the second night. The first night I cooked in the house that we stayed in. Anyway, Danny was late coming back that second night, and I was worried about our table booking in the restaurant—I didn't want to lose it. Oskar and I set off for the hotel and I guessed we'd run into Danny on our way there. And sure enough we did. He was walking towards us along the road—it was quite dark—but as he got near I saw him combing his hair, which was odd because he's not the kind of man you see doing that in public. When we all got into the hotel, where it was bright, I could see that his hair was wet. Almost as if he'd had a shower—only he couldn't have, because he hadn't come back to the house."

"Had it been raining?"

"No. The weather had been quite bright."

"Is there a swimming pool there? He might have gone for a dip."

"That's what I thought at first, but he didn't have swimming trunks or a towel or a bag or anything like that. He was just in his ordinary clothes."

There was silence in the room. All three of them seemed to be thinking of the implications of what Naomi had seen.

Eventually Liz said, "Thank you very much," though she couldn't have said exactly what she was thanking her for. At least now she knew what she was going to do next.

4 9

iz was dead tired by the time she and Peggy got into the car that was to take them across the Thames to the Battersea Heliport. It was after nine o'clock in the evening and she had spent the time since she got back to her office from the Israeli embassy in a stream of telephone calls and meetings. But as she slumped into her seat in the car for the short journey, she had the comfort of knowing that an international operation was in place to thwart whatever plans Kollek had made to damage the conference.

She had started with DG, who had agreed without hesitation that as Liz had seen Kollek, and was best placed to describe him and identify him should he be sighted, she should go up to Gleneagles, taking Peggy with her as backup. In the absence of Charles, an emergency team had been put together to man the Thames House end of things, under the command of Michael Binding, the director of counter terrorism. Not a good choice from Liz's point of view; she regarded Binding as a pompous chauvinist, though she could hardly tell DG that.

During the afternoon, Binding had assembled his small team and they'd all been briefed by Liz. DG had himself spoken to the Head of Mossad in Tel Aviv to get his support. Geoffrey Fane had called Tyrus Oakes, now back at Langley, and had got his agreement to have the Americans represented in the team by a senior FBI officer from the embassy. "You can keep Andy out of it, with my blessing," he'd said. The security teams up at Gleneagles were contacted and alerted to the risk of a threat from a rogue Mossad officer. A4's photographs of Kollek in the stands at the Oval were sent up, together with some posed official pictures from his file at the Israeli embassy, which Ari Block produced. By the time Liz and Peggy had rushed home to collect enough clothes for a few days away, the ground was laid to defeat Kollek's plans.

But what those plans were, no one knew. As she climbed into the military helicopter, its rotors already roaring and vibrating, Liz had the uncomfortable feeling that, with all the backup in the world, it was still going to be up to her to out-think Kollek. She was glad she had Peggy to help her.

As the helicopter circled over the dark grounds of Gleneagles, lit only by the lines of lamps along the drives and paths, a dazzling square of light suddenly appeared below. The helicopter gently dropped and placed itself neatly in the centre of the landing ground, which was almost half a mile from the hotel on the edge of what looked to be a golf course.

Liz climbed stiffly out into the wind of the rotor blades, reflecting that whatever this hotel was normally like, it was now effectively an armed camp. A policeman cradling a Heckler & Koch rifle stepped forward out of the darkness and shepherded Liz and Peggy out of the helicopter's downdraught as it rose up in the air again and turned to fly off to the south.

In a small wooden hut, set up on what looked like a croquet lawn, Liz's and Peggy's documents were examined by a female police officer who offered a car to take them to the time-share houses where they were staying. "I think we'll walk," said Liz, glad to be breathing fresh air again.

"As you like," said the police officer. "I'll let the armed teams know you're coming, but keep to the paths where the lights are on. Everyone's on alert here; we don't want you getting shot by accident."

As opposed to on purpose, thought Liz wryly as she and Peggy set off. They had left a London that was warm, a late Indian summer. But now, in this Scottish evening, there was a crispness in the air that made them both shiver a bit as they walked. The faint smoky aroma of burning leaves added to the autumnal feel.

They passed the hotel, and then went out of its back gate, across a small road and into a development of modern stone houses surrounded by tall firs—time-shares during normal periods. They'd managed to acquire the last two remaining bedrooms in one of the houses commandeered by the MI5 protective security contingent.

The houses all looked the same, which was confusing at first, but thankfully Peggy with her usual thoroughness had printed a map off the hotel website. Liz waited on a small stone bridge across a little stream, breathing in the pine-scented air, while her younger colleague went off to check the door numbers and find their house. Peggy waved and Liz went to join her. They rang the bell. Nothing happened. They rang again and eventually the front door was opened by a man wearing a towel around his waist (and nothing else), his hair a soaking black mop.

Liz burst out laughing. "Hello, Dave."

Dave Armstrong had worked closely with Liz in the past when both were based in counter terrorism. They had become good friends; for a brief time, they might have become more. But since Liz's move to counter espionage, they had rather lost touch.

Now Dave did a double take. "Liz! What on earth are you doing here? They said to expect two more, but they didn't say who. And you've brought your secret weapon as well, I see," he added with a friendly nod at Peggy.

"We weren't expecting you, either."

"Binding," he said crossly, referring to Liz's bête noire, and seemingly now Dave's too. "He's seconded me to protective security during the conference. Come on in, and I'll show you your quarters."

There was a bedroom each for Peggy and Liz on the ground floor. Liz deposited her bag and freshened up, then went upstairs, where Dave, now dressed, was making coffee.

"How very comfortable," said Liz, joining Dave in the kitchen. "Pity we're not here for a holiday."

"I'm sure it fetches a pound or two," said Dave, "when it's not being requisitioned by HMG. You get great views of the mountains through these windows in daylight. The Israelis are in the ones down this row." He pointed towards their neighbours. "The rest have been allocated to assorted anti-terrorist officers, and the bigwigs from the military."

Peggy came up the stairs, and they all sat down at the dining table with their mugs of coffee. Dave said, "You two have certainly put the cat among the pigeons up here. We got the briefing paper and the photographs this afternoon. The old chief constable, who's supposed to be in charge up here, was already in a muck sweat, but now he's absolutely shitting himself."

"Oh God. Is he going to be a nuisance?" asked Liz.

Dave shrugged. "I'll be interested in what you think. He's scared of the Americans, doesn't like the English and acts as if women should never have been allowed the vote. Other than that, he's fine."

"You mean he's perfectly awful," said Peggy.

Dave grinned—he'd known Peggy since she had first been seconded from MI6, fresh-faced, innocent and very literal-minded. He seemed pleased she hadn't entirely lost these qualities. "Don't worry. Nothing your boss here can't handle. I can guarantee that her well-known charm will wear him down,"

"Do shut up, Dave," said Liz.

"I take it the Israelis know their colleague's gone bad?" asked Dave. "So if this guy Kollek does show up, presumably they'll pinch the bugger."

"Yes. They know now." Between Liz's visit to Ari Block, DG's conversation with Tel Aviv and the telexes Teitelbaum had promised Miles he'd send, there couldn't be any doubt among the Israeli delegation that Kollek had gone AWOL.

"What about the military and the foreign office and all the other security folk here?"

"Our beloved Binding is masterminding all the coordination from London, but in the morning Peggy and I will go round and make sure everyone's got the right information and knows what they're looking for. Insofar as any of us does," she added ruefully. "I'm going to bed now. It's been a long day—and it'll probably be a longer one tomorrow."

The chief constable in overall charge of security for the conference was a tall, gaunt man in his fifties wearing a uniform decorated with copious quantities of silver piping and braid. He sat at a large table in a makeshift command post that had been set up in the ballroom of the hotel, reading a document from a pile of papers. Behind him sat rows of police officers, some in uniform, some in mufti.

Liz recognised the man as Jamieson, from the Cabinet Office meeting, an occasion that now seemed months rather than weeks ago. She knew DG had rung to alert him to her arrival, and to tell him that she would brief him in detail on the threat from Kollek, so she was surprised at his manner when she introduced herself, even though Dave had warned her.

Jamieson hardly looked up from his papers, saying, "Just give me a moment, please."

Irritated, Liz surveyed her surroundings, while Jamieson continued reading. The ballroom floor had been covered by temporary planking and on it, dotted around the room, were a number of circular tables, which looked as though they normally saw service in a dining room. Each table bore the initials of a different part of the security operation protecting the conference—local police, the Metropolitan police anti-terrorist command, MI5, military intelligence. Each group had its own table, computers, telephones and communications equipment, and at each table casually dressed men and women sat tapping at keyboards, talking on phones and drinking coffee. And these were just the U.K. elements. The FBI and the Secret Service were in the room as well, but separated from the U.K. contingent by a low screen. Liz noted that the Secret Service had managed to commandeer twice as much space as anyone else. She looked round for the Arab and Israeli teams, but they must have been put in some other command post of their own. This looked like a coordination nightmare; she hoped Chief Constable Jamieson was up to the task.

As he showed no sign of finishing reading, Liz drifted over to the MI5 table where Dave Armstrong was in charge of a small team. "First round to the chief constable," Dave remarked as he offered her his chair. She ignored him and walked round the table to see what was up on the screens. She talked to a junior colleague for a few minutes, then an emissary from Jamieson came to say that the chief constable would see her now. "Kill him, Liz," said Dave in a breathy whisper, as she walked back with the policeman, her footsteps echoing loudly on the planking.

Brushing an impatient hand across his greying moustache, Jamieson said, "Yes, Miss Carling, what can I do for you?"

"It's Carlyle actually, and we've met before, Chief Constable, at the planning meeting at the Cabinet Office."

He sniffed, but said nothing in reply. Liz wondered how much more of this she was going to take. Not a lot, she decided. She said, "I believe my director general has been in touch about a new threat that is particularly concerning us."

"Yes, he rang me last night," Jamieson said grudgingly. "You'll appreciate we have a lot of potential threats right now, Miss Carlyle. What I suggest is that you talk to my deputy, Hamish Alexander, who will produce a risk assessment for me." He gestured to the tables behind his back. "We'll consider it with all the others at our planning meeting this evening."

"We may not have until the end of the day. This requires your urgent attention."

Jamieson shook his head wearily, as if he had heard this all too often in the last few days. "Young lady, I have to prioritise."

The "young lady" did it for Liz. "Has Sir Nicholas Pomfret arrived yet?"

"Yes," he said, looking directly at Liz for the first time. "Why?"

Liz sighed. She'd had this kind of conversation before. On the last occasion it had been with Michael Binding of Thames House. Life might have changed unrecognisably for a professional woman in the past thirty years, but you still met the occasional dinosaur. She said mildly, "I ask because either you and I can discuss this now and agree what to do, or I'll telephone the director general at Thames House, who will then call Sir Nicholas, who will then have a word with you. I'm happy to take that route if you prefer, though I'm sure everyone else involved will think it's a waste of their time."

"Are you trying to push me around, young lady?" he demanded.

"I wouldn't dream of it; I'm merely asking for cooperation. And I'd appreciate it if you would not call me 'young lady.' I'm old enough *not* to be your daughter."

For a moment, Liz thought Jamieson was about to explode, but then some seed of sense must have planted itself. He seemed to think again, and quickly altered his demeanour. "Sorry if I was short. It's just I seem to have the secret services of God knows how many countries trying to tell me what to do. And half of them barely speak English."

"It must be a nightmare," Liz said, trying to show a sympathy she didn't feel. "Now let me make sure that you are fully briefed about this particular problem."

She described Kollek as a Mossad renegade, highly intelligent and trained in covert techniques. She explained his background and the fear that in some sort of revenge for his grandfather's death, he was going to try to sabotage the conference, possibly focusing particularly on the Syrian delegation. In case Jamieson was not up to date, which seemed only too likely, she told him that a brief and photographs had been circulated on intelligence channels. She gave him his own copy of the photographs, suspecting that whatever information loops were operating in the room, he was not necessarily a part of any of them.

Liz said, "I'd like the photographs circulated very widely among all the security on the ground at the hotel, please, and also on the perimeter. It would be very helpful if the local police in the neighbouring towns could have them, too. This man Kollek has been here before, so he knows the layout well. I'll be talking with the hotel managers myself, so you can leave the staff side of things to me. I can't stress too highly that this is a real danger. We don't know where this man is, but we and the Israelis believe he has serious intent."

Jamieson nodded tensely. He looked pale and was rubbing the palms of his hands together nervously. A picture of stress, thought Liz. This was obviously the biggest responsibility Jamieson had ever had; sadly, he seemed to be drowning rather than rising to it.

She went on: "If Kollek's seen, I want him detained and put under guard. If he's stopped, he's certain to have a plausible cover story and all the proper credentials, but on no account should he be allowed to go on his way. He may well be armed, so people should be careful. Kollek's very smooth, but he's also lethal—we think he killed one of his own agents in London just a few weeks ago, so he won't hesitate to kill again."

She was glad to see that she had Jamieson's full attention now. By the time she left the ballroom, she was satisfied that not only did he now take the Kollek threat seriously but he was unlikely to think of much else. His initially patronising manner had infuriated her, but at least he was on board now, and that was the important thing.

The hotel manager, Ian Ryerson, occupied a small windowless office behind the arcade of shops on the ground floor of the hotel, just round the corner from the ballroom command post. He was a dapper man in his forties, with a bland smile and an affable manner that could have been pressed into service in resorts anywhere from the south of Spain to the golf-laden stretch of coast between Fort Lauderdale and Miami.

In welcome contrast to the chief constable, he was eager to help, though it soon transpired there were limits to the assistance he could provide. Yes, Kollek had been up to Gleneagles, he confirmed, and he had toured the facilities with two others from the Israeli embassy.

"Can you tell me exactly what they asked to see?"

Ryerson looked embarrassed. "I'm afraid I can't. You see, I didn't give them the tour. I was rather taken up with the Americans."

"Secret Service?"

He nodded dolefully. Liz gave an understanding laugh. "Could I speak to whoever did show them around?"

"Of course," he said. "It was young Dougal; he's been here only a year. But he's very good," he insisted, lest she think he had fobbed off the Israelis on an incompetent junior.

Summoned by phone, Dougal joined them, looking like a school-boy called to the headmaster's study. He was a gangly youth, with a mop of ginger hair and a serious expression that made his youthful face look oddly middle-aged. Ryerson explained vaguely that Liz was involved with security arrangements.

"We're just checking up on a few things," Liz said casually. "No big deal. I gather you escorted an advance party of Israelis. Can you tell me about them?"

"That's right," said Dougal, starting to relax, since the headmaster's cane was nowhere in sight. He described Naomi and Oskar, then, more hesitantly, the third member of the party, a man they called Danny.

Liz picked up on this. "Tell me about this Danny. Was there anything in particular you noticed about him?"

Dougal thought for a moment. "Nothing I could put my finger on. Except that . . . he seemed more . . . detached. I kept thinking he was looking for something. As though he had some idea in his head that he wasn't letting anyone else in on."

"What sort of idea?"

Dougal shrugged helplessly.

"Was it about the dinner the Israelis are giving the Syrians? The night before the conference."

"I haven't been involved with the dinner. Sorry."

"If it wasn't the dinner, was there anything else he might have been concerned about?"

"Not really. Other than the entertainment, I mean."

"There's entertainment?" said Liz, trying to stay calm. Naomi at the Israeli embassy hadn't said anything about entertainment.

"Well, yes," said Dougal. He looked worried, as if he'd suddenly realised he'd done something wrong. "Falconry and gundogs."

When Liz looked puzzled, Dougal explained how demonstrations of each were going to be given for the guests before the dinner began.

When he'd finished, Liz said crisply, "This afternoon I'd like to visit both the schools."

"Of course," said Ryerson. "I'll ring ahead so they'll know you're coming."

"And I wonder if you could spare Dougal to come with me. That way, we could retrace their steps precisely, and speak to the same people Kollek talked to."

Ryerson agreed. Then Liz took a copy of the photograph of Kollek from her briefcase. "There's another thing. I'd like this circulated among all the staff here at the hotel. If any of them had contact with Kollek while he was here I'd like to know right away. Anyone from the cleaners of his house to a barman—if they remember seeing him, or talking with the man, please ask them to report it immediately. I'll give you my mobile number so you can pass on any reports you get."

"There's a large number of staff, Ms. Carlyle, so it may take a little while—" he said, then stopped speaking as he stared at the photograph Liz had put on his desk. He looked up at her with thoughtful eyes. "He looks familiar," he said.

"You may have seen him when Dougal was showing him around."

"I was busy with the Americans then. I didn't meet any of the Israelis—I didn't have time."

"Still, you might have crossed paths during his stay."

But Ryerson was shaking his head. "No, it wasn't then. I think he was here once before. I remember the face—he was alone, though, I'm sure of it. Here in the hotel. It wasn't that long ago, either. Within the last couple of months."

"Is it possible to check the register of guests? See if you can spot him."

"I was just thinking that. We don't get that many single men staying—though if he was borrowing one of the time-shares, from a friend say, we wouldn't necessarily have any record of him."

Ryerson was obviously pummelling his memory, trying hard to remember when he'd seen Kollek. Liz waited hopefully, but he shook his head. "No, it's gone. But let me go through the register and get back to you."

5 0

iz met up with Peggy at the golf clubhouse, which was in use until the dinner the following day as a sort of officers' mess for the security contingents. They ordered lunch from the bar menu—Liz a sandwich, Peggy a small side salad. "Is that going to be enough to get you through the afternoon?" asked Liz.

Peggy nodded. "I've put on a few pounds lately, thanks to Tim. He bought a pasta machine, and it's been fatal. If I never saw handmade ravioli again, it wouldn't be too soon."

They sat in a conservatory-like annexe that overlooked the last undulating hole of the famed King's Course. The eighteenth green sat like an emerald oval amidst the yellowed grass of the fairways, bleached by the long hot summer.

Peggy plonked a stack of papers on the table. "These are the itineraries for all the delegations," she announced with a sigh. "I'm not sure where to begin."

Liz put her hand on the stack of pages. "I think we should get Dave's team to put those onto one big spreadsheet so that we know where everyone is at any given time. You may find they've done it already. In general, there's no point trying to duplicate what the security people have already done. For the moment, I think we should concentrate on the Syrians' schedule. After all, they are the only specific target that we know Kollek might have. Anything strike you there?"

"Just the dinner here in this restaurant tomorrow."

"That, certainly. But there's to be some sort of entertainment before it. It's being planned by the Israelis to amuse the Syrians. Something to do with birds and dogs, I gather. It seems Kollek was interesting himself in it. I can't think why that Naomi woman didn't tell me. I'm going over to the falconry school and the gundogs after this and find out exactly what they're going to be doing tomorrow. If Kollek's planning something to happen while their demonstration is on, then maybe we can work out what it might be."

"Do you think he'll try to do something himself? He must know now that we'll all be looking for him."

"I just don't know. It would be very difficult for him; the outer security cordon's going up today. I've made sure his photo is being circulated to everyone—provided old Jamieson doesn't sit on it."

"How did you get on with the chief constable?" asked Peggy. "Was he as bad as Dave said?"

"I'll tell you all about him tonight. But I think I sorted him out."

Peggy grinned. "I'll bet you did." She added, "What if Kollek's hidden himself somewhere?"

"I can't see it. Between the police and Special Branch and the Secret Service, there isn't a room anywhere in the entire resort that hasn't been checked, and checked again. The same goes for any explosive device he might have tried to put in place—every inch of interior space will have had sniffer dogs and detectors all over it."

"So what could he do then?"

"I reckon there are only two options. One is that he somehow attacks the Syrians from outside."

"What, with a mortar?" Peggy sounded horrified.

"Too imprecise. He'd have to get within the perimeter cordon to be confident of a shell even landing in the grounds."

"Then a helicopter, or is that too far-fetched?"

Liz shook her head. "I wouldn't put anything past Kollek, but I don't think he'd have a chance of doing that. There's a strict no-fly zone except for conference traffic—he'd get shot down before he even got within sight of this place."

"Hang glider, balloon, microlight?"

"All those things are possible. I suspect he's determined enough, and quite possibly mad enough, to try anything. But I'm pretty sure the protective cordon on the ground and in the air would pick any of that up. And he'll know that."

"Well, that's a relief at least." But Peggy still looked anxious. "What's the other possibility?"

"That he has someone inside to do something for him."

"An accomplice?"

"Possibly, though I'd doubt it was a full-blown partner. Kollek's too much of a lone wolf to take anyone into his confidence. But it might be someone helping him unwittingly."

"Someone in the Israeli delegation?"

"I don't think so. They've all been questioned about Kollek, and briefed in case he gets in contact. More likely someone here at Gleneagles. I've asked the manager to have all the staff interviewed, just in case Kollek struck up a friendship with one of them. The other possibility is Hannah Gold—he cultivated her and then got her invited here."

"Has she arrived?"

"I don't think so, and I'd like you to find out when she's due, and where she's staying—she mentioned a B and B in Auchterarder. While you do that, I'll head off for the falconry school."

As she got up from the table, she saw Dave Armstrong coming into the restaurant. When she waved he came over. He was wearing jeans and trainers and an army-issue olive sweater.

"Have you been on manoeuvres?"

He laughed. "It feels that way. I've been out there with the army." He pointed out the window to the foothills in the middle distance. Clouds were rolling in now, and the bright sunshine of the morning had given way to grey.

"How far is it to those hills?" asked Liz.

"I'd say two or three miles."

"Can a sniper operate at that distance?"

"Funny you should ask. I was discussing that very issue with the brigadier this morning. He said that even five years ago, the answer would have been no. Now it's not so clear cut—the usual terrifying advances in arms technology. You'd need to have been trained as a sniper and have the right rifle, of course, and there'd be an element of luck involved. But it's doable. That's why we've extended the perimeter to the crest of those hills. They'll be patrolled."

"There's a lot of ground to cover."

"I know. But we've got three platoons coming to cover it."

"This one's name is Fatty," said McCash, the handler. "You can see why."

Liz tried to look appreciatively at the eagle, which seemed about three times the size of the other birds of prey. It was brown and black with white stripes on its front shoulders, and had an evil-looking curved yellow beak. It perched like a small fat tank on McCash's outstretched hand, which was encased in a leather gauntlet with a reinforced thumb.

Liz and McCash stood about thirty yards from the school, where birds sat in their individual cells, peering out through the barred windows, glaring enviously at Fatty's freedom. Next to Liz was a flat wooden platform, about the size of a doormat, perched about five feet off the ground on top of a wooden upright. There was a twin as well, roughly fifty feet away. McCash gently extended his arm over the platform and put down a motionless Fatty.

"Follow me," said McCash, and they moved towards the other platform. Liz glanced nervously behind her as they walked; she didn't fancy being attacked from behind by that beak. But Fatty sat as immobile as Simeon Stylites on his pillar.

Using his ungloved hand, McCash reached into the pocket of his Barbour jacket and drew out a small piece of lean meat. He put it on the platform, explaining, "Grouse. It has to be raw—they can't digest anything cooked. Or anything vegetable for that matter. If you feed them pigeon, and the pigeon's been eating grain, they'll regurgitate the grain."

He moved away and Liz went to stand next to him. Turning towards Fatty he clapped his hands loudly. At first, there was no reaction from the bird. Then slowly, almost imperceptibly, it leaned forward and lifted itself up on its two taloned feet. It hesitated, took a small tentative step, then seemed almost to tumble off the edge of the platform.

For a moment Liz thought it would hit the ground, but with one immense sweep of its wings it stayed airborne and began to lumber slowly towards them, staying above the ground by little more than the height of the two platforms. The bird reminded Liz of an immense aeroplane she'd read about in a magazine. Called *The Spruce Goose*, it had been built by Howard Hughes in the 1940s. It flew only once, and that for only about five hundred feet. Those watching its inaugural and final flight had found it hard to believe it would ever get off the ground.

But it had—and so had Fatty. Nearing the target platform, Fatty spread its vast wings and lurched half a foot skywards, then landed with a heavy *whoomf* on the wood, where it immediately scoffed the titbit of grouse and looked round hungrily for more.

McCash laughed. Liz had been there twenty minutes and was beginning to get impatient. She had asked McCash about the programme for the next day, and this demonstration had been the result. Apparently something of the same sort was going to happen, and then the guests would be invited to fly the falcons themselves, if they wanted to. It was difficult to imagine how any real harm could be injected.

She turned to McCash. "Did you meet the Israelis when they came to set this up?" She felt that if she allowed him to pursue his bird obsession much longer, she might as well leave the service and join up as an apprentice falconer. And she still hadn't got to the gundogs.

"Funny people," McCash said now. "There was a woman, not interested in the birds at all. Don't know why she bothered coming down here. Then two blokes—one was a little pipsqueak of a man; he was scared. Don't know why."

I do, thought Liz, looking at Fatty's sharp beak and ferocious talons. "What about the other man?"

"Ah, he was interested all right. Though not in the birds, more the technology. He wanted to know how we could be certain the birds would come back when we unhooded them and let them fly off. I told him, we can't be certain—that's why we've got a transmitter in every bird."

Liz was listening carefully. "Tell me about the transmitters, will you?"

McCash gave her a look. "You're as bad as him. That was all he wanted to know about. It's simple really. If they don't come back, we can go and find them—it's like an old-fashioned tracking device, the sort of thing James Bond sticks on the villain's car. The closer you get, the louder the beep on our detector. It's just a chip inserted beneath their skin—doesn't hurt them. The problem is, they were designed in the States—Utah, I've been told." He gestured towards the surrounding hills and trees. "This isn't exactly similar terrain. The manufacturers claim the transmitters are good for up to twelve miles. Around here, it's much less. Thankfully, when the birds don't come back they're usually just sitting in the trees over there."

"Is there any way it ever works in reverse?" McCash's look made her feel stupid. "I mean—" she began to explain, when her mobile rang in her coat pocket. "Excuse me," she said, and walked away a little.

It was Ryerson, the manager. "I've found him!" he exclaimed excitedly.

"Who?"

"Kollek. I knew I'd seen him before. He was a guest in the hotel a month ago. Only he wasn't called Kollek then. Glick was the name he signed in as. Samuel Glick. He was in room 411. Would you like to see it? It's been allocated to an American, but he's not due until this evening."

"I'll be there in five minutes," said Liz. "Please don't go in the room until I arrive."

She made her excuses to McCash and set off for the hotel ballroom. This time Jamieson paid her prompt attention, and when she emerged from the hotel lift on the fourth floor, she was accompanied by a sniffer dog and his handler, two armed anti-terrorist officers with explosive detection equipment and a uniformed local bobby.

Waiting outside the door of the room, Ryerson looked taken aback to find Liz arriving with an armed entourage. He held out the key to the room and an armed officer took it and cautiously opened the door. It was a spacious room, with light streaming through from its western window. She stood back and let the men get to work. Turning to Ryerson, she said, "Are you sure it was the same man staying in this room?"

"I'm positive it was the man in the photograph you showed me. He paid with a French credit card—one of the girls behind the desk was new so I had to come out to reception and confirm it was okay. That's when I saw him."

"Well done. Now, do you know which American is meant to be staying in this room?"

"Yes, it's somebody from their embassy in London."

"The ambassador?" Her heart beat slightly faster.

"No, no," he said, as if this was out of the question. "*He's* in a suite."

"Of course," said Liz, suppressing a smile. But she was also remembering how the IRA had operated in Brighton. "What about on the floors above this room? Are there suites up there? Is the President or the Prime Minister staying directly above this room?"

He thought about it for a moment, but shook his head. "No, they're just rooms, too."

Liz peered in. One of the men was moving a machine along the far wall, following the trail of the sniffer dog and its handler. Catching Liz's eye, the anti-terrorist officer shook his head. In the middle of the room, the bobby was standing with a bewildered frown on his face;

the second anti-terrorist officer had disappeared into the bathroom. Suddenly from there she heard a shout. "Come in here a minute."

Liz walked in to find the officer lowering himself down from a hole in the ceiling. He landed lightly on his feet and extended an open hand, palm up. "Look at this," he said, puffing slightly.

It was a crumpled wad of cardboard, roughly half the size of an egg carton. "There's a crawl space up there," he said triumphantly. "It's where the air-conditioning vents run through. Somebody's left this behind."

Liz took the cardboard out of his hand and gently squeezed it until it bore a faint resemblance to its original box-like form. There was writing on the box in Hebrew, and numbers.

From behind a hand suddenly reached for the small carton, and Liz turned to find Dave Armstrong. "Let me have a look," he said. He examined the box carefully. "The Hebrew doesn't mean much to me. But the numbers do." He held the box up in the air gingerly. "This held rifle shells. 7.62mm, or .308 to our American friends. They're weighted, designed for a sniper rifle."

51

After the day's excitements, Liz went back to the house feeling tired and anxious. It was as though she were stalking Kollek—walking in his footprints. But they were old footprints, made weeks ago, and she had no sense that she was getting anywhere near the man himself.

She still had no idea where Kollek was or what he was planning to do. The discovery of the shell box in the ceiling of room 411 was alarming. But if the security perimeter remained in place and was effective, Kollek was not going to be able to get close enough to hit anyone with a sniper rifle. And he must know that. Unless he was there already, she thought, before the cordon was put in place . . .

though if he were, he would have been flushed out by now. Dave had gone off to talk to the brigadier again, armed with the shell box.

She found Peggy upstairs in the kitchen, tending an enormous boiling pot and chopping lettuce for a salad. "I hope you didn't want to go out to eat," Peggy said.

"I think I'd fall asleep before I'd even ordered. Thanks for cooking. What is it? It smells good." She sniffed.

"It's . . . pasta."

"I thought you said you'd never eat pasta again. Don't tell me you brought Tim's machine along?"

"No," said Peggy seriously. "I got it in the Co-op in Auchterarder." Then, looking up, she realised Liz was teasing. "I've made enough for Dave if he wants to eat here."

"What about the others?" asked Liz. "Who else is around?"

"I don't know, but I said any of our lot could look in. Some of them are working all night. By the way, I've been to see Hannah Gold. She's installed in the White Hart at Auchterarder. No word from Kollek, but she'll let us know right away if she hears anything. She's coming over here tomorrow to join the peace movement people and meet the Israeli delegation. She's also been invited for drinks before the dinner—though not to the dinner itself."

"Is she going to this entertainment I've been hearing about?"

"She didn't say anything about it. So probably not."

"Okay," said Liz. She could talk with Hannah tomorrow. Just now all she wanted was to eat supper and look at the newspapers Peggy had bought in the town. She sank into the soft sofa in the living room and had just picked up the *Guardian* when the doorbell rang.

"It's probably Dave," said Peggy, as Liz started down the stairs. "I think he left his key in the hall."

But when Liz opened the door she found Dougal, not Dave, standing outside.

"I'm so sorry," he said, looking troubled.

"Come in, Dougal. It's no problem."

They went upstairs, but Dougal refused to sit down, standing uneasily on the carpet in front of the fireplace. "I'm so sorry, Miss Carlyle," he said again and Liz realised it was not the interruption of her evening he was apologising for, but something else he couldn't yet bring himself to say.

"What's the matter?" she said bluntly.

"I just forgot," he said, looking anguished. "I don't know how it slipped my mind."

"Dougal," Liz said sharply, "what is it?"

He looked at her in surprise; Liz realised he had been so consumed by guilt that he had assumed she must know its cause. "The man Kollek, of course. I saw him, that evening after I'd shown them around. He was by the equestrian centre. With Jana." He put his hand to his forehead. "How could I have forgotten?"

"Steady on," said Liz. "Now sit down, Dougal, and tell me everything you saw." Behind him, she could see Peggy tactfully busying herself with supper. "Who's Jana?"

"She's a waitress in one of the hotel restaurants. She's Czech," he said, with a sudden softness to his voice that made Liz think that he must admire her from afar.

"What did you see exactly? What were they doing?"

"They weren't *doing* anything—that's not the point. I could tell from the way they were talking to each other that they *knew each other.*"

"Are you sure about that? You couldn't be . . ."

"Imagining it? No way. I know Jana. There was something between them. I'm sure."

Liz realised there was no point in grilling young Dougal. He'd made up his mind, formed some impression that couldn't be verified, but which was quite likely correct—he seemed very certain. After a moment's thought she asked, "Where is Jana now?"

"At this minute, you mean? She's in the trattoria," Dougal said. "She'll be serving dinner there at least until eleven."

Liz looked at her watch; it was eight-fifteen. She wondered whether to wait until the dinner service was over, or get the girl pulled off her shift straightaway so she could talk to her. There was a risk in waiting.

"Dougal," she said, "is Mr. Ryerson around?"

"Yes. He'll be in his office. He's always there in the evening, in case there's a problem."

"Tell me," she asked. "Is he in charge of the whole hotel? I mean, I know the restaurant will have a maître d', but is Mr. Ryerson in charge of him? If something goes wrong is it Mr. Ryerson who gets called in?"

"Oh yes. Once a guest came in drunk and Tony refused to let us serve him. When the guest cut up, Tony had to call in Mr. Ryerson. He's in charge of everything when there's a real problem. It could be the golf course or the falconry centre—doesn't matter. Mr. Ryerson's the one who decides. He likes to say 'the buck stops here.'"

"All right, Dougal. I'm going to go and find him now. And thank you very much for remembering this. It could be important."

Dougal left, looking happier than he had when he arrived.

She looked at Peggy, who pre-empted her before she could say anything. "I'll cook you some more pasta when you get back."

Unless you were really ill—you couldn't be sick over a customer—you never left your shift. Even in the rough informality of the Moravian tavern, her mother had taught Jana a professionalism she had always stuck to. If you show up for work, you work.

So she had resisted at first when Tony, the maître d', had asked her to leave her tables and go to Mr. Ryerson's office right away. He'd been insistent, and he cut her off when she'd started to object. "I'll wait on your tables myself. Now go."

She felt nervous as she approached the office, and part of her wanted to walk right past the door and head off . . . where? Back to Moravia, to a mother who would say *I told you so* for the next three, or even thirty-three years? No, she couldn't do that, but she sensed trouble lay ahead behind the closed door.

When she knocked, Ryerson called out "Enter" in a grim voice that didn't bode well. She opened the door hesitantly, and felt more nervous still when she saw that Ryerson had someone with him. A woman, probably ten years or so older than her, but trim, attractive—and watching her closely with cool, green eyes.

"Sit down please, Jana," said Ryerson, and she did, facing the two of them. "This is Miss Falconer. She'd like to ask you a few questions."

Jana steeled herself. I have done nothing wrong, she thought to herself, hoping this simple mantra would help—and that it was true. Oh, Sammy, she voiced silently to herself, not even sure if that was his real name, why aren't you here? He had been so confident and knowing. Please God, let this not be about him, prayed Jana.

But it was. Jana knew as soon as the woman named Falconer began to speak. "We're looking for a man," she said quickly. "We believe he stayed here at the hotel, and we have reason to believe you may have been in contact with him."

"Contact?" asked Jana. She thought it best to play dumb for now, pretend she didn't know why they had called her in, didn't understand what this woman was getting at. "I am a waitress, so I see many people, miss. Is that contact?"

"Of course," said Miss Falconer, with an easy smile Jana found disconcerting. "But we're talking about close contact. I'm sure you know what that means."

Jana decided to say nothing. Miss Falconer put a photograph down on the desk and pushed it towards her. "Have a look, please. Have you ever seen this man?"

Jana took her time, but she could see from a glance that the photo was of Sammy. She felt panic moving like an army of ants along her limbs. She was surprised to be pinned down so quickly and accurately. She said faintly, unable to put force in her voice, "I think I've seen his face. Was he a guest here?"

Miss Falconer ignored her reply and said flatly, "You waited on him two nights in a row when he first came here. He was alone, so it would be odd if you didn't remember him, Jana."

The use of her Christian name jolted her. She felt increasingly exposed. Sammy had said he would be nearby, but no one was to know—"hush-hush" he had insisted. Now she tried to shrug.

"The thing is," said the Englishwoman, "we know you know this man. You were *seen* with him. And not in the restaurant."

"What do you mean?" She wanted to sound indignant.

"What was his room number?" Miss Falconer asked sharply.

"Four—" And Jana kicked herself. She felt trapped. "It was only conversation. He had lived in Slovakia," she said, making up the first thing that came to mind. "He spoke Czech. So we talked, that is all."

Miss Falconer smiled, but it was a knowing rather than a friendly smile. Yet her voice softened. "Jana, I know there are rules, and of course they have to be followed. Breaking them once isn't the end of the world. But not telling me the truth now would be very serious indeed."

"I *am* telling you the truth." She paused, wondering how much to give to this woman. "I was in his room." There, she thought, let them make what they liked of that. No one else could know exactly what had happened in room 411.

"All right, so you had an affair with this man."

"I did not say that." How did this woman know so much?

Miss Falconer was shaking her head. "No one's criticising you for that."

Jana was frightened to think where this was leading. Then she realised that if they knew everything, they wouldn't be pressing her like this. Should she come clean? she wondered. *No,* she told herself harshly. That way led only to trouble—she would lose her job, maybe even worse. She could be deported, forced to return home and face the sneers of her mother. She could think of no worse fate.

So give a little, she thought, and hope that would satisfy this woman with the penetrating eyes. Playing on her sympathy would not be enough. There was something steely about this woman, cold and business-like. She would throw her a bone, the same way you chucked a titbit at a barking dog and kept the sirloin safely tucked behind your back.

So she hung her head, forcing tears into her eyes, then looked up defiantly, straight at Liz. "Have you never been in love?" she demanded, letting the tears overflow from her eyes. She had played her trump card and sensed she had played it very well. Let this woman think she was a fool, an innocent, a dupe; let her think anything she liked, so long as she didn't discover what else Sammy had asked her to do. I've got to tell Sammy he has to get out of here, Jana thought, wondering just how "nearby" he was.

52

P oor girl," said Peggy, stifling a yawn.

"I don't know so much about that," replied Liz, twirling her wineglass of sparkling water by its stem. She'd come back from her interview with the Czech girl dissatisfied, and she needed to understand why. Even though she wanted to go to bed and get a good night's sleep to help her cope with whatever the next day would bring, her mind was racing.

"She sounds like a classic victim of a honey trap, only this time it was a man doing the trapping."

Liz shook her head. "I'm not sure. There's something hard and calculating about that girl. I don't see her being taken in that easily."

"Girl?" asked Dave teasingly. He looked half asleep himself, slumped at the end of the sofa. "If I called her that you'd be jumping down my throat."

"No I wouldn't," said Liz. "She is a girl. She can't be more than eighteen or nineteen. Which I know makes her look like the innocent victim of a ruthless man. But there's something about her that doesn't ring true. I'm not sure she wasn't just peddling me a line."

There was a noise outside and Peggy stood up and walked to the window, lifting the corner of a curtain to look out. She turned around with a startled look on her face. "There's a man with a gun out there!"

"He's Israeli security," said Dave calmly. "They would come only if we let them mount their own patrols. They don't trust anybody else—not since the Munich Olympics. And I know their Prime Minister's already here."

"Really? I didn't see a helicopter or a motorcade or anything," said Peggy.

"Low-key. He came a day early. They like to mix things up, so nobody knows for certain in advance who's where when."

"That must be a bit of a problem for all of you doing the conference security," said Peggy, sitting down again.

"We cope," Dave replied, yawning hugely.

Liz said nothing. She was still brooding on her interview. "What could she have been holding back?" Peggy said, trying to be helpful.

"I don't know. She was too quick to get all weepy and pathetic. I didn't believe it. It just didn't ring true somehow. So tomorrow, Peggy, will you keep tabs on her? It's too late to get A4 up here to do it and anyway there may be nothing in it. We can't detain her—we've got no grounds. It's not a criminal offence to have a fling with a customer, though I imagine the hotel may take a dim view of it once we've gone."

"If you're so worried, couldn't we arrange for her to have the day off?"

"It'll be easier to keep an eye on her if we know she's working at lunch and dinner. And I don't want her to think just yet that I suspect her of anything more than what she's told me. No, I'd like you just to know where she is in the afternoon, after she finishes the lunches, particularly where she is as it gets near the time for the entertainment before the dinner at the clubhouse. Okay? You can reach me on my mobile; I'll be around the hotel until I go into Auchterarder to meet Hannah for coffee at eleven."

Peggy nodded and Dave gave a loud sigh. "So now you've got something else to worry about," he said. "As if this sniper business wasn't bad enough. I'm meeting with perimeter security, the army blokes and the Secret Service right after breakfast."

"Why the Secret Service?" asked Peggy.

"Most of the delegations are arriving by car; they'll fly to Edinburgh and drive up. But not the President—he's coming in by chopper. The plan had been for him to land on the King's Course—right in the line of those hills you've got me worried about. I think we're going to move the landing pad, just to be extra careful."

"That makes sense," said Liz. "Though I'm wondering whether we're having the wool pulled over our eyes."

"But don't forget that cartridge box," Peggy protested.

"That's what I mean. It just seems so obvious," said Liz. "Kollek's never been sloppy before."

"Except at the Oval," Peggy reminded her.

"That was a lot of luck on our part. He could easily have gone undetected."

"Are you saying there isn't a sniper threat?" asked Dave.

Liz thought for a moment. There was no point in ignoring the potential danger from a long-distance assassin, whatever her instincts told her. "No," she said. "I'm just worried that that's not the only threat."

. . .

Liz dozed fitfully; the more she thought how much she needed rest, the harder it was to go to sleep. She found herself poring over every aspect of the case, trying to make sense of the bewildering clues Kollek had left behind. She wished there were someone she could talk to, to help her resolve the pattern of this weird jigsaw, of which she had only some of the pieces.

The chief constable wasn't any use; Geoffrey Fane might have fitted the bill but he was still in London. She needed someone sympathetic and intelligent, with lots of experience of untangling this kind of complicated puzzle. Someone like Charles, she thought with a pang. But he'd be at home now, nursing Joanne through her final days; there seemed no doubt that this time she really was dying. She couldn't disturb him. Would he be wondering how they were all getting on? Would he be thinking about her? The thought of that cheered her momentarily, but then she told herself sternly that Charles would be focused on Joanne, just as he should be.

She lay dozing, her thoughts tugging her to and fro until, when she saw the digital clock by her bed reach 6:00, she gave up. Dressing quickly, she went upstairs quietly to make herself coffee, only to find Dave already in the kitchen, in a long white towelling dressing gown. As he heard her behind him, he turned around and smiled. "You too, eh?" he said sympathetically, and she nodded.

An hour later she left the house as daylight was creeping in on a grey blanket of cloud. A cold wind had turned the previous day's hint of autumn into something stronger, and as Liz walked towards the hotel she tightened her raincoat belt around her waist.

Overnight, security had greatly intensified, in expectation of the delegations arriving later in the day. Armed police in bulletproof vests conspicuously patrolled the grounds; on a rear-access drive to the kitchens two dark vans were parked—bomb-disposal units. Everyone Liz passed was wearing the now-mandatory photo ID. As she stopped at the checkpoint at the rear entrance to the hotel she overheard a member of the kitchen staff complaining that he'd been sent home to collect his before they'd let him in.

Even this early, the security centre in the ballroom was humming with tension. The Secret Service agents were looking extra-smart, in crisp suits and polished shoes.

She spent twenty minutes with Chief Constable Jamieson reviewing the arrangements for the Israeli-hosted social events with the Syrian delegation. Security had been beefed up without Liz's even having to ask for it; while she sat with Jamieson, she was gratified to see that even the Secret Service was not allowed to interrupt.

Later that morning the delegations began to arrive. By then Liz had spent more time at the falconry centre, reviewing the planned demonstrations with McCash, ensuring that the entire building and even its feathered occupants would be checked again by explosives experts. She made it to the gundog centre at last, where with the dog handler, a cheerful curly-haired woman, she reviewed arrangements for the canine part of the early evening entertainment. Two out of an endless assortment of ebony Labradors had been selected to retrieve decoys that would be placed in the middle of the little lake a hundred yards away. The handler proudly brought out a larger dog, mocha and white, with a speckled, ugly face but, so it seemed, an almost supernaturally powerful nose. He'd be showing off his skills too.

Walking back to the hotel, Liz was in time to witness the first procession of three black Mercedes limousines moving sombrely down the gravel drive. The bigwigs were arriving. In the background hovered a flotilla of vans and 4×4s containing their accompanying entourages, waiting for the statesmen to be formally greeted before they disgorged their passengers. Next to them were the vans of the television networks, parked there for days already.

She stood and watched as the three limousines eased to a halt on the circular gravel turn at the entrance to the hotel. A porter in a tweed jacket and kilt stepped forward and opened the door to the middle saloon, and a man in a suit and tie got out of the car. He was an Arab, young-looking, tall and thin, with a moustache. From the hotel entrance a man Liz recognised as the Israeli Prime Minister came down the steps to greet him. As their bodyguards looked on, the two men shook hands, though it was noticeable that neither smiled.

Liz had arranged to be driven the three miles to the little town of Auchterarder, where Hannah was staying. As her car drew up outside the small hotel in the long main street, she saw Hannah standing on the steps. She was casually dressed, but with her usual understated elegance—a sage cotton raincoat, heather-coloured slacks and a fawn jumper with a roll-neck top.

"Come inside," she said. "It's quite quiet at the moment. It's usually buzzing—the whole peace delegation is staying here, but the others have gone on a trip out this morning. The place isn't much; not quite the Gleneagles standard. But they do a decent cup of coffee."

They walked into a gloomy lounge, all dark wood and brown upholstered chairs, where a cheerful young girl in a white lace apron took their order. Liz was surprised to find Hannah, usually the most bubbly of women, quiet and subdued, and Liz wondered if her surroundings were getting her down. But as soon as their coffee arrived, she learned why. Hannah said, "Peggy told me all about Danny Kollek. I feel absolutely mortified. How could I have been so taken in?"

"Oh Hannah, you mustn't feel that," said Liz, with genuine sympathy. "You weren't the only one. And that includes a lot of people who are paid not to be fooled. The important thing is that now you know he's working against everything you believe in. He'd destroy this conference given half a chance. That's why it's so crucial that you let me know at once if he gets in touch with you."

Hannah nodded, and reaching into her coat pocket put her mobile phone on the table between them. She sighed. "So far nothing," she said. Her face sagged slightly as she asked, "I realise it wasn't my scintillating personality Danny was attracted to, but what do you think he really wanted?"

Oh dear, thought Liz, she is taking this hard. "I don't know the answer to that. He probably did enjoy your company, you know. But I suppose he was hoping your connection with the peace movement could help him prevent the very thing you're trying to achieve—peace. But how might he try to do that? That's what I'm puzzling over at the moment."

"I never mentioned you to him," said Hannah.

"I'm sure you didn't," said Liz reassuringly, but it struck her that the older woman sounded slightly defensive. So she asked, "Did he know about Sophie, though?"

Hannah blushed and looked away.

"I . . . I might have said something," she admitted. "I thought it was all in the past, you see—Sophie left her job years ago. So I didn't think it could possibly matter if I told him. I suppose I thought he'd be interested." She looked anxiously at Liz. "Oh God, did I screw that up as well?"

Liz reached forward and put a reassuring hand on Hannah's arm. "Not at all," she said soothingly, though now she could see how Kollek had put two and two together. Perhaps he'd wondered whether Sophie was still working for MI5, or at least whether she was still in touch. He must have watched the house, seen Liz visit, probably followed her, discovering where she worked, then where she lived, until in a fake minicab . . . she shivered involuntarily at the thought of the close call she'd had. At least now she knew why it had happened.

Suddenly Liz's phone rang. She picked it up, and as she listened to the voice on the other end, her attention shifted away from Hannah and the gloomy Scottish hotel lounge to the green hills behind the golf courses and what had been going on out there.

53

Mateo didn't mind the climb; in fact he was quite enjoying it. It was difficult to get much real exercise working in the hotel and his short body was getting podgy. But walking up hills was no effort to someone who'd grown up, as he had, in a city on a hillside, where the simplest walk—to the shops, to a tapas bar to meet friends—always involved a steep climb. The gentle roll of these Lowland hills was nothing to him.

But something was spoiling his enjoyment. He was bothered about what he was doing out here in the hills. What was the purpose of his trek? His instructions had been clear: walk south along the A823 and then, where a small stream passes under the road, turn off along a footpath and climb west just as the hills begin, then turn down a track and head north back towards the hotel. The directions were precise: when he turned back along the track, he was to stop after a third of a mile in a little wood that he would reach just after a stream so small he could easily jump across it. The trees were nearly all spruce and fir, it had been explained, so he'd see the only ash tree, hidden by its taller neighbours, once he had entered the wood. It was thirty-five paces from the mound of stones at the entrance of the wood.

Collect the package you'll find at the tree, she had said, and then walk with the sun directly on your left and you'll come back to the edge of the hotel grounds. She would be waiting for him on the southern edge of the golf course, near the tenth tee. Unless he got lost, she'd added tauntingly, he'd be back in time for the lunch service.

When she'd first asked him, he had been unwilling and suspicious—drugs, he had thought. With all this security around, it just wasn't worth it. But Jana's flattery—*I know you are a strong man of stamina*—had been working on him from the start.

Not to mention the money. She had promised to pay him £500. He didn't believe her at first, but she'd shoved the roll of notes under his nose, riffling their edges with her thumb like a deck of cards. His father had died the previous year, and his mother was doing her best to bring up his two younger brothers back in Ronda. If he could send her even half this money, it would make a huge difference.

So he'd squashed his doubts, and as he marched up the hillside, avoiding the clumps of fading purple heather, pushing his way through the high grass, he was thinking of what the money would buy. He was glad he'd worn jeans and not shorts as he brushed against a thistle hidden in the grass. The wind was picking up, and when the low cloud blotted out the sun, it was cold. In Ronda he would be sweating from this walk; here he was glad of his pullover.

He had asked Jana what this strange mission was about, but she'd said from the start that there were two rules: he would get half the money up front, half when he'd completed the task; and he wasn't allowed to ask any questions. He'd insisted on asking one, though—could he get into trouble with the law? Jana had been emphatic: No, only if he insisted on knowing more about it.

In ignorance lay innocence, then, and any qualms Mateo had still felt had been assuaged when Jana had put half the roll of bills into his shirt pocket. And by the kiss she'd given him (he could still feel her lips on his) and by her murmur that he could have "the rest"—and he didn't think for a moment she was talking about £250—after he'd done this for her.

He saw the pile of stones as soon as he reached the crest of the hill, and quickened his pace until he was almost running downhill. The ground levelled off and he slowed down as he entered the small patch of woodland, peering now in the gloom as the sun disappeared behind the thick foliage of the trees. He stopped, waiting until his eyes had adjusted to the dark, and walked slowly, counting. *Four, five . . . fifteen . . . twenty . . . thirty . . .* and before he reached thirty-five he saw the ash tree. Smooth-barked with horizontal branches, bearing leaves rather than needles. As instructed, he looked up and there, on the second branch, perhaps a dozen feet above the forest floor, he saw the package. A long black case, like a thin sports bag, tied to the branch by a carefully spun cocoon of dark green rope. Clever, he thought. You had to look hard to spot it.

He took a deep breath, then lifted himself up in one great heave onto the lowest branch, balancing carefully. Reaching up and feeling with his fingers, he found the knot securing the rope around the case. He used both hands then, teetering for a moment until, managing to steady himself, he undid the knot and pulled the rope slowly as it unwound, slithering around the case until it dangled like a snake from the higher branch. He reached up and grabbed the case by its handle, sliding it carefully off the thick branch. It was so unexpectedly light that he almost lost his balance, but gathering it to him, he half slid, half climbed down onto the soft earth below.

When he emerged on the far side of the wood clutching his prize, he was half blinded by the rising sun to his left, and he stopped to wait for a moment until his eyes had readjusted. But oddly they didn't, and as he blinked, he realised that there was another source of light. It was then he heard the helicopter, as it suddenly appeared over the next hill, low and hovering, with a soldier in its open side door swivelling a mounted gun barrel in his direction and a spotlight shining from its undercarriage with amazing intensity.

Instinctively he turned away from the light and it was then he saw the soldiers—a dozen or more, crouched down along the edge of the wood, their weapons pointing towards him. They were close—maybe a hundred feet away—and coming closer fast, so he didn't even think of running, but raised his hands high in the air, letting the case fall onto the pocket of grass, and wondering if Jana had been betrayed as well.

54

It took Liz no more than five minutes to break through the Spaniard's resistance. He was being held in a caravan set up on the outer edge of the King's Course for the sentries' breaks. By the time she arrived, the platoon leader, a lieutenant named Dawson, had already questioned him. Fruitlessly.

Faced by Liz, the boy at first stuck to his story. His name was Mateo Garcia, he worked in the kitchens of the hotel and he had been out for a walk in the hills when he'd been swooped on by a helicopter and surrounded by armed soldiers. What was he doing carrying a rifle case? asked Liz. He'd found it in the woods; he shouldn't have taken it, he knew, but he had. No, there had been no rifle there. Sorry, he told Liz contritely, but there wasn't anything else to say.

This was no time for subtlety. "I don't believe a word you say," she said sharply. "It will be much the worse for you if you don't tell me the truth now. Do you understand?" Lieutenant Dawson, who was standing close beside his prisoner, moved forward threateningly.

The boy sat back in his chair nervously, unsettled by the ferocity of her tone and the implicit threat from Dawson. He gave a slight nod. Good, thought Liz, knowing that even that small affirmative was a step forward. She went straight on. Holding out a copy of Kollek's photograph, she said, "I want to know when you last saw this man. And what it was he asked you to do."

Reluctantly, Mateo reached out for the picture. As he examined it, Liz watched his face carefully for any flicker of recognition, but there was none—Mateo just looked scared.

"I have never seen this man," he said as if he were swearing an oath. "I don't know who he is." Either Mateo was a gifted actor, or he genuinely didn't know Kollek. Liz's instincts told her that the Spanish boy was telling the truth. Yet she didn't believe for a moment that he had gone into the hills for a walk. So what had he been doing? Why was the rifle case empty and where was the gun?

There was very little time to think—in half an hour the Syrian delegation would be enjoying the hospitality of their long-standing enemies, the Israelis. "I believe you," Liz said. Mateo looked relieved. There was only one other possible angle Liz could try. "But," she added, "your friend Jana knew this man. She was working for him, wasn't she?"

The boy's face froze, and Liz knew she was onto something. "Didn't she tell you?" she demanded, letting her voice rise.

He shook his head feebly. Liz pressed on. "What did she tell you that you were doing, out there in the hills? What was it all supposed to be about?"

Panic filled his eyes, and Liz thought for a moment he was going to cry, but then he seemed to pull himself together. She pressed on quickly, keeping up the pressure. "We know how she was involved," she declared, all too conscious she was bluffing. "But how much do you know? I warn you, you're walking on very thin ice. If you don't cooperate with me and quickly, you'll be on a plane tomorrow to Spain—you'll never set foot in this country again and you'll be spending some interesting time with the Guardia Civil."

She hated dishing out threats she knew she couldn't carry out, but she needed him to talk and this was the only way. *I hope he doesn't know too much about his rights*, she thought.

The boy was clearly terrified now, but was he scared of her or of someone else? She could sense him wavering, trying to make up his mind what to do. Then, to her great relief, he seemed to decide that she was the bigger threat. His voice cracked as he said, "I didn't know why she asked me to go there, except what she said, to collect a package. I know nothing about this man; you must believe me. I trusted her when she said I wasn't to ask any questions."

"And she paid you?"

He nodded, looking beaten and pathetic. "It's my mother—" he started to say, and the words hung limply in the thick air of the caravan.

She'd got everything she could out of him; Mateo was just a pawn. She left him with Dawson and his men, who would hand him over to the police. Outside the caravan she found Dave Armstrong waiting for her, sitting at the wheel of a golf buggy.

"I thought this would be quicker than walking everywhere," he said.

"Good idea. We need to get to the falconry centre right away. The demonstration there will be starting soon."

"What about the rifle? Did the kid say anything? Does he know where it is? There are three platoons out on the hills now searching for it—and for a sniper."

"I don't think there is a rifle or a sniper. But it's right to go on searching, just to be sure—and to take all the obvious precautions. But I think Mateo was a decoy, being used to distract us. Which he certainly has." She reached impatiently for her mobile and hit the key for Peggy.

Peggy answered at once. "Yes, Liz."

"Where's Jana now?"

"Apparently she's ill and lying down in her room. Though when I checked with Ryerson, he said she's almost never ill. Maybe it's the stress of your interview."

"I doubt it. How ill is she supposed to be?"

"Well, it can't be too bad. She worked the lunch shift and then took a walk after it."

"Where did she go?"

"She walked through the tennis courts, then came back a few minutes later to the back of the hotel." Liz realised with a jolt that this route would have taken her right by the falconry school. Peggy said, "I kept at a distance, or she'd have seen me. I just wanted to make sure she wasn't leaving the hotel grounds."

"Has she been out again this afternoon?"

"No, she's stayed in her room. I'm sure of that; I've been in sight of the staff quarters all afternoon."

"I'm going to need to question her again." Liz looked at her watch—there wasn't time to do it now. "Please make sure she stays in her room. If she tries to leave, I want her to be detained. Make up an excuse, we can sort it out later. But I don't want her anywhere near the Syrian delegation. Go and see Jamieson straightaway, and make sure you've got backup available if you need it. And be careful with this woman—she's slippery and she may be dangerous."

Liz was making it up as she went along now. She felt like a goalkeeper taking penalties, with no idea where the ball was going to be kicked next. Dave had driven the buggy across the fairways and they were now coming up to the road that ran past the clubhouse. On the far side armed policemen were stationed every twenty yards. As the golf buggy moved onto the asphalt surface a policeman stepped forward and halted them with a raised arm. Dave braked sharply.

"You can't cross here," the officer said.

"We have to," said Liz sharply. "It's urgent."

He shook his head. "Hear that?" he said, and somewhere in the sky Liz could detect the rumbling blades of a large helicopter. "That's the Prime Minister," the policeman said. "And ten minutes later we're expecting the U.S. President. We've moved the landing zone," he added, pointing to the vast green lawn that lay stretched between them and the hotel.

"I know," said Dave curtly. "It was me that moved it." He pointed to the identification tag on his jacket. "We'll go around the landing strip but we need to cross the road."

The policeman hesitated.

"Call Mr. Jamieson if you like," said Liz, "but get a move on. We're in a hurry."

"No, it's okay," he said. He stepped back onto the road and let them through with an elaborate wave of his hand, to show his colleagues farther down the road that they were crossing with his approval.

Dave pushed the little buggy to the limit of its speed, and they crossed the road and bumped over the crisp turf of the pitch and putt course. The throbbing bass of a helicopter's rotors was now clearly audible, and looking east Liz could see it, less than half a mile away. A landing area the size of an Olympic swimming pool had been hastily marked out with white tape and chalk lines; fifty yards back, ropes were strung to keep the waiting press corps at a distance.

A squad of Secret Service men in dark suits were waiting on the edge of the landing zone. Behind them a covey of British security officers gathered behind a stone balustrade, like commanders watching a battle from a distance. Around the edges of the field armed policemen patrolled, two with Alsatian dogs on short leads.

As Liz and Dave crossed the last corner of the pitch and putt course, another golf buggy pulled out sharply from the path ahead of them, heading in their direction. Next to the driver sat the gaunt figure of the chief constable. He had told Liz he would be personally supervising the security at the falconry and gundog displays, so what was he doing here? Liz tapped Dave's arm and he slowed down until the other buggy stopped next to them.

"All's fine back there," said Jamieson, jerking his thumb to indicate the falconry school. "The delegations are arriving now. I'm off to see the President land—the Secret Service johnnies are insisting I be there. They're in a bit of a state about this rifle that's been found."

There is no rifle, thought Liz. But she didn't have time to argue with the man. He said blithely, "You'll find my deputy Hamish is watching things over there."

As they drove through the last line of trees onto the grassy square in front of the falconry building, she saw phalanxes of security men surrounding the two arriving delegations.

Dave parked at the end of the building as Liz walked quickly down the slope of grass to the area set up for the display. The two delegations were lined up side by side, not mingling—except at the front, where the Syrian President was talking, a little stiffly, with the Israeli Prime Minister. Near them, Liz noticed a balding bull-like man chatting to Ari Block, the Mossad head of London station. Block spotted Liz and gave a small bow.

Hamish Alexander, the chief constable's deputy, was standing on a slight rise, overlooking the small crowd of spectators. He looked dismayingly young but seemed competent—pointing out the armed policeman at each corner of the square, and explaining that behind the small copse of oaks and birch that formed a backdrop, more policemen were stationed as an extra precaution against anyone who had somehow penetrated the perimeter.

The front door of the falconry school opened and McCash came out with a golden eagle perched on an extended gloved hand. Appreciative noises greeted the bird, though as McCash made his way through the crowd of spectators it parted, as people moved back to avoid the razor-sharp talons and beak.

"Look at the size of him," said Dave appreciatively.

"He's called Fatty," said Liz with a grin. But she added tensely, "Dave, I'm nervous about this."

McCash began the display with Fatty, who flew the lumbering solo that Liz had already seen. There was faint laughter from the crowd as the golden eagle seemed just to manage to land on the second platform.

McCash handed Fatty to an assistant as another colleague came out, bearing a hooded hawk. This was the bird intended to be flown by the Syrian President himself, who looked distinctly unenthusiastic when it was explained to him what he had to do.

Dave said, "I overheard one of the Syrians saying the President isn't actually that keen on falconry."

So it wasn't true all Arabs like birds of prey, thought Liz. So much for stereotypes.

As soon as McCash unhooded the falcon, the bird flew straight up in the air, to McCash's obvious surprise, then it tilted, turned and moved like a bullet towards the nearby copse of trees. There it disappeared behind the dense foliage. McCash's face fell, and the spectators watched, puzzled, uncertain whether this was part of the display. McCash signalled towards the falconry school, and an assistant came running out, holding a small device in his hands.

"Young Felix is playing games with us," McCash announced in his soft Highland voice. "But we'll soon have him back. All our birds are electronically tagged, so we can find them when they go AWOL."

Liz could see that McCash was making the best of an embarrassing situation by pretending that nothing had gone wrong. But something *had* gone wrong, she knew, only she couldn't make out what. Alert as she was for something unexpected to happen, the disappearance of the bird made her uneasy. Why had it flown so swiftly off into the wood? What was it doing there? Could Jana have tampered with it in some way during her afternoon stroll? Liz knew that the homing device couldn't call the falcon—it could merely locate it—but she would relax only when Felix returned.

As McCash's assistant moved closer to the trees, Liz could hear a distinct *beep-beep-beep* from his tracker. She had to act. "I want a man ready to shoot down that bird," she said to Hamish Alexander.

He was amazed. "Shoot it down?" he said. "Whatever for? It's only a bird."

"Yes, but it may be doing something dangerous. We can't take the risk," she said without hesitation. She looked around—Jamieson was nowhere to be seen, doubtless having his photo taken with the American President, and she saw no other senior officer in the immediate vicinity. There was no time to worry about her authority to order shots to be fired.

Alexander hesitated, then seemed to make up his mind. He beckoned to one of the armed policemen standing near the door of the school.

McCash's assistant had reached the wood now and he went in among the trees with his hand held high, holding the tracking device. Its beeps were louder; the bird must be very close. What was it doing there? Liz wondered again tensely.

Suddenly there was a rustling and the sound of beating wings and the assistant ducked as the falcon came shooting out of the copse, flying just above his head and aiming straight for the delegations. Then it turned, going straight up like an arrow. As it reached the top of its climb and slowed, Liz could see something metallic dangling from its beak.

The armed officer was standing beside Hamish Alexander waiting for orders. Liz said sharply, "Get ready."

The bird sank slowly on the faintest hint of thermal and moved in a wide descending curve towards them. It passed over the heads of the spectators, all of whom were looking up into the sky, staring at it in fascination. Now the hawk was heading directly towards the Syrian President. The policeman gripped his weapon tightly and swung its barrel up, pointing at the sky. Liz was on the brink of ordering him to fire when the bird suddenly cut sharply back on its own trail, flying at what looked an impossible angle, losing speed until it was directly above McCash. Then out of its beak it dropped the silver package, which tumbled down through the air in a blur until it landed with a soft plop on the grass.

Before anyone could move, McCash bent down casually and picked up the shiny package. He held it aloft and said drily, "Felix has still to learn that this is a no-smoking zone." In his hand was an empty packet of cigarettes, its silver packaging the flash that had glinted in the sun. The audience laughed appreciatively.

Liz, who had been unconsciously holding her breath, let it out in a deep sigh. Her legs were shaking with tension. "That was a close one," said Dave. "I thought for a minute you were going to shoot the President. But well done anyway."

After this false alarm, Felix and the two other birds brought out to join him all behaved in an exemplary fashion. The Syrian President flew Felix briefly, looking uncomfortable, then the Israeli Prime Minister had a go; finally, McCash showed off a falcon that snatched food on the wing from the handler's bare fingers.

As the display finished, Liz left Dave to retrieve the buggy and walked briskly towards the small lake at the end of the grounds, where the gundog demonstration would take place. She was tempted to skip it and head straight for the clubhouse, to make sure nothing had turned up in the distant hills, and that the extra security was in place for the dinner.

Her phone vibrated in her pocket. It was Hannah's voice excitedly saying, "Liz, I've heard from him."

"What did he say?"

"He didn't ring. It was a text. I can't make any sense of it. I've forwarded it to you just now."

Without breaking her stride, Liz looked intently at her mobile's tiny screen. The message was short: *Tell your British friends they should be looking where Kings play—and beyond. The hills are alive . . .*

Balls, thought Liz angrily. He's late. He doesn't know we've caught the Spanish boy. He's trying to distract us, as he has been all along. More than ever, Liz was determined not to play Kollek's game. For far too long she'd allowed this rogue agent to run the operation. Rapidly she got on to Peggy to have Kollek's call traced. But it would take too long. Something was going to happen soon. She was sure of it now. Why else would Kollek have sent the text to Hannah? But what was going to happen and where? Was he here now? She had no answers and her only hope was to keep alert and trust her instincts.

5 5

Where was Sammy? All afternoon she had waited for him in her room. She'd followed his instructions and put the jam jar of flowers on the windowsill the previous evening, in full view of anyone outside, just as he had told her. But he still hadn't come.

It was time to move to what he'd called Plan B. He'd said that if she didn't hear from him within twelve hours of putting out the flowers, she should go back to the group of pine trees behind the equestrian centre at exactly five o'clock and wait there, hidden in the trees, until he showed up.

She'd left her room once that afternoon to see if she was being watched. She couldn't tell for sure: there'd been a young woman in the distance, wearing blue trousers and a black jumper, who seemed to be hanging around by the tennis courts; when Jana had come back from her short stroll, the same woman had been standing outside the staff dining room.

Jana looked at her watch. It was ten to five; by the time she'd walked through the grounds she would be right on time. That was unless someone tried to stop her. The thought increased her anxious need to see Sammy. He would tell her what to do; he would know what she should say if the English security woman questioned her again.

She looked round the room for a weapon—she would do whatever it took to get to her meeting with Sammy. Spying a paperweight on the side table, she picked it up, feeling its weight in her hand. It was roughly the size and shape of a tennis ball that had been cut in half and was made of thick glass, with a snow-covered forest scene painted inside. She remembered how she had once seen Karl, the tavern owner back in Moravia, knock an obstreperous drunk unconscious with a cue ball from the pool table. The paperweight would do; she put it in the pocket of her jacket.

Locking her room behind her, she looked up and down the hall—empty. The other staff were already preparing for the dinner service. It was as she stepped out into the small courtyard that she saw the same young woman from the tennis courts watching her from a back doorway to the hotel. She was wearing a coat now, but Jana knew it was the same person.

Maybe it's just coincidence that she's there, thought Jana, as she set off quickly towards the back of the hotel. But she hadn't taken more than a few steps before a voice behind her called out. "Jana. Stop, please."

She turned around to find the young woman coming towards her. How did she know Jana's name?

"Yes?" she said, trying to sound more sure of herself than she felt.

The woman was approaching her, holding out her ID card. "I'm from security. I'm very sorry, but I'm going to have to ask you to go back inside."

"What on earth for?" Jana demanded, trying to sound confident, the way people spoke in the television dramas she'd seen. She wanted to look at her watch, suddenly fearful that if she were even slightly late, Sammy wouldn't wait.

"I know it's a nuisance," said the young woman sympathetically. "You see, the American President's helicopter is about to arrive, and there's a no-go zone until he's safely inside the hotel."

"But I am going the other way," said Jana, pointing.

The young woman was shaking her head. She still had a half-smile on her face, but her voice was unyielding. "Doesn't matter. The no-go zone extends all round. Sorry."

Jana was thinking fast. There was no other exit from the staff quarters. If she went back to her room she'd be trapped there and would miss her meeting with Sammy. "All right," she said, and turned as if to go back. Then suddenly she pivoted and started to run towards the road behind the hotel. But to her surprise the young woman proved faster than she was, and with three strides she'd grabbed onto Jana's left arm.

"Stop!" the woman commanded.

Jana tried to yank her left arm free, while her right hand reached into her pocket for the glass paperweight. Letting herself be pulled towards the woman, she suddenly swung her right hand in a vicious arc. The other woman tried to duck but was too late, and the paper-weight struck her a smashing blow above her eye, then fell to the ground where it broke into pieces. Blood poured down one side of her face.

Unbelievably, she still refused to let go of Jana's arm. Turning to face her adversary, Jana clawed out with her right hand, grabbing the woman's cheek with her fingers and pinching as hard as she could. As she felt the woman let go of her left arm, she lashed out with that hand as well. The other woman fought back, blocking most of the blows and landing one of her own on Jana's chin. But Jana was taller and heavier, and slowly the woman gave way under the ferocity of the assault. The fight was moving them towards one end of the courtyard, and when the woman's back touched the wall of the hotel Jana suddenly lunged forward, planting both hands on her throat, choking her. She needed to get her out of the way so she could see Sammy, and she squeezed her hands tighter and tighter as the woman struggled to breathe. Yet just as Jana thought the woman must pass out, she seemed to summon a final burst of energy. Rearing her head back she thrust herself forward, and her forehead landed with a sickening crunch on the bridge of Jana's nose.

The pain was agonising. Jana dropped both hands from the woman's throat and stumbled backwards, then fell down onto the floor of the courtyard, completely dazed. She struggled to get up, but a pair of arms was holding her down—a man's arms, strong enough to turn her round until she was pinned facedown on the paving.

Jana could hear but not see the other woman gasping for air. "Thanks, Dave," the woman wheezed.

"You were doing all right without me, Peggy," said the man as he tightened his grip on Jana's arms. "Who the hell taught you how to give a Glasgow kiss?"

5 6

Ahead of her the water in the lake lay like a dark smear. The banks were low and grassy, and at the end nearest the clubhouse where the dinner would later be held was a large square of closely mown lawn—on every other day it was one of the tees of the pitch and putt course. It was here that the delegations would stand to watch the gundog display. Two trestle tables had been set up, covered by white tablecloths. Bottles of soft drinks, fruit juice and sparkling water sat next to a small army of glasses; discreetly in one corner stood half a dozen bottles of white wine.

When Liz arrived the dog handler was already there, holding two slim black Labradors on leads, with the German pointer sitting motionless next to her. The President of Syria was talking on his mobile phone as he walked towards the tee, accompanied by his London ambassador and surrounded by bodyguards. As the Israelis arrived, he snapped his phone shut and turned towards the Israeli Prime Minister, grinning broadly. At least that's going well, thought Liz.

"Tell me," said Liz to the dog handler, "are you the only person who's been with these dogs today?"

"That's right. They get far too excited if I let strangers near them on a show day."

Her reply was firm, but Liz wasn't satisfied and she asked again, "So you are absolutely the only person to have been in contact with the dogs?"

"Yes. I said so," she replied, with a flash of irritation. But then she paused. "Well, except for one of the foreign girls in the hotel. Her mother's got a German pointer back home and she misses him, so she likes to come and see Kreuzer. I let her help me feed him. Why, is something wrong?"

"I hope not," said Liz, frowning. "What's the girl's name?"

"I don't know," the woman replied. "I've never asked her."

I can guess, thought Liz, as she moved back through the people now crowding round the tables, though I hope I'm wrong. She took up a position on a slight incline just below the road and as the delegates moved closer to the lake, Dave joined her. They stood together, watching intently.

The handler clapped her hands and the visitors grew silent. She explained in a loud, cheerful voice that the two Labradors she held on their leads were going to demonstrate their prowess at literally pulling the water off a duck's back. Liz noticed the Syrian President laughing appreciatively, showing his command of English—or Scottish, she thought, for the woman had the musical accent of Scotland's west coast.

In the middle of the lake, some ten yards from its small island, a young man sat in a small rowing boat. At the handler's signal, he threw two life-sized mallard duck decoys into the water. They landed with a splash, then turned upright and bobbed on the surface.

Unleashing both dogs, the handler blew her whistle in a short soprano burst, and the pair sprang forward, entering the water without hesitation, swimming like happy kids at a summer camp. As they neared the rowing boat, they suddenly altered their course, homing in on the pair of plastic ducks. Each dog seized one by the tail, then together they turned and began the trip back to shore, the rowing boat following them in. As they reached shallow water they slowed down, and, back on dry land, they ran to the handler, placing the decoys gently at her feet. On the green tee the audience clapped politely. The Syrian President seemed pleased; the Israeli Prime Minister, anxious until then, now looked pleased as well.

When the applause died down, the handler faced the crowd again. "The next display is something different—it's to demonstrate how the nose can be more important than the eyes for dogs. I've hidden another decoy on that island." She pointed to the lake. "It's completely invisible. But Kreuzer here is going to find it."

She snapped her fingers at the brown and white pointer. At once he trotted to the water's edge and waded straight in.

Suddenly Liz's anxiety increased. Something about the trainer's remarks was bothering her. What exactly was it that Kreuzer was trying to find? She made her way quickly through the spectators until she stood next to the handler. Kreuzer was moving smoothly through the ruffled water of the little lake—not even really a lake, thought Liz; not much more than a pond.

"So Kreuzer will find your decoy purely by smell."

"Yes. He's got the most marvellous nose. On a grouse moor you often can't see where the bird drops, because of the heather, but with a dog like this it doesn't matter. The Israelis told me that they thought the Syrian President would be particularly interested—it seems he shoots a lot."

Liz watched as the dog reached the island and scrambled up onto the low clumps of marsh grass. It began circling, its nose on the ground, and soon it was heading for the solitary tree.

"Oh no," the handler groaned.

"What's wrong?"

"He's gone right past it. I buried it about three feet from the bank where he got out of the water. What's wrong with him?"

But it was clear that Kreuzer was on the scent of something; as he approached the tree his ears pricked up and he was sniffing deeply, rapidly. Suddenly he stopped, stuck his nose deep into the grass and started tugging fiercely with his teeth, once, twice, and then suddenly he raised his head, and in his mouth, gripped firmly but gently in his jaws, was a small package. It was wrapped in some sort of green cloth, and looked rather like a roll of silver cutlery, bound neatly in the middle with a cloth tie.

Liz was thinking hard about Jana—what could she have done? Given the dog another scent. But why? And then she remembered. Kollek's hair—Naomi from the Israeli embassy had said that his hair had been inexplicably wet that evening when he had gone off on his own. He'd been here! Of course. It was Kollek who had chosen this entertainment. He'd been here and he'd swum out to the island to plant his own decoy for the dog. But his would be deadly.

"He's found something else!" the handler exclaimed.

"What if he's been given another scent? After the one you gave him."

"What do you mean?"

"Just what I said," Liz snapped. "If you gave him a scent, but then someone else gave him another scent, would he go for the second one?"

"Yes, of course. It's the last scent he'll track. But I don't see—"

"Can you stop the dog?" Liz interrupted. Kreuzer had re-entered the water and was paddling back, head held high to keep the package in its jaws above the surface.

"What d'you mean?"

"Can you keep the dog from coming here? Tell me! Quick! Can you do it?" No time now to get a marksman to shoot the dog. The handler looked baffled but obeyed. She put two fingers in her mouth and produced a high, braying whistle. The dog stopped swimming, lifting its head, the cloth package still safely in its jaws. But then it started off again, heading steadily back to shore.

"Do it again," said Liz. "Please. Quick. Stop him."

Again the hand went up to the woman's mouth, and again came a high-pitched whistle, even louder. This time the dog stopped, with a questioning look in its eyes. The handler gave a short blast on her whistle, and suddenly the dog swivelled like a seal in the water and began paddling slowly back towards the island. Liz held her breath while the handler looked at her angrily. "What's going on?" she said. "Why are we doing this?"

She suddenly went quiet as Liz raised a warning hand; she was in no mood to be challenged, not until she knew it was safe and that she had been wrong. She would be happy then—more than happy—to take whatever criticism came her way.

The dog reached the island and pulled itself up onto the bank, though more slowly than before—Kreuzer was tired. He panted like a swimmer who'd crossed the Channel, yet he still held the package tightly in his mouth as he vigorously shook the water from his coat. If there was anything wrong with that package we'd know by now, thought Liz, as water sprayed from the dog's taut skin.

Suddenly the ground shook and simultaneously Liz heard the deafening noise of an explosion. On the island, a mound of earth lifted straight into the air and separated into thousands of tiny pieces that fell slowly into the lake, followed by an enormous cloud of dust.

The shock wave rolled over the spectators, rocking Liz back onto her heels as she winced from the sudden pain in both her ears. On the lake, the water rose up like a geyser, momentarily obscuring all sight of the island. When the air cleared at last, a crater the size of a large lorry had been dug out of the island's earth. Of Kreuzer there was no sign.

Next to Liz, the dog handler was staring white-faced at the remains of the island. Behind her, there was complete silence among the spectators. Liz looked back, but they were all standing just as they had been; no one seemed to have been hurt. Fortunately, they had all been far enough away.

The silence was broken by the Syrian President. Turning to the Israeli Prime Minister and smiling broadly, he clapped his hands together in apparent delight, then clapped again. The rest of the Syrian delegation seemed to rouse themselves, and followed their President's lead by clapping dutifully as well, joined a moment later by the Israelis. Soon the applause of all the spectators echoed around the edges of the little lake.

The Syrian President leaned over and said something to the Israeli Prime Minister, who turned and spoke urgently to Ari Block. The Mossad man looked back at Liz. "Wonderful!" he shouted with an enthusiastic smile. "The President asks if there will be more fireworks like this one."

Thank God for diplomacy, thought Liz, as the sound of police sirens echoed round the grounds. She would probably never know how much the Syrians really knew about the background to the explosion, but their President had obviously decided that the evening was going to be a success whatever happened. And as no one had been killed, except poor Kreuzer, a success it would be.

57

It was Private Grossman who saw the footprint. Lieutenant Wilentz was leading the other men to the truck after they'd stopped for a ten-minute break when Grossman called out: "Sir!"

"What is it?" the lieutenant shouted irritably. They'd been out here on the Golan Plateau for over six hours, and everyone wanted to get back—to hot showers, hot food and cold air-conditioning. The dry season had been unusually prolonged and the temperature was an unseasonal eighty-five. In the distance, the snow-covered peaks of the Mount Hermon range shimmered in the heat like a tempting ice cream.

"There's a footprint here," said Grossman, pointing to the dust lying thickly on the packed earth of the track.

Wilentz came over at once. They were two miles from the

Quneitra Crossing, the one official access point between Israel and Syria, though it operated strictly one way—young Syrians living in the occupied Golan Heights were allowed into their former homeland to pursue their studies, but could return to their families only once a year.

There were frequent incursions; most recently Hezbollah had been active in the area, even setting off land mines on the Syrian side in an effort to ratchet up the tension between the neighbouring states. There was growing concern among the Israeli army command that Hezbollah would venture onto the Israeli side as well, which was why Wilentz and his patrol were there.

The officer studied the print, Grossman beside him. "It's pointing towards the border," said the younger man, trying to sound analytic. He was only eighteen.

"Yes, it is," said Lieutenant Wilentz, who tried to be tolerant with the soldiers under his command. Most of them were kids like Grossman, doing their National Service. "But," he added, "that's not the most important thing. Look at the footprint. Does it tell you anything else?"

Grossman looked down at the indentation in the dust, wondering what he was missing. "It looks freshly made," he said.

"Yes. What else?" Suddenly Lieutenant Wilentz stamped down with his boot, about six inches from the print. "Look," he ordered.

Grossman peered down, and then he saw it. "It's almost identical."

"Exactly. It's an army boot that made this print. An *Israeli* army boot."

Wilentz called to the other men in the patrol and barked orders. They left the truck where it was and moved on foot, Wilentz out in front. As they got farther from the road, the footprints became clearer and Wilentz, following the tracks, walked without hesitating.

After half a mile they came to a small rise with a mix of large boulders and loose shingle on its lower slope. The officer signalled his men to halt, then walked back to the group to issue more orders. Five minutes later Private Grossman was clambering up the rocky slope accompanied by Alfi Sternberg, a Haifa conscript he knew from college. Why would a soldier be out here on his own? he wondered. Gone AWOL? But then why was he heading for the Syrian border?

He saw the water bottle first, lying beside a boulder in a small dip in the rock. As he moved towards it, he realised that behind the boulder, sheltered by a larger boulder balanced above it, there was a big space. He gestured with his hand to Sternberg, and together they moved cautiously towards the spot, their rifles at the ready.

Suddenly a hand reached out and grabbed the water bottle, then a man rose to his feet from behind the boulder. He was tall and lean and wore fatigues. He stood facing them with the assurance of a veteran soldier, cradling a T.A.R. assault rifle in his arms.

"Glad to see you," he said laconically. "I've been watching you out there for some time."

Sternberg laughed in relief and relaxed his grip on his rifle. Grossman hesitated; he didn't understand what this man was doing here. "Who are you?" he blurted.

"I'm Leppo," the man said at once. "Sammy Leppo. I'm out here on Special Patrol. You'll know what that means, I'm sure," he added meaningfully.

Sternberg nodded, but Grossman was still uneasy. With Hezbollah in the vicinity, he could understand why Leppo had hidden when he first heard them moving along the plateau—but something about the situation seemed odd. He said, "I'll need to check that out."

Leppo nodded easily, but then he said, "That's not really a good idea."

"Why?" asked Grossman, his suspicions returning.

Leppo suddenly swung his rifle round and covered him and Sternberg. "Drop your weapons," he ordered. There was nothing relaxed about his voice now. Sternberg dropped his rifle at once, and Leppo pointed his rifle at Grossman. "Drop it." Grossman obeyed, suddenly certain this man would kill him without hesitation.

Then a voice said, "*You* drop it."

Behind Leppo, Lieutenant Wilentz appeared; he'd circled the rise and climbed down. Now he stood on top of the boulder behind Leppo and snapped his finger. The four other members of the patrol appeared, weapons pointing at Leppo's back.

Wilentz said, "You'd better come with us. There will be plenty of time for you to tell us all about this Special Patrol."

5 8

This time Ma Folie was not closed; it was doing a busy lunchtime trade. At the bistro on the South Bank, the food was French, old-fashioned and excellent. As Liz took her last bite of *onglet,* grilled in shallot butter, she felt a curious contentment.

The near-disaster at Gleneagles had not derailed the peace confer-ence, though none of the participants would have claimed it a total success. Three days of intensive talks had led to no dramatic break-through, but the discussions had been conducted in a positive spirit by all sides. Enough had been accomplished for another conference to be scheduled in four months' time, long enough to allow informal follow-up talks, but soon enough to ensure that all momentum would not be lost. Liz and her colleagues had sighed with relief when the venue for the next conference had been announced: France.

The Czech girl, Jana, had cracked within minutes at Liz's second interrogation, though what she'd had to say had not added much to what was already known. It served mainly to confirm Kollek's skill at manipulating people. Jana had fallen so completely under his spell that she hadn't hesitated when he'd asked her to wipe a rag over the nose of the German pointer, even though she was rather scared of dogs. She hadn't even questioned why she was doing it, or why he'd given her money to send young Mateo into the hills to collect a package.

Liz assumed she just didn't want to know. Kollek had a lot to answer for, she thought, remembering Jana's face (this time her tears had been genuine), but at least there was the satisfaction of knowing that, having been captured by the army just two miles from the border with Syria, the man would be explaining himself at some length. He was in the hands of Mossad now and it was pretty likely that a certain squat, tough veteran of Israel's many wars would be yet again post-poning his retirement until he had finished the interrogation.

Miles had rung Liz a week after her return to London, and just twenty-four hours after his own from the Middle East. By some unspoken agreement they'd spent most of lunch talking about almost anything *but* the events at Gleneagles. He'd asked about her family, and she'd told him about her mother, and how wrong she herself had been about Edward Treglown—Miles had laughed when she'd described the gold-digging old buffer she'd been expecting. Then he told her all about Damascus, describing a capital city, and indeed a country, which was an odd mélange of the old and new, a land where the latest computer software and the ancient souk were uneasy bedfel-lows, and Islam pushed against a form of Christianity that was equally well established.

It was only now, as she declined the waiter's offer of dessert and they both ordered coffee, that Miles fell silent, and Liz felt it was appropriate to make some reference to the complicated chain of events they had both been involved in.

"You know, you were instrumental in helping us to solve all this Kollek business."

"I was?" Miles looked pleasantly surprised. Liz thought again there was something attractive about his modesty.

"Yes. If you hadn't gone to Tel Aviv and got all that out of Teitelbaum, we'd never have known what was driving Kollek—why he did what he did."

Miles acknowledged this with a reluctant nod. "I suppose that's true," he said, and went silent again. There was a lot to think about. Kollek's plot was probably quite simple to begin with, but it had grown infinitely complicated by the time it concluded so bizarrely—with an explosion that, if it had taken place on land as he'd intended, would have killed both the Syrian President and the Israeli Prime Minister. As it turned out, it was only the dog handler's skill at redirecting the dog back to the island in the little lake that saved them all. In the end, the dog had been the only victim. Sad, even poignant, but a minor disaster. Certainly very far from the worldwide impact that Kollek had hoped for.

But Kollek had been very clever, thought Liz—at least at first. She said as much to Miles.

"What about the Oval?" he said, just as Peggy had done at Gleneagles.

She shook her head. "Even that worked to his advantage. When we spotted them, we immediately suspected Bokus, not him. In fact, every time we found some link with Kollek, we always assumed he was being run by an intelligence service, particularly Mossad of course. But he was playing them—all of us, in fact."

Miles poured Liz the last of the bottle of Crozes Hermitage. She'd ignored her usual limit of a single glass of wine at lunch—what the hell, she'd decided, sensing a valedictory quality to the occasion.

"What I've never understood," Miles declared, "is what Kollek was originally hoping to pull off. I mean, suppose we'd never had the information from Geoffrey Fane's source in Cyprus. We wouldn't have known anything at all of what was going on."

"Oh, I think that's pretty clear. He planted the information on the Syrians that Veshara and Marcham were spying on them, hoping that they would try to kill them. He wanted the hawks in Damascus to win out and the heavies to move in. And he almost succeeded. If both Marcham and Veshara had been assassinated, Israel would have been furious, since they were both giving information to Mossad. Kollek would have made sure the finger was pointed at Damascus, and that might well have been enough to scupper the prospects for peace, certainly this time round. It would have created more bad blood for years to come.

"Of course, that all went awry when news about it leaked from Geoffrey Fane's source in Cyprus, Abboud. And then, bizarrely, Kollek learned of the leak from Bokus. That was his great stroke of fortune, though you could argue that what he did next was a mistake. By telling the Syrians there had been a leak from inside their secret service, he focused their attention on the mole, rather than on Marcham and Veshara. Then he killed Marcham himself, hoping it would look as though the Syrians had done it. But the way he killed him was too subtle for the Syrian heavies, so we never thought it was them."

Liz looked ruefully at her wineglass. "But we let ourselves get preoccupied with Abboud's murder—particularly with trying to work out how the Syrians had discovered that he was working for Geoffrey Fane's colleague. We thought at first the leak could be you and then that it could be Andy Bokus; then when we saw Bokus with Kollek we decided it *had* to be him. Only we were wrong."

Miles said sympathetically, "That's not surprising. Who in a million years would have thought that the source of the story of the supposed threat would find out that his story had been leaked?"

"And Kollek exploited the freak opportunity brilliantly. Here we were, two intelligence services supposedly working together, yet increasingly suspicious of each other, while the real ringmaster stood back and let distrust get to work. We were blind to the fact that it might all be just one person driven by his own weird agenda."

Miles finished his wine and slowly put down his glass. "What I always find surprising is that with all our sophisticated technology and the big bureaucracies we work in, a single person can still do so much damage."

Liz thought about this for a minute. "Well," she said, "when you think about it, so much of our work is about the actions of individuals—not governments or bureaucracies. That's what makes it so fascinating. If it were just about process or gizmos, do you think you'd want to be doing the job?"

"Absolutely not," said Miles emphatically. "And neither would you."

He suddenly sounded rather sad, and she regretted the melancholy note that had crept into their lunch. But then he brightened up again. "There're a couple of loose ends still, aren't there?" he said.

"More than a couple, I'm sure," said Liz. But that was true of every case; there were always threads left hanging. "Which ones are you thinking of?" she asked.

"I was wondering what was the point of Hannah Gold? Why was Kollek so interested in her?"

"I think originally he wanted her as a backup—in case the conference went ahead in spite of his efforts. She'd probably have helped place explosives or trigger them—unintentionally of course. But then quite accidentally, Kollek learned that her daughter-in-law, Sophie, had been in the Security Service. He may even have thought she still was. I imagine he'd been watching Hannah, and he must have seen me visit and put two and two together. He thought of getting rid of me—"

"He didn't just think it, Liz, he tried to do it."

She nodded. "When that didn't work, he dropped the Hannah idea. Too risky. So he used her as a red herring instead."

"He had a lot of those, didn't he? The Spanish 'sniper,' the non-existent rifle—as well as Hannah."

"He was clever and he improvised brilliantly."

"I'd say he was lucky, too."

"Would you?" asked Liz. "I'd have said we were the lucky ones." She thought of the breaks they'd had—her own spotting of the "gardener" at Marcham's house, Abboud's position high up in Syrian intelligence, an envious Dougal happening to spot Jana's assignation with Kollek by the equestrian centre; they were all strokes of luck.

"Perhaps," said Miles. "But the point is, you rode your luck. Not everyone would have managed that, believe me." He raised a hand towards the waiter and gestured for the bill.

"This was lovely," said Liz. "You were right about this place. Next time, it'll be my shout."

Miles gave a funny little smile. "You'll have to visit."

Visit? Her eyes must have betrayed her puzzlement.

"Yes. Visit Damascus." He looked at her intently, and she saw surprise in his eyes. "You mean you don't know?"

"Know what?" she asked. She was tired of mysteries; whenever she thought she had disposed of one, another seemed to crop up, even here during an enjoyable lunch with a man she was starting to like a lot.

"I've been transferred; I'm going back to Damascus. I thought Fane would have told you."

"Geoffrey? What's it got to do with him?"

"He's part of the reason I'm going," said Miles, with a trace of resentment. "It was Bokus's idea to start with—he never liked me, and after the Oval debacle it's got harder than ever to work with him. Then when Ty Oakes went through the Middle East after the peace conference, your head of station there—his name's Whitehouse—mentioned that my presence in Syria would be useful to the joint effort. He told me off the record that Fane had instructed him to make the request. It dovetailed so neatly with Bokus wanting to see the back of me that I assumed it was a put-up job."

It took Liz a moment to follow his logic, for she was still taking in this news. "But why did Geoffrey care?" she managed to ask at last.

Miles gave a small shrug. "I've got my own ideas of why. I think it may have something to do with you. But you'll have to work it out for yourself."

Liz was silent for a moment while she worked it out. Miles could only mean that Fane didn't like their friendship. Did he object for professional reasons or was it personal? She'd have to think about that.

"I'm so sorry," she said eventually, not sure whether she meant she was sorry about Miles's transfer, or about the fact that he'd been forced into it by Bokus and Fane.

Miles gave a wry smile. "Don't be. I like Damascus. Like I say, you'll have to visit. Shall we go?"

Outside, a low, bleak sun did little to take the edge off the chill of a cutting autumn wind. Liz buttoned her coat and tied the belt firmly round her waist. They walked in silence towards the river. At the southern end of Lambeth Bridge she turned, and after a moment's hesitation said goodbye to Miles with a handshake rather than the hug she wanted to give him.

Who knew what might have happened between us, she thought as she crossed the river. Thanks to the professional jealousy of Bokus, and perhaps to the personal jealousy of Geoffrey Fane, it seemed unlikely she would ever find out. It was easy to say she'd get on a plane one day soon and fly to Damascus, but she knew it wasn't going to happen. So many might-have-beens in my life, thought Liz, which made the clear conclusion of the Syrian plot at once satisfying and yet another reminder of her personal life's dismaying lack of progress.

Oh well, she thought, as the bulk of Thames House loomed before her, at least I have a career I'm committed to—and care about. At the entrance as she showed her ID, she laughed at the usual bad joke made by Ralph, the security guard at the door, and as she went up in the lift she found a melancholy comfort at being back in her familiar surroundings. Gleneagles seemed to belong to a different world.

Once in her office, Liz began leafing through the stack of papers that had accumulated in her absence. She had not got far down the pile when there was a tactful knock on the open door of her office, and she saw Peggy in the doorway, white as a sheet.

"What's wrong?" she said with concern.

"Liz, I don't know what to say. I've only just heard the news."

"What news?" demanded Liz, wondering what could have gone wrong now. The peace conference had run its full if unedifying course, Hannah Gold was safe and sound back in Tel Aviv and Danny Kollek had been caught. So what could be the matter?

"It's Charles," said Peggy tearfully. Liz felt her heart start to pound. What could have happened to Charles?

"Joanne's died," Peggy said. "It must be terrible for Charles. I know she's been ill a long time, but now she's gone and he's all alone."